Umbertina

UMBERTINA

A Novel by
Helen Barolini

Afterword by Edvige Giunta

The Feminist Press at
The City University of New York
New York

Published in 1999 by The Feminist Press at The City University of New York
Wingate Hall/City College, Convent Avenue at 138th Street, New York, NY 10031

First Feminist Press edition, 1999

Library of Congress Cataloging-in-Publication Data

Barolini, Helen. 1925–
Umbertina: a novel / by Helen Barolini : afterword by Edvige Giunta.
— 1st Feminist Press ed.
    p.   cm.
    ISBN 1-55861-204-1 (hc. : alk. paper). — ISBN 1-55861-205-X (pbk. : alk. paper)
    1. Italian Americans — New York (State) — Fiction. I. Title.
    PS3552.A725U39 1999
    813'.54—dc21   98-44374
                                                                         CIP

The Feminist Press is grateful to Janet Brown, William L. Hedges, Joanne Markell,
Caroline Urvater, Genevieve Vaughan, and Patricia Wentworth and Mark Fagan for
their generosity in supporting this publication.

Printed on acid-free paper by Donnelley & Sons

Manufactured in the United States of America

05 04 03 02 01 00 99   5 4 3 2 1

It is a wonderful thing to see this reissue of *Umbertina* twenty years after its first appearance. That this story of three women lives again is due to three women: Edvige Giunta, its advocate, Jean Casella, its editor, and Florence Howe, its publisher.

I am happy to see this story of three generations of women journeying to self-knowledge offered to a new generation of readers. Through the image of immigrants reaching a new land to start new lives, the metaphor of all women's journey to be reborn to themselves is retold.

In the spirit of Gertrude Stein's *The Making of Americans*, more than twenty years ago I set out to write an American story that would add a distinct nuance to the national literature through a voice not much heard—one that had the reverberations of an Italian American voice but was, and is, meant for all people.

Helen Barolini
Hastings-on-Hudson, New York
September 1998

In memory of Nicoletta and Stefana,
the immigrants . . .
and for my mother, the storyteller.

With great gratitude to the National Endowment for the Arts, whose grant made possible the writing of this book, and to the Writers Community in New York, where parts of the work in progress were read.

Contents

Prologue

He reached over to the low table where the lamp was always lit, day or evening, because the room was dark—dark and unheated and pervaded with Rome street noises—and where lay the paraphernalia of his profession: heavy black-rimmed glasses, pipe, tobacco pouches, matches, ashtray, pencils, note-pads, and clock. From the low table on the zebra-skin rug that created the island of détente between their facing wicker chairs, he picked up the black appointment book. "*Va bene*, Thursday at five?" he asked. Smooth, self-assured, deep-voiced.

"Don't leave me like this!" Her own voice was anxious and too high-pitched. And she meant: Don't reject me, make love to me! But unable to say so she put it another way: "Tell me something— am I right to go ahead with this divorce?"

"You must do as you feel." It was the refrain of their meetings and it was like an old too-often repeated joke; if she could sort and act on her feelings that neatly she wouldn't be there at all.

It wasn't the answer that mattered. She wanted time to recover herself. The hour had been painful, another stalking of the same no-man's-land. No-woman's-land, she corrected herself. She was aware of the new currents—they had helped, in fact, to precipitate her into the psychiatrist's office.

She searched his dark, lean, Sicilian face. "What I mean is, that in my marriage, at least I have sex if I want it with Alberto. You keep telling me to respond to my instincts—be more primitive, you say!—and yet I'm about to dissolve a marriage without another prospect in sight."

"Well, I can't help you there," he said curtly, sitting back and crossing his legs so that her eyes were drawn, as always, to his bright socks. Priests were known to have large collections of socks. Vicarious sex for the vicars of Christ on earth.

"Thursday at five?" Dr. Verdile repeated.

"No," she said, "I'm going to Florence." She was repaid by his surprise as he looked up from his book and regarded her quizzically, inviting her to continue.

"I think it's time for me to have a vacation from these visits— I'm feeling depressed, I have to get away for a while. And besides I have to see about moving there once I've gotten the legal separation. I want to be settled there with Weezy by the time Tina flies home. Alberto is going to Florence and his expenses are paid for me, too." As usual she had told him too much, given too many explanations. She turned her eyes from his face to his hands.

You're not different from me, she thought, looking at his chewed fingernails. Except that you can hide it better under your analyst's uniform: pipe, turtleneck sweater, thick black-rimmed eyeglasses, white hairs all over your trousers from the Dalmatians you keep at your country place, dispassion, intelligence, aplomb, Swissness.

"Yes, it's a good idea sometimes to take a vacation," he told her equably.

"It's more than that—it's all the *influencing* going on that I can't stand! All those erotic dreams! I never had them before; it's the effect of analysis. I want my life to be my own, not conditioned by these meetings with you and the whole thing pressing on me like a chain I can't lift."

"Now we come to something!" he said sharply. "Now we come to the real matter, and so, typically, you want to escape it. It's not these meetings that create the erotic dreams—that material you've always had in you. The present confrontation only favors its release. But if you refuse to face it now you go back to your favorite escape-hatch, the self-punishment you've inflicted on yourself over the years in order to avoid your main problem. You can go—but you won't have solved anything. You'll simply end up in another place with another analyst going over again and again the reasons for your not facing up."

"But you know my situation! Alberto and I live together in

name only; I've decided on the divorce, and now I'm overwhelmed with dreams of making love to young boys, in Venice, Mexico, England, all over the world—of wanting to make love, of craving it and not being able to do anything about it."

"And why can't you do something about it?"

"But what do you expect? That I put an ad in *Il Messaggero* saying 'Lady available'? Besides, it's too late . . . too late . . ." (If anyone, I'm the white rabbit, she had told him once when he compared her to Alice in Wonderland—timid, tremulous, always late, fearful of duchesses and everything else.)

She wanted to go away and show him that she, Marguerite Morosini, an American transplant filled with fears and desires, who was about to divorce her Italian husband of eighteen years so that she could start again, didn't need him and his professional cool.

She felt stupid. She had put on her long hairpiece; she had done her eyes; she had dressed carefully as she always did for the Monday and Thursday meetings held in the front room of an apartment whose walls admitted the barest attenuated sounds of an invisible young Finnish wife moving somewhere in the adjoining rooms. All the time the echo chamber behind her ears went on sounding: "It's late . . . it's late . . . my word, it's late . . . what will the duchess say?" Now she heard herself ask him abjectly, "What about sex? Sometimes I just want to say to Alberto, 'Oh, come on and sleep with me tonight.'"

"Then do it! Do what you feel," he said energetically.

"But I can't! Don't you understand that if I do he'll never agree to the divorce and I haven't even gotten him yet to sign the first separation agreement." Her restless eyes jumped around the room, lighting on the print of the Indian dancers above the table, the abstract paintings on the far wall, the avocado pit sprouting in a jar of water, futilely searching for the clues that would tell her who this man was, this person into whose hearing she was pouring the pains of her life.

"There's a typical female wile for that. You can get him to sign first and then go to bed. This is something all women understand."

"I . . . I never thought of that," she stammered, confused.

"It's something women have always been able to do. It's a classic stratagem, no?"

She felt a distaste for his masculine presumptuousness. Did he think she would fall into the trap of letting him persuade her about the female role? The hell with the minor roles, she wanted to be a person as much as he.

Marguerite collected herself to go. "I feel so stupid," she said. No, not stupid; keen and smart enough to see straight into the mess of her life, to know she had always been preparing it. Mad Marguerite they used to call her at school. The oddball, the nut! But not stupid.

"We all do at times," he said, smiling generously. "Well, when shall we see each other? Do you want to call me when you get back?" He still had the black book poised in his hand.

"No," she said, defeated (down, down the rabbit hole—would the fall never end?). "I'll be back for Thursday."

Awkwardly she struggled into her coat. He never helped.

They shook hands amicably at the door and said *arrivederci* nice as pie.

The next day Marguerite took the morning train up to Florence. It cost her 5,515 lire. Alberto would join her at the hotel, for he was coming on a later train with some of the other critics and editors who met annually to discuss entries for the literary prize that they judged.

Only Dr. Verdile knew of her divorce plans. She had taken off the gold wedding band and begun to wear again a turquoise ring from long ago, but people hadn't noticed, or if they had, didn't give it any importance. After all, she and Alberto were still at the same address, so who could tell besides Dr. V., and sometimes Alberto, what was going on?

Analysis had intensified everything. She had always been aware of her cover-up—that business receptionist who faced the outside and tried to be pleasing; who hazarded meeting and speaking and giving the correct responses; who engaged in memorized, meaningless routines of life. Now she was another step removed, watching herself watch the receptionist; thinking it was time to fire her and her goddam personality smile.

She opened her newsmagazine in the train: There was Audrey Hepburn divorced, two months from forty, biting her lip in a pretty show of being flustered, looking like a little girl in her pink Cardin mini-dress as she married the handsome young psychiatrist of thirty-one and started life all over again—as perfect as one of her films. No cobwebs in *Roman Holiday*, *Sabrina*, or *Gigi*: all happy endings staged beautifully. Christ, how one would stage one's life if one could! Yet isn't that what she had done? Staged marriage and motherhood for years and years until she had been done in by the fakery. The stage props had dropped and she had been left alone in all the artifice to get out of her sham costume as best she could and find another part, in another theater, with other actors. At forty-two. Jesus! She wasn't Audrey Hepburn.

("You are young, pleasing, elegant—not like some women, who are impossible," Dr. V. had told her. And she had turned on him, furious, accusing him of being Dr. Pangloss, of being so stuck in his optimism that he couldn't begin to see her problems.)

Then suddenly it had been simple: She would get a divorce.

A reddish-haired man entered the compartment of the train and sat next to her. She was aware of him as she drew into her corner and looked out the window.

She thought, of all things, of Umbertina Longobardi, who had emigrated to America as a young wife. Marguerite wondered if her own fears were worse now than those faced then by that Calabrian peasant, her grandmother. Had Umbertina wondered as she lay in steerage, separated from her husband and with her sons by her side, what her life would be like, what its meaning was? Had she wondered how she'd speak? And to whom? Marguerite had never been able to speak to the old woman in her lifetime; they had had different tongues. Now she could, but Umbertina was dead and buried in Cato. Oh, Grandma Longobardi, give me your guts!

As they passed Orvieto, Marguerite applied herself to what she had to do in Florence. She had to find a job. What could she do? Dissemble. Anything else? Translate, teach, type. She had written Tina at Bryn Mawr to ask what she thought about chances over there. Tina, her firstborn. Everything had started to fall apart when Berto died. Her only son. Her last child. Then Tina had left Italy for college. ("Imagine, Dr. Verdile, a child already in college!" "But you're still young," he says, pulling on his English pipe.)

"May I see your paper?" Marguerite said to the man seated next to her in the compartment.

"Of course, of course," he said after a moment of surprise.

She stared at the newsprint; did I ask for the paper or did I ask him to make love to me? Always she asked for love . . . when she asked the shoemaker if the heels on her shoes could be fixed for tomorrow, when she asked the flower man how long the anemones would last, when she asked Alberto's guests if they wanted more ice in their drinks, when she asked Tina's boyfriends to return the books of hers they borrowed.

"They've got a lot of snow in Bologna," she said to the red-haired man. "Do you think there'll be snow in Florence?"

"There was, but I don't think it lasted. Look at it now," and he pointed past her out the window where bright sun was shining over the everlasting sweetness of the Italian countryside. "Do you live in Florence?"

"No, in Rome. I'm just going to visit." Always the explanations. All he really wants to know is how an obvious foreigner like me is just as obviously not a passing tourist. "I teach in Rome," she said extravagantly. "But it's getting so expensive there I'm thinking of moving to Florence." If he wanted to follow it up now, he could. He had said before that he was getting off in Bologna to make a connection for Ferrara.

She thought of a story by Corrado Alvaro in which an Italian salesman going to Germany on business offers some of his Capri wine and oranges to the German girl sitting next to him on the train. He is going to Berlin; she, too, but says that she is getting off in Munich before going on because she wants to break up the journey. Why doesn't he get off in Munich with her, she proposes; it's a beautiful city and she will show it to him. Then after a good night's sleep in a good hotel, they will arrive fresh in Berlin the following day. But the man stays on the train and the girl gets off alone in Munich.

As Marguerite prepared to get off in Florence, she gave the man back his paper. She got down her bag and said good-bye as the train pulled into the station. (Was I saying "Good-bye" or "Why don't you want me?")

The train stopped, she was in Florence, and she decided to be purposeful as befitted her beginning freedom. She was on the way, and though white-rabbit-like she stopped every so often to pull out a pocket watch and see how late it was getting, she still hoped, at bottom, to make it in time. Ever upward, *ad astra per aspera*. She pulled a sheet of mimeographed paper marked "American Schools in Florence" from her handbag and checked an address. Yes, there in Piazza Santa Maria Novella, right across from the station, was an American school run by a Mr. Selph offering courses in English language and literature for Italians. She might get a job there. And what more auspicious than a Mr. Selph as first encounter in her resettlement plans? Old Verdile was always preaching the self and now Mr. Selph, himself, lay right on her path.

Marguerite crossed the piazza. At the address of the American school, she found herself in a dank passageway between a grocery and an auto-parts store and she felt her confidence vanish. There was Selph's name on a letterbox. But there was no doorman, no elevator, no businesslike plaque naming the school; there were no people coming and going. It was a drab, gray hallway in a quasi-tenement and she fled.

She got the runabout bus at the station and gave the name of her hotel, a fancy place on the Lungarno. Her room was 505 and she wondered if she should play lotto with all the fives that were turning up. But it was already two in the afternoon, too late. Clutching her lists, Marguerite skipped lunch and went desperately about her Florentine pursuits.

But everything was wrong. The Arno was thick and muddy, the shops full of tourist stuff, the city dismally flat and dun-colored. Was this Florence, jewel of the Renaissance, as she had known it newly arrived in Italy as a prospective student; when the bombed bridges over the river hadn't yet been rebuilt and there were post-war *ponti di fortuna* connecting the two sides and always thronged with people going on foot from one part of the city to the other?

There on a jerry-built bridge over limpid water in the middle of hurrying crowds, Alberto Morosini had offered her not only love and devotion in marriage but redemption of everything previous to that moment: "I'll make you a positive human being yet," he told her. "You've suffered enough." He would learn her language and she his; she would give him youth and American optimism, he would give him his stable, experienced maturity. All that was long ago. The temporary bridges had been replaced by stone and concrete ones over which an endless traffic of cars, buses, and motorcycles roared, and no one now passed on foot. The air smelled of exhaust; the sallow water was sluggish with mud; and the words that had been said were unrecoverable.

Useless to think of the past, she told herself. What I have is now . . . day by day, for as long as it goes. Useless to think of the years with Alberto—years of being anesthetized, of withdrawing while he emerged in his work, in his books of poetry and criticism, in his encounter with America, where they had lived half their married life, and now in his prestige as a critic and as editor of an Italian review. She saw it as his success story. They could make a movie.

She had always loved the movies; she liked to think of herself as a camera's eye shooting movies of all the people she saw around her. Everything that took place in her life unfolded at a distance from her, as if in a movie. She felt detached from the feelings that could, if she let them, connect her to people. ("Do as you feel," the good doctor said. But how could she if she had stopped her feelings?) She liked to be a spectator, an observer. That way she could put a frame around the parts she liked and discard the parts that didn't come out well, the ugly parts. She could see something in sequence, see it whole and understand it. Rerun it, clip it, splice it. What she really wanted was not to be in it herself, just look on as the others performed: her parents, brothers, teachers, friends and lovers, husband and children.

She would remind herself to pass that on to Dr. Verdile.

On the other side of the brown ditch that was the Arno, on the Palazzo Pitti side, she went to find the well-known English-language school founded some fifty or sixty years before by an educated spinster lady who had undertaken to teach the children of the American colony in Florence. The lady had died, the school was declining, and when Marguerite arrived there was only the cleaning woman to talk to.

While she examined linoleum prints along the wall of a large cold room, the cleaning woman telephoned the director, Mr. Faust, at his home. Another symbolic name, thought Marguerite, and left before Faust came, unable to cope with any other decline and genteel shabbiness than her own; unable to deal with such jokes as Mr. Selph and Mr. Faust.

I will not think of schools for the moment, I will attend to a place to live. She took out another mimeographed sheet, which listed housing agents, and walked down some distance from the Palazzo Pitti to the firm with an American name. The street door opened on a foyer filled with ornamental plants and big pieces of Renaissance furniture. No one was there, but voices came from a mezzanine. Marguerite felt uncomfortable standing there alone with no one to welcome her or ask her to state her business. And what was her business? How could she settle on a place to live if she wasn't yet separated, and how could she think of settling in Florence if she had no work there? Jesus, couldn't she even remember that elementary rule, first things first?

She rushed out the door.

Actually, she told herself, the very first thing to find was work, then the place to live, then the school for Weezy. Maybe she wasn't thinking well because she was hungry and tired. Back on the Uffizi side of the river she walked toward Doney's. But a look in the window at the women gathered in there discouraged her and she crossed the street to the bar at the corner. She had tea and a chicken sandwich and the price was enormous, and she wondered how long she could keep up the pretense that she'd be able to earn enough to live on in Florence even taking into account Alberto's contribution toward schools, sports and music lessons, vacation trips, and God knows what else.

She took a bus at the Duomo and asked the ticket man to tell her when they came to the stop nearest her hotel. He forgot about her, and when she asked again they were two stops and many turnings past, so that she had to walk back. Once again annulled: Like the ticket man, they all forgot she existed and she was reminded of it over and over again—by Alberto; by her family before him; by the lawyer, who kept asking if she were sure she wanted a divorce, thus showing that he didn't recognize her as a person with a precise volition; by Dr. Verdile, who couldn't see her as a woman as well as a white rabbit.

She had no uniform; she had no official presence with which to impress people and help them recognize her. And yet she did: adult woman, longtime wife, past mistress, mother of two living daughters and one dead son, college grad, family flop, translator and sometime substitute teacher, forty-five typed words a minute, *bella presenza*, drives own car, Jungian analysand, job applicant, divorce applicant, life applicant. These were the buttons and stripes of her uniform and still no one saw her. She could no more exist alone than does a painting without viewers, or the Grand Canyon without tourists. Her existence depended on others. How could she get them to know, by Jesus, that she was here?

At the hotel she took a bath and was dressing for dinner when Alberto arrived, snorting and blowing busily through his great nose, his small dark eyes darting restlessly around the room.

"*Ciao, cara*, did you have a good trip? I find it very fatiguing these trips—and then these conferences. This room is not bad, though. I think I caught a cold on that overheated train. I ate like a dog today, let's hope to go someplace decent for dinner. Are you ready?"

She regarded him dispassionately: his stooped shoulders, expanding paunch, receding hair. Alberto at fifty-five. Funny that just this year, of all years, his age should contain her lucky number twice. He didn't believe in the separation. He was being patient about it. He would wait. He had faith. But he would see.

That evening they were at dinner with a group made up of the illustrious and the old, which included even those critics or writers still only in their forties who had managed to catch up in aging. The place was drafty, as all of Florence was, and Marguerite felt the cold seep in and cling to her bones. She watched the agile waiters make small talk at the table of a striking Negro girl and her Italian boyfriend. At her own illustrious old table, instead, the talk was of literary matters.

Bacchetti, a corpulent, solemn old man with the air of a Boccaccio abbot, the author of many novels and a celebrated trilogy, a maestro of the sensual passage, sat at the center of the table and carried on a vast monologue of self-praise, olympically dismissing as asses and prick-heads other writers whose names were sometimes inserted in his pauses. In her Gloversville girlhood the thought of being in such company, knowing such names, being married to one, would have seemed to Marguerite the summit of her aspirations. Now, vaguely excited by the waiters but feeling out of the conversation, she put on her uniform and signaled to be recognized.

"I have read part of your trilogy," she told Bacchetti as he sat back, replete with food, a monolith of majesty.

He smiled benignly. "It's been translated into English, but for some reason it is not well received in America—in England, yes."

"It would make a marvelous movie, and then everyone would read the book."

"As a matter of fact, that emblem of high vulgarity who is Carlo Ponti did propose a film at one time, on the condition, however, that I change the ending. At the time I was foolishly indignant and refused, but now I understand better. It doesn't matter a bit what they do in a film, the book stays what it is."

"But artistically you're right. Why should they change an ending which is right as it is?"

"Oh, I wouldn't mind a bit now. They could change the whole three books if they wanted. You know the story about Ibsen and the Germans? They wanted to put on *A Doll's House* but the ending was too drastic for them—"

"But the ending is what it's all about," she exclaimed, interrupting Bacchetti with what Alberto called her literalness.

"I know, I know," said the old man, "but the German soul or whatever it is couldn't abide the starkness of Nora's simply walking out and leaving her husband. So they asked Ibsen's permission to change the ending: After Nora leaves, she has a change of heart and comes back."

"How terrible! And Ibsen let them?"

"Certainly! He not only let them, but said it was fine for the Germans—exactly what they deserved!"

Marguerite laughed and Bacchetti was pleased, too. This was the life Alberto had always promised her. For a moment she existed in the old man's attention to her. Then he turned to the others at the table and started discussing the season's new novels—all shabby and contemptible, he said—and the most likely contenders among the asses and prick-heads for the coming literary prizes. As the Italian flowed faster and faster around her, she let it slip from her grasp. The pyrotechnics of their wit and brilliant remarks, their irony, sarcasm, and maliciousness swirled about her; she heard the sounds and felt the brilliance, but was, once more, out of it. She let herself subside; the tourists were leaving the Grand Canyon and with their departure annulling it.

Their walk back to the hotel was a slow passage held in interminable suspension by Bacchetti, who walked at the head of the group and stopped frequently to gesture with his cane or gaze distractedly about him. Twenty minutes to cross the street to the hotel. In the lobby someone proposed a whiskey in the bar before retiring.

"Why?" said Bacchetti, making a wry face. "It's gone so well this far, why take a chance? Why risk ruining everything? It's better for us all to go to bed."

The next day Marguerite left Florence, stopping on her way to the station to buy a pair of large white-rimmed sunglasses to hide behind.

"I'm behind in my dreams," she said, consulting her notebook. "All these dreams I had while I was sick after getting back from Florence —we haven't discussed them yet."

"Never mind your notebook," he said brusquely, filling his pipe. "Tell me what you remember without reading."

"There's one I remember. It was while I was sick."

"What happened to you?"

"I caught something in Florence. I was in bed five or six days."

"What was your dream?"

"I am in an Italian classroom. We are all teen-age students, but I am the only foreign one. There is a woman teacher who makes a big thing out of roll call, establishing our identities with a fussy precision and then assigning us permanently to our places. There will be no moving around to empty seats, she says, she'll abolish the leftover places. Then she asks us to call out suggestions for a theme we are to write. We try to impress her and call out words like Love, Justice, Faith, Art, Family, Freedom, and so on, and she writes all these words—they're bright and flickering with psyche-delic colors—on the blackboard. Then, one by one, following our discussions she erases them until only one word remains . . . it seems to be 'Grossness.' I'm not quite sure—it seems to be that: something low, animal, shameful, not nice. Anyway, this turns out to be the subject for our composition. The teacher says to one of the girl students, 'If you do as well as usual, you won't have to come to class regularly, just check in every so often.' I put on big black glasses like yours and start writing. But I have this anxiety. We are at old-fashioned desks, the kind with inkwells in them, and I notice that ink is being passed out among us without any regard to fairness—some get more, some less. I have definitely less and this makes me terribly anxious: Will I run out before I finish the assignment? I keep thinking: But I am a foreigner, I already have a disadvantage, so shouldn't she at least give me more ink or some special consideration? I raise my hand to ask her, but she ignores me. It's getting late. I start writing even though I have this feeling of unfairness."

Marguerite took a cigarette from her bag and Dr. Verdile leaned over to light it for her. She looked at him quietly, waiting for him to take his pipe from his mouth and talk. She thought of the conditions she had set for an acceptable shrink once she had decided on analysis.

"But the face doesn't matter," Alberto had told her impatiently. "What's important is that he knows his profession. If he's good you won't even notice him as a person." How wrong Alberto was about her, as usual. How quick to make everything about her fit only his own necessities so as not to have to waste his time. They never thought in the same way. Where she envisioned a concrete situation and wanted a setting of terms, Alberto saw an idea. He saw analysis as an extension of his Catholicism: a magnetic force into which one released one's soul, hopefully trusting in the roots of one's past and the revelations of the doctor, with firm faith in the future.

No, she knew what her analyst had to be like. He had to be reasonably attractive and agreeable in person or how would she be able to talk? How many times in Washington, during Alberto's years as Italian cultural attaché there, had she met at parties all types of analysts, none of whom she would have ever considered taking into her confidence. Their neighbor in the suburbs was a psychiatrist—a pig-faced, pompous drear who spit out his lisped greetings so that she felt covered with spittle inside and out. Whoever would meet with such a person was more of a punishment seeker than Marguerite.

Marguerite believed in signs—"synchronization" was the word, Dr. Verdile would tell her later—and he, Elio Verdile, had all the right ones: V for victory and Elio for Helios the sun god, the giver of light and warmth, regeneration. And he lived in old Rome on a narrow slum street filled with the sound of artisans and not in fashionable, snobbish Parioli with the rest of the doctors. He was Sicilian, like her father's immigrant grandparents. He spoke English, and she had thought this necessary until she discovered from the moment of their first meeting that it was she who preferred not to speak her mother tongue in analysis. The analysis was done in Italian. Am I avoiding my mother, she asked.

To go twice a week to sit and talk and smoke with such an attractive young man was her good fortune right from the beginning. Her going to him through those dark old Rome alleys reminded her of how, back in Gloversville, she had imagined assignations in Europe: the dark hallway of an unsavory-looking building without a *portiere*; the squalid staircase up to an unheated apartment filled with mysterious doors.

At her initial interview, she had been embarrassed when he had spoken about her going on a journey through a shadowy world whose hidden hazards she could no longer brazen out on her own. The Sicilian Persephone, she thought; down into Hades and then resurrection and rebirth. Life is a dark journey, he continued, at best illuminated only fitfully by a light whose provenance we know nothing of. Helios the sun god? she wondered ironically, until, moved by his composure and confidence and beauty, she let drop her resistance.

"What was your sickness when you had this dream?" he now asked her, coming back to her description of the classroom.

"I had a high fever—flu, I think. Then I got terrible cramps in my stomach and a feeling of being pressed. I had the doctor come, something I never do. He examined me and said there was nothing in my stomach, and right away the cramps dissolved."

"So it was imaginary."

"Not the flu—that I really had."

"Why do you think you imagined those pains in your stomach?"

"But I told you! Everything came at once . . . my feeling lost in Florence . . . my meeting with the lawyer . . . Tina's letter mixing her upheavals with mine . . . my parents' constant harping on Tina as they used to do—still do—with me . . . this analysis. All these things—I probably got sick to get away from it all."

"Your dream, however, seems to cut clear through the difficulties and reach the point without hesitation. The teacher acts decisively in assigning you your place. Interestingly, you are the only foreign student; this has to do with your feeling of alienation and your anxiety as to whether you are American, Italian, or Italo-American. Then, without your objection, she eliminates the grand-sounding words from the blackboard and has you concentrate on grossness. What does that mean to you?"

"Well, I'm not exactly sure it was grossness; maybe it was *grossesse* in the French sense of pregnancy, or *grossolano* in the Italian meaning of coarseness. In any case, a sense of roughness, earthiness, elementariness. Or was it the German *gross*?"

"And what does that say to you?"

"All those abstractions on the blackboard were written in gorgeous blinking neon lights and made to appear fabulously alluring. But in spite of their attraction, the teacher wipes them out. Then, bare and unadorned, only 'Grossness' remains. And the teacher—is it really you?—tells a certain girl (me?) that if she does well on this theme of grossness, she won't have to come to class regularly. Is that it? If I do well, I'll be able to pull out of analysis? What do you think?"

Puffing on his pipe, his legs crossed carelessly, he smiled and said in his teasing manner, "It's what you think that counts."

"I like this dream, this kind of Zen riddle and play on words: gross or grows. The confusion of languages—four different possibilities of meaning in four languages. The Jungian four. It could be a signpost, finally, after all the phoney distractions. Distractions and abstractions. Being pregnant, giving birth, growing. Or something like that. Stripping away the fancy notions and rhetoric and getting down to earth. What do you think?"

"You insist on hearing what I think when it's you who's important."

"Then you are like the teacher who won't answer my question," she said with a smile, pleased at her quickness. "Anyway, I like this dream. I even liked it while I dreamed it."

"Yes, it's a good dream," he said, bending over toward her and stomping more tobacco into his pipe, soiling his hands indifferently. "A good sign. And it would seem that the nut of it is truly getting back to the elemental that perhaps you've lost track of, lured by the neon-lighted abstractions you think you should believe in. The very uncertainty of the final word is important, too—as if nothing precise can be counted on in any one language. It's elusive, it can't be pinned down, it seems to merge into associate meanings, have overtones that keep evolving. And yet the basic sense, or feeling, is clear: Wipe out the labels and stick to the essentials. What are the essentials for you? Who is the essential you?"

"Yes, the essence," she said with a laugh. "It reminds me of when I first got to Europe—my parents sent me to get over my lurid past—and I visited an American girl in Grasse whose job in a perfume factory was showing American tourists how essence is extracted from flowers and stuff. Maybe my dream was Grasse as well as gross to underline the essence bit." She paused, startled. "Or could gross be grocery? My grandmother had a grocery store— and that would really be getting back to the base of everything. That's it!"

She was excited now, feeling an emotion that she hadn't experienced in a long time. Her eyes fixed Verdile's and she leaned forward, talking rapidly. "I always fantasized about my grandmother. I always thought I wanted to get back to her elementary kind of existence . . . her kind of primitive strength. I've always felt that my life was wasted on abstract ideas rather than being rooted in reality; even a brutal reality would have been better than the vagueness I've been floundering in. Naive, my daughters call me. What they mean is soft, mushy. My grandmother, though, was tough. You know, I've always suspected it was my grandmother Umbertina who brought me to Italy in the first place. But I've never even taken the time to go see where she came from. I've never found her."

He smiled back. It always seemed to her that apart from the analysis they had a good thing going between them, like old friends, chatting. A kind of ease that was new to her with a man, even though she was always aware of his being a man.

"I don't know, I don't know," she murmured then as if weights had once more settled on her shoulders. "You know, while I was sick, I had Alberto bring me my father's old remedy, that hot lemonade with whiskey he used to call a hot sling. It was comforting. It was like going back to my childhood. It made me think of my father in a way that was different from usual. Before it used to be in labeled slots: Authority, Filial Duty, Respect to Parents—all those hang-ups I grew up with. Only now I've started to think of him with compassion as another guy caught up in the same goddam struggle and whose life hasn't been easy. I remembered a photo of him in our album, at eighteen on his motorcycle when he had already organized the business but was still only a kid full of God knows what kind of dreams of an exciting future. I thought of him separating himself from the Italians of the North Side to make himself into a real American. He turned reactionary to do it, but he started courageously. He was caught in a terrible trap; he couldn't be either Italian like his father and mother or American like his models without feeling guilty toward one or the other side. And even now he doesn't know how to be American while accepting his Italianness because it's still shameful to him. So there's conflict and bitterness.

"And my mother, too. Beneath her comfortable life, what is she really? Someone who never looked straight at truth and accepted it. And then my childhood, my family, all those years of growing up, marrying, until I'm here talking with you. What has it all been but a trying to fit myself into abstractions, trying to live everyone else's idea of what my life should be. And while I lived it I couldn't see it—it was all written in an invisible ink that's only now coming into sight."

"Yes," he said, considering the floor, "let's see, then, what you see in this newly appearing ink. Don't worry that you're not given enough to write your theme. No matter how little you seemed to have been given, it will be enough."

"You know the line from Antonioni's film *L'Avventura*: 'Do you have any other truths to tell me?' " she asked, smiling.

He looked up, smiled, and said mildly, "Start with your grandmother."

Part One

Umbertina, 1860–1940

Chapter One

She had hazel eyes, fair skin where the sun did not reach, and a strong chin. In the village people said of Umbertina that she had character right from the womb. "She'll be the man of her family," they said.

To herself she was Tinuzza the goat girl, eldest child of the peasant Carlo Nenci and his wife, Benedetta. When she went out into the hills above Castagna with her goats and gathered chestnuts or mushrooms or wild greens, or knitted thick cream-colored stockings to wear in the winter months, that is how she thought of herself and her life: a goat girl.

At sixteen she was strong and full-figured. Her face had the high color of one who is always out in the open. Her bare feet were toughened from exposure, but her large, strong hands were soft from absorbing the oils of the unbleached yarn she knitted. A loose braid of brown hair hung down her back, its thinness at variance with the fullness of her face and body. She was a Calabrian of the mountains and walked erect, unlike the Calabrians of the plains, who were listless and thin, bent by malaria.

Her eyes with their moody amber lights suited her, as did her name with its allusion to shade and shadows and the dark reddish umber of the earth. She was of taciturn nature, reflective, sparing of her feelings, tenacious and tight-lipped. She was used to solitude, and in the hills she would ponder what she heard others say.

"Fatti non foste a viver come bruti/ma seguir virtute e cono-

scenza," Don Antonio, their priest, had preached to them at mass. He was a learned man and they were ignorant, so he explained. "These are the words of the great poet, Dante Alighieri, and they mean you were created by God not to live like brutes, like dumb animals, but to attain to virtue. You people of the Sila are descendants of the tribe known anciently as the Bruttii. But I tell you, you are no longer Bruttii but Christians," he thundered at them. "No longer heathens beyond God's word, but meant, in the words of the immortal Dante, to hear it and follow it. This is God's intention: that you not live as brutish animals deprived of His word, but come to His Church and follow the Church's holy prescripts for you."

Umbertina's father, a weathered and knotted man, who like the other men stayed away from the Church, had laughed sardonically when he heard of the priest's sermon. "Don Antonio is too fine for us. He should have stayed in his seminary in Cosenza. What have we to do with his fine words? Let him impress the women!" And then his laugh had turned to a scowl of bitterness. "*Siamo bruti!*" he said, crashing his fist down on the table and spilling wine. "It's true we are brutish—his words won't change that. We're meant to be dumb like animals. Why else would we follow the Church that tells us to feed our fat Don Antonio? But even as animals we're of less value than Don Antonio's chickens or the baron's hunting dogs."

Umbertina understood nothing of who the Bruttii were or who Dante was, but she understood her father.

Carlo Nenci was a poor man, one of the many poor men of Castagna. His home was a stone hovel and he worked one piece of the large holding belonging to the Baron Mancuso di Valerba, which meant he paid the baron in labor and produce for the privilege of turning that gentleman's idle land into profit. The baron did not work the land and did not know about the land; in return for doing nothing and knowing nothing, but for having had the good fortune to be born who he was and thus owning all the land and trees and streams within sight, the baron was given half of what was produced by Carlo Nenci and the other men of Castagna. Baron Mancuso lived in Rome—he was too great a *signore* to be seen in these parts—but he could be imagined, the people said: Just multiply by a hundred times the airs and orders of his agent, the *fattore,* and that would be the baron. The wife of the baron was obese and the baron had gout, but, went the people's bitter humor, those who worked for them were fortunate because they ate little and so stayed lean and hard. We plant wheat, they said, but never taste white bread; cultivate vines, but rarely drink wine; and raise animals, but eat no meat except the tainted flesh of those that die from sickness.

The baron never came himself to collect all the abundance of his lands—the wheat, the oil, the grapes and figs, walnuts and chestnuts, the wool and cheese and flax; the person who did the collecting was the *fattore*, and to kiss the hand of the *fattore* was to kiss the hand of the absent baron.

For some it was different. For Carlo Nenci's distant relative, Serafino the shepherd, it was different because he had left, following Domenico Saccà, the socialist, to America. Domenico, sometimes called Minguccio, was a shoemaker in the market town of Soveria Mannelli, and the first of the region to go. Hotheaded, quick to flare up, filled with ideals and the frustration of what he called the unfinished revolution, he had emigrated to America because, he said, the new Italy had betrayed Garibaldi, its parent. Domenico Saccà wasn't a laborer who had sweated under the sun or shaken with the cold only to go hungry despite his toil; he could read and write, and he knew of the New World and what to expect of it.

He was not well liked by others of education.

"Let him go to America," Don Antonio said scornfully. "That is an intelligent distance for him to put between us."

In the quiet of the hills, Umbertina would think of faraway America, a place as removed from her as Don Antonio's front parlor. She knitted and thought. Hanging from her waist on a length of yarn was a crudely shaped tin heart joined to a tubular sheath that served as holder for her needles when her hands were occupied gathering wood or pushing aside the brush in her path. A border had been hammered along the outline of the heart, and three circles delineating the forms of a simplified flower, daisies perhaps, made up the design. The tin heart had been given to her by Giosuè, a charcoal maker from the next village who was young and had no prospects beyond the immediate one of being conscripted. When the time was right he would speak to her father for her; in the meantime she wore the tin heart, unaware of what love was but knowing that as all women become wives and mothers, so would she. Working to survive she understood; all the rest was of a foreign world—the world of the gentry whose men worked indoors among books and paper and whose women never used their hands except to embroider. They rode in carriages drawn by horses and looked at the poor with hostile eyes. Umbertina saw them when she drove the goats to market in Soveria Mannelli. The children of the gentry went to boarding schools or took lessons from Don Antonio, but Umbertina and those like her were untaught, for as Don Antonio said, it was not their place to be otherwise.

What Umbertina knew, she had learned through her eyes and ears and hands as she absorbed the rhythms of the life about her. She witnessed its rude forces in the rutting of the goats she herded and in the she-goats' kidding. She read the faces and listened to the words of the women who met at the stream or the well; she saw and read the language of nature and knew its portents. What did she need with books when all the world was about her?

Each day Umbertina rose from the loft she shared with her brothers and sisters above the one room of their stone dwelling, took her piece of dark bread soaked in oil and salt, or a piece of onion or goat's cheese wrapped in a square of dark cloth, released the goats from the pen that was a part of the room dug out from the hillside and separated from it by a partial grating, and went out through the steep narrow streets. At the edge of the village she drank from the fountain, still undisturbed by the girls and women who would come later to fetch water in jugs from it.

Nothing varied in the expectation of her days and nights except as the seasons passed. In the cold months there was a fire in the hearth of that bare room with its packed earth floor, a fire made of the twigs and branches she gathered while herding and packed on her back to bring home. And there were chestnuts to roast in the embers or to boil with wild fennel, those providential chestnuts from the surrounding woods that gave the name Castagna to her village and provided the flour for its dense gray bread.

In all weather, summer and winter, it was good to go up in the hills and woods with the goats. She was glad to be out of the room, which was musty and dark if no fire was lit, and unadorned except for a rough table and chairs, a chest for bread, and her parents' bed with a picture of San Francesco di Paola above it and sacks of chestnuts underneath. Umbertina went barefoot until the coldest weather, her skirt hoisted up into its waistband and showing her short sturdy legs. In the hills she always headed toward the stream whose waters fed the village fountain and then made its way down into the valley, where it vanished into the *torrente* called Corace and flowed past the old ruins of the abbey.

She sat for hours on the bank of the rushing stream looking into the depths, putting her hands in the flow and scooping up the clear, cool liquid to splash against her face, or cupping her hands to drink the pure drops. She loved the stream's clear and rapid course downward, unfettered by obstacles. It was her companion more than the goats, who were often stupid and clumsy, and whom she taunted, calling them names and shouting after them. Or whom she watched as they mated, imagining that's what it was like to be with a man.

Sometimes she lay in the sun and dozed; sometimes she scrambled up to the highest point she could reach, from which, in the fall when the leaves had dropped, she surveyed the country around her. All she saw were hills and woods and small clusters of houses in distant villages; but she knew from what she had heard that there was a huge lake of water, *l'oceano,* which could only be crossed in a journey of many weeks, so immense was it, and that it took one to a new world. The New World. It sounded to her strange and solemn—more solemn than Don Antonio's threats—almost like life after death, it was so remote. She could not imagine the hugeness of that water. Yet she knew that Serafino the shepherd and Domenico Saccà the shoemaker of Soveria Mannelli and some others, too, had crossed it to the new land.

What was its newness, she wondered; did it not have trees and hills and streams? Or goats and mules? Or people who lived in huts and went out to work in the fields? Did they not eat bread? Was the other world new because the land hadn't yet trembled and moved and knocked down the buildings? Down in the valley she could see the crumbling walls of the old monastery, which, it was said, was built in remote times by men from the north called Normans. It was old even before the earthquake of hundreds of years ago had split its walls and caved in the roof, and then other earthquakes had added to its ruin. Now it was only a place where the shepherds took a willing girl. To see the abbey there in the valley meant that Castagna was an old place, not a new one—that Umbertina knew.

What could it be to Tinuzza the goat girl that in antiquity her land was called Magna Graecia; that its city Sybaris had given the world its concept of luxury; that Plato had visited the flourishing center of Locri to learn from the masters there; that in what is now Reggio a woman poet called Nossis had sung in celebrated verses of her loves; that Hannibal had sulked in defeat in Crotone before evacuating Italy; and that Spartacus the gladiator had hid out in the Sila from the might of Rome? Rome to her was only the place where the baron, the pope, and now a king lived, all equally indifferent to the fact of her existence.

She looked about her and saw what was familiar: Over to the west where the sun sank at night was where Giosuè lived in Carlopoli, a village like Castagna perched on an elevated clearing overlooking the valley. Twelve kilometers away was the town of Soveria Mannelli. At the marketplace she saw men in the uniform of Italy, a country she knew no more of than of America. But she heard her father and other men talk, and they would shake their heads and complain about what this new country, Italy, was doing to them. She had been born the year it all happened, in 1860, when the great Garibaldi had crossed over from Sicily, and right there, at Soveria Mannelli, routed the Bourbon troops of the king of Naples in the name of the king of Italy.

It was a new thing to be Italian and the men said it brought new troubles: Taxes had come on salt and even flour milling, so the poor could no longer afford their daily bread, and many of the younger ones had gone up into the mountains, even as far as Aspromonte, to live as bandits rather than be conscripted into the armies of the new nation. There were shepherds, too, like Serafino, who had lost out when some of the old estates that had allowed pasturage on communal lands were broken up and the new money that bought them closed them off.

Don Antonio, who had chickens in his yard and ate white bread and had no worries over taxes on crops, said that it was God's will and that they were all subjects of a king who came from the far north, from Piedmont.

Of the baron's existence, Umbertina was quite sure even though she had never seen him; she grazed the goats upon his hills and gathered wood and nuts from his forests; he existed every time his *fattore* came riding through the village to collect payments and levies, raising a cloud of dust and scattering the chickens and pigs. She knew he and his fat wife existed, for they had to be fed those prodigious amounts of food and wine that her father and the others worked out of the land and turned over to the *fattore*. Umbertina had heard of the baron since her earliest childhood. But the king?

Yet she did not have to see him to know that he, too, existed and had to be fed. He had men who came and gathered taxes in his name while the price of food got higher. "*Ladro governo*," her father muttered about everything, even about the weather or crop failures in his fields. The thieving government that took everything and gave back nothing—not a road or a school or a sewer—was to blame for their misfortunes. It was the *ladro governo* that took bread from the mouths of the poor instead of giving out the lands Garibaldi promised when he told the peasants their day had finally come. The *ladro governo* taxed the poor man's working mule but not the rich man's carriage horse. The *ladro governo* had sent Garibaldi into exile and made land distribution available only to those rich enough to buy great quantities.

"It was better when it was worse," the people of Castagna and the other villages said.

And they suffered as well from nature's heavy hand: from earthquakes, landslides, floods, and droughts against which their prayers and processions rarely prevailed. Umbertina remembered in her tenth year when the earth shook and the tremor had ruined crops and widened the cracks of the poor hovels in the village, knocking the worst into rubble and loosening more stones in the old abbey. Don Antonio called it God's retribution for the sacrilege done against His Church by those who in thought or deed had helped Rome be taken from the pope. Whatever it was, it worked a sense of helplessness in the people: It would always be thus—their land worn out, rent with shocks and tremors; a faraway government in Rome celebrating a victory that was meaningless for Calabria; and with it all, a priest, like all priests, who preached God's wrath and never His mercy. Were they never to have hope? The only "Italy" that would mean anything to them would be not this old land with a new king, but whatever place would give a man bread for his family. They would leave.

Already the shepherds of the Sila, who in winter took their flocks to the coast, had come back and told of what they had heard and seen. The men from the north who were putting down rail for the train line said that many were leaving; the fishermen told of taking people up to Naples in their fishing boats so they could sail from there to America.

It was then that Serafino the shepherd left for America. He was the first from Castagna, and he was bound to go, Umbertina's father said. He had no family. He would be taken in the conscription. And for what? To defend a country that had taken away his pastures and given him taxes instead? Besides, his life had always been difficult up in the mountains with his sheep. He lived alone, nourishing himself from the cheese he made by boiling the sheeps' milk in a great iron kettle and fermenting it with the wild herbs he found. He carved wooden spoons and pipes and made reed flutes to pass the time, but it was a lonely life for a man; if he were to marry, his family would remain below in the village and he would see them only at the change of seasons when he brought his flock down.

Umbertina remembered the clear blue eyes of the tall shepherd Serafino when he had come to say good-bye.

"You are right to go," her father had said. "I am in bondage to a piece of land which is all rocks and to a family which keeps growing. If I were free I would go."

"It is a hard thing to leave one's place," said the shepherd, and his eyes were moist. "A man thinks of marrying, having sons, and being laid to rest where he was born. It is the natural way."

"Go with God," said Carlo Nenci, embracing his friend. Nothing more was heard of Serafino in Castagna, for he could not write back his news, nor would they who knew him have been able to read it.

For those who remained, life stayed the same. Only the weather varied. Summer days were filled with the dappled patterns of sunlight filtering through the trees; winter was cold. Though Umbertina's feet were then covered with goatskin shoes tied on with thongs of leather, and her shoulders were covered with a thick shawl, still her hands turned blue with the cold. Ice formed in the stream where she drank. Without the sun the days filled her with restless longings that she didn't understand.

The change in things had come in her sixteenth year. It was the day, returning from market, when she had had words with her brother Beppino.

"It's not your part to interfere in the bargaining," he had scolded, trying to intimidate, though he was younger. "When I set terms for the sale of the goats that's what it is. I am the man."

She had looked at him with the scorn she never concealed from him. She infuriated Beppino by being more clever than he was. And she didn't care.

"*Scemo*," she jeered. "You forgot the black goat is about to kid—what were you doing, giving the kid away? If I hadn't stepped in, you would have heard about it from our father later on."

"Men have to deal in these things, not women; you should have left the bargaining to me."

"I will leave you to you," she said as they reached the ruins. "Go on by yourself and tell yourself what a man you are. I am going to stop here to wash in the stream."

Scowling, Beppino waded the stream and set off on the mule path up to the village. Umbertina sat on the bank with her feet in the water, looking upstream to where women were soaking and beating their wash. The sound of singing came up behind her. It was Giosuè the charcoal maker coming back along the dirt road from Soveria Mannelli.

> "*Ssu cunocchiella ch'haiu lavuratu*
> *accettala mo' tu, ppe amore mio;*
> *ppe quante puntattelle l'haiu datu,*
> *tanti suspiri m'esciano ppe tie.*"

He was singing the song the young men sang to the girls for whom they whittled carving combs, spoons, or needle holders as signs of their affection.

Young men and women seldom met. On Sunday and holy days there was mass in the village church, where Don Antonio preached life's hard duties and the obedience required of the villagers, while the men looked over the girls and the girls kept their gaze on their beads. Once a year on the feast day of the village saint, San Rocco, they all saw each other at the procession. Sometimes they passed on the dirt road in the valley, or in the village, but they did not stop to talk. Umbertina's and Giosuè paths had crossed several times in the hills, she with her goats and he with a gang of charcoal makers. But they said only the "Good-day" that custom allowed. They had never spoken, but she was aware of his attention. And things could be learned of potential suitors from listening to the women talk around the fountain or at the stream while doing the wash. Even the poor Cristina Muzzi, near her own age and married to a relative of Umbertina's, liked to boast of her knowledge of man though she put it, as always, in a complaining way. "Ai," she said, rubbing her belly, swollen with child, "you see what a man can do! First he looks at you, like the charcoal burner looks at Tinuzza, and then you end up bursting like a too-ripe melon." But Cristina said it proudly; she was not beautiful or clever, but a man had wanted her and she wore the sign of being taken and this was her rank over the virgins. It made Umbertina wonder about the pleasure a man could give if such a miserable creature as Cristina even reflected it. It explained the warm feeling of pleasure and confusion she felt at meeting Giosuè's eyes. Or why she saw his features in her mind after he went on. Or why she imagined how it would be to lie with him. He had beautiful thick wavy black hair that she wanted to touch, he had eyes that looked deeply at her, and lips that were full.

At the stream Umbertina turned her eyes away until he came up to her and said, "I was waiting to see you. At the market there was no chance."

He held something out toward her. It was the tin heart. "I have made it for you," he said.

Silently she shook her head.

But he smiled and said, "I am Giosuè. From Carlopoli. This is for you." He was a thin young man with large dark eyes and there was something in his slightness that touched her. He didn't have the swagger of the other young men of the village.

Umbertina looked at him and then at the tin heart, which he still held out to her. He was young but his face already had a pinched, anxious look. He was also proud. "I have made it for you," he repeated. "You are Tinuzza who takes the goats into the hills."

Umbertina took the heart but looked at him with a kind of defiance. "It is not a pledge," she said. "I take it only for courtesy, not to offend you."

"It is for you," he repeated.

It both pleased and displeased her. She liked it that Giosuè had made the heart for her, but she was also wary. She wore the heart at her waist from then on to hold her needles. Then, when she knitted, it was natural to think of Giosuè. Nothing more had been spoken between them. But when in the hills or along the paths that led down to the valley Umbertina heard the faint strains of songs, like all the other girls of the village she could imagine they were being sung to her.

What would happen, she sometimes thought, if Giosuè spoke to her father? Would she go from being a poor goat girl to someone even poorer, without goats? The only thing certain was that Giosuè would soon be taken for the army and nothing could be settled until he returned.

But even as she kept the heart at her side, she felt that what she wanted was something very different. She was not one to speak aloud her thoughts, either in her family or among the girls at the fountain. Still, she had formed ideas over the years. She learned from Nelda, the priest's housekeeper. Each week when she brought Nelda goat's cheese in exchange for eggs, she learned something of life from the old housekeeper.

The only different world Umbertina could imagine from Castagna was a village all of fine houses—like Don Antonio's, where everyone had chickens and flowers in the yard, or like those in Soveria Mannelli, which belonged to the pharmacist or barber or shopkeepers.

Once she had been there on the feast day of Corpus Christi and she had seen the fine bedspreads and cloths that had been hung out the windows and from the balconies in honor of the procession and to show everyone the importance of each house. And when Umbertina saw those spreads, so brilliant with color and the designs of flowers and leaves, she knew that they were part of what she wanted, too. For her the New World they spoke of as a kind of paradise would be a place where everyone had such spreads and enough to eat each day.

And yet what had she to expect but what she knew and the place in life to which God assigned her? She knew of the struggle to eat, and the occasional joy of a feast day. She knew the patterns of life; everything was as ordained and set as the square kerchief she folded over her head and the black felt caps her father and brothers wore—these were their badges, as the hats of the gentry were theirs. Men were over women in her world, and the rich over the poor. Over everyone was God, and His minister was Don Antonio. It was God's will that girls should marry and work for their husbands and bear children, so that life could be endlessly repeated.

Since it was in the order of things, why should she not accept Giosuè, whose tin heart she wore at her side? What difference would it be to her, in the end, if it were Giosuè or any other young man from her village whom she married? A woman's role was already set, the rhythm to which her life would march already programmed. Even if life was hard, there could be comfort in sharing it with a young man such as Giosuè, a man who had showed his admiration for her. The rest would be the life she already knew.

Then Beppino, to get even for the quarrel over the goat, accused her of meeting Giosuè secretly in the hills.

"*Scemo*," she retorted.

"I saw you talking with him in the ruins," he said accusingly. "You have been seeing him."

"It is not true, but why should it concern you?" she said shortly, impatient of his tone, and infuriating him all the more.

"Women must not dishonor their families," he shouted at her.

"I have caused no dishonor," she said.

"It is not decent for *femmine* to go meeting men in the valley. I saw you the day you stopped at the stream and I went ahead."

"It was by chance," she started to explain, and then she was disgusted at herself for having to put things right with Beppino, whom she had always bettered and bossed. She shrugged her shoulders silently and walked away.

She was not sentimental; pleasure was not the first thought in her mind, and she knew that whatever pleasure she and Giosuè would eventually share would not be the kind that could be stored up like dried figs or flour in sacks to nourish them through bad times. Yet she resented what she understood in her brother's outburst —that her wishes counted not at all. That she was bound by men's notions of what women must be.

Up in the hills, she wondered what it could come to. Did she want to marry Giosuè? If she did marry him would her father be displeased and not give her a *dote*, those few household things a girl brought in marriage to her husband? In her world, she began to see, a woman could not afford the displeasure of any man—even the insignificant and sneaky Beppino.

Troubled by her thoughts, Umbertina's sensitivity to her surroundings was lulled. She did not sense the ominous stillness and the heavy pressure in the air before it was too late. The clap of thunder took her by surprise and startled the goats she was herding. One scampered away, and in her haste, as she scrambled up the hillside toward the flock to get them together, she lost her footing and slipped on the mountainous terrain, dislodging rocks that pelted her as she fell and rolled down. The thud of rocks and her own cries fell on no ears except her own. God is punishing me, she thought to herself. When her fall was finally stopped, she was bruised and cut; the rain was falling hard and the goats were bleating in panic as she stumbled back to get them together.

She could not account to herself why she was so sure that God had spoken to her through the storm. As she limped along, getting the goats together and leading them down to the village, she seemed to be thinking in the manner of those old women who believed God was always there turning their neighbors' milk sour and sparing their own, or causing children to be born crippled or simpleminded in return for some slight. Was that God's work, to mete out such misfortunes, or to send a storm in order to straighten out her thoughts?

Umbertina could not believe all the miracles the old women were always recounting, because she could see that much of it was how things were done, well or badly—or simply luck, good or bad. But she could and did believe in signs that were powerful.

Her thinking had been changed; it was God's sign to her, through the storm, that she should not think further of Giosuè.

She accepted this as naturally as she did Beppino's telling their father there was talk in the village about his sister and the charcoal burner from Carlopoli. That same night her father told Umbertina that it was time for him to think of finding her a husband.

Umbertina, a realist, accepted what her father said.

Chapter Two

Umbertina was herding the goats back into the village when she saw a tall man coming up the path from the valley. She noticed him because he was not dressed like someone of the region. He wore long trousers and a cap that was not the usual soft one that fell in a fold upon the shoulder, but a strange little one with a brim that tilted to one side; and yet he could not be a *signore* since he was walking. She thought he must be a foreigner, someone from the coast or even the North, until he came nearer. He stopped and took off his cap and wiped his brow with a cloth. His thin, graying hair receded from his forehead. Then, though his face was worn and thin, she recognized by the blue of his eyes that it was Serafino Longobardi, the shepherd who had gone to America.

Serafino's name was his nature; in a land of violent feelings and emotions that came quickly, he was instead seraphic. It was as if his temperament derived from the ingenuous candor of his blue eyes. They were of a blue seldom found in Italians, especially those of the South, and were the reason he was known as *il normanno*. The Normans who had built the abbey in the valley had also added blue eyes and tall stature to the Bruttian stock. Still, Serafino, whose name was Longobardi, must have descended from those other Northmen, the Lombard hordes who had swept through the old empire earlier than the Normans, devastating it while disseminating their seed.

Serafino was breathing hard and coughing into the patterned

cloth that he now held to his mouth. He continued to rest, and saw, as he looked around, a strong-limbed girl balancing a load of brush upon the square cloth on her head and urging on a small flock of goats. She stood tall and straight though she was of short build; her bust was high and rounded, and full hips swelled beneath her skirt, promising the fertility of her race. The roundness of her face softened the thrust of her aggressive chin. Her eyes seemed to carry the lights of the forest, greenish and brownish tones mingling in variegated shades, and as they caught Serafino's eyes, she lowered them in shyness.

A light of recognition came over his face and he broke into a broad grin.

"Tinù, Tinuzza!" he exclaimed, giving her the affectionate diminutive by which he called her as a child. And then to be sure, "Carlo's daughter?"

She looked up at him and nodded, and in that moment he saw she wore no ring. In another moment he knew he would ask for her hand. He had come back from America to marry a woman of his village and to start a family. Now that he saw this strong girl glowing with health and womanliness he thought, Why not the daughter of my friend?

"Still with the goats," he said, smiling. "Everything the same— the ruins, the old mule track . . . the good air."

Serafino walked beside her as they went toward the village. Viewing the familiar scene, he felt a great relief and at the same time a sadness. It wasn't the first time that he had returned. As a young man of eighteen or nineteen he had left Castagna to join General Garibaldi and his Redshirts after they crossed the Strait of Messina from their victories in Sicily, marching through Calabria and sweeping the Bourbons away before them. The news of the approach had crumbled the reserve of that people as nothing before. Serafino had already heard of the Garibaldini at the coast, where he took his flock. When the general himself arrived in Soveria Mannelli, Serafino sold his sheep and went off with him.

No one had ever thought of Serafino the shepherd as a soldier, much less a revolutionary. He was an easygoing, gentle man whose movements were slow. He spoke with long pauses, as if reflectively, or as if words did not come easily to him. He was used to the long silences of his stay in the mountains with his sheep; his thoughts were simple.

"Serafì, what made you go with the troops?" Domenico Saccà, the socialist, asked him when he returned.

"I thought it was time to go. They said for a few men to own all the land was not good and that we should all be free. I think that is right."

But not everyone had his simple faith, and when the general's victories were betrayed by the statesmen, the cynics laughed at the fools, at those who had believed that things could change. "The more it changes, the more it's the same," they said.

But Serafino never regretted going. Among the Redshirts he had met men from other parts of Italy whom he could hardly understand, so different was their language from his. But he listened and learned from those strangers, and got along well with them; with his blue eyes and tall stature he was more like them than like the small, dark, nervous, bitter, and sad-eyed men of Calabria. *Il normanno* his *paesani* called him, and in the words were a secret envy, an acknowledgment that he was different—that his nature was not, like theirs, intense and tormented.

After Garibaldi's troops disbanded, Serafino returned to Castagna, and since he no longer had a flock became a day laborer by putting himself out for hire each day in the market square at Soveria Mannelli. It was the lowest of all the castes of misery, lower than the herders and sharecroppers; it was the lot of those who owned nothing.

Often as he waited in the square he would see Domenico Saccà, who was always agitating and talking about injustice.

"Garibaldi was betrayed," said the fiery shoemaker. "He will not be sent here to govern and oversee the partition of lands, as he thought. He has been sent into exile by the man he made king. The troops who are coming here now are not the old ones, of Garibaldi's Thousand. They are the king's troops being sent to stop the protests and help with the conscription. As for me, I will leave now—for America."

"America," Serafino had repeated, his voice full of wonder.

"You can go too, Serafì," Domenico had exclaimed, his voice sharp with urgency. "What keeps you here? You are not *senza sale* —witless—like the ones who stick here."

"What good could it do me to leave?" asked the shepherd.

"Listen! There has to be one place in all the world where a good man, a strong man like you, can start fresh and be better than he was."

Serafino was a mild man, a man of sentiment attached to the place where he had been born and to what was familiar to him. He lived in a poor shack on the edge of the village and his day work kept him alive, although there was never enough extra to think of buying sheep or even taking a wife. But as the years passed and nothing changed, he slowly came to accept the idea that he would leave. Along the coasts were agents who told of work for immigrants to America the minute they got off the boat in Brazil or Argentina or New York, for railroads were being built in all those countries. The agents would even advance the cost of passage, to be paid back from salaries.

Serafino chose New York because Domenico Saccà had gone there, and because in his time with the Redshirts he had heard the story of how the general, before his triumph, had gone in exile near Nuova Yorka, where he made candles until he could get back to Italy.

Now, many years later, walking with Umbertina, Serafino thought of the night he had told Carlo Nenci that he would go to America for work. The little girl Umbertina and her mother had been baking loaves of chestnut bread on the hearth, and Umbertina's father had said sourly, "*Tutto il mondo è paese*—it will be the same everywhere, even America is hard for such as we. The poor have no place to rest except the grave."

"But if a man wants work he should have it. If a man can earn, he can change," Serafino said slowly, trying to repeat in his own words what he had heard so many times from the shoemaker.

All this went through Serafino's mind as he walked with Umbertina to the village. His heart had been touched when he had left the main road from Soveria Mannelli and turned into the valley where the Corace flowed past the Norman ruins. Inside, barely visible, was the dim souvenir of some past civilization that long ago had frescoed the walls with the life of Our Lord. Serafino's eye recognized and took in gratefully the pilasters and arches of the transept, the vaulted apse, the fading fresco, the ogival windows and portals—none of which he could name or identify, but which spoke to his heart as nothing in the New World had.

From the valley distance had softened the contours of Castagna, giving it a serene and nestled look among the trees on its height above—so unlike the hard, raw sight of the ugly wooden towns thrown up across those vast lands in the middle of America where he had lived and worked building railroads for six years. Even New

York and Chicago gave a feeling of makeshift, of being temporarily put together quickly, rather than being chosen sites where men set out gardens and sanctuaries for their saints. The homes were flimsy, of wood, not thick-walled stone.

Now Serafino's tubercular lungs breathed the mountain air and he was cheered by the sight of the enduring mountains, rivers, and forests, and by the hand of man in the grace of the abbey.

But the reality of Castagna was another vision: What he saw as he walked again in the dirt streets among the stone hovels was not the picturesque and distant view of centuries, but the ugly countenance of *miseria* close up.

What was he to believe? His heart had felt the beauty of Italy the moment he had touched her shore. He could not put words to what he felt: that no matter in what forsaken village there was the feel of a long bond with nature that gave meaning to the endurance of poor men and women. In America, the land was vast, and it was unknown and unshaped except for the frenzied hurtling across it of buildings and tracks such as Serafino laid. Unlike the solitude of the mountains where he had tended sheep, the solitude of America's wide expanses was broken by the furor of men pushing the railroad through, putting up towns, looking for fortunes.

But he had forgotten what *la miseria* was until he saw it again.

Back in Calabria he saw again the burnt-out fields in the plains, the thin and bent *contadini*, the ports filled with people fleeing the misery. If America was consumed by an almost brutalizing energy, a drive to change the wilderness and tame it, here instead, his eyes told him, there was no change. Even though his own lungs harbored the disease of hardship, he was still shocked at the evidence of malaria, trachoma, and rickets among the people he passed on his way inland. He had forgotten.

And what was he to believe of himself? He brought two things to his village that they had never had there: the money in his pockets and the tuberculosis in his lungs. America had given him hard work and money until the depression came, when the Italian laborers were the first to be laid off. In exchange, he had given the new country the health of a once-strong man and his very soul in sadness.

That night, gazing at the fire of his friend's hearth, Serafino sat with a Carlo who was the same as before, no richer and with no money in his pocket, but a Carlo who was the head of his home, the father of a family, and a man who still tilled the soil of his native land. He was, in the light of the village world they both knew, a man following his given destiny. He would live and die where he had been born, hearing only the tongue he knew and seeing only the faces that were familiar to him. Serafino, tasting the coarse dark bread of Castagna, the sharp goat cheese, and the strong sour red wine that was saved for such occasions, savored it all and thought of how no food of the New World had ever eased his hunger.

"Tell us, Serafì, how it was," said Carlo.

After a long pause of looking into the fire and collecting his thoughts, Serafino spoke the idea that had accumulated in his years of exile. "It is a strange thing," he said slowly, shaking his head; "here I was nothing, a poor devil with no flock, no land, no family . . . waiting in the marketplace each day to see if I would get work and would eat that night. But over there I was less than nothing. Here I had a name, and in the memory of people of this village I had been a shepherd and a follower of Garibaldi.

"There I wasn't even a Christian with a name, but just a pair of arms for the bosses to trade off. I was already promised to the railroads to pay back my passage. I didn't speak the language of America, it was the *padrone* who spoke for me. Every week we gave him the *bossatura*, the boss's part of our pay, because we can't speak to the Americans, we are dumb as animals and treated so. The Americans have nothing to do with us. And I have heard it said that America is named for one of us, an Italian! We paid the boss for the tools we worked with, the rotten food we ate, the stinking railroad cars we slept in, and even the train fare to where the railroad company wanted us to work. And still I saved money!" Here he stopped to cough into his handkerchief and to shake his head in disbelief. "That's the difference, my friend—money. Here you have *miseria* all your life and with nothing saved at the end. There you have hell, but at the end you're saved because you have money."

Serafino rubbed his forehead as he gazed down in the fire and shook his head from side to side, as if to activate the memories he had put from him. Umbertina, all the while, stayed in the shadows and listened while she kneaded the loaves from the chestnut flour.

"Where did you live?" Carlo asked.

"In the middle of that enormous land. We slept in the railroad cars and worked, that was our life. To eat we were given company bread, so bad it would turn the stomach of the goats in your pen," he said, jerking his head in the direction of the grating. "Some nights the tears would roll down my face as I remembered the clean air of the mountains where I pastured the sheep. I thought of the good cheese I made, of our bread . . . of wine. I thought of what a bad life it is for a man in a strange land that despises him, in a place with no family to take care of him when he is sick or to remember him when he is gone. What good then is money?"

He stopped, ashamed to speak further.

He thought of the filthy boxcar without windows where he and the other men had slept on straw bags placed on boards across boxes; the first time he had entered the car the stench had choked him; heaps of rubbish covered the ground around the cars and among those heaps were rusty tin boxes propped up with stones where the men cooked. When it rained the men's clothes were drenched and they had to sleep like that . . . doors closed at night, no windows, no air, the coverings live with vermin. That's how his lungs had gone. From five in the morning to noon with nothing in their stomachs but coffee to start them, they labored like beasts until they were given a sausage and bread and then went back to work. In such an existence there was no religion, no God. Serafino from time to time in Chicago and other towns had had the cheap and ugly women who were as hard as the money they traded in and as bitter as the despair they caused him. But none of this would he tell his listeners.

Serafino looked up at his friends. They were solemn and grave, as befit people who hear such a story and see a man who has sickened and come back to them. Yet what had they to offer that was any better than the misery of the American railroad gangs? They recognized their common fate as the poor of the earth and were silent for a time as they contemplated it.

"How is America to look at?" asked Carlo after a few minutes.

"Ah, my friend," said Serafino, his mouth finally breaking into a smile. "It is immense—there is land there for everyone, and pastures and forests. The rivers are like the sea between here and Sicily. You cannot imagine how far the land goes, and it is green, not yellow and dried as in our plains. And I have seen heaps of fruit under the apple trees—so much fruit that people don't bother gathering it all—it just lies there. And here, as a boy, I was whipped for taking an apple from the pharmacist's tree. Yes, for some people it will be a promised land. . . . It is a place where, if you speak the language, you call everyone 'you'; there is no special way of addressing the priest or the boss. And they say that this land was named for an Italian. That is what I learned there."

The next day, when Umbertina had gone off with the goats, Serafino came by and spoke for her. It seemed to Carlo Nenci that Providence had sent Serafino back just for this purpose. But it was unseemly to be too quick to agree, and he offered instead a courteous objection.

"She is young, Serafì, like your daughter," he said.

"She is a good and strong girl and she can come to me as she is, without dowry. I will purchase the linen that is brought to the marriage."

There could be no reasonable objection after that. They would marry when Serafino had regained his health and had purchased some land that would soon be put up at auction.

As for Umbertina, when Serafino's offer was announced to her she never considered not accepting. She knew that if she had strongly objected her father would not have forced her. But why should she object? What was important to her was that Serafino represented something new in her life. He had been to America, he knew the way.

In life there were few choices. In the hills and woods and village that were the only world she knew, she grew up with gravity already in her spirit; she observed the hardness of life with seriousness; and if it ever should happen, as it had to Serafino when he went to the New World, that she be given a choice of things, she would make the best choice and not repent afterward. And so she accepted her betrothal to Serafino.

Besides, she liked him. She liked his blue eyes and mild ways. She trusted him and she understood, too, the advantage of marrying *l'americano*, as Serafino was now known in the village. He was a man who had gone beyond the confines of his country and had learned something of men, and the world beyond. And he had brought back savings.

When she next saw Giosuè she said, "It is my father's wish that I marry Serafino Longobardi." She wanted to give back the tin heart, but Giosuè made an angry gesture with his hand, stopping her. She respected his anger and turned away. In his eyes mixed with the anger was the resignation of those who have nothing to hope for.

Umbertina looked ahead. She went to Nelda, the priest's housekeeper, who had a loom. "I want a *coperta matrimoniale* for the wedding bed," Umbertina said, "such as I have seen hanging from balconies in Soveria Mannelli on Corpus Christi day." The bedspread was the one thing she would bring to her new home and she wanted it beautiful and strong, to last forever. It was to be the traditional design of the countryside: brightly colored yarn embroidered in bunches of grapes, fig leaves, twining ivy, flowers, and the stylized hearts on the bright yellow-orange ground of thick homespun.

She went to visit Nelda every week, to see how the spread was coming. She liked going to Don Antonio's home, which stood next to the church beneath a giant and ancient tree that spread its branches over the whole of the tiny piazza overlooking the valley. Don Antonio's garden was filled with rows of tomatoes, beans, eggplant, basil, and bushes of fragrant rosemary that bloomed with a blue flower in the spring. Sheltered against the wall were fig trees and lemons. He had flowers, too, which Nelda picked each Sunday for the mass. He ate well, for he kept chickens and rabbits, and even his chickens ate well. Umbertina had seen Nelda scattering crusts of stale white bread from the priest's table—a bread she had never tasted—on the gravel around the house in which the chickens scratched. Nelda baked fresh loaves of white bread once a week, and Don Antonio was given wine by the peasants as payment for baptism. He had books in his rooms and he gave lessons in Latin to the sons of those who could afford it, like the pharmacist or tobacconist. Don Antonio was the highest person in the village and next to him Umbertina's father was nothing. Not so Serafino. Though he was illiterate and had been a poor shepherd, the pittance of money he brought from America made a difference.

And he looked different, with his American clothes and even in the way he acted. He walked differently, more freely. He could compare things, whereas the rest of them had to accept only what they saw before them or what they had always known. He came and went as he pleased to Soveria Mannelli, to Cosenza, even to the coast. No matter what stories of sacrifice and hard times he told of his experience in the New World, and no matter what harsh truth his feelings about America conveyed, what was true for Umbertina was what she saw, and she saw that he was respected and listened to because he had savings to buy land. And his health was returning in the good mountain air; his confidence also, as his marriage approached and he made the down payment on the parcel of land he obtained at auction.

It was a promising time despite Don Antonio's sour prediction in the pulpit that those blasphemers who bought secularized Church lands at auction would not be blessed with them. "You cannot take from God and expect to prosper," he said. And many believed, for the Church was powerful and there were more ways than one for it to get revenge on those who dared think they could buy its expropriated property.

"They say those who bought ten years ago are already ruined," Carlo told Serafino.

"They tried to get too much from their soil—they wore it out," Serafino answered confidently.

"Even trying to get little from soil is no good," Carlo rejoined. "This is a thin soil, a soil that washes away. Only the rich can manage it. They can afford irrigation. They can afford a large holding and keep some of it fallow. But a peasant has little and has to work it all—continually. And it dies."

"My friend, what would you have me do? Return to the mountains with a flock? One must try," Serafino answered. "Times are changing."

"All that's changed is that instead of barons being the landholders, now it's the *borghesi*—the bourgeois—who buy out the ruined peasants. For us it's always the same."

At the auction of a large ecclesiastical estate, Serafino was able to put up the minimum deposit required of bidders. Then, when he had bought the land, he put down a tenth of the purchase price on his few acres, agreeing to pay off the balance in eighteen years at 25 percent interest. He had enough to make a start. Work would do the rest.

Umbertina on the eve of her marriage went to get the finished spread from Nelda and pay her what lire her father had let her keep from the sale of some goats. "There is another thing I would like from here," she told the old housekeeper, who was at her work in the kitchen. "I would like some of Don Antonio's rosemary to plant where I will live from now on."

Nelda laughed in a raucous, rough-edged way. "They used to say you had a character because of your strong chin. And it's true, for now you want rosemary. The saying is that in the house where rosemary thrives, the women of that house are its strength."

Umbertina reddened; her desire for the rosemary was something else. She had heard Nelda say that she seasoned Don Antonio's roast chickens and rabbit stews with it, and so, proudly, Umbertina had wanted some, too, for the day when she would have chicken just as the priest did.

Nelda told the story at the fountain the next day, and the women laughed and said Serafino was not getting a wife, he was getting another man in the family.

When the words got back to him, Serafino was unconcerned. "I am not worried," he said. "My land will need all the men it can get."

The *parroco* married them in the village church, and their wedding feast, paid for by Serafino, was held alfresco on his new land. They drank the thick red wine of the region and had pasta served with ricotta, hare stuffed with chestnuts and roasted over the hearth, dried figs stuffed with almonds, and *panicelli d'uva passato*, the exquisite little bundles of grapes wrapped in leaves and slowly roasted in ovens until they became juicy raisins still filled with the taste of sun and now sweet and savory from their wrappings and the permeating smoke of the chestnut twigs.

Near the doorway of the dwelling Serafino had built for them, Umbertina planted her rosemary. That night she lay in her husband's bed. For the first time she felt Serafino's hands on her body. They were no longer the soft hands of a shepherd who has absorbed the oils of the wool he shears, but the work-toughened ones of a laborer. Yet they were gentle on her body, caressing. And when he took her as his woman, his bride, she felt his tenderness envelop her. Armed only with the notion of marriage as a state meant for childbearing, she had imagined sex as something as primitive and crude as the rutting of goats in her flock. But it was not only duty and submission to become the wife of Serafino. For the first time in her life, in her bridal bed, Umbertina felt gentleness and the warmth of affection that binds man and woman more than passion. She would never know another way. Though she did not experience what she had heard the women at the fountain describe, she was still content. It was enough to be with a good man.

In time Serafino found a market for his first crops and was able to meet his interest payments. In more time, two sons, Giacomo and Benedetto, were born to them.

Serafino now had home, family, and work. But his eyes at times clouded with bewilderment. He was a man who had thought of love often, alone in the mountains with his sheep and alone in the middle of America. And Umbertina puzzled him; her face was soft, her body was soft, but there was in her a separate will that was hard and unyielding to him. It was not that she resisted his embraces, but that she took them only as part of the marriage bargain. He was tender with her; he wanted to treat her as a girl-wife, to hold her on his knee as he had done when she was a child, to caress her, but she did not want this from him. She brought him her strength and loyalty instead.

When Serafino's American savings were gone he found he needed loans for farm animals and seed. These were charged at high interest. Then there was a fall in the price of farm goods on the market, while the dread land tax, the *catasto*, stayed as high as ever. To that was added the tax on draft animals, and to these taxes that Rome took were added the supertaxes of the provinces and communes.

Serafino struggled to keep up the installments. Then, in desperation, he began to hire out as a day laborer, going each dawn to the marketplace in Soveria Mannelli to be bid for. And Umbertina, with Giacomo and Benedetto kept in sight at the field's edge, took to working their land alone.

Two more pregnancies ended in miscarriages before the third son, Paolo, was born. Umbertina's strength ebbed and Serafino's confidence was gone.

"It is time to think of leaving," she told him.

Serafino resisted. What would he have to leave his sons, he would ask in anguish of Umbertina, if they gave up their land and went to America?

"Don't worry," she reassured him. "You gave your sweat and muscle to that new country—now it can give something back to you for your sons."

Slowly, he was persuaded. This was the bitter lesson of his life that he must swallow for the sake of the sons already here and for the children who would come after.

Reluctantly he agreed to leave: "Italy doesn't want us—it makes us bandits or beggars in our own country. It pretends to give us land in exchange for our money and work, then takes it back with taxes and interest while the rich are exempt."

"We cannot live here," said Umbertina. No longer were there

the old communal rights of gathering wood, food, or stone on feudal lands as she had done in her years as a goat herder.

And though Serafino marveled at her willingness to go, it had all been decided in her long before, at the time she agreed to be his wife. It was a hope she had always kept alive within her even during the years of trying to succeed on the land.

When the time came for departure from the little stone house where she had lived seven years with Serafino and where her sons had been born, the scent of rosemary filled the air from the bush which had grown from the shoot Nelda gave her. How do I know, she thought, if there will be rosemary where I am going? She dug a root and carefully wrapped it close to the dampness of Paolo's swaddling clothes. Just to be sure, she would take her own with them. And she took the tin heart, which had always been at her side reminding her that she had made her choice. The marriage spread was packed with their few clothes, the whole covered by a sheet and looking like a bundle of laundry.

It was she who reassured Serafino about their leavetaking. He no longer wore American clothes, nor had American money in his pocket. He wore his country rig of years past—the high pants held up by a thick leather belt around his waist, and his shoulders covered by a mantle. And still he worried, remembering the crowded chaotic streets of New York when he landed there fifteen years earlier: the wagons, the throngs of hurrying people, the miles of buildings, and not a field in sight. How would Umbertina, who had lived all her life in the open, live in New York? But they had to go, and this time it was for good.

As if in answer to his thoughts, her own responded: She would make the change that was called for, she would change her place for her children's sake. But she wondered to herself if it would be pleasing to God, or not, that they change their place in the world. Would God see her and know her in the strangeness of the New World where Serafino said there were no churches for such as they? Or would they add to their sins and end up more miserably? She had to believe that God would bless them, and, as if to seal a bargain, she made a sign of the cross.

They left Castagna with their last possession, a donkey, bearing the children and bundles. They descended the path into the valley and passed by the ivy-covered ruins of the Norman abbey on the banks of the Corace.

Serafino stopped and told her to take a last look up at the village.

She said she would like a drink before they went on, and filled a jug at the water and drank from it, offering it also to her husband and the small Giacomo. Then they left the valley. She did not look back, but Serafino did and his blue eyes filled with tears, for he knew there was no coming back. And he knew that his strength was less now than it had been fifteen years ago; if he hadn't won America over then, how would he do so now?

Chapter Three

Each step reinforced the feeling of the great wrench their lives had been given. Uprooted, they were set loose from their land and their people. For Serafino it was defeat; for Umbertina, confidence grew from the moment the children and bundles were put on the donkey and they walked the road to Soveria Mannelli, there to join the other emigrants headed for Cosenza and then the coast.

From that day Umbertina was never again alone, but always with others; among people talking, complaining, weeping, swearing, praying, eating, laughing, vomiting, urinating, lamenting. Sometimes she felt a longing beyond words or prayers, like a physical ache, to go back in time to the days of her solitude in the hills. Then she would be ashamed; she was a woman, with a husband and three sons, not a girl among goats. She never spoke of her feelings; she kept her thoughts in silence. But Serafino, simple as he was, could read the fleeting shadow of distress in her face and would bend over and say, "*Coraggio, coraggio.*" When he did so, her shame at her weakness was doubled. He was her companion, her friend.

At Soveria Mannelli they sold their last possession, the donkey, and bought bread and dried figs for the trip. Another bit of the money went to pay their way in the wagon that would take them to the sea. Umbertina was troubled at the small price Serafino got for the donkey. She saw how those who left their homes were truly without place or meaning, or protection—at the mercy of whomever they met in their journey, and with whom they could not bargain.

They were transients in the land of their fathers, heading away from it, and it gave them a queer sense to be adrift between the old country and the new, belonging to neither. The journey impressed her with the feeling of place: Wherever it might be, one had to have a place in the world.

They were joined in Soveria Mannelli by two young brothers, Zeno and Bruno Saccà, cousins of Domenico the shoemaker, who were going to join him in the town where he had settled, a place called Cato in what they called the state of New York. Then there was Gino Gualtiero, a handsome young man who was leaving behind his new wife with the promise to send for her when he had work; and Cristina Muzzi, who had with her the three children born from each of her immigrant husband's visits back to the old country and who would have been satisfied to live that way indefinitely if Giovanni Muzzi hadn't had Domenico write a letter to Don Antonio in Castagna asking him to read this message to his wife: "Either come with the children to live with me here or you won't see any more of me or of the money I've been sending you. This is the last remittance—use it for the passage money, or good-bye for good. Your husband, Giovanni."

Umbertina, related to Giovanni Muzzi, gave a hand to the whining, crying Cristina, who had always been a poor creature in Castagna, without salt or backbone. Now Umbertina liked her even less for her continual lamenting and her thin, pinched face and the way she frightened her children by her moans and sighs of "*Gesù! Gesù!*"

"Are you still a girl living under your father's roof?" Umbertina chided her, and as she spoke she knew she was chiding herself too. "Or are you the wife of your husband and mother of his children, and a woman with work to do?"

"It is a curse to leave one's home and the place where one is known to go among strangers," said Cristina. And in her heart Umbertina acknowledged this truth. But she only answered, "We are doing this for our children, and they will not be strangers where they grow and work."

"*Che Dio voglia!*" said Cristina, her thin face made even more scrawny and pinched-looking as it contorted with weeping. Her two girls were about the age of Giacomo and Benedetto, and like Umbertina, Cristina also had an infant in her arms.

They soon left the green forests along the mountain road that twisted down to the valley where Cosenza spread at the confluence of two rivers. There they rested in a public park filled with marvelous plants Umbertina had never seen before—acacia, tall palms, eucalyptus, and cassia; she filled her leather flasks with water from the fountains, and as the family ate their coarse bread she looked at the finely dressed people who strolled through the gardens as if they had nothing else to do with their time. In the wide, paved streets horse-drawn buggies rang with the sounds of bells on harnesses and passengers sat under gay, tasseled canopies that sheltered them from the sun. The sun was strong there, in the lowland.

Cosenza, a provincial capital in the heart of Calabria, looked already foreign to Umbertina's eyes. But it was after they made their way through the plains and toward the mountain range in the distance which separated them from Paola and the sea that she began to feel in a very different world. Gone were the trees and fresh cool air of her hills; they were in a parched and desolate land of baked dry earth crisscrossed by gullies. Farmhouses stood on burntout mounds of yellowish soil where not a piece of green grew; nearly dry riverbeds were thick with flowering oleander bushes and rocks among the trickles of water or stagnant pools. And the people they passed were not like the people of the Sila, their people; these in the plains looked as yellow and dried-out as the soil. They were stunted, thin, weak creatures with sallow skin and deep-set, glazed eyes. A few exchanged greetings and asked where they were going. "America, ah yes," they replied, as if sharing some secret; "we will follow if God is willing."

"God!" said Zeno Saccà in a tone that sounded to Umbertina like blasphemy. "God has forgotten them and their land."

"I did not know there were others worse off," she said to Serafino. And he remained silent, keeping to himself what lay before them in New York.

Umbertina looked and considered as they journeyed; she saw why what they passed through was called the old country. The land was parched, thin, worn-out, dying. And she wondered if it had dried out because it was so aged; if so, how long before the New World would itself become old? And when that happened, when the new was used up and dried out, where would people go? Would that be the end of the world that Don Antonio was always preaching?

The sound of singing that came from a patch of olive trees they approached was like a wail solacing itself in the face of God's indifference. It came from the heart of that scourged land as if from some antechamber of hell. It was a love song, but even love songs were wails of despair—the invitation to mate, to couple with one's man to produce the children who would go on perpetuating, without knowing why, the misery of lost lands, lost prospects, lost lives.

The olive grove was at the edge of a barren plain, where it began to ascend into the mountains to the west of Cosenza, and then again they were among trees and shade. The road was incessantly winding, often doubling back upon itself up sides of gorges and skirting precipices. Once they passed a cross that Serafino said must have been set up to mark the place where a traveler was killed by bandits. But they, too poor to rob, passed unmolested.

It was still light when they descended into the coastal town whose Calabrian saint, Francesco di Paola, was namesake of Paolo, the infant Umbertina carried in her arms. The boat from Messina would stop in Paola and take them on to Naples for their departure across the ocean. They were weary from the long trip in the wagon, sitting on the bundles of belongings. The wagon driver from Soveria Mannelli left them at the marina below the town and they arranged their things around them, sitting in a silent circle facing the sea, which most of them had never seen before. There was no harbor; some fishing boats were pulled up on the sand; some people from the town had come down to wait at the shore for the boat from Messina. Dressed in uniform, the *dazio* officials, contemptuous and discourteous, poked through the poor bundles of the emigrants and asked what they had to declare.

"We are not traders," said Bruno Saccà, always ready to jump to the attack, hotheaded like all his family. "We are emigrants and these are our belongings."

"Yes, the treasures you are taking to America," said an officer sarcastically, and the others, bored with their ridiculous job of searching poor peasants and claiming a few miserable coins off each bunch of onions or grapes to be traded in the marketplace, started laughing.

"Will we find pigs of tax collectors over there in America?" Saccà asked Serafino.

"No, you can move from place to place without being stopped and searched," he answered. "But you have to beware of the *padroni* —our countrymen from the cities who can read and write and have learned enough English to serve the American bosses and make their fortunes off our ignorance. There are some good *padroni*, but mostly bad ones. Watch out for the *napoletani* and *siciliani*."

Umbertina's eyes, the colors of water mixing with the strand of sandy beach, took in the new wonders of the sea, the thick orange groves, the olive trees banked up the hillside, the flowering cactus and bougainvillea that splashed gaudily over the whitewashed houses on the hill. Vendors started coming down to the beach, approaching their group and other groups, and waiting for travelers who might arrive in that unlikely place on the Messina boat. Serafino saw Umbertina's eyes taking everything in as she sat nursing the baby. The two little boys, Giacomo and Benedetto, played in the sand near her.

Serafino walked toward a vendor, took some money from his pocket, and came back with oranges. He peeled one and gave her and the boys some sections of the fruit. "Eat this," he said, "it's an orange."

"You shouldn't have wasted our money," she said shortly, as was her way. "It wasn't necessary."

"Not because it's necessary," he replied. "Because you've never had an orange and they are good."

She blushed with shame. He had done her a kindness and she had answered him like a shrew. As she bit into the juicy section and savored its sweetness, she looked up at him and said, "Yes, it is good. Will they have oranges in America?"

"Yes, yes. There is everything there," he said.

For a moment she who was so practical, so resolute and realistic, joined his fantasy—because it was fearful leaving a known place and having only one person to depend upon in all the world; because the long journey lay ahead; because they were gambling on the future without knowing what was there. Her thoughts went to Giosuè. What had happened to him? Where did he live? What was his life? If she had accepted him years ago she might not be sitting on this shore now. *Stupida!* she chided herself. She had no time in her life for romance and daydreams. She had made the right choice.

The small steamer arrived and was anchored offshore while the fishermen's boats went out and discharged the freight and the few passengers. There were other emigrant groups on the beach besides the one from Soveria Mannelli. The others had come from villages in the plains or from along the coast. Their dialect had a somewhat different intonation from that of the hills. But they were all emigrants, all homeless now, with the men dressed as if in mourning in the dark clothes that were their best, the short jacket and trousers they had been married in. The women wore the aprons and bodices of that time, and shawls, some very beautiful and colorful. Umbertina's treasure of color, the matrimonial spread, was in the bundle Serafino carried with the few other possessions they had. She carried the sack of their food and water.

No one spoke. The weather changed as they sat there—a sudden squall had come up and it began to rain. Wet and shivering they cloaked themselves in their coarse mantles and shawls and sat patiently among their bundles, knowing as always that they could do nothing against the elements. Patience had always been their lot.

Zeno Saccà wandered among the other groups, talking with the men. When he came back, he said to Serafino, "A priest is coming to give benediction before we leave."

Cristina Muzzi was moaning and holding her head in her hands. "It is a sign, this storm. It is bad luck. I never wanted to go from my home. It is not right to be forced. . . ." She was frightening the children. "Will you go back to Castagna then?" Umbertina asked impatiently, constraining her to silence.

They waited while the *dazio* checked the discharged cargo and passengers from the Messina boat. The two boys dozed, huddled against Umbertina while she sheltered the baby against her heart beneath the protection of her shawl.

They stayed there in the growing dark, the whole group of them huddled together with their children clutching them, their few sacks of belongings at their feet. A few children whimpered, many slept in their mothers' arms. They were waiting for the priest and his voice of reassurance. It was somehow fitting that they should leave at night, slipping away like shadows from the country that had not wanted to hold them.

Serafino squatted next to Umbertina. "Are you tired?" he asked her.

She shrugged her shoulders in a noncommittal gesture. The women of Calabria are not often asked how they feel, and again Umbertina was ashamed of her behavior, for Serafino was not like the other men. There was a cry from one of the groups: "The priest is coming!"

The priest was a simple unshaven man who looked almost as

poor as the group on the beach. The rain had stopped, but the sea was turbulent and a wind was growing, making some of the men mutter with apprehension while the women shivered and moaned among themselves. A man approached the priest and said, "We would feel better about setting out from our land if it were not on a sea like this, which will frighten our women and children, who have, already, enough fears of what is beyond. Can you persuade the captain to stay over until morning?"

The captain had come ashore with the last rowboat to consign some papers to the officials. When the priest put the matter to him he answered roughly, "Tomorrow morning I'm expected in Naples and that's where I'll be." Then he signaled to the emigrants to get into the boats that would take them to the steamer.

"You might add 'If Gods wills it,' " the priest said quietly.

"If He wills it or not, I'll be in Naples tomorrow," the captain said curtly, and the people quickly blessed themselves and murmured at that defiance. They, in their lives, had never before knowingly defied fate; now they saw the journey itself as a great defiance of Providence.

When they knelt on the shore for the priest's benediction, there was fear in their hearts. Some kissed the priest's hand; some pressed their last coin into it and asked that a candle be lit in the church for their intention.

"These are bad times," said the priest at the end. "I will pray for you and may the Good Lord attend you. You heard how the captain spoke. This is what happens from imprisoning the pope and setting up priest-hating governments."

Zeno Saccà turned to his brother and gave a disgusted grunt. "*La politica!*" he said. "Even as we're leaving!"

From the boat rowing out to the steamer, Umbertina could see the black shapes of mountains looming behind the few flickering lights of the town. She said a prayer to St. Francis.

"Good-bye to the old country," said Zeno Saccà buoyantly, "and long live the new!" From deep within her Umbertina echoed his assurance that the new, though unknown, was going to be better. Perhaps it was the taste of the orange, its sweetness still in her mouth, that made the future seem to her so full of promise.

"I wonder how the New World will be," Bruno said reflectively.

Serafino, standing nearby, answered, "A land where we arrive like infants, and where we have no past."

"Then we will make our memories and our history," Zeno retorted.

In Naples there commenced the noise and crowds that Umbertina would ever after associate with *lo strappo*, the uprooting. In Castagna people had been poor, too, but quiet and proud; here instead, in the city, were street urchins, beggars, cripples, and whores all gesturing and importuning. Some Neapolitans, cocky and already using their sharp city ways to prey upon the country people, whom they called *terroni*, were among the *Abruzzesi*, the Calabrians, and the emigrants from the Lazio, Campana, and Basilicata regions; all were destined for America, as if all of Italy were going across the sea. The tiny group from Castagna and Soveria Mannelli clung to each other among those other "Italians," who were, in fact, the first foreigners they met. All was different now for Umbertina, who had begun to live among strangers.

She saw them there, on the boat, a herd of people all headed in one direction for different purposes: those with trades and skills, who could be barbers or tailors in America and looked down on the peasants; those who went seasonally for immediate gain—to get some money and then return, better off, to their old home; those from the city who accompanied the peasants like parasites, sensing that they could profit from their ignorance in the New World; those like Serafino, who went humbly looking for any honest labor by which to earn bread; those like the Saccà brothers, who went with a kind of idealism, looking for a government of men more just than the one they were rejecting; those like Cristina Muzzi, who went passively, caught up in a drama they didn't even recognize, destined to be the same in the New World as they had been wherever they came from in the Old; and finally, there were some like Umbertina, who believed they were the sacrificial catalysts of change, the ones who were to give their children two births—life itself and new life in the New World.

Chapter Four

In years to come Umbertina would say she could not remember the long weeks of the passage over, only that it was miserable sharing those stifling dormitory quarters in the hold with the other women and children (the men were put elsewhere); trying to sleep without privacy; trying to feed and care for the children, wash diapers and menstrual napkins and clothes stained with vomit from seasickness and the nausea caused by the fetid air; trying to keep a decency of person and clothes that they no longer felt, since the way they were made to bunk like animals soon gave them the conviction of being animals. At the end the captain had to order some of the worst to clean themselves and to throw the worst of their garments overboard before the quarantine officer set foot on the ship. Some who were fearful of being sent back had hidden their sick ones; others struggled to stand up and look well.

The day was fair and clear when they reached New York Harbor, and the little group from Castagna was at the rail of the deck to see the approach, their eyes fixed gravely with the importance of the moment.

For years they had been hearing from Domenico Saccà about the wonders of Cato, where there were factories and great houses and gas-lit streets and everyone had work. Now, as they sailed into New York Harbor, Cristina Muzzi looked about her, awed, and said, "If this is only New York, what can Cato be like?" In their safe old age, they would remember what Cristina had said and laugh. But at the moment there was no laughter, only relief and thankfulness.

"*È bella*," Umbertina exclaimed almost in surprise as they steamed past the harbor islands and she saw, in the thick green on shore and the fine wooded hills that arose from the New Jersey side of the Hudson, the promise of a beneficent and plentiful nature; and in the wonder of the newly completed Brooklyn Bridge her eyes read the marvels to be accomplished in this world of new men. All about them in the busy harbor were signs of industry and commerce in the great traffic of tugs, steamers, cargo barges, and ferryboats.

By the time they boarded the tender that took all the immigrants ashore to the landing stage of Castle Garden at the Battery, Umbertina's anxieties had turned to hopefulness. Even as they were herded into the Rotunda and lined up to give their names and birthplaces to a registrar who noted them down in a large ledger, her spirits kept up. Then they were asked their places of destination. Serafino said New York. The others from Castagna said Cato and were told where to go to get train tickets.

She and Serafino embraced the Saccà brothers, Gino Gualtiero, and the weeping Cristina Muzzi and her children before they separated. The Longobardis, penniless now, had to stay in New York until Serafino made enough money for the trip upstate.

"Tell Minguccio we'll be coming," he told Zeno.

"Don't forget to come, Serafì," said the others.

Umbertina realized then that when they departed the last connection to the old home would be gone. They would be alone.

Serafino made his way toward the Labor Exchange and there he found who he was looking for, a *padrone*. "There he is," he said to Umbertina, pointing to a dark, short man with wide mustaches who was wearing a black bowler, the first hat of that kind she had ever seen. "He is the man who can get me work."

Umbertina stood back with the children, as was proper, while Serafino engaged in some words with the short man around whom were collected several strong-looking young immigrant men who had been on the ship. They looked dazed and wondering; they were alone, without families, and needed work. All of them needed the *padrone* and Umbertina could tell already that he would simply be an agent, like the baron's *fattore*, living and getting rich off the labor of others by taking from them part of what they worked for. Her brows knit in a frown of disapproval as she looked sharply at the man in the strange hat. Good, she thought to herself with her ironic bent, we have crossed the ocean to trade the *fattore* for a *padrone*.

Serafino was, as usual, trusting. "He will get me work," Serafino told Umbertina. "He knows the American bosses. They are building an underground railroad in New York and he can get me work."

"You did not want to work ever again on the railroad," she said irrationally, knowing as she did that there was no choice now.

"It is only until we have the money to leave for Cato," he said. "A few months."

In the Rotunda the sorting out of the silent and stoic-looking immigrants by the *padroni* from various regions was still taking place. They were claiming workers according to where they came from in the old country and what dialect they spoke. Now these little groups of people, mostly men but some with women and a few children, left Castle Garden, each behind its leader.

Out in the open Umbertina's eyes were assaulted by a throng of buildings all around them. The steeple of old Trinity Church could be discerned down the end of a street, and the large seven-story Washington building and Produce Exchange loomed above them. There seemed to be a forest of ships' masts at anchor in the harbor, and the tugs and ferries still were going back and forth frenetically. Never had she seen such busyness, heard such noises and clamor, and felt such a press of buildings around her. The eyes of all the newcomers, glazed with seeing so much, darted around as if in search of some still center on which to locate. But everything was moving.

Serafino and Umbertina got into the *padrone*'s open, horse-drawn wagon with the children and bundles, and the others of his *clienti*, and began the trip from the docks on the Battery at the end of the island some forty blocks across town up Broadway. They were headed for Mott Street where it ended in Bleecker, just a block or so west of the Bowery. Umbertina had Paolo in a sling across her chest, while her hands still gripped the end of the bundle, flung over her back, that contained their clothing and what bread remained. Her eyes ached with the endlessness of buildings that shut out the sky and sun, with the crowds of people, wagons, and carriages. They passed horse-drawn street sprinklers, warehouses with bales and barrels of goods spilling out into the streets, a forest of telegraph poles and wires, horse-drawn trolleys, awninged storefronts, and fine large Renaissance or Gothic buildings that housed banks.

Umbertina was truly awed by the number of rich-looking *signori* she saw walking, riding in carriages, or descending from trolley cars. They passed cigar-store Indians, signs and posters of every sort. Pushcarts and peddlers with all kinds of wares.

Could any city be so rich and vast, she thought as she passed one splendid building after another, some colonnaded like Greek temples and adorned with marble and reclining figures in cornices; others spired, pinnacled, and strewn with finials like cathedrals; others with cast-iron facades or mansard roofs and story-high arched windows like the block-long McCreery's Department Store. Even the elevated train that crashed over their heads had station stops fashioned like Swiss chalets.

Her head throbbed with the noise. By the time they had gone up Canal Street to Mott the scene changed. Rickety old wooden buildings of two and three stories were wedged between taller brick buildings whose fronts were festooned with the black tangles of fire escapes, over which clothing, mattresses, bedding, and people were draped. The entrances were covered with awnings, a solid line of them down the street, and the sidewalks were jammed with stands of merchandise and with rubbish cans, forcing people into the street, which was itself thronged with pushcarts, delivery wagons, peddlers with trays over their shoulders, running urchins, and dogs. Heaps of rubbish, paper, and moldering vegetables—the only green she saw—were everywhere.

"Where are the trees?" she murmured to Serafino as they inched through that inferno of bodies, her eyes heavy with the multitude of things imprinted on them.

"Not here," he answered, "out there," and he jerked his head with his chin pointing ahead toward imagined distances to the north.

When they crossed Prince Street the man in the bowler hat gestured around him and said, "Sicilians. The street of Sicilians." At Mulberry he said scornfully, "This is the street of the *napoletani*, a bad street—full of fights and bandits."

Thus Umbertina learned that she was in America but living in a little Italy, in streets filled with Italians arranged according to where they had come from in the old country. The children were whimpering with fatigue by the time they reached the end of Mott Street where the Calabrians lived.

The voice of the *padrone* cut into her thoughts. "*Le Baracche,*" he was saying, the Barracks. And her eyes followed to where he was pointing—to a large brick building almost at the end of Mott Street, three stories high, with windows lining the front, from which plants, mattresses, rags, and people hung. On the street level, women sat on the front stoops holding babies and working at garments piled near them; other women walked through the streets bearing bundles of fabric on their heads as Umbertina had once carried kindling wood in the old country; the sidewalk was littered with papers and refuse, and children squatted among barrels and broken-up crates to pitch stones. Between buildings there were alleys crisscrossed with clothes where the sun never penetrated, and narrow passages littered with empty bottles, garbage, and occasional tramps—sometimes a woman—lying on the stones in a drunken sleep. There were stores with long salamis and cheeses hanging in the window; old clothes were sold on the sidewalk; and even stale bread lying on dirty mattress ticking in huge wreaths and loaves, guarded by ragged old women who called out "*Pane vecchio,*" was sold for a penny. For the rest, the *padrone* would amiably point out *la banca, la posta, la polizia.* He spoke proudly of Nuova York, saying it already had more Italians than Rome; this was just one section of a city that stretched on and on. "The city is growing. There is work for everyone," he said cheerfully. "The elevated railroad, the subway, the bridges, the factories. The Americans are always building and tearing down and starting again."

To Umbertina, in her fatigue, it sounded like God's curse, a curse of dissatisfaction and restlessness. It was a matter of indifference to her how great Nuova York was. If it was a great city, why didn't it have a park with plants and a fountain so that weary people like them could rest and drink as they had done in Cosenza. Here when bells rang in the street, it was not canopied horse-carriages that passed, but the ragpickers' carts. Her eyes were dulled with so much seeing, and all her senses hammered by the constant din.

Serafino, who had seen it all before, was unmoved, resigned.

"We won't stay here," she said to him. "We will get to the country."

The *padrone* heard her and laughed with the contempt of the learned for the ignorant. "Did you come to America to remain peasants, to work in the fields?" he asked. "Here there's money. Here there's work."

"I want to start," Serafino said.

"Get yourself a pick and shovel and you can work tomorrow. I'm taking a gang up for the subway."

They came to Bleecker Street, and at the end of the block where the street terminated in the Bowery they could see the girders and rails of the Elevated. The house they entered was one of the older ones, a narrow, three-story wooden structure of old New York, once the private home of some well-to-do merchant and his family. The broad brownstone steps were worn; the once-graceful columns alongside the front door were rotted, and the lunette above it the only sign of a once-fine residence. The house was now partitioned off and forty people were squeezed into its spaces. The only space not rented out as lodgings was the first-floor saloon, which opened onto the side alley. The roar and rush of the elevated train shook the house as they were entering and filled Umbertina's head, frightening the baby in her arms.

The hall they walked into was stained with the marks of a thousand grimy hands that had passed that way; the stairs were decaying. Under the stairwell a dirty, tattered curtain closed off a sleeping-space that was home to the cobbler who at that moment occupied the hall with his bench and tools and looked up briefly as they passed.

As they went up the stairway the heavy smells of cooking enveloped them, and an undefinable stench that they would soon recognize as that of human bodies, unwashed, closely packed in un-aired spaces; it got darker and the air closer and they could hear clearly the sounds of tenement life: babies wailing, men cursing, women screaming out windows.

"You have a room to yourselves," the *padrone* was telling them. "It's at the top—you won't have people above you." He opened the door to an attic room under the roof, stifling hot, with a dormer window that let in what little light and air could filter between the taller buildings all around them. The room had a bed, a table, a wood-burning stove with a pipe that went out through the wall, and some battered old pans that hung from a wall whose papering was peeling off in shreds.

"*Padrone*," said Serafino, "I want to work. I need money for the pick and shovel."

"Here," said the man, his face wrinkled in disgust at the heat and stench of the room they stood in. "This will come out of your first pay. The month's rent here is $10 and that will come out of your pay, too. Then there's the $2 each month you owe me for finding you work. Agreed?"

"Can I not agree?" said Serafino, overwhelmed at the news of the high rent for that miserable room.

"Agreed then," said the *padrone*. "You'll have credit at the saloon downstairs and at the *groceria*—just tell them you're working for me." As he left, he turned back and said, "I guarantee credit for all my men as long as there's no trouble."

Serafino watched him leave. In his head he had figured up already that almost half of what he could earn in a month would be gone between the rent and the *padrone*.

Umbertina understood that before they had even started their American life they were mortgaged to a *padrone*. How would Nuova York have been built, she wondered, if there hadn't been people desperate enough to enslave themselves in its building? Still, they had shelter of sorts, and after the *padrone* left, Umbertina went down to the old courtyard in the rear of the house to the hand pump to get water for them. Where a garden and orchard had stood in the house's better days, the high brick walls of a rear tenement now encroached. The sheds in the back of the old house had been turned into outhouses, whose stink lay trapped in the heavy air between buildings. The space between buildings was clotted with wash hanging from lines strung between walls—banners of defiance against a harsh lot that hung there in brave and touching statements.

The women in the courtyard, who were washing over stone-slab sinks, looked up as Umbertina came to the pump. Dirty children and bony dogs ran among the dripping clothes, and the cramped space was crowded with heaps of refuse, tubs, pails, sacks of rags and bones and bottles from the scavengers' rounds, and empty pushcarts. Umbertina worked the hand pump vigorously, but no matter what the effort only a trickle came out.

"It always happens in the summer when we need it most," a woman called out to her in the familiar dialect of Calabria.

"What do you do?" Umbertina asked.

"There's always stale beer, no shortage of that," another woman laughed grimly.

And Umbertina, gathering what she could from the trickling pump, thought of the clean air and sun in the hills above Castagna and the taste of the clear spring-water in which she used to bathe her face on summer days, kneeling and cupping her hands to fill them with the cool, sweet water that ran its way down to the valley.

It was in the courtyard, among the women at their wash, that Umbertina learned many things. She heard how the woman who was there constantly, washing load after load, was a widow whose husband had been killed on a construction job and who now, to feed herself and four children, did laundry for 35¢ a load—out of which she had to deduct the cost of coal, soap, starch, and blueing— and then walked uptown to deliver the wash at the back doors of the rich. Other women took in single men as lodgers for 75¢ a week. Umbertina was shocked at this violation of family privacy and said so.

"*Che vuoi?*" she was answered. "It helps pay the rent and it's better than doing piecework for a *padrona* who gives you a few cents and then makes her own profit selling it to the Americans."

Umbertina had to agree. If there was one thing she was learning about American life, it was the need to be her own boss.

"It's worse for a woman," said the washerwoman. "It takes a woman three days in a sweatshop—if she's lucky and not fined— to get what a man does in one day."

"That's because there are too many people who want work," said another. "The bosses don't have to pay us to live, there are always more people coming in."

It was also in the courtyard, some days later, that Umbertina learned that the true rent for their attic room was $7 a month, not $10, which meant the *padrone* was pocketing the difference. When she got Serafino to mention the rent difference to the *padrone*, Serafino suddenly found himself off the work-gang. The American boss wouldn't rehire him without the *padrone*'s word, since he didn't want troublemakers or anarchists on the job making every-one dissatisfied. To get back on the gang would now cost Serafino an extra $1 a month in kickback.

"We are in his hands," Umbertina said when she learned how things had gone. "How will we save enough to get out?"

They ate frugally and Umbertina took in wash, and somehow every week they managed to save some of Serafino's pay even after the debts were deducted. But Umbertina was wrong when she told the women with whom she washed that they would soon be leaving. It took them two years.

Chapter Five

From the first Umbertina had kept her marriage bedspread on the one bed of that room. It not only kept them warm in winter, it was her one thing of beauty in all that squalor; it was her remembrance of leaves and flowers and the sun overhead, just as it was the image of what they had come for—something better than they had known.

During their first summer, when babies in the tenements dropped like flies, the city's summer doctors came with free advice and medicine; following them came nurses from the Board of Health's Italian department. The visiting nurse who came to Umbertina's block was an Italian woman named Anna Giordani. Her family had arrived in the earlier, political immigration of 1848 when Garibaldi himself had arrived in America after defeat in the siege of Rome. The Giordanis were northern Italians of the Protestant Waldensian sect; they were educated and had some money. Anna Giordani was a middle-aged spinster who was devoting her life to work among the new Italian immigrants, the southerners, who were as removed from her experience as the Negroes of New York were from the whites. She felt in conflict about these people, who, politically, she had to consider her countrymen, and spiritually her brothers. She never managed to like them, but she did her duty unflinchingly, as a kind of penance and discipline for her soul. She was tall, lean, fair-skinned, with watery light eyes and graying brown hair. She was fastidious; she wore white gloves and every bit of her person was clean and orderly when she came to work in the slum tenements.

It astonished Umbertina to see such a lady in her attic room the first day Anna Giordani came to call on her. From the start, Anna respected Umbertina. She saw in her the stubbornness of not wanting to succumb to the tenements, of being determined to leave them behind.

"*Brava, signora*," she said encouragingly. "Things will get better for you because you want them to." And she admired the bedspread from Castagna, which shone like an ensign of hope in the dingy room.

It was Anna Giordani who helped Umbertina get Paolo through that critical first summer. She showed Umbertina how to get to the East River with the baby and children so they'd get a breath of moving air to fill their deprived and pinched bodies. Umbertina was still nursing Paolo, but she would buy milk for the other boys and take them all to the river, where they would watch the boats with their cargoes of garbage being picked over by Italian ragpickers for what they could scavenge; or they would see the unmarked coffins of the poor being taken on barges to Potters' Field, where they would be dumped in a trench at city expense, crowded in death as they had been in life to save space that had more value for the city than their lives; or, from the new piers on the East River, they'd watch the naked boys who swam from them until the police came to chase them away.

Once she saw tramps and vagrants and a group of lunatics being taken by guards out to the penal workhouses and asylums on the islands in the East River, which looked green and inviting with their trees and which her eyes strained toward. In Calabria the harshness of life had made people sick in body; here, she saw, the life sickened the heart and soul.

She was learning the American story—money was the key to everything. If you were fortunate enough to keep your health and reason in the midst of the purgatorial tenements you were forced to pass through in the New York sojourn, you might be able to get to some other place with the money you saved.

But the tenement got and kept most lives; it made people into its own image, lower than when they had arrived. Anna Giordani was always exclaiming, "Why do you Italians put up with the worst conditions, take the worst jobs, and then either send your money back to Italy or let yourself be robbed of it by a *padrone!*"

"*My* money won't go back," Umbertina told her fiercely. "It's to get us out of here. We are not like the *napoletani* on Mulberry

Street. They came from the slums of Naples and are happy in the slums of New York. But we are country people. We don't live like this."

That winter and the next they froze, trying to keep warm in the attic room with whatever coal or wood Umbertina and the boys were able to scavenge from the streets. Serafino's gang work stopped when the snow came, so that all he could earn during the winter was whatever he got from shoveling snow. The children loved the sight of snow falling out of the sky, and Umbertina, too, found peace in its softness and the quiet it brought. It seemed right that Christmas should come in such softness. She learned from her neighbors to make a *granita di caffè* with the freshly fallen snow, some coffee, and sugar. But soon the white blanket turned to black slush, making the streets worse than ever and clinging to her skirts.

It was in winter that the city's Sanitary Police came around at night, banging on doors and calling *"Apri porta!"* to gather evidence of illegal overcrowding in the tenements. For when work was scarce and people kept arriving in the city, the only solution was for the jobless to take in lodgers at night and for the homeless to pay their nickel a spot to lie on someone's floor or to sleep sitting up squeezed in an alcove or someone's doorway. One night, in the room below them, Umbertina saw the police evict twelve people and send them off to a police station probably as overcrowded and as filthy as the hole they had been driven from. And she wondered what kind of country it was that tried to do good by recognizing evil, but whose remedies were as bad as the original evil. It strengthened her resolution that they had to take care of themselves and be their own salvation.

But the summers were the worst, with the cooking, sleeping, working, living all together in the sweltering tenements and streets, unable to breathe. In the newer tenements, the Barracks, those who could moved to the roofs and fire escapes to sleep, but those in the old frame houses were trapped there in rooms heavy with sweat and stale, fetid air. This was the time of year when babies slipped from windows and adults rolled off rooftops in their sleep. And in the streets the Americanized children chanted at their games, "July, July, go to Hell and die!"

People who had worked all their lives in open fields became tubercular. Almost every front doorway on every block bore the grimy white bow with streamers that announced an infant's death in the building.

Despite Umbertina's constant wish to get away, they slipped into the rhythm of the place. Serafino stopped nightly in the saloon downstairs to pay 2¢ for a mug of stale beer and talk to his comrades; Giacomo and Benedetto had begun to go to the American school and speak English and wanted to be called Jake and Ben; Umbertina found some solace in the company of other Calabrian women, with whom she sat out on the sidewalk and chatted while she mended or shelled beans or picked over the greens for their meal.

She learned from them a dozen ways to cook escarole. And she heard with a feeling of shock how they derided the American teachers of their children.

"*Uh-ei!*" said one of the tough *comari*. "These American *femmine* know nothing. My Vito comes home and says his teacher told the class they should have meat, potatoes, and a vegetable on their plates every night, all together. Like pigs eating from a trough, I tell him. In my house I have a *minestra*, a second dish, and a third dish. And beans if I want to! Madonna, that skinny American telling us what to eat!"

"These teachers are not good," said another. "They make the kids cry because they can't pronounce Italian names and make them ashamed. Annunziata says her teacher makes a face like she's vomiting when she calls her name. *Miserabile!*"

Umbertina's great frustration was that her hands weren't trained enough for the piecework the other women did to earn money and that she who had worked the fields and herded goats in Calabria could only do wash in the city.

The street had a life of its own that reminded her of the dusty streets of Castagna when they had sat out and gossiped as they did their work and minded the children. But Castagna was becoming more unreal and insubstantial as time passed, and her memory glossed over past fatigues to fasten on to the present ones. If one had asked her how Castagna was, she would have answered, "Quiet . . . quiet as the woods and the ruined abbey in the valley." And to her mind now, constantly battered by the sounds of the New York streets, it did seem that Castagna was a place where only the wind in the trees or the rush of the stream was heard.

On Bleecker Street, together with the constant roar of the

Broadway Elevated, there were the wagons and peddlers, the organ grinder and monkey, and a continual chorus of calls from the vendors: roasted peanuts, *ceci*, chestnuts on a charcoal brazier; baked sweet-potatoes or, in season, watermelon, peaches, and cherries. Even for the poor, abundance flowed through the streets, replenishing afresh the dream that had brought them there.

Yes, it was hard; but how could one doubt? Umbertina watched the color and bustle of everyday life and saw, despite the wretchedness, the look of expectancy on everyone's face that seemed to replace the old look of stolid resignation which was native to Calabria. And then there were the feast days, when the neighborhoods took on a gaudy, brazen look with illuminated arches over the streets, flags, banners, and huge ornate candles, fruits, flowers, and pastries in profusion to honor the old country's saints. They paraded and feasted for *martedì grasso* just before Lent, for Corpus Christi, for Our Lady of Mount Carmel, and then each street had its own special *festa*: the Sicilians for Santa Rosalia, the Neapolitans for San Gennaro, the Calabrians for San Rocco. Processions were formed; the children skipped alongside, bright-eyed with wonder; and everyone joined in.

There was solidarity among the countrymen who stuck together in their neighborhood. None of them strayed out into the alien city, despite Anna Giordani's chidings that things were better uptown or over on the West Side. They had already been wrenched once from their homes; they could not give up their last comfort—the protective feeling of being together where their language was understood.

Each payday a dime or even a quarter went into the savings Umbertina kept with their countryman Ranucci, who had a bank in his grocery store on the corner. Then, one day, Serafino came home with a message from some new arrivals from Soveria Mannelli.

"Beppino wants us to send some money so he can come over."

Umbertina looked up with a scowl from the table where she was rolling pasta. She looked to see if Serafino—the husband to whom, by custom and Church law, she owed deference and obedience— had taken the correct estimate of this preposterous message from her brother.

"I could take something from what we have at Ranucci's," he said, "and send him a money order." He spoke as if it were the most natural thing in the world.

For the first time in their married life, Umbertina looked at him with anger. He was a man of over forty and she a young woman in her twenties, already thick with childbearing and heavy now with her newest pregnancy.

Her face flushed and she screamed, "Let Beppino make his way as we did! He hasn't a wife or children. He can work." It was the first time she had shown rage at him and her eyes filled with tears at her feelings. "You are a fool!"

Serafino felt the same hurt as a child who is turned upon by someone he loves. He was astounded at her reaction and what he considered her hardheartedness. "*Non hai sentimenti,*" he said chidingly.

"Feelings!" she threw at him in anger. "Why should I have feelings for a grown man like Beppino who lives in his own home while my children live in the land of strangers in this sty," she screamed. "*You* have the sentiment and no brains to go with it!"

For years she had been silent and stoic, bearing everything. But now the time had come for her to take charge, and she would do so whether it meant disrespect to her husband or not.

Serafino was crushed. He did not fight back or give her the blow she deserved. "What do you want from me, *Signore Dio!*" he said in a self-pitying tone.

"I want you to get us out of the city. Now I am having another child and we are still here. Giacomo is eight and Benedetto six . . . maybe they remember what it was to see trees and the sun shining. But this new baby and Paolo—what will it be for them? To live in this room or on the streets? Even the goats in my father's pen were let out into the hills. Are we worse than the animals?"

"We will go, we will go," Serafino muttered in a tired, defeated way. He was already forty-four and he had never recovered all of his strength after his health had broken. Could he be sure to find other work if he left what he had? The work was steady now in New York; he had his *paesani* in the saloon with whom he found pleasure playing cards.

But Umbertina had different ideas: to have a piece of land, to be again in the open air under the sun working the soil—most of all, to use their strength for themselves.

Before the beginning of a third summer was upon them, Umbertina took things into her own hands and had Anna Giordani write to Domenico Saccà in Cato for her. She couldn't send a written message to her relative Giovanni Muzzi directly because he was as illiterate as she. She told Anna Giordani to write Domenico, asking him to find out what work Serafino could have in Cato and to see if Giovanni Muzzi could find them a place to live. Domenico could answer through Anna Giordani.

Umbertina's fourth son came before the answer to her letter. Named Rocco for the saint of the impossible, the child was born in June. Anna Giordani had helped at the birth and then found the wet-nurse for the baby, because Umbertina, having nursed Paolo through his second summer, had no more milk.

Anna had been there to visit Umbertina on the day when Serafino learned that their savings were gone. Ranucci's store hadn't opened one day because he had taken all the money from his bank and gone back to Italy.

Umbertina, already weakened, felt defeated by the news. She resigned herself to sinking like the others into the life of the slums, not making the effort any longer to get out.

There was too much to fight against. Despite the wet-nurse the baby was wasting quickly, and Paolo himself, never strong, was sickly and pale. I have mocked God, Umbertina thought as she watched Rocco whimper and struggle for air. I wanted to change our place in the order of things and to be something more than what God wished. And God is punishing me with these calamities.

But if that is true, her stubbornness told her, what kind of God is He?

Chapter Six

The children sat wide-eyed and quiet next to Serafino, impressed by the importance of being in a train.

Umbertina sat impassively with Paolo in her lap, her excitement abated by the thought of the dead infant left behind. Only Serafino, guileless and open-natured, showed pleasure looking out the train window as they left New York and began the journey upstate to Cato.

Umbertina was thinking that for the rest of her life she wouldn't be able to cast off the feel of the room where she had given birth to Rocco: Her memory would always reverberate with the roar of the elevated train that was the expression of the city's blind, on-rushing unconcern as it hurtled over the streets of the poor in a city built by pick-and-shovel men like Serafino—Italian laborers, Anna Giordani had told her, whom the Americans despised and treated worse than the black people. "You take the lowest wages, the worst housing, the most loathsome jobs, and you are the worst citizens," she would go on and on, sermonizing relentlessly, her thin lips drawn in disapproval, her dress and person a statement of fanatic neatness and cleanliness with which to detach herself from the reeking surroundings she plunged into each day, only to emerge at five or so in the afternoon to rejoin civilization on Twenty-third Street. "And why? Because you stay ignorant!"

"We are poor, *signorina*," Umbertina would patiently point out to her.

Anger made Anna Giordani's voice cold as she retorted, "And you will stay that way unless you educate yourselves."

"What can we do?"

"You can at least let Giacomo, and even Benedetto, come to the mission tent for free reading and writing lessons."

"Ah, the *vangelisti!*" Umbertina replied with a frown.

"Protestants are not devils; we are Christians like you, despite what your Catholic priest tells you," Anna would answer.

But Umbertina, who had risked so much, would not risk sending her sons among the evangelists, where they would surely be turned into Protestants and thus burn forever after death in Hell.

"You people are impossible. It is you, from the South, who have given us Italians in this city a bad name. You live where the Germans and Irish and even the Jews, no matter how poor, won't live. You break the picket lines where workers are trying to force decent wages out of their bosses, and when you are robbed and even murdered, you won't go to the police—you want to take care of it among yourselves in your disgusting little vendettas. But surely you're different, *signora*; I see how you want to get out and be something better than a slum dweller. I see you making an effort to be clean and take care of your children. But why won't you help your children break out of ignorance?"

"We cannot be changed overnight, *signorina*. We can change some things . . . but my children must be of my faith."

Umbertina wondered why this woman, who felt so superior because she was English-speaking and Protestant, still bothered to call herself Italian. She felt a mixture of both pity and contempt for Anna Giordani because she was a plain, angular woman, tall and thin, with drab light hair and fishy gray eyes, who was working among the poor because she didn't have her own children and husband to look after; who labored each day among conditions she could not change, venting her anger on the victims of those conditions.

Umbertina resented the cold appraisals of this joyless woman, and yet she respected her, too. No one else, as much as Anna Giordani, had taught Umbertina the real facts of American life; had stimulated her desire to overcome her disadvantages and make good; had, in a real sense, protected her and her sons against the worst dangers of slum life. And Umbertina knew she was right to scorn those who clung to the slum only for the comfort of its teeming life and in fear of the coldness outside . . . and yet Umbertina also knew that when you are poor and have nothing it is natural to hang on to what is familiar and known. There were always two sides to everything.

Now, safe on the train, Umbertina remembered when Anna Giordani had brought her the answer from Domenico Saccà. "Your countrymen from Castagna, Carlopoli and Soveria Mannelli," Domenico had written and Anna read, "are here in Cato and have found work in the knitting mills or on construction jobs. Gino Gualtiero and some others have moved out near Canastota and Emory, where they have started farms on the rich black land out there. It is a long winter here and not an easy life even for a shoe-maker like me, but things go well and we live in our own homes."

Those words came to Umbertina on a day of bleak depression when all hope seemed to have sputtered out and died. But as she listened an idea came to her and she knew immediately what she had to do.

"*Signorina*," she said, "do you know anyone who will buy my marriage spread?"

Anna Giordani had raised her eyebrows in surprise and then glanced over at that bright image of some lost and beautiful world of fruits and flowers. "Why, yes, yes . . . yes, I might know some-one. There is a Quaker lady I know, very refined and cultured, who has traveled to Italy and collects things of this rustic nature as well as fine things. She has bought shawls and embroideries and things of that kind from Italian immigrants over here. I think she will buy your spread. But why do you want to sell it?"

"To get out—to go to Cato."

"Don't you have anything else?" She knew what the spread meant to Umbertina; she also knew it was her duty to help Umbertina make this sacrifice in order to better her lot.

"Nothing," said Umbertina. But then, perversely, she seemed to retract the offer. "Why would a lady want a spread such as mine, the spread of a poor woman?" she asked Anna. "She could buy better ones. This one was made for me by Nelda in my village." The words rushed out harshly, in anger.

"It is very beautiful, *signora*," said Anna. "It is all hand-done on hand-loomed fabric. You cannot find something like this in the cities, and no tourist goes to places like your village. This is a unique spread, an individual spread not made in batches for the shops."

Umbertina felt a momentary shame at her attachment to the

spread. Yes, it was hers, made only for her by Nelda, but if that was the price of their getting out, she would pay it. How could she say to Anna Giordani that she wanted her children's health, the price of train tickets to Cato, and still be allowed to keep her spread? The poor could not have so much.

"Ah, America!" said Umbertina, taking the spread from the bed and folding it carefully, caressingly, passing her hands over its richness to smooth it and feel it, as if to impress forever into her memory the raised embroidery of its design. She gave the spread to Anna Giordani.

Later that night, lying sleepless in the stifling room listening to the baby's whimper and the punctuating roar of the Elevated, she wondered about the woman who would buy the belongings of the poor. It seemed indecent—worse than the greed of Baron Mancuso, whose stomach all of Castagna had fed with its labor; worse than the indifference of Don Antonio and the bishop. For they had taken the work and obedience of the poor but never the things from a poor man's home. What were Americans, she wondered, that they had so few feelings?

Umbertina forgot courtesy and gratitude as she voiced this to Anna Giordani, who came to bring her the money from the sale of the spread. "Come along, *signora*," Anna had answered shortly, put out by the question, "you were lucky to have a buyer when you needed one. This is a place where you can buy and sell anything. You needed the money more than the spread and you simply made a trade. That is how you have to look at it."

And it was true. In the old country, where could she have gotten money when she wanted it? Sitting in the train, safe now from the city, Umbertina realized the great truth of American practicality, and decided again that sentimentality would have no room in her life in this country; what was done was done, and no good would come of looking back like a Cristina Muzzi who was always crying for the past.

Her Rocco was now of the past.

He had died before he was three months old, on a hot August day, and a white ribbon had gone up on their door. But there was no need for Umbertina to drape her gold earrings in black as the women did in mourning, for hers had long ago been sold for medicine.

As Umbertina looked from the train window and saw the buildings of the city recede behind her, she thought of how she had lived two years in New York and had never known till now its size or shape or the look of it except for those few blocks around Bleecker Street. As she saw its extent she thought, So many people packed in those buildings. What have they found there that keeps them tied to so much stone and cement? What are their lives?

Leaving, she felt again the stirring of hope. She was a woman of faith and she had seen in Rocco's death a heavy penance exacted, just as she had seen absolution in the miracle that had taken place on the day of the baby's burial, when her two older boys had come back to the room with bunches of daisies in their hands.

"*Margherite!*" she had exclaimed in a sudden vision of the spring hillsides of Castagna, where daisies burst from the earth with the new grain and red poppies.

"A policeman gave them out," Giacomo told her. "At the station on Mulberry Street he's giving flowers to everyone. They come from people in the country who wanted the city children to have some flowers."

A smile came to Umbertina's pressed lips. God was giving her a sign: He would not abandon them after all, but sent the fruit of His good world as proof that He saw and cared for them.

It was as if a window had opened and let in reviving air; no food or clothing—the usual gifts of charity—could have done more for Umbertina than the sight of field flowers her eyes had been without for so long.

And then irony sent a final message. Ranucci's store was sold and the proceeds were divided among those whose savings had been stolen. When this unexpected windfall came upon them, Umbertina sought out Anna Giordani and said, "Let me buy back my spread. Tell the American lady it was only desperation that made me sell it. Tell her my son died but the spread will go to my first daughter for her own marriage bed."

"I will try, *signora*."

But when she saw Umbertina again, Anna Giordani acted annoyed and short-tempered. "Look here, don't keep bothering me about that spread. The woman says you're not to be an Indian giver."

"What have I to do with Indians?" Umbertina asked in disgust.

"She says no," Anna said irritably. "She bought it fairly and she paid a lot besides to have it thoroughly cleaned. She wants to keep it. She won't give it up, and I can tell you she was very upset at the suggestion. She said a bargain is a bargain in this country and she paid enough for it so that you can buy another much more practical spread." The gaunt woman, so much taller and thinner than Umbertina, tried to speak dispassionately, but Umbertina sensed the struggle in her, sensed that Anna Giordani, too, felt the Quaker lady was not right.

"I can pay for the cleaning," Umbertina protested, "and whatever else she wants extra. The spread is something of my life and nothing to her."

Anna Giordani looked at the stubborn and tenacious Umbertina. She had spent years among the Italian immigrants and she had learned their differences: The Sicilians were ornately, elaborately civil, but hotheaded; the Neapolitans vain and sly; the Romans overbearing; and those of the North, her own kind, stolid and dull. But of them all, the Calabrians were the most given to nursing long grudges against wrongs. It was Umbertina's nature to hold tight to her resentments.

"Really, *signora*, why carry on so about a spread! The woman said you people shouldn't be so attached to showy things but should work to get ahead and then buy things that are more practical. You should be glad to be rid of something that is so expensive to clean." Anna lowered her eyes before Umbertina's direct stare. "In any case, she wants it and has no intention of giving it up."

"This is a country without heart," Umbertina spit out. "Only buying and selling is understood here." Anna Giordani silently agreed.

When Umbertina packed for the train trip to Cato, she had only a few sheets of rough and coarse hand-woven cotton left of her *dote*; those and the tin heart alone had survived the ocean voyage and the years in New York. It was enough, she thought; we still have our health.

On the train her heart slowly began to lift as they left the city behind and her eyes rested on the waters of the Hudson, which she had not seen since their arrival. Her eyes were fixed to the window, gazing at the wooded banks on the opposite shore. It was early September and there were patches of tall purple, white, and yellow wild-flowers along the tracks. The train passed through one little town after another where wharfs projected out into the river, clustered about with barges loading or discharging cargo. Boats sailed upon the river. On the land beyond the tracks she caught glimpses of great homes, and there were some large factories along the riverbanks. This is beautiful country, she thought, not dry and burnt-out like Calabria. Abundance was everywhere—the piles of stones, lumber, and bricks in the yards alongside stations showed that growth was in the air. She saw men fishing along the banks; she saw the walls and towers of the fortresslike building that was Sing Sing prison. She saw trees and flowering weeds and the tangle of vines and bushes.

Above Peekskill she saw the rounded hills of the Hudson Highlands and the higher crests of the Catskill Mountains. The river was majestic and beautiful; she thought of the little streams that had met at Cosenza and been called rivers; she thought of the even smaller stream in the valley below Castagna. But here, she thought, everything is bigger—the rivers, the cities, the men, the greed, the hopes. It was as if in a new country one had to express everything in nature and in man in a larger way. Somewhere between Peekskill and Poughkeepsie they passed a castle on an islet near the shore. Again and again a pretty little town, or a glimpse of a fine home and expanse of smooth grass. After Poughkeepsie there were some factories, and in the river there was a lighthouse that was a real home, with a mansard roof set on a pile of cement blocks. Then she saw something that remained impressed on her mind ever after: a whole islet of bricks—jettisoned bricks that had come ashore on the islet and lay there, useless and wasted. In a light thicket were the ruins of various brick buildings. It seemed to her as if a brick factory had been there and then had stopped and all the bricks had been left, dumped in the river. But why? Why such waste? It was her first experience of willful waste—of seeing things abandoned that might be recovered and used—and it shocked her.

Everything was a first experience. She had seen a Negro porter for the first time on the train. She had been timid about looking directly at his black face, but he helped her and the children, and when she nodded to him her thanks he smiled and said something back. It took her aback—he spoke English and she did not.

She had taken the children to the lavatory on the train and it was clean and unsmelling. Everything is better, she thought. It is true that you can start fresh.

And her optimism was confirmed by what she saw from the

window; this was truly a new, fresh world. *Ci siamo!* she thought. We're here.

Surely now they would not be preyed upon. She had seen good country all around her and people who lived in little towns. Surely now there would be an end to the interpreters who had been needed at every step of the way and who had preyed on their ignorance and trust—from Ranucci their *paesano*, who had warned them against putting their savings in an American bank, to the Italian priest who had threatened them if they let their children go to the Evangelists in the summer school mission tent where they would be taught to read and write English, and the brewery agents who sold them beer by telling them that the air in America was so strong that they all had to drink beer—children, too—to survive the hard winters.

They crossed the river at a large and imposing town, Albany. And then the country, as they proceeded westward along the Mohawk River and Erie Canal, became even greener and wider. She had the sense of vastness of continent, of lands stretching for immense distances and forests not yet felled. There was a still-uncultivated look to the land and the great luxury of many fields given over entirely to pasturing cows, not made to produce beyond their fertility. Finally she got her first glimpse of corn. "*Grano turco,*" Serafino said as he pointed to the tall stalks of ripened corn at its prime, and she thought it was the most beautiful sight she had ever seen. The richness! Fields could be left with patches of trees between them or whole strands of woods, blocking out her view of the river. Here the fields weren't rocky, walled, dusty patches with thin rivulets of irrigation as they were in Calabria, where nothing could be allowed to lie fallow and recover its strength. There farming had been plundering, sacking the dry earth beyond its endurance; here she saw such abundance of wild green that it put her soul at ease—it would never dry out and force them to be uprooted again.

"The first thing we will do is get a piece of land to grow our food," Umbertina said.

Serafino nodded, satisfied to see her serene at last. He patted her hand, tough and hardened now like his. And she smiled fondly at the man she had made her destiny.

They went past canal locks, bridges, and neat homes on green grassy patches of land that weren't cultivated for food but could be left for beauty; they passed barges, the main streets and tidy village greens that were the piazzas of upstate New York, factories on the river with high arched windows and tall smokestacks that were as imposing as the palaces and temples of the old country, and the clean white spires of the churches.

Serafino pointed out to her fine large buildings, as noble as monasteries or churches, and amazed her by saying they were *stalle*, cow barns. Even the animals live well here, she reflected—not made to pull loads, but, as she saw, free to graze on hills or lie, sleek and fat, on the grassy meadows, well-fed and content. How much better off they were than the poor Christians and Jews cramped in the stink and murk of the New York tenements! And she thought of the Jewish ragman who had come to the courtyard behind the tenement to sort through the refuse and had found her tending basil and slips of geraniums in some old cans. He had said something to her, smiled, and nodded. Later she was told what he said: "You Italians make something grow wherever you are."

A richness she hadn't conceived of was everywhere—even fruit trees, abandoned along the tracks, displayed their unpicked bounty to her wondering eyes. Green was everywhere; a yellow-orange light played over the foliage that was just beginning to show some red in the clear pre-autumn air under a huge sky billowing with clouds. Tall golden sunflowers filled her sight. Umbertina felt the blood coursing through her veins in her desire to dig the earth, to plant seed, to cultivate, tend, and harvest.

For the first time since they had left Castagna she felt at peace. She had never spoken aloud her worst fear; it had simply lived with her, deep in her heart, the fear that they had offended God and broken His design for them. She knew, by the Church's teaching, that there was a great design in life, wrought by God just as surely as the seasons followed one on another and plants sprouted from seed and women brought forth children.

But now she saw her journey not as a curse or a rent in God's design, but instead as the addition of another motif that would enrich the great pattern. After all, the nut falls from the parent tree to start its own growth; and the wind blows about the seedlings of plants that fall to earth far distant from where they started. So it must be with some people, for surely the Lord wanted His earth populated and tilled, not left idle. And as she looked from the train window and saw the expanses of land, the old fear left her heart and certainty of her future took its place.

She was reminded of the old story of the three orphans that she had heard so many times among the women of Castagna. She looked at the restless older boys and said, "Sit still, here, near me, and I'll tell you a story so that you can learn to have faith in God's Providence." And she found contentment in the rhythms and phrases of the folktale she began to tell.

"There were three orphan boys, each of whom set out, one at a time, the eldest first, to find his fortune. 'Whoever wants me for a servant, him will I serve,' cried the first orphan as he came to a town. A fine *signore* came to a balcony and said he'd take the boy on if he would obey in everything, and the boy agreed.

"The next morning the master called the boy and said, 'Take this letter, mount this horse, and let him take you where you must go to deliver the letter. But do not touch the reins because it will make him turn back.'

"The boy rode off until they arrived on the edge of a ravine, where, frightened, he pulled the reins and the horse turned back to town. His master then said, 'You didn't go where I sent you, you must leave my service. Go to that pile of money, take what you want, and then go.'

"The orphan filled his pockets and left, but as he did so he went straight to Hell.

"When the other two orphans saw that their older brother didn't return, the second decided to go out and seek his fortune, too. And he was hired by the same master and given the same instructions. But he, too, pulled the horse's reins on the edge of the ravine and was brought back to town, where he was let go, told to take what money he wanted, and after leaving, went straight to Hell.

"Then the youngest brother set out on the same road to town, was taken in by the same master, and was told: 'I'll give wages, give you food and whatever you want, but you must obey me.'

"The orphan accepted, and was given the letter and the instructions about not touching the horse's reins. When he arrived at the same ravine as his brothers had, the boy looked down and felt gooseflesh on his skin, but he thought, 'I'll trust in God,' and he closed his eyes. When he opened them he was on the other side.

"Then he arrived at a body of water as large as the sea and he thought, 'I'll surely drown. In my case, I put my trust in God.' And, at that, the water parted and he got across.

"Going on, he came to a river of blood and thought, 'My trust is in God!' and the river opened a path to his horse.

"Then he came to a thick forest, so thick that not even a bird could get through. 'Now I'm lost,' he thought. 'Yet if I'm lost, so is the horse, so I'll trust in God.' And he went on into the woods, where he met an old man who was cutting a tree with a stalk of wheat. 'What are you doing,' he asked, 'cutting a tree with that stalk of wheat?'

"To which the old man replied, 'Another word and I'll cut off your head as well.'

"The orphan galloped off, and then he saw an arch of fire with two lions on each side of it. 'If I go through that arch I'll burn,' he thought, 'but if I burn so will the horse, so let's go with trust in God!'

"He galloped on until he saw a woman on her knees praying, before whom the horse stopped. The orphan knew then that the letter was for that woman and he gave it to her. The woman opened the letter, read it, then took a handful of sand and threw it in the air. The orphan mounted the horse again and returned to town.

"When he got back, he saw that his master was the Lord, who told him: 'The ravine you saw was the fall into Hell, the large body of water the tears of my Blessed Mother, the river of blood was from my five wounds, the thick forest was the thorns of my crown, the man cutting the tree with the stalk of wheat was Death, the arch of fire was Hell and the two lions your brothers, and the kneeling woman was my Mother. You obeyed me, now take what you want from that pile of gold.'

"The orphan wanted nothing, but finally he picked up one gold coin and then took his leave of the Lord.

"On the next day, when he went to buy his bread, he spent his coin and yet it still remained in his pocket. And thus it was ever after, and thus he lived happy and well."

Umbertina smiled at the end, content with the story. But Benedetto, always the suspicious one, the one of her sons who had most inherited her dark and brooding nature, spoke up shrilly. "Why did it have to be the two older brothers who go to Hell? Is that Jake and me?"

"Is it?" repeated Jake, who was older but slower to draw conclusions than Ben.

"*Stupidi!*" said Umbertina indulgently. "Are you orphans?" And she laughed at seeing them so uncertain and eyeing Paolo warily as he slept in her lap.

It was a long journey, and it was evening when they got to the big station, flanked by tall brick buildings. The conductor called out "Cay . . . tow! Ca-ato . . . this way for Cato," and they recognized the sound. They could see by the length of the station platform and by the marble columns of the station itself that it must be a large and fine city. The station was very grand and it was filled with well-dressed people. And among them were Giovanni Muzzi with Domenico Saccà.

"Eh, Longobardi!" the shoemaker called out cheerfully, and they embraced loudly and tearfully. The long journey from Castagna was over.

Chapter Seven

Bleecker Street in Cato, like Bleecker Street in New York, was named for the same wealthy upstate Dutchman, Rutger Bleecker. There the similarity ended. In Cato the street was a wide thoroughfare, a handsome business block of prospering tradesmen inspired with civic pride. The Italians of Cato had settled just east of Bleecker, and bordering on it.

When the Longobardi family arrived, Cato had the same boisterous confidence and bravado of any other nineteenth-century American town or city; progress seemed unlimited, optimism unrestrained. First settled as Fort Herkimer before the Revolution, Cato got its name from a slip of paper drawn from a hat at McTaggert's Tavern after the War of Independence had ended. Buildings went up and then were moved, turned about, or torn down before two generations had passed. The old was supposed to be succeeded by newer, finer buildings symbolic of growth and expansion. Wagon and blacksmith shops were replaced by churches, and churches by new business enterprises; carriage factories, tin and stove stores, flour and feed stores all thrived.

The open market and old state armory had been on Bleecker Street; likewise the town lockup and the social hall, the New American Hotel, the YMCA building, John Owens' marble shop, several saloons, a butcher shop, a druggist, a brass and bell foundry, a tobacco factory, a crockery concern, and a furrier. Then parts of that jumble were replaced by the Arcade, only a decade old and still grand when Umbertina and Serafino first set eyes on it. Cato was richer by far than the part of New York they had known.

A whole area of the city, south of Rutger to Pleasant Street, bordered on the west by Oneida Street and on the east by Mohawk Street, was still known as Corn Hill from the cornfields that had covered the whole area in midcentury and still remained on a good portion when the Longobardis got there.

From the beginning Umbertina liked the tree-lined streets, the bustle of business, the nearness of canal and railroad and farmland, the invigorating northern air, and the frame houses and brick warehouses of Cato. She even liked the name, Cato, though she couldn't nasalize the *a*-sound as the Americans did. It sounded to her like the dialect word for cat.

The night they arrived, the city was illuminated with gaslights as Giovanni Muzzi's horse-drawn wagon took them down part of Bleecker and then over to Third Street. They went down a hill into a section that looked completely different from what they had passed through.

"This is *il Buco*—the Hollow," he told them. "This is where the Italians live. The Americans don't want it, it's not good enough for them."

The part of town they were in bordered on Cato Creek and was in a dip, or hollow, between two hills. Considered too difficult to build on, it had been left as a dump area and was cheap land. Now over two hundred Calabrian families had occupied the area, carting off the junk, shoring up the creek banks, terracing the land, building on it.

Five streets—Yale, Denny, and Canal on one side of the creek and Mohawk and John on the other—made up the heart of the Hollow. It looked like an Italian hill village. No matter how harshly the homeland had treated them, once away, the immigrants could do no more than reproduce their lost home in the new land.

Umbertina saw the solid, closed housefronts facing the street, while in the rear a conglomerate of little gardens, arbors, fruit trees, vines, sitting spaces, clotheslines, and woodpiles flourished. Good, she thought. It was the sign of a people used to want, used to making every foothold of soil flower and bear fruit. Not like the American homes she had passed, where wide expanses of grass, instead of being used for pasturing animals, were kept idle, like green rugs.

The Hollow was comfortable and familiar. The homes were close together, creating a packed density as if they were still huddled in land-poor Calabria. Scorning the plentiful wood of the boundless American forests, the Italians still built stone walls and stucco houses and laid cement where an American might have let grass grow.

Everywhere was the sense of bounds that had been the sign of property in Italy; even the cement tubs for flowers, the rock-studded planters, or the flowerbeds marked out by bricks showed the passerby a sense of order and propriety. It was the order of peasants used to protecting every bit of land that could be called one's own.

Umbertina gazed with pleasure at the plants growing on front ledges from tomato cans, oil tins, basins, or tubs. But the real miracle was behind the stone and cement in the cascade of cultivation that flowed from the terraces down to the creek. This was the true culture of the uprooted, patiently preserved.

As they went up Yale Street and she passed the homes, Umbertina recognized something in their construction. Brick pillars along the walk would be topped with cement and then studded with rocks, the largest set in the center as a finial. It was as if her countrymen were exalting the very rocks that had caused their poverty in the fields of Italy and of which they had built their hovels. Here their ancient enemy was rendered harmless and stuck into the walls that surrounded their homes like captive totems.

Some of the original wood houses of the area had brick facades added onto them and the grace of arches. The brick was worked with open designs and a pattern above the archways; or patterned cement was shaped into squat, square columns supporting a balcony-porch. Most homes were built in stucco—plain, homely, facing the street guardedly in their homeliness and knowing that they were strong enough, impenetrable enough, not to care about prettiness. At one house, a silver-painted Minerva reclined in a semi-couchant pose with her lion shield on the top of a cement pillar. Other stone walls sported cannonball ornaments of cement at intervals, or baby-bath-size cement tubs for plantings. From the homes came the sound of the sizzle of cooking, the murmur of women, the muffled tones of children.

The dwellings closer to the creek were warrens of entrances and stairways on every level, with balconies and porches and rooftop spaces. Single homes had been made into multiple dwellings by the canny addition of stairways and entrances, and cantilevered space had been achieved where there was none.

On the "better" side of the street, the side farther uphill from the creek, stone walls braced up the hillside and were often topped by shrubs that gave a certain privacy of "estate" to the homes, which were larger than those on the other side of the street, often rising to three stories of flats, but nonetheless immigrant homes. Yet they were distinctly better, if only because by their size they afforded so much room to rent out to boarders, and by their position they could look down on the houses in front of them.

But even at best, and in the good season, the Hollow at a quick glance from the street seemed drab and poor—the other side of the tracks. It was picturesque to the outsider, the American who lived uptown on an elm-lined street with wide lawns and front porches where everyone sat and swung in view of everyone else, where windows were large enough to show the rooms inside, and where backyards were wasteful with little fringes of flowerbeds but no vegetables or grapevines or fruit trees. Guinea Gulch, as the Americans called the Hollow, was to them a part of town where peddlers trundled handcarts through the streets calling out *"Es-ca-ro-la! Verdura!"* and where women in dark dresses with aprons around their waists and kerchiefs over their hair could be seen carrying home bundles of dandelion greens in thick loads on their heads.

It was mysterious, too, in the Hollow. The houses had the closed look of fortresses—front windows shuttered or draped, no front porch for sitting, no front yard, no opening to the stranger. It was the suspiciousness of the Old World come to the New—the still-dominant peasant mentality that no one should see the extent of a person's fortune.

At John Street the embraces Serafino's family exchanged with their countrymen were again full of feeling. Tears of gratitude silently streamed down Umbertina's cheeks when Cristina Muzzi and her daughters pressed food and drink on them as the ritual feeding of long-lost *paesani* began.

Lodgings had been found for the Longobardis in a three-story wooden structure which, they were amazed to learn, Annicharico the baker owned. It was like a *palazzo*—wood, yes, but still high as a *palazzo*.

On Labor Day, a few days after their arrival, a large *festa* was organized in Muskieville, just across the river from Cato, on the lands Giovanni Muzzi rented at the farm of James Brown. They pulled up to a field beyond Brown's farmhouse and barn, and there were other wagons full of people to welcome them. The *calabresi* of Cato, both familiar and unfamiliar, expressed their feelings of satisfaction at the safe arrival of more of them in the exchange of sarcasms and twittings that buoyed up spirits, recharged confidence, and allayed the sense of lost birthplace that the sight of newcomers always brought to mind.

It was a beautiful day of late summer, one of those unique upstate days when skies are perfectly limpid and the horizon stretches far and nature is a marvel of beauty with just the hint of being at its peak and therefore fleeting. Umbertina gave thanks in her heart as she looked over the fields and saw what the earth produced here. *Ci siamo!*—we've made it—she thought over and over.

Gino Gualtiero had his accordion and was playing a lively tune, the women were putting out the *coperte* in the fields to spread the breads and cheese and salamis upon, and Domenico Saccà was making a fire to boil water in a cauldron for the heaps of still-unshucked corn next to him. The children ran about gathering field daisies. Umbertina reveled in the feel of sun and in the clean air. She looked with pleasure at Giovanni's tilled rows of tomatoes, well staked and growing fuller and rounder than she had ever seen tomatoes before; beans climbing up poles, peppers, eggplants, even the feathery rows of finocchio and the dense clusters of rughetta, basil, and escarole; and he had tall stalks of broccoli and cabbage, and beyond these a small vine of grapes carefully trained along stakes.

There were no walls or gates around James Brown's farmhouse, nor around the other farms they had passed on their way from the city. Everything was open and peaceful, and Umbertina compared it silently to the walls with jagged bits of glass embedded in the top that separated a landowner's place in Calabria from the landless. "This is what we need," Umbertina told Serafino. "A field to grow our food on."

"And here when you hoe the ground you can truly say everything is a mouthful for me and mine and no one else," said Giovanni Muzzi.

"And what about him?" asked Serafino, nodding toward Brown's farmhouse.

"All I have to pay him is the rent—not half my crop like in the old country. And we swap, me and the American. He gives me eggs and milk for some of my vegetables."

The others nodded, recognizing the good fortune of being in such a land.

Umbertina tasted the corn that Domenico had boiled and offered her. She said to herself that she would refuse nothing this land had to offer, would taste everything out of gratitude for being there. But she did not think she would like the *grano turco*, which appeared strange and coarse and had to be gnawed at as a rodent would gnaw at something. It was out of politeness that she accepted the corn which Domenico pressed on her.

"Here you are, Tinuzza, this is corn, a truly American food . . . the food of the redskins. Eat it like this, spread with butter and a little salt." He demonstrated and the others watched. "Some of your *paesani* won't eat it because what they didn't know back in Castagna, they don't want to know here. But you're not like that."

Umbertina imitated Domenico and ate her first ear of corn. She was pleased. The kernels were sweet and she liked the look of these golden nuggets. It looked like America—bright and filled with golden promise.

"It is good," she said. "I will have it in my garden."

"*Brava*, Umbertina! *Brava!*" said Domenico, his broad face crinkled into a beaming smile. He was a handsome man with intelligent eyes and his face was always alight with some emotion or excitement—pleasure, sorrow, rage, shame, compassion, or eagerness. He wore his passions openly, not at all like the guarded mountain folk who were his *paesani*.

Annicharico was at the picnic and had brought loaves of his long crusty bread, which his wife was splitting, filling with large gobs of roasted peppers, and handing out. Pasquale Luppizzi, the ward boss, was there too.

"Remember," he was telling Serafino, "in this country you vote Republican because they're the ones who have the money and they're the ones who give the jobs."

"And what jobs are there?" Serafino asked.

"Look around you . . . everyone here has some work. One young Saccà is a carpenter and the other is a mason; Domenico has his own shoe store; Giovanni Muzzi peddles his own produce in season and other things in the cold seasons; his brother Sam is a mason. Others are ice cutters, gardeners, coal shovelers on the barges, or factory hands."

"I have nothing with me, not even the pick and shovel which I sold in New York."

"You don't need anything to work in the cotton mills."

"Then I'll go there."

"And be exploited by the American mill owners!" Domenico cut in sharply. "The mill owners who work you a twelve-hour day and pay you less than the Irish because you're Italian."

"Only to start," said Serafino patiently.

"It could be your end—the workers in the mill get chest sickness," said Domenico.

"That's not for you, then," said Umbertina decisively. She wished they could have their own farm.

But how many wishes I have! she thought as she looked about her at the trees, the laden berry bushes, the fields of ripe corn. First it had been enough to get out of the city slums; now she wanted a piece of land to work, and beyond that, independence for her family. How many things! Still, it all began to seem possible. And as she looked she saw a deer come from the trees at the end of the field and stand poised, head high and still. "It's beautiful," Umbertina said.

"To a certain point—the deer also eat our plants," Giovanni Muzzi told her.

"And deer are good to eat," Gino added. But Umbertina thought that was one thing she would not eat.

She learned at the picnic that school would begin the next week. Most of the children from the Hollow went to the parochial school of Our Lady of Mount Carmel, Father Di Simeone's new Italian church at the end of Third Street. They were fortunate to have an Italian church; Emory or Schenectady didn't yet, they said. "The only reason you have it," said Domenico scornfully, "is that the Irish didn't want you in their church—not even in their basement where you had to go to baptize your children as if they weren't Christian enough for upstairs." He started to laugh. "There's a saying in town that so many Irish gave contributions to Mount Carmel that when the bishop came to dedicate the church he said to Father Di Simeone, 'This seems to be a church erected by the Italians of County Cork.'"

Umbertina frowned at Domenico's story; he was still dissatisfied, she thought.

"The Italians are always the worst off," he was saying. "Other peoples came from Europe accompanied by doctors, priests, engineers, and teachers. But not the Italians! They came in a herd of peasants. Father Di Simeone is a rarity. He had to get special permission from the Church to come over and help the immigrants—no one in the government cared anything about them."

"Weh! Domenico, *esagerato!*" the women muttered. "You exaggerate."

Umbertina discovered that day that it was easier to be as she and Serafino were than to be Domenico in the New World.

The next day she went to the Convent of Our Lady of Mount Carmel, which was a modest frame house next to the little wooden church that looked, to her eyes, quite miserable for the Lord's House, not anywhere near as substantial as the banks and the business establishments of the town.

The nun who introduced herself as the teacher of the elementary grades surprised Umbertina. She was a young woman, no more than twenty-two or twenty-three perhaps, and she was tall and fine-featured, with a bearing that reminded Umbertina instantly of some of the signoras she used to glimpse in their carriages in Soveria Mannelli. This nun—whose name, she told Umbertina, was Sister Carmela, and who spoke Italian, not dialect—was not a southern Italian, but one from the North like Anna Giordani. Of good family, Umbertina could see immediately.

"Your name is like the Church," said Umbertina, shy before the imposing presence of the beautiful nun who was not much younger than she, and not knowing what else to say.

"It is not my real name, of course. My parents were from Milan and would not have given me the name of girls from *bassa Italia*. My name was Chiara, but my brother used to call me Carmelooch to tease me and make me angry, since all the *meridionali* seemed to be named Carmela. When I entered the convent my superiors gave me the religious name of Sister Carmela and I thought, Oh, dear, now I'm Carmelooch for life! And now I'm here at the School of Our Lady of Mount Carmel—it all seems to have been intended by the Good Lord."

Umbertina was perplexed at this fine ladylike nun confiding such things to her. But that wasn't all. Umbertina could see the wisps of very fair, fine hair that were barely visible beneath her coif, and she thought, She is a blonde. Her eyes were blue behind the glasses she wore and her skin was pale and soft. Umbertina could not imagine this fine person teaching the children of the poor. In Italy no one taught the poor.

"But I'm glad to have been sent on this mission," the nun went on. "I think it was God's plan to name me Sister Carmela to remind me that my life is to be spent educating the children of the South. Now I can teach proper Italian to these children who speak only dialect."

Umbertina's shyness vanished in an instant. "Oh, no, Sister, not Italian! It is American our children need. They have to go out and earn their living in America and they have to read and write for us who have no learning. Leave the Italian to us at home, and teach them the language of how to do business in this country."

"Why, Mrs. Longobardi"—the nun laughed condescendingly—"none of you speak proper Italian at home! You speak dialect. And you don't read or write. It is the cultural heritage of these children to know their mother tongue."

"*Pazienza*, Sister Carmela. The culture will come after we make a living, God willing."

The aristocratic nun wrinkled her brows and her light eyes looked steely with disapproval for an instant. And then she said, "I suppose this will be my cross, as much as my name! But so be it."

Umbertina went away marveling that she, a poor goat-girl from the hills of what that fine person had called *bassa Italia*, low Italy, had been able to prevail over a northern lady. This was truly the country of equalizing! It was a miracle. She resolved to remember Sister Carmela on every July sixteenth, the feast day of Our Lady of Mount Carmel, with a great bouquet of garden flowers to help soften the indignity of her name. She'd send her special pastries at Christmas and Easter.

The day following her meeting with Sister Carmela she bought a broom and had Serafino cut off part of the long handle so that she'd have a rolling pin to make pasta and *chinolelli*, her stuffed pastries for feast days. And she sent Jake and Ben off to school with the bunch of field flowers they had picked in the country for their teacher.

Serafino found a job as a laborer in the railroad yards, and every day Umbertina got up early to make dough for the crusty white pizza he liked so much. She prepared enough for his lunch, too, and sprinkled it with oil, oregano, and a touch of ground red pepper. Or else she varied the pizza for Serafino's lunch by making it with onions, or with potatoes and rosemary, or with pieces of scamozza cheese, or olives and anchovies—but never with tomato sauce as the Neapolitans did, for that disguised the good taste of fresh dough and turned it soggy and soft. Sometimes instead of pizza she made bread and gave Serafino *panini* of meat, or egg and escarole, or peppers.

Serafino was envied for his freshly made pizza or *panino* among his fellow workers; their women let them pick up bread from Annicharico and cheese or salami somewhere else along the way to work. Soon they were asking Serafino to bring them the same lunch as he had—they'd pay. Before long the news of Umbertina's baking reached others, too, and through Serafino, the laborers who stopped in at Scalise's bar for beer on their lunch break started giving orders for Umbertina.

How often, as she got up in the cold dark of a winter's day to start the fire in the wood-burning stove or went out to shop, did she thank God for her health and energy and think with contempt of the laziness of the other wives, who preferred to sleep rather than fix their men's food.

Umbertina kept the men's orders in her mind; she had great powers of concentration and a memory that took the place of reading and writing. She charged everyone the same flat rate of 75¢ per week for their lunches to simplify pricing. To get the mill workers' lunches ready for Serafino to take with him, she'd get up at five in the morning to start the baking and get to the market. She never got an order wrong.

For Umbertina it was an article of faith to eat well, and now that she could afford it she always had in her kitchen the most virgin of olive oils, the most aged and mellow of cheeses, the best salami and freshly baked bread, crusty and not doughy inside the way the bakers left it to increase its weight.

This was a northern climate, she said. And they needed to eat more, including meat, to keep up their strength.

If there was one flaw in her paradise—and she seldom mentioned it, feeling it wrong to complain—it was the vagaries of the upstate New York climate; the weather was erratic, and its crazy quirks would make her restless and edgy. There would be chill, gray days in August or such balminess in February that the trees and bushes would go berserk and produce buds at the wrong time, only to have them die in the frost. April was warm one day, cold the next.

"It is because it is a new world, a new country," Umbertina would half grumble to Serafino. "It has not yet found its *clima*," that steady, predictable flow of the seasons she remembered from her years in Castagna. And she thought that the weather might have something to do with the jerky movements, restlessness, and rigidness she noted in the few *americani* she ever saw. Or maybe they didn't eat well—she had seen their bread, a characterless, soft, spongy, dead-white concoction that she wouldn't have fed her pigs in Castagna and that she considered a desecration of God's good grain.

She never stinted on food for her family. They had everything fresh or homemade. On special occasions, like Thanksgiving, which she called Chicken Day, she made ravioli filled with ricotta and other cheeses, never mixing it with spinach as the *abruzzesi* did, for she didn't believe in mixing her greens—dandelions, good strong chicory, spinach, and broccoli—with anything. Fresh greens were a miracle of the earth and had to be separate to be relished properly and have their best effect on bodies after a long winter without. But into the *minestra* went everything: beans, greens, vegetables, and pieces of meat, along with the soup bones to enrich it. She made *cacciatore* dishes with her tomatoes and peppers, or if there was rabbit, with fragrant stems of rosemary and white wine. The rosemary in her garden was not the sprig from Nelda's garden in Castagna, which had not survived the journeys and moves, but a new American growth. It would never be the glorious blue flower-laden bush of the warm Italian countryside, but it still had the aroma she remembered and was still the totem of her strength. "In the house where the rosemary grows, the women of the house are its strength," Nelda had told her, and that's what she now believed.

Her oldest son would be summoned occasionally by her excited shouts as he was getting ready for school when it suddenly occurred to her that some laborer hadn't stopped by for his *panino*. She'd scream, *"Eh, Giaco, ven'acà! Su!"* and have him run down to the railroad before he went off to school.

She worked hard, she made money, and she was quick to see that profits would be even greater if she had her own store of provisions instead of going out to buy them. She decided to open a *spaccio*—a space, as it was known in the old country—in a little storefront on Third Street, near Scalise's bar.

When summer came they leased a piece of Brown's farmland in Muskieville and bought a horse and wagon for getting there and back. All the defeatism of the former years was worked out of her straining, sweating body as she bent and stooped and ached and felt the joy of hard exertion against the earth, defying and prodding it to bear. Umbertina felt strength flow back into her as she worked under the hot sun.

This challenge she could understand: the one that pitted her and Serafino and their arms and craft against the caprices of nature. They had to outwit upstate weather, stay vigilant against weeds and insects, look out for the young shoots. In two summers they expanded the *spaccio* into the Longobardi *groceria*, a grocery store. And here, too, she had to concentrate and remember and plan ahead and pay attention when the salesmen called and not let them play tricks on her. She was a sharp questioner and compared prices and had one of the boys read what she couldn't when necessary. But she could do it. The adversary she could not contend with had been the dark slums of the city.

As she hated waste and had none in her home, so she also could not tolerate stinginess and was an abundant provider to her family. What she and Serafino raised they consumed or conserved for the winter or sold, or even bartered with Mrs. Brown for fresh eggs and milk. Umbertina would nod and smile and say, "Yessa, yessa" to Mrs. Brown when they met, but she would be thinking to herself how ugly American women were—so sharp and angular with thin little faces and pinched noses and lips; she wondered how they gave birth from such bony frames.

She herself had girth; she rounded and billowed beneath her full skirts despite the hard work. She wore no corsets as the other Italian women did, but let herself flow in generous waves of flesh. Two more children, her daughters Pina and Anna, were born in the early years of the store. Her face was still full and round-cheeked and her skin still had the fairness of the people from the Sila. Her cheeks and chin always had a pink tinge to them, and on feast days she dabbed the juice of pomegranate seeds onto her lips to make them redder. Her dark nature turned jovial as the years became good; bitterness drained from her as the visible proof of success accumulated in savings and she laughed heartily, shaking all over while her chin flushed an even deeper pink. She wore her still-dark hair in a pompadour held up with tortoise shell pins and combs, though strands of it kept straggling down so that she was always pushing it back.

Umbertina now gave orders and directed the family. As both family and grocery store grew, Serafino gave up his job at the railroad for seasonal laboring so as to be able to help more at the store when needed. Serafino let his wife take charge—somewhat because he was an easygoing fellow, somewhat because she would have done what she wanted anyway. She was younger; she still had the energy and confidence that he had long ago expended on the railroads. Besides, she was more intelligent than he; he had always said so.

Serafino did odd jobs at the store. He'd go down to the farmers' market with the horse and wagon and get provisions or down to the warehouses near the station and buy sacks of flour and sugar and coffee beans and other staples the Longobardi store now stocked. In the winter he would sit inside the store roasting chestnuts in the potbellied stove, on top of which he'd throw a long slice of orange peel to release the aroma of its oils into the air. Or he'd crush cardamom seeds on the hot surface, releasing their spicy fragrance like a waft of the exotic East, and talk with his customers and friends. In good weather he roasted peanuts outside the store on the sidewalk, greeting people and sometimes letting them take a turn on the handle of the roaster. No sooner were the peanuts done than they were sold out and a new batch started. Work always seemed rewarded—it never failed to amaze Umbertina.

The salesmen of olive oil and cheese, who represented importing companies from New York, stopped at the store, and soon Umbertina expanded into imports. She carried pastas of all shapes and sizes in glass-fronted drawers, and genuine semolina flour for those who still made pasta at home.

Umbertina worked constantly, never missing any time in the store or in the fields at Muskieville except for her confinements after each birth. Then the babies were kept in the store with her while she worked; later, when she was past nursing them, Serafino would look after them or take them for walks.

There was only one fly in the ointment as far as she was concerned and that was Domenico Saccà, who kept sounding off his complaints and quarrels with the powers-that-be like a bothersome gnat in their midst. First he had to grumble because they sent their children to the parochial school instead of to the public schools where the American children went. Did they want to increase the power of the Church over them so they'd never be free, he asked. Didn't they realize that finally they had free, open schools paid for out of their property taxes—not like Castagna, where they paid taxes and got nothing back. But they just nodded and said, "Father Di Simeone is our friend; we can't go against him." For who knows, they thought, when we'll need such a friend.

Then, because Domenico was educated and could read and write and got the Italian paper from New York, *L'Eco d'Italia*, sent to him, he would always be ready to tell them of the latest catastrophes that had befallen their countrymen.

"Now they are rounding up the poor Italians of Buffalo," Domenico would report, "calling us undersirables and demanding that immigration from Italy be stopped. They say that we all carry weapons, that we're all part of the Mafia, as if we had anything to do with the Sicilians."

Umbertina would frown and mutter "*A diavolo, disgraziato*" when she saw Domenico coming toward them, for she was sure there would be more preaching and more listing of calamities. But Serafino respected him and always insisted that he be invited to their baptisms and confirmations. Domenico was like the leader of the little band from Castagna, which was yearly increasing. He it was who could be their eyes and tongues, writing home for them and relaying back the messages from family they'd never see again.

Serafino and others in the store would listen spellbound while Domenico read about arrests, lynchings, and dragnets in Italian neighborhoods, or confiscations and wholesale expulsions of Italians from towns. Umbertina went about her business trying to seem unattentive, but in her heart she asked, Could this be America? What was the reason for such hate? And yet some of it she knew by herself: The Italians were pouring in, more and more each year, and they were taking the jobs away from the Americans. But was this a cause to hate and kill them? After all, the Italians were doing the jobs that all the others scorned and refused. And wasn't there supposed to be reward for hard work and making good in the American way? Wasn't that what America was all about?

"You have to become citizens and get the vote so that we can all protect ourselves—that is the only way," Domenico would say, and for once she agreed with him. Serafino had gotten his citizenship papers, and she had told him to vote as Pasquale Luppizzi wanted so that Luppizzi would protect them against the extortionist Black Hand Corvo family. But Domenico derided her idea of the vote as a favor to pass on to Pasquale Luppizzi. "You have to educate yourself to think for yourself, not let someone else do it," he told her while she mentally scorned him as a dreamer.

For Umbertina these were all words—not bread to put in her children's mouths and not the protection that would keep the Corvos from coming around and demanding money so that her windows wouldn't be broken, her bins of flour ruined with rat poison, and her vegetables dumped into the street. She had to work and stay safe, not go to school to learn to read and then be unhappy with the things she couldn't prevent anyway.

She did not want Domenico as her conscience; she did not want to hear that there were ugly patches in the American design, that there was discrimination and hate and prejudice. She liked her life now, she liked being her own boss and making money and seeing things go well. Why should she listen to the gloomy talk of Domenico, who was like the fox that said the grapes he couldn't reach were sour? Just because Domenico, learned though he was, was still only a shoemaker and not making the money they did, did that give him any right to come and spoil their good times with his bad news?

Serafino was all ears when Domenico came.

"Does it make you feel like you're back with Garibaldi?" she would ask him dryly after the shoemaker left.

"Domenico reads things we don't know about," he answered. "He understands things. We should listen."

"Yes, and then do what? Go out in the streets and shout because in New Orleans they have lynched some Mafiosi Sicilians who probably deserved it? Is that what you want, with five children to feed and another one coming?"

"*Andiamo*, Tinuzza!" he said placatingly. "Domenico is right. We must defend ourselves."

In her heart she also knew Domenico was right; she didn't want America to become what the old country had been, because although she found the climate harsh and erratic and the people graceless and ugly, still it was a country that gave *benessere* in return for hard work. She knew Domenico was right just by the sense of self-consciousness she felt when she went out of the Hollow on occasion and experienced the disapproving stares and sneers of the Americans, who were contemptuous of her way of dress and the halting way she spoke her few words of English. Not all Americans were that way; not Mrs. Brown. But most were. And it was because she felt this and wanted so strongly for it not to be true of the country she loved that she reacted so unreasonably to Domenico. What he said was true. And she didn't want it to be. Therefore she wouldn't listen.

Anyway, her future was in her sons. They were becoming as American as anyone else. Jake, at fourteen, had finished eighth grade at Mount Carmel, where he had been made to memorize Washington's Farewell Address by Sister Carmela to impress upon him in his future life, she said, the importance of religion. He took a job on the streetcar by day to add to the family earnings, which all went back into the store, and studied a business course by night. Then Ben did likewise, and when they both started working in the store at night they continued their education through correspondence courses.

Paolo, now called Paul, was more delicate, Umbertina maintained, and she favored him. Curiously, for a woman whose faith was hard work, she kept him from exertion. Paul was bright, inquisitive, adept, and he often read and wrote for her. Since the business was going well by the time he was of age, he was allowed to finish high school while Pina and Anna helped out in the store.

Umbertina, who had become a strong woman, did not ever consider that her daughters should be so; the future of the name and business was in her sons.

Chapter Eight

Three more daughters were born to Umbertina and Serafino in Cato. In the old-country way of name giving, Pina and Anna had been named for deceased grandparents. But when Margherita was born, she was named for no one but Umbertina's memory of the arrival of daisies, *le margherite*, the day Rocco died. She was followed by Sara and finally Carla. The last girl was born shortly after Beppino arrived in Cato, bringing Umbertina word of their father's passing as well as other news.

"Do you remember Giosuè, the charcoal burner from Carlopoli?" he asked, fixing his sister with an ironic smile. Umbertina was now forty, a woman thickened by childbearing and unconcerned with style. But a flush came to her cheeks at Beppino's words and the image of the tin heart passed through her mind; yes, she remembered Giosuè.

"He is doing well," Beppino reported. "He inherited a house and land in Castagna and has moved there."

Umbertina nodded curtly at Beppino. So what does this *cretino* mean when he gives me such news? she thought. That my life is not set into its own pattern? That I should have regrets? *Disgraziato*, she muttered silently to this brother of hers who brought the shadows of old rancors into the peacefulness of her life. There was more.

His presence, made commanding by the thick black handlebar mustache that caused the children to call him Zio Moustacchio, reminded them all that she hadn't let Serafino send the passage money for him years before, and that the two of them had never gotten along anyway. No matter. He was taken into their large new home and given a room. He was still unmarried and they were his family. But it galled Umbertina that he had learned to read and write in Canada, where he first immigrated. "Thank God I've got a head on my shoulders and don't need to scratch marks on paper to remember things," she'd mutter. But secretly she envied Beppino and disliked him all the more for his being able to go among the *americani* as she could not without a son or daughter.

The reason for his arrival among them soon came out. Beppino was now thirty-eight. He had saved money working in Canada and it was time for him to marry. A man went home to marry, to be sure of getting a woman from his own area, and since Cato was the place where many *castagnesi* had settled, one calling another until there were almost as many in Cato as back in Castagna, Beppino was there to find a bride.

In the first year of the new century, Umbertina was middle-aged when her last child, Carla, was born and baptized in the grand new stone edifice of Mount Carmel, built on the site of the old wood structure and completed with Italian money. In that year it seemed to her that a design, like the rich intricacy of the long-lost matrimonial spread, was complete. Her life's pattern was outlined, and it was satisfying and beautiful to her. It was in that year, 1900, that she and Serafino moved out of the Hollow and put $1,500 of patiently saved money into the purchase of a $4,000 property, an old stone mansion on Broad Street in what had once been the finest part of Cato. That move, hallowed by the fact that the American bank on Main Street had given them a mortgage, was a proud day in Umbertina's life. It was the transaction involving money that made her feel American; she had never cared much for the rhetoric that she sometimes heard in church or that Ben read from Cato's Italian paper, *La Luce*, about such vague things as patriotism, justice, and liberty. As far as she was concerned, all of what America stood for was the fact that she and Serafino could go to a bank that looked like a temple and not be treated like animals but be received, seated, and given a mortgage based on their hard work and thrift. *Figurati in Italia!*—Yes, just imagine such a thing in the old country.

The stone house was a former mansion on grounds where trees of magnificent girth and height and age still stood, and where there was a carriage house in the rear for keeping Bessie, the horse, and the wagon. Across from the property were the businesses that had ruined it as a residence: the Cato Paving Company and the sheds of the Mohawk Trolley Company, whose conductor's cap and brass-buttoned uniform Jake now wore as an employee.

That same year S. Longobardi & Sons became an importing business, and Jake and Ben spent all day at the business, which was expanding into a private neighborhood bank and steamship-ticket agency as well. At night Jake went to his trolley job and Ben worked as an insurance salesman; what money they made went into the common till to build up the family business. Umbertina's triumph was complete. Her sons had not entered the cotton mills, as the sons of other immigrants were doing, and soon they would be working entirely for themselves, the family.

She could not write, but she yearned to tell them in Castagna of her progress. Of how work had succeeded. Often, in the New York tenements, she had sent her thoughts and longings back in her imagination, but she was glad now that she hadn't been able to write of her despair and sorrow at that time. Why send the record of defeat and humiliation?

No, she would document only her success. She summoned the itinerant photographer who showed up in Cato once or twice a year and had him photograph her family on the steps of the Broad Street mansion. Then she had him take a picture of the store.

She did not wish to be deleted from the memory of her *paese*; Castagna should have some knowledge of her—the kind she provided.

She became expansive with good fortune. With the sons now in the business, Umbertina told Serafino he could retire. "You've done your work, old man," she said with her brusque affection, "now retire and let your sons work for you."

Sometimes as he napped after dinner and she was going over business matters with Jake and Ben, she'd look over in his direction and say with pretended scorn and a toss of her head, "*Guarda, guarda, occhi chiusi*—look, look at old shut-eyes!"

The new century began auspiciously. It was a prosperous year all around: The first tentative Italian businesses on upper Bleecker Street had succeeded and were followed by several *caffè* and then the fine Hotel and Restaurant Roma. Pay was up to $1.50 or $1.75 a day for laborers and Jake was bringing home $12 a week just from his streetcar job. *La Luce* came out weekly and was a great help to business, for it printed announcements on its front page of arrivals at the Longobardi store: caciocavallo cheese and pasta from Naples; nuts from Sorrento; *baccalà* from Livorno; beans, figs, semolina, oregano, pignoli, anchovies, *camomilla*, and Fernet-Branca from Milan; *cipolletti* from Basilicata, and chestnuts from Calabria.

And in this land of plenty, Paul read to Umbertina that in Italy the tax on consumption of bread and pasta had finally been abolished, at which she shook her head grimly, remembering her father, *poveretto*, and his bitterness. And then they heard that the bandit Musolino had been captured again after his third attempt to escape, and Serafino's eyes turned vague, looking into the distance as he remembered the mountains of Aspromonte where he had shepherded sheep and where fugitives from the law had hidden. Bravo, Musolino! he would think; if only you can make good your next escape to the mountains you will be safe.

Also in the paper were disquieting notices of lost persons—persons who had emigrated to the United States years ago and not been heard of since by relatives in Italy. Where had they gone? What had happened that they had lost all ties to their families?

The year and its happenings were celebrated at a christening party for Carla in the new house on the day of the Ascension. The *paesani* of the Hollow, and even those like the Longobardis who were beginning to venture beyond, were invited to the great stone mansion. All except the ignorant godparents of a short-lived infant born between Anna and Margherita—who, over some insignificant business having to do with a purchase at the store, had quarreled with Umbertina and earned her scorn and the ridicule of the neighborhood by saying, "Since your child died, we are no longer *padrini*."

But the others came. "Weh!" breathed Cristina Muzzi as she looked about the large entrance hall and into the big rooms, "it must have been a church once. That *portone* looks like it was made for a church." She pointed to the great thick heavy wood door at the entrance. "And look at these places for statues, *Madonna mia!*" She was looking at several arched niches recessed in the walls.

"*Ma che dici,*" said Umbertina irritably, annoyed as always at the ignorant Cristina, who came to every affair—christening or wedding or funeral—still dressed like a poor countrywoman with a black kerchief tied under her chin and always whining about something. Any misfortune was hers; she relished misery. *La strega*, the witch, Umbertina called her. Cristina's face had become more cavernous with the years—a gauntness due, Umbertina used to say, to her being too stingy to eat properly—and her teeth were gone, so that her mouth was sunken and her nose, disproportionately large in the hollowed face, looked like a hook bending over to meet her sharp chin.

Umbertina's prosperity showed not only in the large rooms of the mansion but in the expansiveness of the table she spread for the christening feast, replete with pastries such as *chinolelli* and anise biscuits that she and the older girls had been making for days. There were almond cookies, sponge cakes, ricotta pies, sweet dessert wines like Marsala, and colorful punches; there were gelati, spumoni, and biscuit tortoni; there were brandied cherries and peaches, and the pink sugar almond candies that signified the birth of a girl.

Among the company and in keeping with the upward advance of the Longobardis was Father Di Simeone, who had performed the baptism; Dr. Rossi; the Mazzello family, who came from near Rome and always managed to refer to it proudly when among the Calabrians; several businessmen; and the well-off Colombo family with their stunning women. Chief of these was Francesca Colombo, who was called *la fanatica* because of the exceeding care she took of her person and her dress. She had beautiful thick hair that was turning gray and she wore it marcelled in waves. This was the one thing Umbertina envied, for her own hair was thin and wispy though still dark. Umbertina kept her color, she said, because she never washed her hair, only brushed it; by keeping the natural oils, she believed she kept the color.

"Oh, Ma," Anna used to protest, "where do you get such ideas?"

But Umbertina knew what she knew. Her daughters would never know as much.

Now, despite being busy with greeting and feeding everyone, Umbertina had time to notice how Beppino was already acting as if he, too, owned that house. He liked to dress up and smoke cigars, and there he was talking with important people like Dr. Rossi or Father Di Simeone as if he were one of them.

"I can remember," Father Di Simeone was saying to Beppino, shaking his head with incredulity, "when a Sunday collection at the Italian mass netted only ten or twelve dollars. No one thought the Italians would ever make enough money to build a proper church. As soon as the Irish had raised enough for that first wooden barracks where we used to say mass, they weren't interested in financing anything else. All they wanted was for the Italians to be out of St. John's. So what happened? We learned from the Americans. We had suppers with all the women donating the food —why Umbertina by herself sent up wagonfuls! Then lotteries, picnics, and bazaars, and we kept going until we got the church your niece was baptized in this morning."

"That's the church I'll be married in, Father," Beppino said.

"About time!" Gino Gualtiero boomed, clapping him on the shoulder. Umbertina noticed Beppino eyeing and playing up to Grazia Saccà, Domenico's daughter, and she felt he was doing it for spite. He knew that she wanted Grazia for her Jake.

Umbertina did not hide her resentment against her brother. Serafino, more affable, would tell her, "It's only because you can't command him and order him about, as you do the rest of us, that you resent him. But he is your brother."

Whereupon Umbertina made it clear to Beppino that he could, until he was settled elsewhere, have a room in the big house and eat at her table. But not forever. "This is a country where there's room for everyone; we don't have to stay all together as in our father's house," she told him.

"No matter what country, your tongue is always the same, Umbertina," he answered, offended.

Now, in front of her eyes, as if to show her disrespect, there was Beppino courting Grazia.

"*Disgraziato*," Umbertina muttered under her breath as she watched him. It bothered her that Beppino had not had to undergo the same baptism of pain as she; he had always worked and saved for himself without sharing and now here he was in Cato starting out in comfort and courting one of the Saccà family.

For Domenico Saccà, despite his preaching and book learning, an alliance with the Longobardis was now desirable. Though he had arrived first with the advantage of his trade, he had seen himself bypassed. Hard work and canniness had made the *cafoni* businessmen. The Longobardi family had become importers; Samuele Muzzi, a onetime railroad-tie cutter and handyman, was now a building contractor; the Gaultiero family had gone into real estate.

Peddlers opened stores, and Calabrians like the Micheluzzi changed their names to Michaels, married into Irish families, and from stonemasonry went into construction. Yet Domenico had not even remained a shoemaker; with the growth of shoe factories, his custom-shoe trade had dwindled and he was now left with only shoe repairing.

His bitterness was taken out in polemics against the ignorant in high places and in inveighing against the inequities of government, taxes, and politics in general—to the vast annoyance of Umbertina, who still understood nothing about politics but everything about being better off.

It was Domenico's idea to found a Circolo Socialista Italiano as a kind of mutual-aid society, with dues at 25¢ per month and benefits to be paid to widows and orphans of those who were victims on the job and whose employers did not provide compensation. He hoped through such a program of direct help to enlighten the poor landless *cafoni* about the inequities of the capitalist system that was exploiting them. And several times the *circolo* did make payments of $100 to bereaved persons; but the lessons never seemed to take. The *cafoni* continued to vote Republican, to work for wages no one else would accept, and to raise money for the church instead of for the club. The club they came to as a social center where they could talk and drink beer and play *scopa*. Worst of all, they laughed when he told them how bad off they were. "Oh, Domenico," they said, "to be bad off here is still better than we were there." And he despaired of ever teaching them to aspire to live more democratically. The only one who listened was his son, Dom, who was in law school. And that had to be enough for the old socialist.

"Do you call this a free country?" Domenico was raging, over in a corner of Umbertina's living room with his cronies. "Every ward boss knows how to buy votes. Look at Serafino. He got his citizenship papers—and how did he, without speaking English, without knowing how to read or write any language, get his papers? Simple. All he had to do was promise his vote to Luppizzi . . . that's how, who told him what to memorize, and maybe greased the judge's palm a bit. And *ecco!* Serafino Longobardi is an American!"

Some laughed at Domenico's jibing; others paid no attention.

"And that is why we get editorials in the *Cato Citizen-Press*," he went on, "against the immigration of ignorant Italians. They call us 'nondesirables'—*persone non grate*—and why? Because of ignorance! And I say it's time to stop being the mules of this country—it's school or stables, *a scuola, o nella stalla!*"

"Tell the *Citizen-Press* to ask the railroad tracks who put them down," cried an indignant voice, "or the buildings and bridges who put them up, or the parks and gardens who laid them out, or the mines who digs them!"

"That is the point," said Domenico patiently. "You will be the beasts of burden of this country until you learn other things and learn how to vote against those who use you and then call you undesirable."

"What is he, an anarchist?" Dr. Rossi asked Father Di Simeone.

"You can't dignify him by that term; he's just envious—a rebel and a loud one at that."

"Well, he makes a certain sense. But probably too idealistic to be a ward boss himself."

Then the suave Lucio Mazzello, a *galantuomo* if there ever was one, a tailor by trade and elegant to a fault in his piped jackets and well-cut trousers, proposed a toast. "Let's drink to this little child whose birth is synonymous with the light of the new electricity on Bleecker Street. She is truly a child of fortune to be born not only in the year of the new century but in the new era of progress. *Alla salute e alla fortuna!*"

"*Alla salute!*" everyone echoed, and they raised their glasses of wine.

And the toast was not just to the baby in Umbertina's arms; it was to the Longobardis and their future, it was to the new century and the new country and their place in it and the confidence that rose in each breast like an excitement that couldn't be stilled.

Serafino still busied himself around the expanded store on Third Street, but the days of brutal work in all weather, long hours for a dollar, and large doses of humiliation were over; his name was on the storefront—that much he could read—and he was proud. He spent more time now at Scalise's bar, talking to his cronies and remembering the old days. His face was round, his head bald and shining, his light eyes hooded now by the droopy eyelids that gave him his last nickname, Occhi Chiusi, old shut-eyes.

Umbertina got pleasure from hard work, from giving orders

and supervising her growing family, who were like so many soldiers in her own army waging the war of American success. Her son Paul laughed and said she should have been a union organizer, for though she was suspicious of politics and group action she believed in justice and fair play for workers. She despised those who broke strikes in order to work for low wages, who didn't speak up their grievances, were self-denying, and still dependent on a *padrone*. But her concern was only for her family, not for some abstract common good.

Jake and Ben still turned in their paychecks to the common fund. Everything, Umbertina said, should go into the common till and be doled out according to need, and she took offense when Domenico told her she was a good *socialista*. Pina and Anna helped in the store, did the housework, and took care of the babies. Umbertina expected a lot from everyone, but with Serafino she was now indulgent. "Rest, rest, old man," she'd tell him. And as he sat dozing in his rocking chair near the stove in the grocery she would nod her head toward him and tell her customers proudly, "His sons work for him now."

The neighborhood women would come into the store and when they pinched their pennies or complained of prices, she would scold them and tell them to think of their children's health. She saw all of her *paesani* from Castagna and the nearby villages. Most of them were workers in the mills or slate quarries or laborers on construction jobs. The Muzzis were doing well, but Cristina Muzzi was the same in Cato as she had been in Castagna, still having sick children in a land of plenty. Not because they didn't have money, but because of their mentality. *Miserabili*, Umbertina would say of them—afraid to spend for good food, saving for the doctor and the pharmacist by not spending on God's bounty. Their children would forever go on looking like stunted Calabrians and not Americans.

The neighborhood women also would come to the store for counsel. "*Comare* Umbertì," they would say, "what shall I do about my child who is ailing . . . shall I see a doctor?" "What do you think of the young woman my son is seeing? Is it suitable?" "Now I have money in the bank. Shall I go back and buy property in Castagna or shall I buy here?"

She scoffed at them for sending money back to their relatives in Italy; never a cent of hers would go back, she said. And in fact it was well known, and talked about in the neighborhood, that

Umbertina Longobardi never sent anything back except her photographs.

"A question of $26 for her brother's fare and she couldn't even send that," they whispered about her.

"*È dura*," the women agreed, "she's a hard one."

"Have you made your money here?" she would ask the women with a cold courtesy that barely masked her contempt. "Have you found fortune and *benessere* here? Then use it here. For your sons and grandsons who are Americans."

She saw men and women who had come over at her time, or later, remain peasants. They sent their money back or they went back, after saving and scrimping, and bought patches of dry, worn-out land in the old country instead of property in the new. And, improvident, they let their sons continue to work for others. Umbertina had learned what it was to fill the stomachs and pockets of barons and bosses.

Once the uprooting had taken place, everything from then on had to go toward regaining strength in the transplantation. She was not of peasant stock for nothing; she did not tend her own fields without learning. Her family had been uprooted by misfortunes, they had suffered loss and shock; now they must concentrate on new root growth, here in this soil that favored them. What nonsense did Cristina and Domenico and all the others talk of sending money back, going back, buying land and starting again back there? Can one keep moving one's roots and buds? Not and produce good fruit—that much she knew.

Even Serafino might have wavered but for her. He might have been content to take their earnings and go back where the winters were gentler. But she jeered at such softness and told him he was a foolish old man; there were his sons to consider. Did he want them conscripted for the Italian army the minute they set foot on the land they had been born in and which still claimed them? Italy had given them nothing, she told him, but it would be quick to take his sons for soldiers and his money for taxes.

When Cristina Muzzi would come by the store, crying over something she missed from the old country or saying that the chestnuts here could never compare to those of Castagna, Umbertina would look at her witheringly, for she hadn't progressed.

The only disagreeable thing about living in the Broad Street mansion was the quarrels she had there with Beppino. Maybe she was jealous because Serafino and the boys got along with him and the girls loved him because of his dashing, pirate appearance with those huge mustaches. But Umbertina called him a sponge and told him to get out on his own. Indignant, he finally did so, marrying Grazia Saccà, and as Umbertina said, finally opening his money-bags.

Again she was jealous; instead of working day and night and sweating through manual work, all he did was buy and sell real estate and second mortgages. He came by the store to tell Paul about a notice in the Italian paper concerning lots for sale off Broad Street north of the bridge over the canal.

"All I had to do," Beppino said in his blustery way as Umbertina turned her back and pretended not to listen while she filled sacks with dried beans, "was go down to the lots—they were all marked out with yellow flags—and take the flags from the posts on the lots I wanted back to the office on Bleecker Street with $10 down for each lot. The contracts and deed documents were included free. The lots were selling for $150 to $300, and you'll see, by next year I'll sell them for more than double. They're right between the Erie Canal and the railroad, where all the business and factories are opening up."

What bothered Umbertina most was how Paul listened to him.

The ensuing years in the mansion were happy and busy ones. Umbertina loved the tall trees around the house and the huge, ancient wisteria that coiled over the portico and veranda; she loved the big rooms and the spaces up in the attic where the little girls could disappear for hours at a time and read their books or play with friends who came and went in the easy American manner that first puzzled but finally pleased Umbertina. She loved the great porch where they sat on summer evenings and felt the breeze from the oaks and elms and heard the muted sounds from the canal and railroad. It didn't bother her that the formerly grand neighborhood was now zoned commercial; she liked it all the more with the sense of purpose and work all about them.

The old house was associated with good things: getting Bessie from the carriage house and hitching her to the wagon for the trip out to Muskieville in the spring for the tilling and planting, with the children in the back coming along to help and to play in the fields; then, later, the weekly weeding and the re-sowing of greens; and finally the fall harvest, when the girls gathered pretty leaves to wax and take to school for their teachers or looked for horse chestnuts or picked the last wild asters or cat-o'-nine-tails in the ditches along the roads while Serafino buried the cabbage and potatoes and carrots for the winter months.

Serafino was like a benevolent old grandfather to his younger children, and they were often with him at home while Umbertina bustled around the store. It had become his special task to make the ricotta, and he had a big copper kettle, jealously excluded from any other use and kept meticulously shining and clean, which he used on the wood-burning stove in the kitchen. It was like his time as a shepherd in the mountains. On days when the milk was delivered in huge quantities he'd start the fire and have the children keep it continuously fed. Then he'd stir, stir the huge amount of milk in the copper kettle with a beautiful constant rhythm that he had to keep just so, he said, so that the ricotta would come smooth and sweet. The harmony fascinated the children, and they would watch the hypnotic stirring until he aroused them shouting for more wood. When the whole process was over and the ricotta put in hole-punched containers for the draining, Sara and Carla and Margherita got the leftover whey with its chunks of good, sweet ricotta to eat on fresh bread. Then the copper kettle was carefully cleaned and put away for the next time.

Serafino was an easygoing old man who rode his little girls on his foot and told them stories. He wasn't as strict and bossy as Umbertina, but he never criticized her. They had grown comfortable together. And when they sat, at times, talking, they remembered the same things.

Margherita, Sara, and Carla were expected to get the ripe tomatoes ready for the winter store of *conserva*, the thick dark tomato paste that Umbertina would use when the fresh tomatoes were gone. The tomatoes had to be skinned after dipping in boiling water and then cooked down to the dense paste. This would be spread on trays that went outside to dry under cheesecloth between stakes. The girls would be stationed there to keep the birds and insects away from the trays, fussing because they couldn't leave to play.

The kitchen was the family's center, just as their aesthetic was the land. Not the house or the rooms they occupied, or the furniture they surrounded themselves with, or the clothing they wore were for Umbertina and Serafino as important in a deep, essential sense as the grooming and tending of land, which yielded them its fruits as God's visible sign of life and grace.

And not just Umbertina, but all who had left their land had to return to it to find their order and identity. Sometimes it was only a backyard plot, for not everyone could afford the horse and a wagon and rented farmland at Muskieville; but even so, an Italian yard was always distinguishable from a non-Italian one, where lawn meant leisure and money enough to cultivate the arts rather than the soil.

But cultivation for Umbertina was something else: It was direct contact with the land, an almost angry wrenching of well-being from the earth and whatever ruled it. Behind the plain frame houses of Yale and Denny streets in the old Italian neighborhood grapevines were lovingly splayed on stakes and gently formed; or there would be a pergola upon which the vines were trained so that the beauty of the vine was combined with the practicality of shade. Nothing was left to chance or to waste. Flowers were grown for beauty, yes, but also for the church.

In his backyard, tending his plot, the Italian felt himself again a man, not a foreigner among strangers. America was vast and alien, but the former peasants kept their footing there by little patches of zucchini and broccoli—vegetables the Americans knew nothing of.

Only a few immigrants, like Gino Gualtiero, had gone immediately to the rich lands near Emory and Canastota and become farmers; most of the former peasants were now city laborers. But all kept their culture, which was the tending of the land. Domenico used to say they were all like Don Antonio's chickens—they needed dirt to scratch in.

Even Muskieville wasn't enough for the great urge in Umbertina's heart to harvest as much of the wealth of this prodigious country as she could. With such riches should one close one's eyes? No, she felt young and strong and she had strong children. Summers she gathered them all up for a ten-day foray into the hop-fields near Oriskany Falls, where the farmers needed seasonal pickers. She had Pina buy the tickets as they stood in the station with little Carla hidden in their midst while the ticket seller counted heads; and then in the train Carla went under the seat when the conductor came through, covered by her mother's long skirt.

Agents had come by the store and told her where pickers were needed and made arrangements for her with the farmers. It was a chance for the children to have a real vacation in the country, they said, and to make money as well. She agreed. No opportunity was ever lost to add to the savings.

It was an all-day trip to Oriskany Falls in those days and they went on the milk train, finally being picked up by a farmer and taken to the bunkhouses—men in one building and women in another, just as in the old days in steerage. And as Umbertina and Serafino had done on the boat trip, they brought their own staples with them—their bread, pasta, beans, and oil. Fresh milk, cheese, and salad greens they got at the farm. It was on such an excursion that the child Carla had what she considered ever after an authentic American experience: She who had eaten Italian food all her life was given a fresh molasses cookie made by the farmer's wife. It was her Americanization.

Umbertina and Serafino, like the other workers, picked hops from dawn to dusk. The children picked some, too, and played around in the fields. The hops were pretty, the girls thought, like white fluffy flowers; it was what Umbertina called "clean" picking. And the hop picking was also fun for the children because they joined the other kids and ran in the fields, picked wild flowers, followed brooks and sailed leaves in them, played, and talked.

It was truly the golden country. And in the family they would tell over and over the story of Serafino's being sent to the store, when they had first gotten to Cato, for lard to fry zucchini-flower fritters in. At the store, he had pointed to what he thought lard was in America, something bright and golden. So instead of lard he had brought back butter, which burned in the pan. Now they could laugh about the burning; it was no longer a tragedy.

Jake and Ben had given up their outside jobs, and with the Longobardi wholesale and importing business thriving they both thought of marriage. Both approached it pragmatically and took girls they knew and had grown up with: no surprises, but good workers. Both furthered the relationship with the Muzzis—Jake by marrying Amelia and Ben by marrying Jenny. So there it was: Umbertina was now more firmly connected to Cristina Muzzi and all her complaints than ever before.

But the girls, Amelia and Jenny, were docile, easygoing girls born to breed large families and never give trouble. They were neither whiners like Cristina nor headstrong and domineering like Umbertina. They raised no objections about living all together under Umbertina's roof and seeing their husbands' earnings doled out and supervised by their mother-in-law while they themselves depended upon her, too, for other expense money.

The marriages, however, started Umbertina thinking about leaving the Broad Street place and finding more suitable housing for them all.

Chapter Nine

As if luck had been too lavishly given to the Longobardis and a compensatory toll must be exacted, it came suddenly and claimed the thirteen-year-old Margherita, a beautiful healthy girl who took sick and died of quick consumption before Dr. Rossi could do anything for her.

In death she was laid out in the front parlor of the Broad Street house, where the neighbors and *paesani* came to pay their respects and cross themselves in the silent prayer that such a thing would not be visited upon their own families. Tuberculosis was prevalent among the mill workers and the mill workers' children, with whom their own children, like Margherita, had contact in school. The women in black said their rosaries before the girl's coffin and prayed to be spared. It was the last family function in the old house.

For Umbertina it was a crushing sorrow, reminding her of the terrible days in the tenements when she had lost Rocco. Why was it, she asked Serafino, that the Lord blessed them with one hand and took away with the other? Was there some kind of balance that had to be kept? Margherita was the favorite of her daughters, as Paul was of her sons. She was the girl in whom Umbertina saw herself—the same eyes, the same quiet, tenacious will, and the same love for the outdoors.

Serafino opened his hands wide in the age-old gesture of helplessness; he said nothing. He went with Jake to Calvary Cemetery and chose a site at its highest point, nearest the huge wooden cross that gave the cemetery its name. He bought a large grassy plot with places enough for twenty-four family members, and Margherita was the first of the Longobardis to be laid to rest in Cato.

It was a loss that angered Umbertina as well as grieved her. Why should that bloom of a girl—well fed, well housed, and well taken care of—be snatched away? Had she suffered deprivation as Rocco, *poveretto*, had? Why? Why, with all their successes, did such a warning of humility come from God?

"There is no reason," Domenico Saccà said when he came to make his call of condolence. Domenico had experienced his own sour run of luck and tried, philosophically, to come to terms with it as a person of some education would, not superstitiously as the ex-peasants did. "It is the *imprevedibile*, the unforeseen and unaccountable . . . what God in His mercy hides from us. It happens in all lives, no matter how fortunate." Umbertina's heart agreed, but it was still a defeat.

Serafino, aging, began to diminish: The great broad shoulders of *il normanno*, so distinctive among his shorter countrymen, became curved; his stature lessened, and he receded in spirit as well as physique. His once-full face was now pinched, his old benign look had changed to one of quizzical bewilderment. When he was taken to a studio photographer at the age of seventy-two, the resulting portrait fixed him with the dignity of a banker in his dark suit with a gold watch fob across his vest; yet a faint look of astonishment and displeasure was also registered on his face, as if in dissent from his garb and pose and the whole question of being there. He sat erect, his shoulders once again high, but his light eyes were questioning, wondering.

He had given his name to a business, and "S. Longobardi & Sons" could be seen painted on wagons that delivered produce all over town. S. Longobardi & Sons had expanded into wholesale produce—the logical extension of a retail grocery store. The Longobardi Wholesale was the first of its kind in the central Mohawk valley, and it soon became the purveyor to institutions, hotels, restaurants, and other food markets. To all appearances the shepherd from Calabria had led his family to their fertile pasture.

But circumstances also helped at the right time. Cato was growing, and to accommodate the stream of workers who poured in to work in the knitting mills, the city council decided to cut a new street parallel to Broad and open it to housing construction. That meant that the rear portion of the Longobardi property on Broad Street, through which the new Catherine Street was to be cut, greatly increased in value and was sold at good profit. The family was still left with the old mansion and the remaining land, which now had entrances on two streets.

Umbertina immediately sensed what to do. She had Samuele Muzzi start to build what she called a *palazzo* on the part of their land that fronted Catherine Street.

It was a brown-shingled structure, large, ungainly, and absolutely without embellishment. It stood three stories high in strident ugliness, its only gesture toward amenity being the protruding street entrance that supported small porches for each of the floors above. It was frontier-type housing, made to consolidate good fortune and provide maximum space with minimum show for both business and living quarters. The ground floor would house the grocery on one side and the ticket agency and bank on the other; the first and second floors would have two apartments, each on either side of the stairway. It would be, under Umbertina's direction, the Longobardis' last endeavor to practice thrift and plain living. "You don't go around showing your fortune to the world," Umbertina said of her quasi-*palazzo*.

When it was completed, they all moved in: Jake and Ben and their families in their own apartments on the third floor, and Serafino's family on the second, with the extra apartment rented out.

Carla was only a child of eight at the time, but even so, moving from the Broad Street house to Catherine Street impressed her as a ruinous and improper idea. Although she used to mind being teased by her girl friends when they came over to Broad Street after school and asked why she lived in a "church," nevertheless she loved the old house with its imposing door and large rooms and nooks for disappearing into when her mother or sisters called.

The year Carla started school at Mount Carmel was the twentieth anniversary of the church's founding, and Sister Carmela, in appreciation of Umbertina's continual remembrances and the Longobardi donations over the years, chose Carla to be a flower girl in the pageant commemorating the occasion.

From their first meeting Carla had been awed by the nun's beauty and bearing. The dignified way she talked in a low, unhurried voice, the fine script of her handwriting, the delicate ceremonies with flowers and candles and embroidered cloths before the classroom shrine of the Virgin all spoke to the child of something beyond the everyday things of life. And the house on Broad Street was like that, too. So she couldn't understand why her mother was making them move to the ugly place on Catherine Street where they'd have a plain apartment with no dining room and no upstairs or attic.

"We don't need such a big house," Umbertina told her. "Such places are just show for people like the *vanitose*. We bought it for little and now we can sell it for more. What really matters is good food on the table and not what room the table is in."

It was the first time the little girl understood that her mother, who ran everything in their lives, never could know the things that Sister Carmela did—that there were other fine things in life as well as food. Then, when Carla learned that the old mansion was not going to be sold but was going to become the wholesale-produce warehouse, she cried and had her first experience of powerlessness before what was called progress.

After Margherita's death, Umbertina threw herself into work at the new place on Catherine Street with extra vehemence. The enterprises were divided: Ben managed the bank and steamship agency, while Jake ran the wholesale-produce business. Umbertina took charge of the grocery store, and the older girls ran the house and filled in at the store.

Then, in correct immigrant interpretation of values, quickly incorporating American nonsentimentality and disregard for the past into their thinking, they had the lovely stone mansion gutted inside to become the wholesale warehouse. Wagons and trucks of produce now went up the drive from along which the specimen trees had been cut down for parking space; they went to a loading dock that was built onto the veranda where in 1825 the stately double doors, now removed, had seen the entrance of the marquis de Lafayette and dignitaries of Cato to a celebration in honor of the opening of the Erie Canal and the fiftieth anniversary of the Revolutionary War. Gone, too, was the hung stairway of the entrance hall and the niched walls that had held classical statuary; the mansion now housed crates of fruits and vegetables.

It was the correct move in terms of getting on with fortune

building in the first immigrant generation; but it also set family values squarely into what they called business sense. Despite Paul's suggestion that they preserve the mansion for their residence and put the Wholesale in the ugly Catherine Street structure, it was clearly more practical to have the Wholesale facing Broad Street, where business was concentrated and where there was close access to the railroad and canal. This was the smart way of looking at things and it made Paul seem impractical—even to Umbertina, who favored him.

Umbertina had very little sentimentality in her toward people, and none at all for buildings. The older girls didn't mind the move; they would be married and out of their mother's house soon. Besides Paul and Carla, only Serafino might have wanted to keep the old mansion, which in some way reminded him of the old Norman abbey in the valley below Castagna; but he was retired now, and like Carla, what he thought really didn't count.

Having little to do, Serafino would hang around the Wholesale watching the loading and unloading of wagons, enjoying the bustle and bickering of selling; or he'd pretend to supervise his grandsons and the neighborhood kids as they sorted fruit into bushels. In pretended rage he'd sometimes flick off the wide leather belt he still wore, mountain style, with pants top hoisted above it, and snap it near the boys to hurry them up and make them jump in laughter.

Much of his time he spent playing *scopa* and drinking beer at Scalise's, which he and his friends called the Poor Man's Club with an irony that delighted them, for weren't they all past poorness, in one degree or another? Hadn't America proved itself?

In his last years Serafino and his friends at Scalise's bar used to debate long and hard over their beer and roasted lupine seeds on the story of their leaving the old country—it was the great story of their lives, an odyssey that was still real and vivid in their memories, a perpetual drama to be retold and acted out in all its shadings of sorrow and joy.

"The climate here is bad and there is no wine worth drinking," someone would say by way of starting the story.

"What wine could you, a *cafone* without land and vines, ever have drunk in the old country?" another would jeer. "You would be lucky to have goats' milk." And so the story of their *miseria* and how they had left would be picked up and repeated.

But if Domenico Saccà were there, it wouldn't be the simple

story of how it had been in the old times and how they had gotten where they were; it would become a political exhortation.

"*Stupidi!*" he shouted at the men, all common laborers and illiterate. "You are not educated! What do you know of the real wrongs of this country? It isn't because of the wine or the climate that it's bad; it's because here you are treated worse than the niggers. The niggers at least speak English, the bosses say, and that makes them more intelligent and worth more . . . and they are loyal Americans who don't send their money out of the country like the dagos do. So that's why you dagos get $1.15 for a twelve-hour day and the others get $1.50. And you not only take it, you're glad to get it and don't even ask why it's like that."

Sometimes Scalise, the wiry bartender, would get so exasperated he would himself lean over the bar and respond to Domenico. "When times are good and people have jobs and their stomachs are full, then there are complaints! Why don't you go back to the old country and organize your protest?"

"Oh, Domenico," someone else would call out, "you were the first one here and the one who's been here the longest; tell us again why you settled in this miserable climate. Why didn't you have the sense to go to California and then have us come over?"

Amid the laughter and catcalls, Domenico would continue his harangues, all his frustrations seething within him as he shouted and pounded his fist on the bar. "That's easy for you to say now, Signor Smart-Aleck," he said, "but maybe you don't remember when you let your bellies decide for you. This is where the work was and this is where you came. Sure! Now that your bellies are full and your heads empty you have time to think about the weather instead of the serious things."

A few others started singing, "Oh, where do you work-a-John?/ On the Delaware-Lackawhan. . . ."

"The D L W," said another—"Delay, Linger, and Wait."

"Sure, sure," Domenico went on, "the railroads, the mills, the quarries—there's still work wherever you look. But instead of organizing to make the work conditions better and making the Circolo Socialista a weapon against the bosses, you're sitting back and listening to your bellies and thinking your job is over."

"What good is socialism?" said Scalise. "You can't get into politics around here on that ticket, so what good is it?"

"When I first got to this country," Serafino said, "the *padrone* told us that when the time came for us to vote we should vote Republican so we'd always be sure of having jobs. The Republicans have the money, he said. And without money to build we wouldn't have jobs. It seemed right to me, anyway," Serafino mused, dragging on his old pipe, "because I fought for the great Garibaldi to make a republic in Italy. He was betrayed by the king and Italy still has a king, but here it's a republic and here I vote Republican."

"We all vote Republican," Scalise added dryly. "Who wants to vote Democrat like the Irish?"

"What's the difference, one way or the other?" Domenico broke in excitedly. "Democrat or Republican, it's still the *padrone* who makes the jobs."

"Not anymore," said Serafino. "I had the *padrone*, but my sons don't."

"You're lucky, all right," Scalise put in, "that you've got two sons, at least, who are working."

Whenever any reference was made to his two working sons by the men at Scalise's, Serafino would inwardly fume because what they said was true: His third son, Paul, was still a bachelor living at home and still not contributing anything to the family. He was personable and charming and liked to dress up and walk about town talking to people. He was a good talker and he was full of ideas, schemes that never worked out. First he persuaded Jake to carry an expensive line of candies at the Wholesale; when that failed, he got his brothers to invest family funds in a dying cotton mill. His last venture was The Blue Bird Cafeteria, which he opened on Bleecker Street with family backing and then watched wither and die because Bleecker Street itself was dying by then. Whenever one of Paul's business schemes failed, Jake and Ben and others simply worked harder to make up the losses. Paul was not blamed; he was more educated than the others, Umbertina said, and it was simply a question of bad luck, not bad judgment, that he hadn't succeeded. In any case, Umbertina wouldn't have allowed any censure of him; the only thing that displeased her in Paul was his courtship of Mary Pauline Colombo.

Mary Pauline's mother was Francesca Colombo, who would sometimes come to visit in her gray silk gowns with her gray hair handsomely marcelled, sitting there regally accepting coffee and little pastries while Umbertina, in her frumpy full skirts, would bustle around, her hair spilling out of its combs in long, untidy straggles. The Colombos were all fashion on the outside, Umbertina muttered, but without substance where it counted—by which she meant linens for a dowry.

For even though the Colombos were well off, they had never produced for their girls the dowry that Umbertina was assembling for each of her daughters. Even worse, the mother, being a *fanatica*, had produced a daughter who was bold—a daughter who one Sunday after mass at Mount Carmel had come to Catherine Street to ask for Paul, and when told he was still sleeping had horrified Umbertina by going to his room to wake him.

But the attachment was real, and when Mary Pauline dropped the first part of her name so that she'd be Pauline to his Paul, and then moved her birthday back so that she wouldn't be any months older than he (for he had to take precedence in everything), Umbertina knew she had to accept the inevitable. She became resigned to the idea: The girl was clever and intelligent and completely loyal to Paul, and that was what was needed.

For Paul was a dreamer, always reading, and filled with ambitions for himself that had nothing to do with the kind of hard work and drudgery the rest of his family engaged in. He was different in everything, not only in his attitude toward work. He could not be commanded as the others were; without ever outwardly disagreeing with or angering his mother, he managed to elude her as well as he did the others.

Things had been comfortable enough by the time he was in high school so that unlike his brothers, who had been made to leave school and start work, he was allowed to finish and even take some extra courses—not in business subjects, as Jake and Ben did, but in the arts and literature, which he passionately enjoyed. He was the exception to the family unity of hard work and cooperation. Umbertina said it was because of his health, which had been damaged when he was an infant in New York; and though she was indefatigable herself and demanded as much of others, including her daughters, Umbertina not only let Paul get away without contributing his time or his physical strength to the family enterprises, but also managed to make the others feel guilty if they questioned Paul's privileges.

Jake, like his father, was the plodder; and like Serafino he was of an open and simple nature, his full face smiling and jovial. He was a good front-man, for he inspired trust in all his dealings; with the young he kidded around in American slang, and with the old *paesani* he reminisced of his early childhood in Castagna, when he remembered riding a donkey out to the fields bringing water to his father.

Ben was like his mother had been in the early days, dour and suspicious; he was keen on systems and he was the one who insisted on installing books in the business and keeping records. With Ben in charge of the office, the family was no longer allowed to help themselves from the great big handsome brass National cash register that sat like a golden idol adorned with ornate scrolls and festoons on a counter of the grocery store. Even as a young man Ben had been painstaking and pedantic; he took a night course in calligraphy to improve his penmanship and insisted that the girls do nightly practice in making circles and up-and-down strokes to prepare them for working later in the Wholesale office as secretaries. He himself was in demand to write letters back to the old country in his flowing hand, and he became secretary of finance for the Mount Carmel congregation. He was efficient, intelligent, systematic, and fair. And yet, like Umbertina, he had a streak in him that held grudges and fed on resentment—especially, in his case, toward Paul.

Still, it was as much a surprise to Ben as to the others when Serafino finally put Paul out of the house.

For years it had angered and puzzled Serafino in a way he didn't understand that Paul slept late, made friends among outsiders, and generally acted different from the rest. Perhaps Serafino felt this way because of what he had suffered in his own youth, when work had been both a blessing and a curse. Anyone who got work was blessed, for how did you live without it? And yet, in those days to work was like going to war—you didn't know if you would survive the harshness of it.

Paul, instead, easily succumbed to the flattery of politicians, who told him he was too smart to waste his time around two-bit family stores; he should be in politics. He let himself be persuaded to run for the state assembly and this touched off an ugly threat in the family ranks: Ben, disgusted at Paul's attitude, threatened to disclose something that Paul had kept hidden from his political cronies—that he had been born in Italy and so was not eligible to run for office. Umbertina squelched Ben's threat and Paul ran but didn't win. It was another scheme that hadn't worked, but this time Serafino had had enough.

"Why don't you work like the others? Why always these ideas that waste the money your brothers earn?"

"Pa," Paul explained to the old man, "there are other things I'd like to do; why does it have to be the store or nothing? We can still be a family without my having to work in the store with Jake and Ben."

"Leave him alone," Umbertina said, "he's not as strong as the others. *È più delicato.* He needs a different kind of work."

"Maybe he should be a priest, then," Serafino answered sarcastically. "They're the ones who know best how to get out of work."

Despite Umbertina's efforts, this time Serafino had his way about Paul. "If you don't work with the family, don't stay with the family," he said. When Paul left, Umbertina added to her devotions a special one for Paul to bring him home and to his senses.

Umbertina and Serafino observed all the religious feast days and went regularly to Sunday mass at Our Lady of Mount Carmel, where they had given a window in memory of Margherita. Umbertina observed the saints' days, especially those for whom her children were named and those who had special protective powers—like San Biagio, the patron of throats, on February 3, who could keep them from strep-throat infections at that bad time of the year. Particularly important was the feast of San Serafino, which fell on October 12, the day the Americans commemorated Columbus' discovery of the New World. It was a day when Umbertina could rejoice in the spectacle of the American fall, so much more brilliant and rich than the gentle autumn of the Sila, and gave thanks that her fields had been harvested and her foods preserved by that time. Then there were other important days, like the Assumption of the Virgin on August 15, when Sara (actually baptized Assunta) was born; San Francesco di Paola on April 2; and, in June, the great summer feast of San Giovanni.

The devotion that Umbertina was most attached to after Margherita's death was not to a saint of the old country but to a Venerable of this new land, the Mohawk Indian maiden named Kateri Tekakwitha, whose shrine was nearby at Auriesville. Each year for many years, on the Sunday before Labor Day, Umbertina and her unmarried daughters would set out for Auriesville to attend the Kateri Mass in honor of the martyred Indian maiden and to pray for the special intention of Margherita Longobardi. It was not just the mass

that moved Umbertina. It was that short trip into the Mohawk valley which made her heart expand and gladden as she re-evoked her
own journey up from New York and the way her eyes had beheld
the green hills and fields of the valley in rejoicing and thanksgiving.
At Auriesville she looked out over the expanse of green from the
height where the shrine stood and saw always trees, trees, trees; and
something in her remembered similar long green vistas in the hills
above Castagna from her girlhood. She loved the sad beauty of these
excursions. She never stopped marveling at the old barns that stood
like weathered abbeys, grand and imposing. It was the equivalent
moment of standing in the hills above Castagna as a girl.

Some years after Margherita's death something happened that
seemed to Umbertina another great lesson of life. Serafino burst
into the store one day, excited and flushed, to say that he had just
heard at Scalise's that Domenico Saccà was at the station about to
board a train to leave the country and go back to Italy. Domenico
had been brooding for months over the end of his Circolo Socialista,
which had come about when the old members defected and set up a
new club, the Società Castagnese, which was strictly social with no
politics allowed. It hurt Domenico, and then with the death of his
wife he had, in fury and frustration, decided to return to Italy.

"*Imbecile!*" said Umbertina in disgust at such a senseless act. At
the same time she was moved, for despite the aggravation he pro-
voked in her, Umbertina knew they all owed their start to Domenico. Serafino was beside himself at the thought of the shoemaker's
leaving.

"Run to the station!" he shouted at Ben, who was in the midst of
dealing with a salesman from New York. "Keep him from getting
on the train! Bring him back!"

Somehow Ben did it, reaching Domenico on the platform and
persuading him to return with him to the store.

"*Pazzo,*" Serafino greeted him gruffly, but there were tears in his
eyes as he put his arm around the shoemaker's shoulder. "Were you
going off to spite yourself? Stay so that you can tell your grandchildren how the stupidest thing Serafino Longobardi ever did was
to send his son to the station to keep you here so you could go on
insulting him at Scalise's."

In that incident with Domenico, Serafino understood the fullness
of his own good fortune; he felt that he, the unlettered shepherd,
had been propelled by a destiny he didn't understand, while Dome-

nico, who deserved more, was left behind. Serafino wanted his friend to understand that he esteemed him and that he knew that fortune had been capricious in rewarding only backs and muscles. But such feeling made Umbertina impatient.

In the winter, in the warmth of her home, Umbertina wondered, as great storms of snow fell on that city of upstate New York, about being laid to rest in a land where snow would cover her grave. She began to think of death as she watched Serafino age and get weaker. She would glance at the tin heart she had worn as a goat girl, which now hung in her kitchen, and think of herself then and now. Sometimes she wondered how it would have been to be wife to a younger man. Would she have done as much? No, no, she thought; my life went as it had to, and it is the right way.

When the great war broke out in Europe in 1914, Umbertina gave thanks for their being there, in America, safe and well fed, her family growing in grandchildren—and for the return home of Paul. Chastened by lack of success and ailing, he had come back to a great family celebration promoted by Umbertina in which Serafino was made to feel ashamed for what he had done. Paul was brought into the wholesale business and made a salesman for the territory around Cato, canvassing the small towns and getting orders.

When the United States entered the war, Paul was drafted. Just a few months of training broke down his health to such an extent that he was given a medical discharge for a heart condition and sent home, where Dr. Rossi visited him and said he wouldn't last the year unless he went west and had a complete rest in the sunshine of Arizona. Pauline Colombo insisted that their marriage take place before he left. She refused to believe he wouldn't get well, and her stubbornness earned the enduring respect of Umbertina, who had always understood defiance as a necessary tool of life. Paul, who was supported by the family when he and Pauline were married and he was out West recovering his health, was never to see his father again.

As Serafino grew weaker, something seemed to give way inside him, as if his sweet nature had finally been apprised of the horrors and treacheries of life. At times the old man's mind would wander and tears would come to his eyes as he remembered the years of his youth, the loneliness and the hardship. It was as if the scars of those years were opened and throbbing with the pain of what was past.

Umbertina no longer reproved him when the tears came to his

eyes and his voice choked as he said in his rough dialect of the hills, "It was a tough life . . . all alone in the mountains . . . working months and months without stop on the railroad."

Toward the end he spoke only in dialect, his English words forgotten, and he spoke rarely. "Why did Christ let me suffer so . . . was it worth it all just to make money? Just to end up an old man like this?" He would repeat the same phrases over and over.

At first Umbertina had countered this rambling by saying, "But you have your family, your home. What more does a man want?" Then she realized that he was not listening or hearing, that her words made no impression, for he had slipped back to another time when he had nothing.

Just as abruptly he would come back to the present and say, "Domenico was right—we should have all worked together as in Garibaldi's day when we had some hope. Instead we worked for ourselves. All that hard work . . . that tough life . . . and all you have at the end is money."

He who had been the mildest of men even in adversity refused to go to mass at Our Lady of Mount Carmel anymore. "What the priest says I've heard before," he said.

Serafino died toward the end of the war, when the Wholesale had grown and profits were so large that Ben had closed out the paralyzed steamship and banking operations and joined Jake. They started dealing in sugar and flour at the war's beginning, and then, when the influenza epidemic broke out, they foresaw the call for lemons and contracted for carload lots so that each lemon was like a nugget of gold on the market. When, as *La Luce* put it, Serafino passed to a better life, the family was secure, its fortune started.

As was customary, his obituary credited him with the business success and his wife only with having been his working companion. The piece in *La Luce* read, "Serafino Longobardi knew how, with his honest and untiring work, to launch his sons into business and open for them the way to that excellent place in everyone's esteem that the Longobardi family enjoys today. Of scrupulously upright character, gentle and affectionate toward all, he leaves a great emptiness in all who had the fortune of knowing him. To his stricken family—to Signora Umbertina his good companion, and especially to his sons Giacomo, Benedetto, and Paul, who have so worthily followed the paternal example—we offer our most sincere condolences."

He was laid to rest under a large polished granite monument that bore his name and dates as well as Umbertina's unconcluded ones, and was topped by a winged seraph in honor of his saint. His monument stood in the center of the cemetery plot, a plot that was in itself another visible proof of earthly success. Who in the old country would have had the money to have such a piece of good land just for burial? The angel that recalled his name looked toward the city below.

It is a good place to lie, Umbertina thought as she watched the casket be put to earth. "Rest, rest, old man," she said to him. He was more than her husband and the father of her children; he was her friend, the only true companion of her adventure and laboring. He had brought her to the New World, and now, despite her sons and daughters and the grandchildren, she was alone.

The cemetery was a high place—almost as high as the village they had come from, and from which they had looked down to the valley where the river ran and the ruined abbey stood on its banks. But here there were no ruins; there was a city still growing fast and work still to be done.

Chapter Ten

Umbertina Longobardi had few words of advice to give her daughters before they married. She believed in good food on the table and good linen on the bed; all the rest of housekeeping was so much *fronzoli* for which she had neither time nor temperament. The importance of family and of loyalty to one's husband, her daughters would have acquired from her example; anything else they had to know they would find out for themselves.

Pina was the first to marry, and her husband was the very dapper, nattily dressed son of Lucio Mazzello the tailor, about whom Umbertina shook her head, for the son gave no indication of being the serious man his father was. Soon after, Anna married a tall, good-looking northern Italian who had come from Connecticut for a visit to relatives in Cato and then returned to court Anna, to marry her, and to take her back to Chester. As children, Sara and Carla remembered their sisters selecting their trousseaux from the Mc-Cutcheon's salesman who came with a suitcase full of beautiful linens from New York.

It wasn't their turn to have linens until they got to the new house on Rutger Street, Jake's house.

After Serafino's death, Umbertina gave Jake notice. "I can't stay alone in a flat with these unmarried girls," she told him. "It's not right without a man as head of the family. Your family is growing and you'll have to find a larger place anyway, so what you have to do is get a house large enough for all of us—for your family and for the girls and me. I'll buy the food and do the cooking and the girls will take care of the house. That will give Amelia time for the children."

That was the bargain she made with Jake, and it could only have been with Jake and the amiable Amelia that such a household could have been set up, for the others were already moving in directions of their own. Catherine Street no longer suited the Longobardi prosperity. When Paul had come back from the West with his health restored, he and Pauline had bought a bungalow in a new part of town. Ben and Jenny were building a home in a residential section near Belleview Park. Jake would have moved long ago, but he had been too busy at the Wholesale to think about a house, and Amelia, who already had four children and was pregnant with the fifth, could never get away.

Finally Umbertina put her foot down and sent the two girls, Sara and Carla, now aged twenty and seventeen, to select Jake and Amelia's house for them.

The house they chose was a romantic one, and it was on Rutger Street, a fine, old established street not far from Bleecker Street and Mount Carmel parish. Even though the house was not at the most fashionable end toward Rutger Park, but more easterly where lots and yards were smaller and there were no rear carriage-houses, still it was a definite social advancement from the old neighborhood.

The street was arched over with towering old elms, and the house at number 675 had a large backyard that the girls knew was a necessity for their mother's garden; it also had a spacious and dignified front porch of the confident, ebullient era when families sat out and spoke to their neighbors, and a handsome approach up wide stairs between red sandstone balustrades that terminated in pillars topped by graceful white columns, continued at intervals along the porch. It was a Queen Anne structure, with the scalloped shingles, festoons, and garlands typical of that revival style. The house rounded and curved with bays and turrets, and had gables, chimneys, and useless balconies along parts of the second floor. Umbertina laughed when she saw it, and laughed again when Carla explained that it was the most romantic house she had ever seen; she and Sara wanted it because it had a huge golden-oak staircase with banisters and a landing that curved in a bay beneath a stained-glass window that would be perfect for the descent on their wedding days.

Her two youngest daughters made Umbertina uneasy. They sometimes took her to American movies where love and marriage was shown as a game played between men and women instead of the serious matter it was. "*Oche*," she chided them. "You have to respect marriage, not be geese about it."

It was to prepare for weddings that long sessions in the kitchen with the McCutcheon's salesman took place, since no one store in Cato had linens fine enough for Umbertina's taste. The long table in the kitchen, where ten of them now sat to meals, was cleared and a clean cloth set out upon which the contents of his suitcase could be shown. The girls would sit there occasionally interpreting while their mother questioned, inspected, rejected, or approved. Umbertina, who couldn't sew a seam or do a stich of embroidery, knew instinctively, however, how things should be; she had an absolute feel for *biancheria* and knew what kind of mitering was right, what types of linens should accompany a woman in life, how fine the hemstitching should be, what monogramming was suitable, and what quality of material was appropriate. Always it was the best and most expensive quality that she ordered, and the most obsolete: dream stuff of another way of life that included damask dinner cloths with banquet-size monogrammed napkins, exquisite Madeira tea sets, blanket covers and tray sets for breakfast in bed, napkin envelopes with cutwork, and linen hand-towels with long strands of flax fringe which, she told Sara and Carla, were to be used by the doctor when he washed his hands after a home visit; they also required, after laundering, the patient combing-out of fringe strands that no daughter of hers, in their modest homes, was ever to have time for.

She insisted on ordering for them several beautifully embroidered and hand-stitched capelets, called matinées, which were to be worn over garments for the morning brushing of the hair. Even though their hair was bobbed after the war and the girls didn't spend time brushing and tending it, Umbertina, by not accepting new ways, seemed to think she had eliminated them. Imperturbable in her convictions and in the revenge she plotted over the loss of her tenement days, she continued to buy and store up linens for her daughters and send out the sheets and pillowcases to be hand-monogrammed by her countrywoman, old Vincenzina, who had been taught handwork in a convent and with whom not even McCutcheon's could compete.

Umbertina often told her daughters the story of her dowry bed-spread and its loss during the hard times in New York; and she had told them that the bed-linen and spreads she provided must remain with them and then be passed on to their own daughters. She was never as concerned with furniture as with what she believed were the real, substantial bases of life: eating well and sleeping well. The business she had built up and the property she had worked to accumulate would be for the sons, but her daughters would get the finest *biancheria* possible.

This apportionment wasn't contemplated out of meanness, or the desire to slight her daughters, who had also worked in the family business right along. Rather, she had the conviction that family property should stay with the family name, and that the husbands of her daughters should be expected to provide for them after they had brought their marriage dowries to their new homes. That was the way things were done in a right and ordered world.

By the time they moved to Rutger Street, Umbertina no longer kept a horse and wagon to go to the fields in Muskieville, and her gardening was done in the back of Jake's house, where she laid out her rows of pole beans, tomatoes, and corn.

With Serafino gone, Umbertina's life changed; Jake became the visible head of the family and she who had always bossed her sons now consulted with them. The grocery had been closed out and the family business was now completely at the Wholesale, which was moved from Broad Street to a warehouse down near the station, where, in huge letters, "S. Longobardi & Sons" greeted train travelers coming and going through Cato. She had no work now, except in the garden, and though she made the kitchen her domain, things were not the same. Nor could they ever be again.

Umbertina was still a strong woman, in good health, and with a clear mind and undiminished ambition. But now her sons, as was right, were in the forefront, and she spoke only to keep loyalty and solidarity among them. She became the grandmother in the kitchen, the old woman dressed in black with wispy gray hair straggling down from the knob on top of her head, a household fixture standing at the stove stirring sauces or sitting in her white chair listening to the station in Schenectady on the radio.

"Gia-nee!" she would call her grandson Johnny, Italian fashion, bossing him and his brothers around as she no longer could her grown sons. She made them come and help her weed the garden or make *conserva* while the boys fumed and fussed, wanting to get away and play ball. Disrespectful, she would call them, and they didn't know what she meant.

Sometimes in the kitchen she would sit still and think; she would think how strange it was that although Serafino hadn't worked for years and all the early decisions and planning had been hers, it was his name which triumphed and it was his presence, as a man, which had been necessary to give her the standing from which to command.

It was a man's world, they said, and this had never troubled her when she was actually in command and actively wielding her own will; but to be deposed now as a widow, because there was not the figurehead of her husband, was hard to take. She saw now that there was much that was not honest in this world, and she remembered Domenico, whom she had scorned when she was in full vigor, saying that in a just world women would be valued for themselves and all things would be open to them. Now she sat in the kitchen and felt that a woman alone was a poor and wasted thing.

Though her daughter-in-law never said anything, Umbertina sensed that Amelia would have liked control of her own house, and would have enjoyed being in the kitchen alone sometimes to have a supper of milk-toast or to make the thinner tomato sauce or simpler dishes she preferred to Umbertina's rich concoctions. For her own part, one of the indignities for Umbertina of not being in her own home was having to put up with the insult of Cristina Muzzi's visits to Amelia; Cristina would draw her daughter into her bedroom to talk behind a closed door for hours instead of sitting in the kitchen with her as decency would demand. Umbertina saw each visit of *la strega* as an invasion of Longobardi territory, and she rankled with fury at the idea of the stories they told behind that closed door.

The only respite they all had from each other was the two weeks each summer when Umbertina took Sara and Carla by train to nearby Richfield Springs, a spa in Cherry Valley that for some curious reason was filled with wealthy Cubans come to take the waters there instead of at Saratoga.

Other things weighed on Umbertina's mind. She blamed herself for having unwittingly provided the first visible sign of family disunity by quarreling with her brother, Beppino. It was years now since they had seen each other, and this was wrong. She who had always held the family inviolate, one for all and all for one, had undermined its structure with her quarrelsome and grudging nature. She saw signs among her sons that made her uneasy.

Paul was prospering independently of the others with real estate and stock market investments. With the excuse of his health, he stayed home from work and studied investment reports while the others worked at the Wholesale. Yet all this time he was receiving his share from the Wholesale, too.

As Paul and Pauline were advancing rapidly in Cato's social circles, Pina went into the limbo of abandoned women. Her husband had gone west, promising to send for her and the children, but had disappeared completely. Pina, like Umbertina, became a woman without a man, and though she was taken care of out of the business her status was irretrievably fallen. She couldn't leave her children to resume work at the Wholesale, so Carla was pressed into leaving school and taking Pina's place at the office.

"We need you at the Wholesale," Jake kept saying. "Sara can't manage alone, and that other girl who kept the books was making mistakes that looked like fraud. We can't prove anything, but it's better to have one of the family doing that work, anyway."

"But I want to finish high school . . . I want to go to college," Carla told him.

"Listen, Carla, we'll give you whatever you want. You can open charge accounts at all the stores downtown: Marvin Miller's, Grant's Bookstore—everywhere. You can have that whole set of Dickens you wanted; you help us out and you won't regret it."

It was Umbertina who made the decision. "You help your brothers," Umbertina told her. "We're living in Jake's house and he's head of the family now. And don't talk foolishness about college. No daughter of mine is going off to sleep out of town under strange roofs. Girls should be married."

Before she was married, Carla Longobardi had two fur coats and several Paris gowns from Marvin Miller all charged to S. Longobardi & Sons. She and Sara spent every Saturday afternoon going downtown shopping, and on their way they would always stop for a minute at the shrine of St. Rita in St. John's Church to pray for good fortune in courtships. Good fortune was all around them; all they needed was to have it provide them the right man.

Jake had bought the house on Rutger Street with $7,000 in cash and then ordered three Stearns-Knight automobiles for the three brothers. Everything prospered, the Longobardis were known all over Cato and the other towns of the Mohawk valley, and Umbertina was even interviewed by a woman reporter from the *Cato Citizen-Press* for a Columbus Day feature on the achievements of the town's Italians.

Carla was there to explain and interpret when the reporter, an emancipated young woman with bobbed hair and the hard, brittle look of plucked eyebrows and bright lips, came to the house.

"We know, Mrs. Longobardi, what America has given many Italian families, for their success is now familiar to Catonians," she said to Umbertina, who sat there impassively in her black, not leaning back in the armchair but sitting up straight on the edge—wanting, Carla knew, to be back in her kitchen or garden and not wasting time sitting in the front room. "But, as a typical successful Italian, what would you say your countrymen have given their new country in return?"

Carla gave Umbertina the gist as Umbertina nodded and looked hard at the young woman: her hair, her lips, her colored nails, her pencil poised over pad, her bony knees showing from her shortened skirt. She seemed to Umbertina to be in her own way a *fanatica*, but with less style than the oldtime women like the Colombos.

Curtly Umbertina gave her answer. "Hard work," she told the young American woman, "and good bread."

Carla was faintly embarrassed. Wasn't there something else? Could they mention Marconi or the poet Carducci who had won a Nobel Prize? But no, the famous Italians were in Italy and they certainly weren't Calabrians, anyhow; for the first time Carla wondered what they, the Italians of America, could point to besides their cars and furs and big houses. But that feeling didn't last long, and it was her simultaneous courtship by two suitors which put things in perspective for her.

It was Carla Longobardi who was the more polished and sure of herself when Sam Scalzo from Gloversville came courting her. She was attractive, as all the sisters were, and she had her mother's good skin; for the rest, she was dark-eyed, dark-haired, and rather sharp of feature like Zio Moustacchio's side of the family. Sam first came to Cato as a novice in the produce business, hoping to become connected with Longobardi & Sons as his initial supplier. And Jake, kindhearted and generous as he was, invited Sam home for dinner.

Umbertina liked the shy young man and felt sorry for him because he looked so thin and sickly. "Be kind," she admonished her daughters, who were giggling between themselves at his turtleneck sweater and strange shoes. "He's just lost his mother!" Though he owned his own business and drove a Packard, he looked like a kid.

The Longobardi girls, known in Cato, like an order of rich novices, as the Sisters of Longobardi, dressed elegantly and had callers who vied to be seen with them. Yet Carla's most importunate suitor, Stanos Saxenian, a recent graduate of Colgate College and the one with the most highly directed ambition, made her uncomfortable with the intensity of his drive, his dark looks, his damp handshake, and the pressures he laid upon her by encouraging her self-education. On her twenty-first birthday he gave her a set of the Harvard Classics and in a note said that this was the first step toward her getting her high school diploma and then going on to even more. He said that if they married, they would honeymoon in New York, where he would be in law school and she could take undergraduate courses at New York University. They would live in The Village, where she would become acquainted with artists and writers and new social thought. The prospect frightened her exceedingly, but she was flattered by his attentions and the natty way he dressed when he came to call. "Greasy spats," her nephews at Rutger Street snickered when they saw him coming up the front steps; and in her heart she agreed that he was greasy, and ludicrous, too, with the spats he wore over his shoes.

She was more comfortable with Sam Scalzo, who was quiet and undemanding; he was making good money without ever having finished school himself, and he looked at her in a gentle, appealing way that touched her. No matter how successful his Gloversville business might become, he would never outdo the celebrity and success of the Longobardis in Cato, and this reassured her. She accepted, not Stanos the prospective lawyer, but Sam.

Sam Scalzo had been a self-made man from the age of twenty and head of his business at what he called The Place. Sam stood in no awe of the Longobardi brothers. He dealt with them in business but they didn't own his soul, he said. He had made his way alone, whereas there were three of them and they had had the first boost from Umbertina.

Sam had a precise notion of duty and how to discharge it. When his mother had lain dying he made up his mind to leave for California right after her death; she was the only thing holding him in upstate New York, and with his own small reserve of cash and his knowhow he could set himself up wherever he wanted to be, which was out West. But his mother—a handsome, melancholy, strong-featured woman in her forties—had called him to her deathbed and in a few words had set his life. "You've always been a good boy, Samuele. Promise me when I'm gone you'll take care of your brothers and sisters. I can't trust your father . . . promise me you'll make a home for them."

She was dying of a heart condition, her life embittered by a husband who hadn't gotten ahead in America and who, it was known, had taken up with another woman. "Be the ever-present instrument of my justice!" the dying woman seemed to be saying, her dark eyes burning with the eloquent passion of retaliation as she laid the burden of it upon her eldest child, the son who revered her.

Sam's mother was a simple woman and he saw in Carla qualities that reminded him of her; she was trusting and had the accepting nature of a basically honest and modest person. Appealingly, Carla was without the dark part of his mother's nature: the intense pride and melodramatic sense of wrongdoing and betrayal that were in her Sicilian blood.

If Sam hadn't identified Carla with his mother he might have courted Sara, the family beauty, as would have been more seemly since she was the elder and by Umbertina's rule no younger sister could be married before the older ones had husbands. Sara, however, snubbed Sam and even tried to persuade Carla to choose Stanos, a college man, over him. Carla's engagement to Sam went on for almost a year until Sara married a handsome insurance salesman related to Gino Gualtiero who almost immediately began to mistreat her.

In their wedding picture Sam and Carla are a handsome couple. She is attired in an expensive gown with a veil of handmade lace; her eyes are demurely downcast into her bridal bouquet; and her hair is marcelled into row upon row of waves. Her eyes are brown and his are too, but hers are the brown of docile, romantic dreaminess and his are restless and sharp, with a depth of melancholy. He smoked cigars, hoping they would create a businesslike look for him. He was all wrapped up in The Place. He disapproved of his father and wished to live up to his mother's expectations. Responsibility was to shape his life forever. For him, love was duty. For Carla, love was a Gloria Swanson movie.

And what had love been for Umbertina? She reacted as if to an indecent question when Carla, teasing, asked her if she had been in love with her husband.

Umbertina's firm round chin turned pink. *"Faccia tosta!"* she scolded. "What has that to do with anything? He was a good man —a little sentimental, but good; and I did my duty. That's what marriage is, not all this love and romance. Marriage is to start a family, it's not a *carosello*, a merry-go-round. It's a woman's duty!"

Umbertina's fair skin flushed at what she considered the undue intimacy of this talk. She was a reticent woman, she did not discuss emotions. Carla, she said, read too much. It gave her foolish ideas of the world and people.

"Oh, Ma, you're so practical! Didn't Poppa ever give you a gift or do anything nice for you?"

"Yes, he came back from America for me." Umbertina's flushed chin was the only sign of her embarrassment and emotions.

"What about that tin heart you have? Did he give you that?"

"No," said Umbertina, "that was someone else."

She said no more. But for Carla there was conjured up the shadowy figure of some other man and of something uncompleted in her mother's life. Why else was the useless tin heart still with her mother, except as a memory of something not done—some reminder that not everything in her life had been a direct line of advance, that compromise also is progress of a sort.

"Were you happy with Poppa?" Carla went on, trying to fathom before her marriage what lay ahead of her.

What innocent and simple children she had, Umbertina thought; listen to this girl speaking of love and happiness as if they were the things that counted in this world! But she was the baby, come late in life when the worst was over. She saw a table with food and slept in a clean bed and warm room at night. She didn't know about survival so she dreams of love and happiness, as if such things could come bound up in any one man.

Happiness was not that, Umbertina knew. It wasn't a prize you were given and could hold on to, but a feeling of satisfaction that receded or advanced according to each day's design. Her happiness was in being part of something entire, something that was you and more than you.

"The important thing," she told her daughter, "is to find your place. Everything depends on that. You find your place, you work, and like planting seeds, everything grows. But you have to be watchful and stick to it."

"What about Paul? He was always moving around and trying out different things. He's never worked like Jake and Ben."

"Never mind about Paolo. He is different, but now he, too, is settled down and working. His place is here with the others."

"And my place?"

"Where your husband will be."

The hardest thing about marriage for Carla was that it took her from Cato and from being a Longobardi.

Marriage, Carla soon found out, was more than just the distance from Gloversville to Cato; it was exile from laughter—from the warm, high spirits and joking and good times of Longobardi life, first at Catherine and Broad streets, then at Rutger Street with Jake's family—to the gloomy, dark, Sicilian moodiness of Sam's family.

The splendid old days of getting on and up in the world had stopped with marriage, and real life had begun; there was housework and child-rearing in a new place and in a new era called the Depression. Hard times coincided with a fire at Sam's place, and were something quite different from the bustling times of Carla's girl-hood when they were all working hard to get ahead and the expectations were positive. Now, as a woman, Carla learned that there was an end to expectations, to going forward, to always succeeding and wrestling destiny to the ground. And it didn't depend on one's character, as Umbertina had led them to believe by belittling the old-country people who didn't get ahead—it depended also on outside forces before which they were powerless.

There was one event to look forward to that took on a kind of mythic quality in Carla's life: the annual picnic at a meadow on the shores of Lake Petulia, midway between Cato and Gloversville. Umbertina's children and grandchildren gathered together there to celebrate themselves as a family, to meet and eat and pay homage to Umbertina, the old lady in black who sat under a tree and was served food all day and given babies to kiss.

For Umbertina the picnic scene was her lifetime spread before her. She sat in the meadow on the shore of the lake under the shade of a large leafy elm tree, dressed in black on a warm summer day as she was always dressed in black when she sat in the kitchen at Rutger Street and waited for the foreign children of her own half-foreign sons and daughters to come in and greet her with their mumbled, memorized phrases of unintelligible Italian. In the kitchen, when she wasn't cooking, she sat immobile on a white chair, resting in thought. There in the meadow she sat on a folding camp chair that had been brought along for her. The others sat on the running boards of their Oldsmobiles and Buicks, or on blankets on the ground.

Umbertina's older grandchildren, Jake's and Ben's sons and daughters, were young people in their twenties, teens. The older boys wore knickerbockers and played banjos or formed a group by themselves and played cards. The older girls gave a hand to their mothers and looked after their younger cousins.

Marguerite and Sammy were Carla's small children. Both were foreign to Umbertina; was it the food, the air, the dress of the New World that produced grandchildren she could not recognize? She couldn't speak to them, nor they to her, but they went through a ritual at each meeting.

Carla, with her beautiful wide smile, would lead her children by the hand to where her mother sat. "Say hello to Granma," she would say.

The children were shy. The little girl, Marguerite, had the round face and light eyes of her grandfather Serafino. The little boy, Sammy, was dark—dark as a child of the Calabrian plains; it must be his Sicilian blood on the Scalzo side, Umbertina thought. The Sicilians, she had heard long ago in New York, were often spoken of as Africans. They were quarrelsome, though not as bad as the Neapolitans and those from Campagna, like Pauline's family, the Colombos.

"Say hello," Carla prodded. "Say '*Come stai*, Granma.'"

"Coe-may-sty, Granma," the children said in unison, not knowing what they were saying.

The old woman smiled broadly and nodded her head, reaching over to pat them and pull affectionately at their cheeks. "*Bene, bene*," she said over and over, reassuring them.

It was their ritual; it was all they could say to each other. But the affection was there in the pats and the smiles. Later Marguerite would ask her mother, "Why does Granma look so strange?" And she meant: She doesn't look like other grandmothers, the American grandmothers in schoolbooks.

"Your grandmother came from Italy," Carla would say, leaving the child to wonder what place that was.

Umbertina sat regally under her tree like an old Indian squaw, and mounds of food were placed around her like offerings. Daughters and daughters-in-law in sleeveless white frocks and white stockings kept coming up in a steady stream with the trays of food they had prepared. There were about fifty of the family gathered there, and Umbertina looked contentedly about her. They brought fried chicken parts, her favorite fried sweet peppers to be eaten in huge chunks of fresh-baked crusty bread, tomatoes sliced and dressed with chopped basil, fresh corn on the cob, eggplant fritters, stuffed zucchini, huge tubs of fresh salad greens, whole forms of caciocavallo cheese. It was like Thanksgiving; the Longobardi Thanksgiving took place in the summer in a meadow where all the family gathered around the head of the family, Umbertina, and offered her their services, goods, and children—all that food, those cars, the well-dressed young people who, like Jake's older sons, went to college to become businessmen. She had never taken to the American Thanksgiving and its strange foods. "In this country they even have *una festa delle galline*," she used to say sarcastically each time it came around. She didn't like November, when the earth couldn't be worked and the trees were stripped of leaves and the skies were leaden gray. Umbertina liked the sun on her shoulders, the grass green under her feet in a meadow, a lake before her eyes, and blue skies above.

The picnic in the meadow at Lake Petulia had grown out of her remembrance of the lunches eaten in the fields in Muskieville when she and Serafino and their children had gone out to work their leased land. Then, when the daughters had grown and married and both Carla and Anna had moved away from Cato to their husbands' towns, Umbertina had spoken her wish: that they should come back each summer when travel was easier and meet in a meadow large enough for them and all the cars, to have a picnic. In her old age, it was the event that pleased her most, more than Christmas or Easter or any of the saints' days. She lived with the memory of it through the long winters; and by the time spring came and she could go out in her backyard and start the rows of corn, put in the stakes for the beans and tomatoes, and nurse the first tender lettuces and herbs, she would be planting for the coming picnic.

The weather was always good—they had never had to cancel a picnic on account of rain or misfortune—and the food was always good; but as Umbertina sat under her tree and looked at her progeny, she knew bitterness as well as contentment. All that work and sacrifice that she and Serafino had known. Did any of these gay, chattering, well-dressed, and happy people around her know any of it? Jake and Ben, maybe, yes—they might remember the early days in the tenements; and she often thought that Ben, with his dour and dark temperament, might have been forever burned by that experience. Jake, though, was like Serafino, open and optimistic and not given to looking back and brooding. But where was the companion of her strength? She had married a man much older than she and now she was left. There was Paul being waited on by Pauline, the only one in the group besides Umbertina who had a chair to sit on because of his still-delicate health.

When Prohibition had ended, Paul, through his wide political connections, got Longobardi & Sons licensed for wholesaling liquor. With this further expansion, the Longobardis had reached the peak of success, financially and socially, in a period when others were still recovering from the Depression.

Paul and Pauline had become the fine ones of the family. And even though Jake was the senior son and the nominal head of the family, it was at Paul's large country home that family occasions other than the picnic were held. He lived just outside of Cato in a 1830 Classical Revival house that he had enlarged with elegance and taste, making use, at last, of the architectural studies of his youth. His home pleased him because it had the tradition and class of an American epoch preceding immigration. Still visible in his home were the hand-hewn matched flushboard sidings and thirty-foot columns, made from single tulip trees, that upheld the graceful two-story portico surrounding the original structure. Inside were hand-carved woodwork and seven fireplaces. This edifice was called the Soames House and was on grounds that had once been part of the thousand acres of a patent granted to General Thaddeus Kosciusko, officer in the American Revolutionary Army, and then passed by means of inheritance and marriage connections to the Soames family of Cato. Paul, of course, belonged to the Kosciusko Club, as did the best society of Cato—the English, Scotch, and Welsh society of Cato's mill owners.

Yet Umbertina was not impressed, even though she had a great deal of wary respect for Pauline, recognizing in her the same determination and unflinching family partisanship that she herself had. As she scanned the group at the picnic, Umbertina thought that none of her own sons and grandsons looked as purposeful as her son-in-law Sam Scalzo—he was the self-made one; he was his own boss, not an inheritor like her sons. And her daughters, she reflected, had married men who were stronger than they, and they had simply accepted secondary roles as wives and mothers. Look at Sara with that arrogant little *napoletano* who slapped her around! None of them worked alongside their husbands as Umbertina had done; none of them had the drive and ambition to succeed that Umbertina had felt. How, she wondered, had it been that her daughters had not absorbed any of her strength? Margherita was more like her than any of the others and she had been taken. Carla, yes, had once said she wanted to go away to college but it was only a romantic notion, not connected to any work she saw for herself in the future, since in the future she wanted only to be courted, to dress well, and to marry. Sara had a certain spunkiness but all it led to was quarrelsomeness and disrespect to her husband.

And yet the girls had all helped out in the stores and offices and had helped build the Longobardi & Sons business. Perhaps the fault had been hers, Umbertina's: She had chosen their dowries, taught them about the importance of good food and good linens, bossed them and demanded obedience. She had never allowed them to be stronger than she was; it was always she who had spoken and they who had listened, even when they had gone to school and become educated and she had remained illiterate.

She looked at her two daughters-in-law Amelia and Jenny, poor dead Cristina Muzzi's children. They were good wives to her sons Jake and Ben. Amelia had given Jake nine children, and Umbertina the command of her house. A dark, worn little woman, Amelia was always smiling and agreeable. Jenny was sharper featured, but she, too, was mild-tempered and patient. Both so unlike that whining Cristina who had died still unsatisfied and complaining, unable, at least, to pass the curse of discontent on to her daughters.

They were submissive women; they often cried. Carla, for instance, her youngest, a married woman with two children and a good husband who was working hard in his own business to get ahead, was always homesick and missing her old family—she who lived only fifty miles from Cato and came for visits each Sunday! What did she know of real uprooting? Of leaving your birthplace and family to put an ocean and three thousand miles and no possibility of return between you? Of depriving yourself of your native air and sun and food and language in order to live in the land of strangers where even your grandchildren could not speak to you?

That Umbertina missed the haranguing and needling of the querulous old Domenico Saccà, now many years dead, was surprising to her but true. She could imagine him there looking about skeptically and saying, "You call this success, Tinuzza, but in Italy there's a different *benessere* and the word is more gracious, not so materialistic. Well-being of the total person—not just money, but spirit, too. How crude is the success of money compared with real *benessere*." Ah, Domenico, she thought, this *is* well-being.

As she sat and watched she remembered the first prosperous years when she had sent her photos back to Castagna. Now, she wondered, who do I have to tell my story to?

No one. Not one of her sons and daughters, let alone her alien grandchildren. Carla, with her Paris gowns, had made Sam take her to Castagna as part of their honeymoon trip and then fled as soon as she got there without understanding anything. And then there was one of Jake's sons sending off money for a family coat of arms, the *imbecile*, as if they had come from *signori* instead of a shepherd and a goat girl. And some of the other grandchildren— that pale and dreamy Marguerite, named for her own lost child, and Anna's northern Italian children, who looked more American than Italian . . .

She had won, but who could she tell the story to? At times the doubt came to her whether she really had won, after all. All her life had been a struggle for family, and now in her old age she saw some signs that made her uneasy. She knew of Ben's feelings toward Paul and his envy of Jake's five healthy sons after his only son—Ben, Junior—had died. As long as she was alive, she could keep him in line. But after? Would the brothers quarrel and divide? She saw poor Pina alone and treated with disdain; why hadn't she taught Pina to be more resourceful and independent so that she could make her own way and not be a charity case the rest of her life? All was not well with Sara's marriage. And there was a certain ruthlessness in Paul, her favorite. . . . She had always known it, but she hadn't stopped it in time. Now there was war in Europe again—the Second World War, they called it. Maybe America would be called in another time. Would everything she had set in motion end all right?

Yes, she was treated like a *signora*, like the Baronessa Mancuso herself. But deep in her heart Umbertina knew there were mistakes she was leaving behind as well as the successes. Ah! Serafino, she said to him silently, her thoughts flying about behind the impassive exterior of her face. It is a mysterious thing to be born in this life, work hard, and then at the end see that it has been a mere moment and all that one has done can come undone like the briefness of a flower.

Umbertina thought often of Serafino in her own old age. She did not falter as he did and break down in tears and question the trials of her life. She regretted nothing. Even the mistakes she was too stubborn to regret—she merely acknowledged their presence. She was old, she would not start amending now; she was the way she was.

She had seven living children and twenty-seven grandchildren, but to none of them could she really speak. There wasn't much to say anymore, anyway. At the end of her life she was much alone, and when her eyes fell on the little tin heart, she would think of the quiet of the hills she had come from. Who was it who had given her that heart? It was hard to remember. Ah, yes—the charcoal maker.

She had never gone around moaning the way the other women had done, and missing the old country; she hadn't been scared or disheartened—those weren't her words—but she had at times been angered at what it had been given her to fight against. Her loyalty to the new country was nevertheless without end, and as soon as they gave the vote to women she, too, had voted as an American citizen.

And at the end she understood Serafino.

It was 1940. Italy, she heard, had entered the war. How enraged Domenico would be! How everything seemed to repeat itself!

Nearly eighty, as she lay dying, her vision dimmed so that Jake and Amelia and Ben and Carla and the others at her bedstead became dim gray shadows, and then a sudden brightening came to her eyes as in a vision of light she saw the lost *coperta* of her matrimonial bed with all the intensity of its colors and bright twining of leaves and flowers and archaic designs in its patterns. "Ah!" she gasped, at its beauty.

As Jake leaned over to hear her better, she asked for a cup of water from the spring.

"What spring, Mama?" he asked.

"Castagna," she whispered. Then she was gone.

Part Two

Marguerite, 1927–1973

Chapter Eleven

Marguerite was the middle child, born soon after Sammy and a few years before Steve. "You're the ham in the sandwich," Sammy used to joke when they were kids.

She didn't think so; ham was something familiar, something her father liked between pieces of Italian bread for his Saturday lunch before he went to play golf. And in her family she felt not familiar, but different.

Marguerite was not popular as her brothers were. "You have no personality," her father would tell her, hoping to open her up. But Marguerite would take it wrong: "*Everyone* has a personality," she told him, "you just don't like mine."

It made her sad in a way to be unlike the others, but also proud. It made her think that her life was going to go in diverse ways from what she saw around her—it might not be popular but it would be richer in experiences, more intricate, like an exotic dish or a fabulous place such as she saw in the pages of *Holiday* magazine.

"Why aren't you like everyone else?" her mother puzzled. "Where did we go wrong with you?" But these weren't questions a child could answer.

The house on Prospect Avenue in Gloversville where Marguerite and her brothers grew up had, according to her mother, only one prospect—to be gotten out of as soon as possible.

Marguerite liked it because it was a two-family house and her Vitale cousins lived upstairs. Nunzio Vitale had married Sam

Scalzo's sister Emma; but Uncle Nunzio was, Carla Scalzo said, right off the boat. He spoke with a thick accent, was a manual laborer at Sam's place, and a whole generation behind the others in his Americanization. What was worse, he didn't care; he was cheerful and unambitious, and tended his fruit trees and plants at home without even knowing that beyond his fence there were golf clubs and bowling leagues to join for his exercise if he could only change his name, his looks, his accent.

Marguerite learned that it was not nice to look too Italian and to speak bad English the way Uncle Nunzio did. Italians were not a serious people, her father would say—look at Jimmy Durante and Al Capone; Sacco and Vanzetti. Italians were buffoons, anarchists and gangsters, womanizers. "What are we, Dad, aren't we Italian?" she would ask. "We're Americans," he'd say firmly, making her wonder about all the people in the shadows who came before him. Grandma Umbertina was exempt, even though she didn't speak English, because she had made good.

Some of Marguerite's earliest memories were of picnics with Grandma Umbertina at Lake Petulia. She had a photograph of herself when she was a child of three or four—a pretty round-faced girl in a wispy dress, barefoot, sitting on the trunk of a fallen tree that jutted into the lake. She remembered those occasions so well: the big boys among her Longobardi cousins playing touch tackle in the field, the girls wading and squealing foolishly; her mother and aunts busying themselves with hampers of food. The men spread blankets on the ground and played poker. And Grandma Umbertina was a large, motionless, black figure peering through spectacles like a solemn owl. She was always seated in the shade of a giant tree eating and watching.

Marguerite had always felt attracted to that mysterious old woman with whom she couldn't even speak. There was a picture of her up in the attic in an oval gilt frame; she was a young woman then, standing straight and stiff at the side of nine-month-old Uncle Paul, who was propped up in a wicker high-chair and looking dazedly out from yards of white clothing. It was with that handsome, proud, direct-gazing, unflinching peasant face that Marguerite wanted kinship.

Their house on Prospect Avenue adjoined the park named for Friedrich von Schiller, for it was in a mixed German and Italian neighborhood, modest but not run-down. Prospect Avenue climbed a hill, and at the top, where Schiller's statue stood, was the prospect over the city that gave the street its name. Perhaps it had once been a grand view, worthy of Schiller's gaze.

By the time Marguerite knew it, it overlooked factory sites, the large creamy mass of General Hospital, and the old-fashioned dwellings and stores of the Italian North Side. Prospect Avenue itself was a quiet clean street of neat houses, porches, and trim gardens. The yard Uncle Nunzio tended was an exotic diversion from the adjoining Germanic ones. He had a fig tree (which he buried in the winter), grapevines, and other fruits instead of zinnias like his neighbors. And he made wine in the cellar, strong and sour-smelling.

All that appealed to Marguerite. At the same time she sensed how un-American it was and how her parents disapproved.

After Sam Scalzo moved his family to a Tudor house in a fine residential area, Carla still sent Marguerite and Sammy back to the house on Prospect Avenue every Saturday to play with their cousins.

On good mornings they played cowboys in the park; when it rained they played in a kind of catch-all room next to the kitchen. In the kitchen, with its warm and comfortable smells of sausage making, they ate at Aunt Emma's long oilcloth-covered table.

And every Saturday afternoon, rain or shine, they went down the street a few blocks to the old Schiller movie house. They saw the Charlie Chan detective films; they saw Shirley Temple, Tarzan, and Fred Astaire with Ginger Rogers. They even went to see the mushy love stories that starred Ann Harding or Kay Francis or Anita Louise. They saw everything and they ate bags of penny candy or popcorn. Deleterious and addicting as a narcotic, those Saturday-afternoon films in the shabby theater seeped their culture into Sammy and Marguerite, into Tony and Vic Vitale, imprinting indelibly on their minds the look and feel of American life. They believed what the movies showed them: Real American lives were effortlessly happy ones. This only reinforced the odd quality of her own life for Marguerite.

The other part of education for her was the story of *The Little Engine That Could*—that chugging, struggling little prig of an engine full of dutiful fortitude and New World optimism whose painful sense of responsibility to others overcame the odds and got him over the mountain in time to deliver his load of toys to the children for Christmas. You were supposed to be responsible, dependable in life, no matter what. (Years later, looking for something to read her own child, Marguerite came upon that tale in a story-book collection. "The hell with the choo-choo train," she told Tina, "let's read something wicked." "I thought you were a serious person, an activist," Alberto said, amused. "That was before I married a decadent like you, Alberto. You saved my life." And she tore the story from the book.)

If all her childhood she had been quiet and dreamy, by the time she was sent to the Franciscan sisters for high school she had become sullen and withdrawn. Carla liked to look on the bright side of things and could never understand her daughter's discontent. "Smile," she'd tell her, "you catch more flies with honey than with vinegar." And Marguerite would answer, "Who cares about flies . . . or being popular . . . I'm not some damn Homecoming Queen. All you want me to do is smile, play golf, and have dates as if that's what life is all about."

"What is life about?" her mother asked.

"I don't know . . . but I'll find out, and it won't be what you think."

Too serious for a girl, they all agreed.

At school, where all the daughters of the top Irish families went, including the mayor's daughter, she got to be known as Mad Marguerite—because she read books no one else had heard of (Voltaire, Spengler, T. S. Eliot, Ivy Compton-Burnett) and because she defied convent ways. She wore her uniform too tight, she studied too hard, her answers were delivered in a deprecating way, and for religion class she had written the notorious answer on a test that the Virgin Birth could be explained by *coitus ante portam* —"intercourse outside the door," i.e., without penetration.

The nuns crossed themselves, said their prayers, and only kept her on in the school because of the large food donations Sam sent them from The Place. But Marguerite's soul, if not her presence, had already left them.

Pale, nervous, thin, Marguerite trembled in a confusion of roles, unsure of herself and withdrawn, while her brothers changed from dark skinny kids into tall, athletic, handsome boys full of masculine confidence. She began to think of herself as the family freak-out, a throwback to Grandpa Scalzo, the Old Man, who had come to America and never made good and so was given a broom and the job of sweeping down at The Place.

"Why don't you have any friends? We're spending money to send you to school where you'll meet worthwhile girls. You can have them over, we have a nice home now," her mother said.

It was, in fact, Carla's idea of Home at last: There was a sweeping staircase down to the hall, a paneled study where the Harvard Classics were displayed, a glassed-in flagstone sunporch, a breakfast room, a fireplace downstairs and another in the master bedroom, a rock garden, a goldfish pond, and a two-car garage.

It was a home in which they never lit fires in the fireplaces. It began to strike Marguerite that in her family all of them, including herself, were as unlit and unnatural as the clean white birch logs neatly arranged on the brass andirons of fireplaces that served no purpose. Fires of understanding and affection never glowed in that household, throwing off either light and warmth or those shadows of conflict and passion that come from deep involvement. They didn't touch. But separately they were all susceptible to the sudden combustions of rage and crisis.

For all their material well-being, a vague despair stuck to them like a low-temperature contagion. It hung there constantly, a bitter aroma ever-present in the air with Sam's cigar smoke, curling around them with each sarcasm voiced, each judgment passed, each repression, and permeating their lives with something as bitter as the cigar smoke in their clothes.

"We only want you to be happy," her father would say, and she felt the terrible pressure of trying, somehow, to produce happiness for him. She wanted his approval. She didn't want to exasperate him. But where could she find happiness? Was it a standard brand she could go out and buy herself? It was as if life was still and always Saturday afternoon at the Schiller.

There seemed gulfs between her and her family. They were completely into the American way of progress: college fraternities, Rotary Club, country clubs, *Ladies' Home Journal*. She didn't know yet what she wanted, but it was none of those.

Sam and Carla Scalzo counted, added, figured interest and dividends, and always came out on the credit side for having given so much to their children. They pushed their generosity, shaping the family around it; and if they had been told that the only gift a parent can make his child—the unconditional affection that alone generates freedom—had been withheld while they figured the dollar costs of camps, private schools, sailboats, clothes, sports cars, and allowances, they would have been indignant: "That's gratitude for all we've done!"

Marguerite hated that about them—the constant figuring of returns. But she also loved them and needed them, and it hurt her to see the gulf widening.

"Why is your nose always in a book?" Carla chided. "You think you're better than anyone else but you'll never get where your father has and he never even finished school."

"I don't want to be where he is! I'm not him! Why are you always comparing me to him? He's what he is and I'm what I am. That's simple enough, isn't it?"

"Don't talk to me like that! While you're living in this house, you owe us respect."

There it was—family talk was always in words of commercial transaction. Children *owed* parents respect; children *paid back* what was done for them by studying hard and leading good lives; children had to *capitalize* on their talents; doing so bore *dividends* in life; you didn't go around with certain people because there was no *profit* in it. The family motto could have been "Money Talks."

Then there was religion. For Marguerite her family's religion was like their fireless fireplaces, without warmth or comfort or honesty. Just show.

"You won't have good luck in life," her mother prophesied when she stopped going to mass. "That's why you're unhappy."

Carla Scalzo put in her time in church just in case the Last Judgment, rewards, punishments, and all the rest did turn out to be true. Besides, like the other family women she liked the tangibility of a rich and powerful organization that looked after immediate earthly functions so well. Weddings, baptisms, and funerals were taken care of with really impressive ceremonies. The day her sister Pina's daughter married outside the Church in a second-rate service without candles or flowers on the altar, all the women wept at the visible signs of disgrace.

It seemed as if Marguerite would never marry. She had gone to college costing Sam a pile of money, which brought him nothing in return, for after four years as a misfit ("Someday you'll find your place in the world," her place-card at the Senior Banquet read) Marguerite still had not found her place, which should have been marriage. She came home to Gloversville and got a job at the library.

"Maybe you should go to business school," her mother said. "Or at least go out and have some fun."

"I don't want to go out."

"What are you going to be, Marg, an old maid?" Sammy laughed.

"No," she said, out of the blue, "I'm going to marry a poet."

"So impractical." Her mother shook her head in disgust.

Sammy was practical. He had let his father talk him out of taking a job on the West Coast and he had gone into business down at The Place. But what Sammy did that was really outstanding was to capitalize on his golfing acquaintance with Art Burke by marrying his sister, Betty. It was beyond any expectation Carla had ever had of her children marrying well. Betty's late grandfather had been vice-president of the United States and the family still lived in his beautiful old home outside Gloversville. That Sammy got married in an Episcopal church was more than graciously accommodated by Carla. "They're hardly different at all from Catholics," she said. That there was no papal blessing was a small thing compared to the luster of the Burkes.

For years Carla had avoided the Scalzo clan and their Italianness. But with Sammy's marriage she felt she could invite them all, for the reception was to be held at the Burkes' country place. If Betty Burke chose to marry Sammy it meant that Burke receptiveness was broad enough to accommodate even those Scalzo and Vitale relatives Sam and Carla wouldn't want in their own home.

Carla went even further in her Italian sentiment and advised Betty to have Josie Strombaluppi from the North Side bake her wedding cake. "For tradition's sake," she told Betty, since her own wedding cake had been done by Josie's father. And yet it was not tradition, but the firm assurance that the old times could never again touch her, that made Carla suggest it. Betty was delighted at the quaintness of that touch.

The cake was the one thing about the wedding that interested Marguerite. Josie's store, down on the North Side behind the glove factory, smelling of almond-paste and anise and so different from an American bakery, had always seemed an exciting place to her. And the wedding cake that Josie's father had baked for her mother was a fabulous confection that had become part of the mythology of her childhood.

"How was your wedding cake, Mother? Tell us about it."

"Well, it weighed as much as I did—I was slimmer then, before I had children. And when I cut it, lovebirds came out."

Marguerite, enraptured, would think to herself of those birds waiting there in the gloom and soft innards of the cake; lodged there helpless like raisins in batter. She never wanted to say anything because she was a shy and reticent child, but she used to think: Wonder if they dirtied there, while they were waiting—how could anyone eat the cake? Or maybe the guests wouldn't know it was bird stuff, would think it was part of the mixture and eat it anyway. But what about her mother, didn't she know? Finally she asked.

"Silly!" her mother laughed at her. "Those birds weren't real! They were mechanical. They were wound up and made to come out when I cut the cake in a certain place and released the spring."

It was still a romantic story.

At Sammy's wedding Marguerite looked around and saw the old relatives who had disappeared from sight once her father had moved to a better neighborhood. Now there they were again, the derelicts and left-behinds. As a child she had begun to learn that bettering oneself meant getting out of the Italian neighborhood. Then in school, with her Irish classmates, the Italians, by contrast, had embarrassed her by their foreignness. Now her foreignness joined theirs on the huge Burke lawn.

There was dark Uncle Nunzio, with his thick black eyebrows like shaggy caterpillars across his face; there were the Scalzos who were laborers or carpenters; there were the ones who spoke broken English and had gold teeth in their mouths; the women with their mustaches and the men with baggy pants; the Old Man, that poor guy with the broom she used to see at her father's place. Grandpa Scalzo had never made good in America like her mother's family, the Longobardis.

"It's a good thing your father works as hard as he does, or who would take care of his family?" her mother always said. "Not any one of them could make good on their own—they all depend on your father to look after them." Marguerite, as a child, had not only felt sorry for her father and his having to work so hard to provide jobs for everyone else, but had also felt from her mother's tone how terrifying it must be not ever to make good and to be despised for it.

Marguerite observed the Burkes and their friends at the reception; what distinguished them from the Italian group was their indifference to class. They had made it so long ago and were so well established that it didn't matter to them that Betty was marrying beneath them. A charming deviation was just that: charming. For the

Longobardis and Scalzos, still involved in evolution, it was a different matter. Still, you couldn't say the Scalzos were the way they were because they had so recently been Italian, Marguerite thought. It was also something they had chosen. The Italian-American complex was too intricate a notion for her to unravel in that scene, and it was a relief to hear herself called.

"Marguerite, come over here and meet a friend," her cousin Louis Longobardi was saying. Louis was smooth—a well-spoken, witty med-school student, the first son of her Uncle Paul and Aunt Pauline Longobardi. "This is Lennart Norenson," he said, indicating a very tall, loose-limbed laughing man at his side. "He's a classmate from Dartmouth and was in Cato. I thought he should have some fun, too; isn't that right, Len?"

"Right you are! Nothing I like better than weddings—as long as they're someone else's!" He laughed heavily, his soft pale face puckered like a squeegee doll's, his light hair falling boyishly over his forehead.

"That's my cousin's line!" Louis snickered, nodding toward Marguerite.

"So we're off to a good start," Lennart said. "Let's drink to that."

"Careful, Marguerite," Louis said. "He turns melancholy with drink like all Nordics."

It turned worse than that.

No one could ever understand how Marguerite, with all the advantages she had had, could have run off with Lennart Norenson like that. Nor could Marguerite understand. That was the only good part of it.

She and Lennart had left the reception to go to Keeler's in Albany and had ended up in New Jersey. She felt he understood her ("Listen, kiddo, what are you doing here? What kind of a life is this for you alone with your folks in that big house and nothing to do?"). He was the first to have looked at her as a person and she valued him for it. Excited with drink and his attention, she had suddenly wanted to believe in the freedom and spontaneity of her life—she wanted to experience the precariousness of existence, outside the law and order of the Tudor house.

There was a quickie marriage, she forgot where. Mentally she made the necessary maneuvers and translated Len's vulgarity into vigor, his ignorance into genuineness, and his height into protectiveness. Transformed to her needs, she took him. They spent a few nights in a tourist home that looked like the old house on Prospect Avenue. Len snored. He was heavy on top of her. His clean white flesh was soft and hairless and she felt embraced by mounds, suffocating mounds of cotton batting. She felt no pleasure.

Love and sex—she had often thought of them. Love and sex; the two were separate though perhaps not equal, as in well-meaning segregation; they were non-meeting, ever-propinquitous parallel lines which, to infinity, would never join. Sex was an insistent mechanism that pulsated through her and filled her with the mystery of its senseless imperative. It was also her ID card. If love were unattainable, there was always sex; and if it meant she got less, it also meant she'd be asked less, be less hurt.

First, sex had been imaginary. She had imagined it with her cousin Vic and combined it with her religious heresy: Like First Communion, she and Vic would have First Coming together. When she stayed overnight at the Vitales' she'd think of Vic coming down the hall in the quiet night to her room and softly pulling down the blankets and lifting up her nightgown to look at her. She would take his hands and guide them to her and she would put her hands on him. He would get into bed with her. Afterward he'd be conscience-stricken and talk of having to go to confession.

("Why do you have to confess, Vic?" . . . "My God, are you kidding? Marguerite! It's a sin what we did!" . . . "Why? Didn't you like it?" . . . "Of course I liked it! But it's still a sin." . . . "Don't you want some more? Put your hand here and feel me." . . . "Are you crazy? It's a mortal sin! Just touching yourself, just even thinking about it. And you go to a Catholic school!" . . . "That's why I don't believe all this sin business. All the boarders, and probably the nuns, too, do it every night with the crosses hanging over their beds." . . . "God, Marguerite, you better stop talking like that!" . . . "Are you afraid lightning's going to strike you, Vic? Let's go down to the cellar and put wine on ourselves and then lick it off." . . . "Jeez, Marguerite, it's a mortal sin, just talking like this is a sin." . . . "You're just superstitious, Vic, like all Italians." . . . "Aren't you Italian, too?" . . . "But not superstitious like you—come on down to the cellar, I'll show you." . . . "It's a sin, don't say I didn't tell you.")

Then there was Lennart, who referred to her body as her shape and had to drink to function, so that sex with him was his drunken breath and bumbling, drunken maneuvers, his big hands, the lines of anguish on his squeegee face.

After a week she and Lennart drove back to Gloversville.

Success, she thought as she looked at the ring on her finger. Now she was married and she could tell her aunts and Sammy and her mother and all the rest of them to go fry ice. She had done it—she had gotten out of the Tudor house. How would they live? Where? And she'd look at the big man by her side and wonder who he was.

She had time, as they drove up the Storm King Highway on their way to Gloversville, to consider the ever-present miseries of Man. In the first dimness of twilight she had glimpsed a person, his pants lowered, his head hung down, defecating, with one hand clutching at the fence against which he cowered, the other at the shame of his lowered pants. And the sight went with her. As did the sweet-sick smell of the aftermaths of Lennart's intercourse with her. There it all was: ingesting, voiding, vomiting, copulating, laboring, farting, nose picking, pimply skin, bad breath. Always present. No matter how you arranged your life, no matter how grand a Tudor house you arrived at, the low gross part was at the bottom of everything.

Sam and Carla Scalzo could never understand the elopement and didn't want to, but they moved quickly to have it annulled. No trouble; they liquidated Lennart with a good sum, had Marguerite go through a physical to make sure she wasn't pregnant or infected, and promised her a trip to California or a new car.

She wanted nothing. She got a job in a store, where she met an Italian printer named Matteo de Mariani who stopped in weekly to pick up copy for the *Gazzettino* that he put out. Marguerite persuaded him to give her Italian lessons. ("Why Italian?" her father said. "Where will that get you?") For a whole winter, several nights a week, she sat with the gentle, elderly De Mariani in the clean kitchen where his wife had just cleared away the supper and learned Italian. He wanted no money, and under his patient teaching she learned the verbs, the "impure *S*," the pejoratives and the amelioratives, and began to read with him in the empyrean of Italian opera libretti.

"Italy is a great and sad country," De Mariani told her. "I do not hate her."

Nor, anymore, did Marguerite. In June she took her parents' offer of a trip and headed not west, but east to Europe. An unselected candidate for American happiness, a family failure, she sailed for England harboring the certainty that her destination was surely Italy.

Chapter Twelve

They had met in the bar of the cabin-class lounge on the ship sailing to England.

"Need some help there, miss?" he said as she tried unsuccessfully to light a cigarette from her lighter. He was a short, grinning man with a thick thatch of sandy hair and the marked accent of northern England. "I couldn't help noticing you." She noticed him, too: the two missing front teeth, the scruffy necktie, the reddish face, and the roguish cocky air. "The name's Alec Dunn."

Alexander Dunn. The meeting with Alec, any Alec, was inevitable.

"Are you a smart aleck?" Marguerite asked him, laughing.

"Now, then, what do you mean by that? Want me to ask you if you're like the English twirps? They won't lay down and go about lovemaking properly because of their scruples about going to bed with a guy. Prefer to stand up and go it in doorways or in the tube stations, they do."

"There, you see! You are a smart aleck!"

Sex with Alec was something she didn't have to think about—could keep her feelings from. Sex pure and simple. Alec the maestro of acrobatics, life skills.

"Come on now, Maggie, you can do better than that—that's the girl! Right on!" Achieving orgasm meant doing well. ("Well done, my girl!" "Thanks, Alec.") Like getting the bull's-eye throwing darts in a pub. It might have repulsed her, but it didn't. It was physically exciting. His vulgarity and excesses matched her desolation and brought her sources of epidermic, nervous, unreasoning sensuous feeling that she had not known with her brief husband.

"But why is sex so important?" she'd groan, alarmed at herself.

"Come along there, Maggie, it's perfectly simple—a case of cocks and cunts. Made for each other, they are."

But she knew something else. Sex was the way to unpeel all those layers of lies that had been plastered on her consciousness. Family, God, Money, Success, Marriage—all she had to do to strip these plastered-on slogans from her was to derobe and screw them off. Fucking *is* fucking Mother, Middle-Class Virtues, a College Education, and Marrying Well, with its square coitus and family life around the backyard picnic-table. So you screw to unpeel; that's classic, and sometimes even good. If you're lucky, each time the overlay gets scraped away some more.

Work-outs, work-ins, work up, work down, work your way around the globe. "Come on, old girl, I'll work your fucking ha'penny off," Alec would invite her. The work principle; work as the Protestant Ethic; work as morality, well-being, purpose, Americanness, chosenness.

Marguerite thought of her father's words: "No one is going to hand you everything on a tray. If you want to be happy and make something of yourself, you have to work at it. That's what being American is all about—the chance to get someplace."

To climax, for instance.

There were no illusions with Alec, nor did she want any. A five-day crossing and then good-bye.

She met Gillo Gatti in the British Museum. He was tall, his hair long and dark blond, and he wore a well-fitting gray flannel suit. As he approached her in front of a display of Greek vases with an air of studied detachment, she thought of a line from an Aldous Huxley novel: one goes to museums to find Old Masters and young mistresses.

After the encounter they walked through the halls of the museum speaking guardedly of who they were. His plans, unlike hers, were so definite! He knew what he was in London for: The courses he was following at the university would get him the fellowship that would eventually win him a chair in English at an Italian university; he knew who and where the specialists were in their fields and which of them were most likely to help him; he knew how long he had to hold out in English on a teaching fellowship and just what book (Wordsworth) he had to write to get him back to Italy. He knew why for everything.

"Even why you spoke to me in front of the vases?" she asked. He wore a beret, he was Italian. She could imagine loving him. She already loved him.

"Of course. You are attractive and you looked as foreign and out-of-place as I. It was my luck you even know some Italian."

"My luck is better—you know more Italian."

Gillo invited her to tea in the commons at the nearby university, where they had to stand for a while in a long line of students. He looked about impatiently, his amber eyes cold and derisive. He was already a *dottore*, he had told her.

"I don't know how it is in Italy," she said, trying to lighten the wait, "but here you queue for everything—buses, stamps, and even tea with trifle."

"Italians don't queue," he said scornfully, "not for trifle and not for the pope."

"What else are Italians like?"

"Melancholy."

"Why?"

"If we didn't have our melancholy what would we be? A race of clowns. It's the only thing that redeems us."

The next evening Marguerite put on dangle earrings and a black dress to dine with Gillo on wilted hors d'oeuvres and dance stiffly to South American tunes in a medium-fancy restaurant off Piccadilly Circus to which he had invited her.

Leaving, they hurled a pocketful of small change at the ticket window in the underground, sure they were being gouged, but no matter; Goodge Street, please. Good. Goodge. Gouge. He had a bottle of grappa, and they stopped for a moment in Russell Square to drink from it. "*Che gelida manina*," she said from her opera studies with De Mariani as she put her cold hand in his. He laughed, and outside the School for African Studies he caught her to him and kissed her hard. They went to his room in the dorm.

"Here we are in East Africa," he laughed, explaining that an African student had had it before him. But gaiety was gone; her muscles, nerves, bones—even her teeth, she noted with curiosity— felt rigid with apprehension.

He didn't notice but started taking off her dress, unzipping it in back, tugging at it impatiently when it jammed. Marguerite was aware of how stupidly she was dressed for that night; she had dressed not for lovemaking with Gillo but for a date in Gloversville. Everything was snaps and buttons and zippers, even her girdle. Gillo tugged, and any feeling she might have had toward lovemaking now centered on the goddam zippers and her discomfort as she lay on the narrow bed while he tried to get at her. "No . . . no . . . no," she was saying, not knowing why. Finally, Gillo had torn off everything, flinging garments all over the floor, and was upon her, welded to her in perspiration, fused. They were drawn together by the suction of their sweating nude bodies that squeaked and sucked as they moved toward their union.

Her flesh felt scaly, cold through the sweat. The sucking seemed a monstrous noise drowning out the cheerful girl and boy voices calling to each other in the hall outside Gillo's door. She thought the whole house must be reverberating and echoing the sucking and smacking of their bodies. Is this better than Len? The thought came quickly and she just as quickly smothered it.

The sound of their bodies continued as they came together then broke away, in rhythm to his thrusts, the air rushing between them. Warmth, then cold. She felt his spasms and then he was still. Sprawled across her, he seemed to sleep. She waited. After a time she extricated herself. Naked, she got up to look out the window. The house was quiet.

Streetlight. Shadows of branches. The dim outline of an owl. Minerva and wisdom. She stood for a while and then quietly dressed. She washed in the deserted john and wished she had a toothbrush to take away the bits of lettuce leaves from dinner that were still between her teeth. How would she get back to her place in full daylight in her torn and too-dressy clothes? She should have thought it out better. But it wasn't the first time she hadn't.

Gillo was snoring lightly. She covered him with the bathrobe that hung from a peg on his door. She sat at his desk near the window, put her head down on her folded arms, and dozed off.

That morning Gillo brought her coffee in the room. "How are you?" he asked. Distances were still in his eyes.

After that, they met sometimes in his room, sometimes in her hotel, or sometimes not at all, when he would say he was busy because he had to meet the person from the British Council in Venice who had gotten him the grant to study in England and wanted to keep in touch with his progress.

When Marguerite and Gillo were together they went to the

pubs, or they walked Shaftesbury Avenue to Piccadilly Circus late at night to play the penny machines in the squalid little amusement galleries, hoping to win cigarettes, still hard to find in England. Sometimes they sat in the park at Great Russell Square across from the British Museum. Often he spoke aloud in Italian with the sad, cadenced tones of his Veneto accent about some private woes she could not understand. But the intuitions of those nights hurt her, left her startled and uncertain. He filled her with tenderness one moment, and because of the cynicism that showed in his eyes, with unease the next.

"Why are you unhappy?" she asked.

"You'd prefer me to smile like the American guys, isn't it true? The Happy Man is my real part. I should remember it when I get too serious. They told me at Padua that I could be the most valuable man of my generation—and look at me, what do you see besides a buffoon like everyone else?"

"Why are you like this, Gillo? Because you wanted to write as an artist, not as a critic or a professor? You can do both!"

"Yes, you pioneering Americans! Always ready to go on. Have you never understood the beauty of futility and of not wishing anymore for anything?"

"I wish I understood you, Gillo, but you won't let me."

"No, my baby, you are wrong. I have let you in the best, most complete way. It is up to you to know it."

The burden of their relationship was on her. It was for her to know if she loved Gillo. The question was, Did she? That oldtime library book, *What a Girl Should Know About Sex*, had put it to her: "If your mother was loving and kind and you learned to love her, you learned to love. This is the greatest asset of your life." The old lingo of assets. What the book hadn't mentioned was deficits: parental duties attended to, but the very sweetness of life withheld. What if her capacity for love had shrunk, atrophied from disuse; what if she were not able to receive or return love because she wasn't familiar with it?

They decided to go for a weekend to Lavenham. She made the arrangements, chose the inn, found out the train schedules, and got them to the right station at the right time.

"Why Lavenham?" he had said on the train, a light smile playing over his features, the sarcasm ready.

"It's got a famous inn, a famous church, and even some famous people."

"Who?"

"Somebody who's supposed to be Shakespeare, for one; and the lady who wrote 'Twinkle, twinkle, little star.'"

"I think I prefer her."

"And I prefer you. Even though you don't know I'm here half the time."

"I do feel something for you."

"Oh, what does that mean?" she said, laughing at him. "You and your beret! What are they going to think of you in Lavenham?"

"That I am a distinguished foreign author and you are my secretary. And since I compose also at night—better at night—you must share my room with me."

But in the room, which she thought charming, he looked around disconsolately and said, "What a place. Did you bring any cigarettes?"

"Why don't we go for a walk and see the church and then we can get some cigarettes."

"Why don't we just stay here and think about the walk and imagine the place; I'm sure it's better that way."

"You always think things are better in your thoughts than they are in reality!"

"And you?"

"Of course not, or I'd turn into a cynic like you, and one of us has to stay cheerful." As she said it, the thought came: Love should be better than it is.

"Do you know me?" He had an arrogant air, as if daring her. Cold, intellectual Gillo, whose very egoism made him exciting and desirable to her. He was never concerned with what he did or said to hurt her, but very much with hearing what he was. "Why am I so?" he'd ask Marguerite intensely, fascinated by himself as she and others saw him. It was in those moments he was closest to her.

"Yes, a little," she answered.

"Then you know I'm only a buffoon."

"You'd like to be."

"Then if I'm not even that, I'm nothing. And that suits me best."

She loved him in Lavenham. Sometimes as they lay together he'd say lines of poetry in Italian. These she sometimes understood. But not when he talked at length in his language.

"What do you say, Gillo, when you speak in Italian? Tell me."

"I am just missing a part of my country, that part that is sun and light and of which this miserable England knows nothing."

"I wish I knew your country; it is mine, too, in a way."

"We shall see it together when this course is finished."

"Italy!"

"Sun and light—for me it is essential. I cannot live without them. But not only in the real, physical sense. In the metaphysical sense, too. Now I am in exile, in this country of damnation where they say it is summer, but how can you tell? Italy, no . . . Italy is sun and light."

In Italy I will love him better and he will love me, she thought. It would be her homecoming, as it was his. It was his promise to her of an opening toward light, of an Italy that was no longer the shady, misunderstood one of her childhood. After Lavenham, Italy was waiting for them both.

Chapter Thirteen

A familiar scene: the Arno, the backdrop of lights on the Piazzale Michelangelo glittering in a Florentine night, the soft curve of hills outside the city, the shadowy bulk of Ponte Vecchio. It's 1949 and Florence still has wartime scars; other than Ponte Vecchio, the bridges over the river are makeshift, and the areas adjacent to either bank are gutted shells; but the grimness lends itself to the essential toughness, the cult of *grinta*, in the Tuscan character.

It is a windy, chill evening of February; jammed in the throng crossing an improvised bridge are a balding, middle-aged Italian poet named Alberto Morosini and the American student of Italian, Marguerite Scalzo, in a bright green polo coat and wearing Gillo's old beret over her long hair.

Alberto has gripped her arm and is talking vehemently of the life they could live together. Marguerite now knows Italian well enough to understand that. He stops abruptly, emphatically, every few steps to gesture and reinforce some point he is making. His words pour from him unimpeded by the streams of people passing in both directions, who brush by or collide with them. The progress of Alberto and Marguerite across the bridge seems agonizingly eternal to her. But she is, nonetheless, attentive to his proposal of marriage.

It would be hard to support her, he is saying, because she, an American, is used to a comfortable life and she has only to look around her—here he stops again and opens his arms toward the ruins on the riverbank—to see what condition Italy is still in. His teaching job in a Rome *liceo*, though prestigious and honorable and augmented by the courses he gives at the Dante Society, does not pay much. On the other hand, he contributes articles to leading cultural reviews and this is an important opening for him. He even has important friends in the Rome ministries. Everything would eventually work out. In the beginning they could live in the room he has in the apartment of his Danish bachelor friends.

What has led to this wild, windswept, shivering, jostled, dark-night proposal of marriage in a language she is still learning? Its improbability, and the improbability of Alberto Morosini, entrances Marguerite even though she knows the consecutive steps which have brought her where she is.

Gillo had not come to Italy with her. During the last days of his summer course, the British Council person had returned to London and was arranging interviews for him for his future post, he said, and so he couldn't leave on the boat-train with Marguerite. He had to stay on in England and then he would join her in Rome. After a holiday in Italy they would go back to England together to wherever he would be teaching. He arranged for her to be met in Rome by his friend Alberto Morosini, who would be helpful to her. Alberto would be at the station to meet her train with a red flower in his buttonhole, and she was to carry a white one. In case they missed each other, Gillo gave her Alberto's address and telephone number.

But the trip to Italy was long, and she became resentful of the disarrangement of all their plans. She had wanted Gillo to be with her in Italy, not some stranger named Alberto Morosini. Impulsively she got off the train in Florence instead of going on to Rome and signed up there for the course for foreign students at the university. Soon she was tired, lonely, and sorry she had snubbed poor Alberto.

She wrote to him. He answered saying he was glad to know she had arrived safely, and as things would have it, he would be coming to Florence for a meeting concerning a literary prize. He would come and call on Marguerite.

He came not only to her little hotel-pension between the station and the market that sprawled around San Lorenzo but right to the door of her room, knocking at it insistently. Marguerite had been dressing to meet him downstairs at the time they had set. Flustered at his banging, she called out *"Un momento!"* and when he continued she found herself suddenly unable to put together enough Italian or French or Spanish to tell him to go away, she'd come when she was ready. She simply opened the door as she was, in slippers, her hair uncombed.

Never (and the premonition was intense in the air as Alberto Morosini bowed over her hand and entered the besieged room), from their first meeting, from when they first laid eyes on each other, would things go exactly as planned between Marguerite and Alberto. As if they were in a film, there was always some element of unpredictable comedy and havoc that filtered into whatever scene they were playing. There was, forever after between them, a sensation of *improviso*, of crazy ad lib, of things getting out of control and taking their own unsuspected direction.

That evening in the *pensione* a short, businesslike, and soberly dressed man carrying a leather case had entered her room. He sat down, opened his case, and took out a book. It was, he said, the volume of his recently published poems, and he asked if she wanted to hear some. Of course, she said, wanting to comb her hair. He read odes to Keats, Shakespeare, Catullus, and Goethe; a ballad for springtime, an elegy to his dead mother, lyrics to the unknown love he still awaited. All the time she was aware of the chill in the unheated room and the growing hunger in her stomach as the evening grew late.

When he stopped she told him they were very beautiful. He said she was sensitive as well as lovely and inscribed the book for her: *"A Lesbia Purissima."*

They went out to dinner, and the problem of conversation between them wearied and depressed her. When she didn't understand Italian he tried French, crushing every drop of elegance from that language in the grip of his merciless pronunciation. Later (years and years later), Alberto Morosini would maintain with conviction that they had spoken Latin at their first meeting, that he had courted his wife in the language of Catullus to Lesbia. He called her Margherita though she corrected him.

"And Gillo?" he said in one of the lulls of their conversation. "How is he? I saw his wife not long ago and she said his future plans were still uncertain."

Marguerite stared unbelievingly at the chattering man next to her. What wife? What plans? Wasn't the plan that Gillo come to Italy as soon as he could and then he and Marguerite would return together to England to wherever he had his appointment? He had never said so but wasn't it marriage they were heading to?

Alberto's chatter imploded, shattering inward to the pit of her stomach as he continued, oblivious, raising his voice louder in the silly effort to help her understand. "They've had a hard life, you know, Gillo and his wife. They married very young before the child was born, while he was still studying. He wasn't ready . . . it's been a trap for him, the end of certain hopes. He's had to abandon testing himself out as a writer and to prepare himself for something more practical. He's been lucky only in having the Englishwoman who got him a grant for studying in London."

With that Marguerite understood about the Englishwoman from the British Council, too.

"Gillo's plans are to teach in England," she told Alberto stubbornly. She searched her mind to recall if he had ever hinted at a wife, a child, a mistress. Wouldn't Gillo have realized that in her meeting with his friend Alberto this part of his life was bound to come out? Was that what Gillo was counting on? Was that why he hadn't come with her to Italy, after all? He wanted her to get the news from someone else. That would give her time to have absorbed the worst and gotten used to it, accepted it, before he got there.

"Why wasn't his wife with him in England?" Marguerite asked hostilely.

"She is living with her parents and has work here. It's better for her and the child to stay here while Gillo is in England. It won't be forever. He has only to perfect his English and get his book finished. That will open the way for him in Italy. He is extremely intelligent."

"Yes, I know." Intelligent enough to use the Englishwoman to get to England; as he would have used me and my American cigarettes to keep him company and type his notes in Manchester or Liverpool or wherever the hell he's going. Then, with his career all set, he'd come back to his wife and child, and that would be that. A life full of sun and light.

Oh, Christ, I love him! Would he leave his wife? Is that why he wanted me to go back with him? I could go back for the winter and see what happens by the time next summer comes. Even if he doesn't leave his wife, we could have that time together and not think ahead.

As the possibilities of choice presented themselves to her while she sat silently next to Alberto, Marguerite felt that it would be impossible for her to love Gillo within time limits, knowing the end was already predetermined. It was too much to expect to have him. There it was, the old phrase of her convent schooling: *Domine non sum dignus*—exclusion from grace because she didn't merit it.

She couldn't remember how she got through the rest of the evening with Alberto Morosini.

She spent Christmas at Alberto's old home in Venice, where his sister still lived and where a few relatives stopped by to greet him. "Why, she's just a girl!" an aunt of Alberto's had said on meeting Marguerite.

In January he invited her to Rome for the opera to hear *Don Giovanni*.

Marguerite's idea of what Gillo's friend Alberto Morosini would be like (an older man, yes, but Walter Pidgeon) continued to linger. Each time they remet she was startled again by the splay-footed professor who snorted and blew through his nose and had small brown furtive eyes sunk in the hollows on either side of that huge nose. In winter Alberto wore a thick brown loden coat and a hat whose brim turned up all the way around. His walk, with that rocking toed-out gait, made him seem ludicrous like a performing Russian bear, but he was unaware of anything except being himself.

The day she got on the *rapido* to go to Rome, she went with no precise plan in mind, but with at least a willing suspension of disbelief in Alberto Morosini. She could be reached now if he felt like reaching.

Pazienza, she thought with the shrug of shoulders she was learning from Italian life; if things hadn't gone exactly as they should have, it still wasn't Gloversville. She saw the Italian women, how sure they were of themselves, how well they dressed and carried themselves; and she despised her soft, round, childish face and Italian-American uneasiness. She could learn from Alberto. And he was a poet.

When Marguerite arrived in Rome the skies were blue and the Roman wall through which her taxi passed to get to Corso d'Italia was tawny with the elegant light of late day. She went straight to Alberto's place and was shown to his room in the Danes' apartment by the scowling housekeeper, Rina. ("She's fine with bachelors," Alberto had said of her, "but she doesn't like women. I'm the only one in the household with a vocation for women.")

Alberto's room was a large one at the end of the passage. A deep studio couch faced a low table, on which anemones were arranged in a bowl next to a silver candlestick and piles of books. The furniture was large and old-fashioned: an enormous wardrobe, a writing desk that occupied the whole end of the room in front of flowery drapes drawn across the windows, and a great stuffed armchair with a leather floor-lamp next to it. In a corner there was a sideboard and a small table spread with a blue and white embroidered tea cloth on which stood a hot plate, a silver sugar bowl, a teaspoon, and a jar of *petits-beurres*. Marguerite felt a pull of tenderness for the man whose room this was. It was charming and orderly, and like Alberto, restfully *démodé*. She sank into the fat armchair and her glance was caught by a painting on the wall opposite. It was a painting in tenuous pastel of a young girl with thoughtful eyes and a small mouth, seated and holding in her lap a large, almost voluptuous lemon. It looks like me, she thought.

She felt warm and protected in the steam-heated apartment after the austerity of her *pensione* and the Florentine winter like a severe Morandi painting. She needed a sensible, stodgy person like Alberto to help protect her against the romanticism of which she was always a victim. Everything about Alberto helped: his walk, his talk, the view of long underwear sometimes visible when he crossed his legs, and his careful rituals against indigestion when they ate out.

Sauntering in with his familiar step, Alberto went over and kissed Marguerite on the forehead. "*Ciao, cara,*" he said. "Have you been waiting long?"

"Not so long."

He complimented her on her improving Italian as he looked over the unopened mail on his desk. He tore up what didn't interest him and methodically straightened his piles of notes and folders. He spoke to her absentmindedly, pedantically.

"How did you know Gillo?" she asked suddenly.

He looked at her, bemused. "Well, someday perhaps I'll tell you, but not now."

"Why not? What is there you can't tell me? Gillo and I were lovers in London. Didn't you know? Didn't he tell you?" He left off fussing at the desk to look at her in astonishment.

"No, I didn't know; Gillo didn't tell me anything. But maybe that's what he meant when he wrote he was having me meet an American girl with whom I could have a good time."

"Is that what he said? Do you think he's right?"

"Not in the way he meant it. I expected a completely different type—one of those smart, sophisticated women you see in fashion magazines. Not a schoolgirl."

"I'm not a schoolgirl. And if Gillo meant something else, I didn't deserve that from him."

"No—you didn't."

Marguerite began to cry softly. "I didn't know he was married. I loved him."

Alberto came and sat next to her and held her hands, looking at her with concern and kindness. "*Su, su,* Margherita, Gillo is not bad, but he is cynical and embittered now because his life has taken a turn in a way he didn't foresee and certainly didn't want."

"That is no reason for having deceived me—why didn't he tell me the truth first?"

"It probably didn't occur to him. It's his misfortune that he has always used people. He always thought he had to; his life was not easy, ever, and now he has this family to support."

"Where did you meet him?"

"In a whorehouse in Florence. He was like a young Apollo. I noticed him immediately for his beauty and then when we talked together I found he had a first-rate intelligence. Gillo gave me an enormous insight into my own poetry. His criticisms were in every case improvements."

"It's more important to be a poet than a critic."

"Gillo knows this, too. He feels his creative life is smothered, bottled up, by his having to make a university career for himself." He looked at her again, his face showing a concern that wrinkled and crossed it. "But you—what are you doing in Italy alone?"

"I came to be with Gillo," she started, and then stopped abruptly. "No—I would have come anyway. Catullus brought me here." She smiled.

"Perhaps he is not too good an example for you. The true classic temperament is detachment, not passion. In any case he is a great poet. In the spring we can go to see his village, Sirmione, on Lake

Garda. However, there is more for you to discover than Catullus. There's all of Dante, Leopardi. . . ."

"And Alberto Morosini."

"Well, maybe, but not so big as those others."

"To be a poet is enough. What else is there?"

"One could hope to be a poet and a good man. Life is more important than art. If I had to choose, I would choose life over art; otherwise one becomes arid, a mere aesthete, *un letterato*. Yes, it is more important to do one's duty to one's family, to be loved. . . ."

Marguerite stopped listening. Alberto treated her like a child, as if the difference in age between them was the most significant thing about them. He fussed, he sorted and filed, he snorted through his big nose. He didn't look or act like a poet—it was Gillo who did.

As she blew her nose mournfully, Alberto pulled out a big gold watch from his pocket and exclaimed, "*Per carità*! It's almost time for dinner and I have two other guests coming." He looked at her and then said, "If you want to use the bathroom, it's just next door."

Always alone, she thought as she looked into the bathroom mirror. She had come to Rome on Alberto's invitation and now she discovered he had other guests, too. She thought she was Gillo's while he was loving her, but now she knew she had been only a temporary replacement for him, the summer companion.

She dried her tears and refixed her face and hair. It was true; she looked like a schoolgirl. Solemn, apprehensive, wondering green eyes, slightly tilted like those of many Sicilians in whom Mediterranean races have crossed, looked out from a pale face. There was no sophistication, only vulnerability in her gaze.

Marguerite observed in silence as Aurelia Eccli, one of the guests, examined the dinner china, told Alberto how to dress for the opera the following night, pronounced a Boucher painting that hung in the room valuable but dull, and said that Americans were idiots and Russians beasts and she didn't know which was worse. Her husband, Leone, was brilliant.

But all Italians were. They darted effortlessly from subject to subject like gorgeous butterflies glittering with wit and daring paradox, never staying long enough to be challenged and caught by the slower, deeper thinkers. . . . What a beautiful, quick people, Marguerite reflected. I am not: I am ponderous. I have not the retort quick, the blandishment supreme, the aphorism ready. They leap around like graceful hares and I am the slow tortuous turtle who will get there eventually but with no class, no performance, no verve. I haven't the nerve, nor the skill, to make their mistakes. But maybe I'll learn.

Marguerite wondered if, as Alberto's wife, holding superb dinners for his friends, she could ever be so brilliant. She tried to think of herself as a handsome, arrogant woman taunting young men and bowing ironically to their exclamations of delight. She would hold salons and wear impeccably made black gowns with a single great jewel. She would be a poet's wife, *Lesbia Purissima*, bearing in fierce pride and dignity the pains of her unhappy past.

Tomorrow, she thought, there's *Don Giovanni*. In the spring I'll see Sirmione. It won't be bad, not bad at all.

All that had led up to the declaration on the temporary bridge across the Arno that windy February night when Alberto proposed to her. She had been prepared.

"I have been in despair," he told her on the bridge. "I have seen my family disappear and my friends die in the war. I have felt alone in the world. And then you came like an unexpected gift into my life when I had given up all hope of finding the woman I could love and with whom I could start a new family, new hope. What you have told me about your life proves nothing more than what I knew from the beginning—you are pure, limpid, and serene. You have not only sensibility and freshness, you have a deep innocence that can't be touched by any Gillo. The rest of what makes a woman, maturity, you will learn through marriage, as I will learn— or try to—your American optimism."

It couldn't be wrong if he needed her, too, she thought.

When she wrote home of her plans, her parents wrote back that it was completely out of order for her to marry a man they didn't know, and typical of her. "Italy has no future and never will," her father wrote. And her mother: "There is the family to account to, and all our friends. What will they think if we don't have the wedding here? It looks like you're running away again, or have something to hide. You owe us some consideration."

"This marriage is mine," she wrote back with little grace.

Chapter Fourteen

Marguerite's pursuit of culture had amused Alberto when she was living in Florence before their marriage.

"You Americans," he'd say affably, "the trouble with you Americans is that you read too much, see too much, listen too much, and want too much. You're like geese stuffing yourselves to make intellectual foie gras."

Marguerite knew he disapproved of her mindless energy, her helter-skelter accumulation of notions, facts, art reproductions—the merchandise of culture. In return, she esteemed his disapproval. She felt graceless at times with him; her walk too fast, her mind too logical, her curiosity too encompassing, her interests too immense. She felt the contrast of her American vigor with the twilight delicacy of this refined, civilized man, who, as he often declared proudly (completely unaware of the horror, to her, of his words), was the end product of a millennium, at least, of good, stolid middle-class Catholic tradition.

"You laugh at Americans because you already have your culture —it's all around you," she told him. "But we have to form ours."

"What I have I owe to my friends," he answered in a thoughtful way. "Before the war we spent beautiful times together talking and discussing. They opened my mind and taught me about writers and thinkers who were forbidden in Fascist Italy. Bertrand Russell. All the American writers. Even Croce was suspect. We were partisans in the war and only I'm left now. Eight friends! Killed fighting or taken away to concentration camps and never heard of again. It's a loss I can never make up. The lines I have given to their memory in my poetry are nothing to what I owe them."

Would she be able to give him as much? she wondered. Some things she was already learning from him. Once she got two tickets to a soccer game to be played in Renaissance costume in the Piazza della Signoria during the weekend of one of Alberto's visits to her. When he arrived he was casually contemptuous of the idea: "Margherita, *mia cara*, just think—shabby little page boys and a whole tribune of fake De' Medicis. Do you think we really want to spend our time that way when we might be making love?"

Then, to cheer her up, he said, "Let's go up to Fiesole. On such a fine day we can eat out in a garden and then walk up to sit in the Roman amphitheater and talk."

He bought her an armful of anemones from a street vendor, a straw hat to protect her from the strong sun, and they drank *spumante* at lunchtime and decided to stay overnight. It was the day he really married her, he would always say later, in their own ceremony in the cool interior of the abbey church they visited.

Later that night she slipped out of bed and took the unused soccer tickets from her bag. Getting back under the covers with Alberto, she tore them into little pieces and sprinkled them over him. "Every wedding needs confetti," she said.

He held her close to him and said, "I will make a real human being out of you. We will live a life of art together. You are a creative person with much to express. Only remember that one has to love the other's defects as well as his virtues—maybe more. Remember, too, the classic position is detachment."

"Even in bed?" she asked, responding to his caresses.

Marguerite continued her Italian courses in Florence. She liked this interlude of aloneness with Florence during the week and Alberto's being with her on weekends.

Things went well between them except when he unwittingly offended her sensibilities about the culture she was acquiring.

"What rubbish to give foreigners!" he said when she told him she was reading Pulci, Ficino, Poliziano. "You don't want to turn out like those American Express ladies who go through the Uffizi and think they have to look at every single work in every room when it's enough to go straight to the *Primavera* and one or two others." She felt ridiculed.

"But, Alberto," she protested—her eyes troubled, her voice unsteady with a kind of smothered indignation—"it's different for you. These things were part of your background from always. But just think of what my background was—nothing! We don't even know who we are any further than my grandparents, and you've got family trees right back to the thirteenth century. It's only with my parents that reading and writing and speaking correctly began for us. That's the difference between us!"

He understood her resentment because he was a compassionate man, even when he told her in jest, "That's a big difference. It's a good thing your Calabrian grandparents emigrated to America and made it possible for a northern Italian like me to marry you. Not many northerners would let themselves in for marriage with a *terrone*."

"*Tant pis* for them—you northern intellectuals could use new blood and brains. My grandmother, for one, had native intelligence."

"Then we are a good combination for our children: my beauty and your native Calabrian intelligence. And once we do have children all this cultural mania of yours will evaporate."

"Oh, you're impossible, Alberto! Don't you understand I don't want it to evaporate! What am I paying for?" She sounded just like a Scalzo.

"*Già*," he laughed. "Americans can buy anything."

Each time he arrived in Florence Marguerite looked anew at this man who was to be her husband as if to impress the fact upon herself by studying him as hard as possible. He was almost forty but sometimes she thought of him as a sixty-year-old who looked trimmer and younger; at other times he seemed thirtyish and prematurely bald, but a thirty-year-old who carried himself with authority and sobriety. The paradox went further: His monkish head, fringed by a narrow band of curly black hair, gave him a Franciscan air maliciously complemented by something furtive and foxy—and yes, lewd—in his small, dark eyes. He was a man of sensibility, a latinized young Spencer Tracy whose good looks had gone slightly askew, whose features gave the impression of perpetual caricature. But Alberto's smile had grace and warmth and the hint of a genial satyr, and it was to this Pan who lurked in the monastic shadow that Marguerite was continually attracted.

Alberto liked her freshness. "You are like a child playing with Florence," he would say fondly when he came to visit her and found her room packed like a corner of the straw-market with all manner of baskets, mats, hats, and flowers.

Marguerite would buy him beautiful things as she roamed the old streets: a box of lapis lazuli to keep on his desk; a little gold pen to write his poems; a white tooled-leather frame with her picture in it; a desk calendar that she had turned back to the February date of their engagement on the bridge to inscribe *"Pazienza con Margherita"* followed by weeks of *"ancora pazienza."*

Her only reservation was that she felt he wanted not only to civilize but also to constrain her. Despite his garrulity and easy sociability, Alberto was inclined to a pessimistic view of things. "You optimistic Americans," he'd say damningly—blaming her countrymen for the foolish simplicity they were inflicting every-where—"no philosophical preparation at all, and you're supposed to lead the world."

Their civil marriage took place in May. They were married by the mayor of Venice, who wore a tricolor sash around his waist, and then there was a gay parade through the Piazza San Marco, scattering pigeons, to Florian's, where they were toasted by Alberto's sister Lauretta, some cousins, and the two friends of his who had been witnesses. It was a warm day and Marguerite had worn a plain white dress (called in those days a *princesse*) and short white gloves. Long hair, no jewelry, no matching wedding band for Alberto. Much laughter and good cheer . . . Alberto looking slim and elegant . . . his friends amused. And that was that.

Except that such a marriage didn't exist for the Scalzos. They insisted that she come back and do it properly—in their church and in a wedding gown with a reception at the club for all their friends. The correspondence about such a plan went on all summer until by fall Marguerite wrote, No, she wouldn't come (she was pregnant and sick), but if it meant so much to them she and Alberto would be married again in a religious ceremony so that it could be announced in the Gloversville paper.

That event could have furnished the title for a film: *The Bride Wore Black.* It had the right bizarre ring of unexpected situations and acerbic irony. The marriage took place in a chilly, unadorned chapel into which she and Alberto were banished by the bishop for having given public scandal by contracting civil marriage six months earlier. It was a drizzly, dull November day; Marguerite, pale from morning sickness, wore a gray flannel suit with black accessories. When Carla Scalzo received the photos of that non-event, she wrote back to note that Alberto's uncle, who had given the bride away, was on her wrong side, but probably in Italy they didn't know how to do those things correctly, and in any case, wearing black at one's wedding brought bad luck.

So it did. Immediately. At the wedding dinner overseen by Lauretta, the fish course had to be abandoned when everyone concurred that the fish had a peculiar taste ("*Sa di fango*"—it tastes of mud—they kept saying with what Marguerite thought a shocking lack of delicacy). And the tableware didn't match because a cousin had made off with the silver to pawn it. A few days after the wedding they heard that the little boy who had served the mass had been run over and was in the hospital. A month or so later, Alberto's uncle caught cold while marching hatless in a religious procession and died of pneumonia.

Despite the sinister auguries, Marguerite's faith was in the future. And Alberto sensed that she was beginning to take form, take shape, in the way he desired. He had found almost embarrassing her lack of philosophical notions and her incapacity for stillness and contemplation. But now, with her pregnancy, he felt she would emerge a more reflective being.

Marguerite's marriage to an Italian had unexpectedly brought into focus that fundamental American creed, present in the air at her birth and in her parents' admonishments, that happiness was a noble and attainable pursuit. Her mistake was thinking that happiness could come through Alberto's informed and caring guidance, instead of through her own sense of direction.

There is always the phenomenon of adaptation in marriage, and especially so in a mixed one like Marguerite's and Alberto's. And it is, most times, the woman who undergoes mutation, despite her private resolves, just because of the circumstances of life: The wife lives in the husband's country because his work is there and so her life becomes his. Her ways of life, the foreign ones, are renounced because clinging to them in the face of different hours, language, customs, foods, friends, attitudes, and practices would be intolerably difficult.

The foreign partner gives up, one at a time, the old comforting habits and interests, and takes on the same protective coloring as her husband. Except that he is always in his ambiance, while she, fatally, is like some poor drab set off by his brilliance and preening stance; she is consort, nest warmer, and a distant, dim reflection of his coloring and glory.

They had started married life in Rome. But for the birth of their first child, Tina, Marguerite had persuaded him to find an assignment in the States. Three and a half years later, when another daughter was born, they were back in Italy. And so it went; every so often Marguerite would urge a change, and Alberto, though he would have preferred staying where he was, would always give in to her.

Marguerite began to recede from outward life and to turn back into herself. Life centered around Alberto; even her hopes and aspirations focused on him. These were the years she was also occupied with the two little girls, and Alberto left them and the management of outward life completely to her—forgetting somewhere, like an umbrella it's a nuisance to pay attention to when skies are so clear, the inner life in her he had also pledged himself to support.

After some years, by skillful politicking in the ministries and a timely prize for his newly published study on Zanella, the Veneto poet, Alberto was rewarded with the post of cultural attaché at the Italian Embassy in Washington.

Again in the States, encountering American activism and purposeful pursuits, Marguerite found that she thirsted for them like a recluse let out of a cell. She tried gardening, the Great Books course, French lessons, helping at the library, art seminars at the National Gallery, and translating Alberto's poetry.

Only this last enterprise had success: an irony that more puzzled than pleased her. She could do for Alberto what she couldn't do for herself. It was some sick joke of which she was the butt—all implicit in the doomsday wedding.

Her translation of his poetry was securing him a name in the States and even reverberating back to Italy to reinforce his literary position there. His cultural work in Washington was satisfying and brought him important contacts. But Alberto himself had not changed. He remained what he always was: the man from Venice who was proud of his traditional ties. And if this acceptance of himself was essential because of the serenity and confidence it gave him, it also bound him to the past and to a narrowness of view. He saw no reason to explore, to try and discard, to range. Restlessness, he said, was the reason for Marguerite's unhappiness.

"No," she said. "Staying still is."

Alberto wrote of provincial Veneto life with a nostalgia attuned to other times and other people. For their time he was irrelevant, a backwash. When Cesare Servi, the Italian critic, wrote that Alberto's work "stood out scandalously from the modernity of the rest of contemporary Italian writing," Alberto couldn't have been more in agreement. That's how he wanted it.

Their third child, a son named for Alberto, was born after they had been in the States a few years. One summer when Marguerite took the children to Gloversville for a visit to the grandparents, she overheard a conversation in a beauty parlor that seemed to highlight the hurt of her life, the unfairness of being left behind while Alberto thrived. Hadn't he promised to make a person of her?

"Why don't you go to a charm school?" a woman at the beauty shop was saying to the young male hairdresser who worked on her in the chair next to Marguerite's. "It's too much to expect someone to live with you thirty, forty years or so and you're boring. It's not fair. Everyone should improve themselves, do something, not just stand there and bore people to death. Especially the ones who've got to live with you."

"You've put me right in the dumps," said the hairdresser. And Marguerite with him.

"Well, everyone should try to have some personality," the woman continued. "With all the articles there are now in *Reader's Digest* and everything, you don't even have to read a whole book— just get the gist of it in a magazine."

"I guess I'm just tired when I get home," said the hairdresser.

Marguerite compared that exchange with Alberto's offhandedness. "I love you as you are," he'd tell her, "with all your defects."

She felt it was his global acceptance of her that was her ruin. He never sharpened her, needled her; he took her for what she was, and if she was nothing, that was all right with him too. But not for her. She wanted him to want her better than she was. She wanted the fulfillment of her old college prophecy: "Someday you'll find your place in the world."

Little by little she became convinced that this place was not with Alberto. One Christmas vacation she went off to Bermuda alone for a week. To rest, she said. And when Alberto came to pick her up at the airport, she told him on the drive back home that it was time for them to quit. That night he cried, saying she was all he had and loved in the world; and she couldn't stand that, so she stopped thinking of real solutions and imagined others.

Flashback scene: At the Senior Banquet she is in an evening dress hunting for her place-card at the long table. Each name on the cards is accompanied by an appropriate remark. Marguerite finds and reads her card: "Someday you'll find your place in the world." Everyone laughs. Zoom in on present scene: The lovely still-young widow is dressed all in white at the funeral of her husband, noted poet and critic. She is graciously receiving the condolences of eminent Italians; many writer friends of her defunct husband come up and embrace her warmly. His close friend, the noted womanizer Leone Eccli, gives an extra pressure to her hand as he kisses her on both cheeks and looks into her eyes. Her husband has died of a heart attack after the great emotion of hearing that he won the Nobel Prize for Literature. . . .

What had marriage become? Not even the fury of hate or violent unhappiness. A vague discontent. Middle-age malaise. Scenes from Cheever stories.

"*Andiamo, bambina mia,*" Alberto would say when he saw her dispirited. "You love me, too—you just won't admit it to yourself. I would do anything to make you happy; you know that. But it's you who resist seeing the happiness you have. You're always wanting something impossible. You must accept what you have—and first of all, yourself."

He wanted her to be happy much in the same way her father had.

"I'm not your sister or some old cousin in Venice," she would retort. "For me the unexamined life is not worth living—Aristotle!"

"No, Socrates. You Americans know nothing of philosophy, but you should at least get your facts right."

"Don't give me that sarcasm!"

"But what is it you need to be happy? Don't you have everything?"

Fifteen years after she had decided on marriage over love, if you asked Marguerite Morosini what it had brought her she would have answered bitterly: being a hausfrau, an au pair, mother hen, sister goose, and pumpkin pie; the shadow and steppingstone of her husband, a victim of multiple cultural shock, an innocent and trusting American stooge to cynical Italian guile, Daisy Miller to Alberto's Machiavelli. An ex-American, a non-Italian, a crossbreed.

Or wasn't it that she wanted to be just that—unfixed and directionless, even in her aspirations? A wanderer and perpetual wonderer.

Chapter Fifteen

"There is no such thing as an artistic age," said Marguerite confidently as she impaled a fresh fig on her fork, and leaning toward Alberto, began to peel it, wrinkling her forehead in concentration. "The real artist has always transcended his time and place."

"And still I feel I was born a hundred years too late," Alberto reflected, gazing morosely about the flower- and leaf-shaded dining terrace of their hotel in Ponza.

They were back in Italy. Berto, their young son, had died in Washington the winter before of complications from pneumonia, and Marguerite, rich with grief, had told Alberto she wouldn't live there any longer. He gave up his post and took the editorship of a literary review in Rome. He was in his fifties. His glasses hung on a cord over his expanding paunch; his hair had receded and deep lines creased a face which, despite the August sun, still bore the pallor of winter. The vigor and enthusiasms of his American experience were past. He had had a mild heart attack just after Berto's death. In his life and in his writing he was returning to the formal commitments of his boyhood Catholicism.

"Now everyone can write," he was saying, "and well enough, too."

"Don't worry, Alberto, you're still out of the general run of things. You've gotten yourself labeled a Catholic writer and that's a bag just you and a few other reactionaries have all to yourselves. Now even Italians are better informed. Religion isn't relevant anymore. The Beatles *are* more popular than Jesus Christ . . . and they aren't the queer he was, either."

Alberto looked up quickly, his face pinched in outrage. "You have no right to offend me in what I believe!"

"I'm only saying what's true."

"At a certain point you're not even offensive, just ignorant. If you know so well what the world and times require of an artist, why aren't you one?"

Marguerite wondered, too.

It's true, she thought, that Alberto never encouraged me once we got off that bridge in Florence where he spoke of our creative life together, but if *I* had wanted to, couldn't I have done it just the same? What happened? The children . . . translating his work . . . the years just went. Or is Alberto right? That it's easier for me to be a victim than anything else?

Under the spectacular arbor of bougainvillea, she looked about at the other diners—slim, tanned, brightly dressed, laughing vacationers—and wondered: He has his belief, and what is mine? Art? And what is Art? A part of, or apart from, life?

Marguerite remembered a dinner party in Rome at which the Great Man of Italian Letters and his young blonde companion, Lalla Fonti, had been present—not only present, but peremptory in their presences: he wearing a great wide Roberta da Camerino necktie over a canary-yellow shirt under a brown velvet suit; she with a phallic charm around her neck. The Great Man, a formidable name when presented on college reading lists, was in excellent spirits. Over *tortellini alla crema* he told everyone at the table how his wife had wanted to be married in church in front of the altar where the intestines of St. Ignatius Loyola were conserved in a glass urn. But he had declined; he hadn't the guts for it, he said jovially.

"Arnaldo," someone had then asked, "you're a Roman, but is it true you've never been to the Capitoline Hill?"

"Of course I have—it's my legend that says I've never been there. Sometimes I forget what's legend and what's real. In any case, like any Roman I don't care for Old Rome; that's for the foreigners. But I've been to the Capitoline—that, yes, though never to be married. I marry in church."

For six or seven years he had been living with Lalla. The connection had launched her as a full-blown star into the international literary scene, consecrated by his favor no matter what she did; and she did everything from parodying Tennessee Williams to writing poetry and novels, dabbling in women's lib, making films, and doing political reportage and High Pornography. If being with Lalla had made the Great Man a more affable, entertaining, charming, and humanly accessible person, it had, on the other hand, also greatly diminished his own art.

So there was the old conundrum: Life over art or vice versa.

But, Marguerite considered, no matter how it came out for the Great Man, he had made it. He had written his finest work while married to a myopic woman who was herself a writer, perhaps even more so than the Great Man himself, but so ugly and scruffy-looking as to take the heart from any man, despite her soul. She was Art.

Lalla, pretty and cheerful, and twenty-three years younger than Arnaldo, was a writer, too, but not an artist. She was a good biological force in the Great Man's life—a blue-eyed St. George so committed and willing, so much the good Girl Scout of Revolt and Protest and Reform, so sincerely battling against bigotry, that you forgot the rest.

Everyone credited her with changing Arnaldo's life. "She's turned Arnaldo from a compulsive grouch into a human being," Leone Eccli sanctioned. So, thought Marguerite, life *is* more than art; but that was too simple a solution since the Great Man had both.

She knew something else. Alberto was no superman, no superpoet. But he was both a man and a poet, and she could not, with all her rage, deny it. Nor could she ever have touched his inner conviction of what he was. Elegantly and patiently, he listened to the inner evidence and explored with constancy the possibility of himself. She called it his egoism. But her label was her envy at his knowledge and acceptance of himself.

Now, in Ponza, as they mouthed the worn-out phrases of their dialectic, she knew that, too, for what it was: their form of communion . . . what held them together.

"Everything revolves about what you want to do," Alberto was saying, poking skeptically at the sole that was being served them. "I didn't want to come here in the first place."

True enough. It was Marguerite who wanted to be in Ponza. Alberto was happy to abstain from everything. The change had come after his heart attack and their subsequent return to Italy, as if the quasi-experience of death, following so soon upon Berto's death, had frightened him back into the religious superstructure of his boyhood. She was excluded—both from that period of time in which she hadn't known him and from the explicitness of belief she didn't share. Only in polemics did they now join spirits.

The change had made her realize that their previous life together had not been all a desert. There had been companionship and tenderness. (Was she to forget his painted messages and love poems? The flowers and fruits and phone calls when he was away on one of his official trips? Once he had been gone three weeks; miserable at home with the children, pregnant with Berto, she'd gotten his call from Atlanta: "Margherita, *cara*, how are you? And the girls? Are you eating? Do you sleep well?" "Yes, Alberto, yes," she answered wearily, only half listening. "I'll be back tomorrow." There was a long pause. "Tomorrow!" she cried out. "Did you say tomorrow?" And the joy in her voice was as much a surprise to her as to him.) Now, however, his silence and inner retraction stood between them. It bothered her that his new book would be on the nineteenth-century Catholic writer Tommaseo.

"Alberto," she said in a conciliatory tone, "can't we two be here in Ponza for a weekend together without Tina and Weezy and try to enjoy it? Angela Cambio, the Ecclis—everyone's here."

"Why couldn't you have come with them? What am I here for?"

She thought of their arrival on the hydrofoil and how the place had come to sight: the great rocks that were the outer islands of the Ponza group rising from the sea. Behind the outlying rocks was Ponza itself, with the pink and white town, the boat-filled harbor, and the flowering backbone of cactus and wild broom that grew among the lava-rock of the island. It was a place of fishing nets and high-style boutiques, nightclubs, fishermen's taverns, stalks of gladioli stuck ridiculously in crystal vases on the deck tables of moored yachts, vegetable stands, and clotheslines full of sarongs, hats, bikinis, and sandals for sale along the docks.

It was a beautiful place. It broke on her vision like a dream of some paradise. The limpid, agate water; the white houses of the fishermen outlined around doors and windows in bright colors and covered with fragrant greenery; calm little coves crammed with fishing boats or the relics of old schooners; the tiny streets climbing up the lava wall of the island and ending in shrub and cactus; bamboo, purple bougainvillea, huge marigolds, huger zinnias, cascading geraniums; clumps of pink or yellow houses stuck here and there on the gaunt island top; laughing people. All beautiful.

When they arrived she had wanted to sit on the eighteenth-century mole built by the Bourbon kings in Naples and see if anyone they knew passed by, but Alberto was full of anxieties about getting a lift to their hotel: Hotel Pontius Pilate.

And what *is* truth, Pilate, an inhabitant of the island, had once asked. This island, thought Marguerite, is truth—a belief, while it lasts, like any other.

The hotel was a strong white in the dusk, a multileveled dwelling carved out of the hillside and utilizing several preexisting fishermen's homes; it was built around open areas ablaze with the blooms and wild vinery of the island's rampant growth. Their room was on the top floor and from the terrace she could see the round church dome, which seemed to rise from the hotel itself, and the lights of the harbor and ships like reflections of the star-filled sky. Just below, in the whitewashed church, bells began to ring; the sweet smell of acacia filled the suave night.

"Alberto," she said, turning to where he sat on the edge of the bed in the dim room, "how beautiful it is!"

"How can they go to the trouble of making a hotel like this and then not put a tub in the bathroom?" he said peevishly, his shoulders hunched over. "I'm not well. I haven't felt well since we stopped for lunch at Anzio."

The next day they rented a *moschone* to row out into the bay and over to the beach in the next cove. Marguerite was thinking of the photos in their album at home that showed Alberto as a beautifully tanned muscular young man in a sailboat off the Lido. She had never known his youth and she felt overwhelming nostalgia for it as she watched the pale, paunchy person he'd become guide them over the gorgeous water to a strand of beach. Once there, Alberto sat in the shade of a straw-matted shelter while she swam.

"Alberto," she called to him from the water, "the boat—it's drifting away."

Annoyed, he floundered around grabbing the line on the boat and called, "Get yourself a porter next time—or an athlete! I'm not supposed to exert myself."

"The doctors have told you the opposite. They've told you to exercise and not just sit still, writing. My cousin Louis Longobardi went back to playing tennis after his heart attack."

"I'm not Louis Longobardi. I can't take so much sun, so much exercise. I don't need this escapism; I'm fine in my own home."

The delight she took in the sea and sun on her body, in the sights before her, was undone. Sun and light. She remembered Gillo Gatti yearning for sun and light; she thought of love and wondered if, before it was too late, she'd have it. She thought of how such a place could be with a man she loved—a man to swim with, walk with, drink with, talk with, laugh with, make love to.

At dinner she said, "It's all a mistake between us. All we have together now is a common address. Tina is going to college in a month, Weezy is old enough so that staying together serves no purpose. I want a divorce; I want to get out." The tears came to her eyes, not his, this time.

"You're tired from all that sun," he said. "Let's go up and rest. When we get back to Rome you can see that psychiatrist we heard about. You're still upset over the loss of Berto."

There was no further use in asking Alberto to walk to town, to find the Ecclis, to join the dancers, to look at the night, to do anything. They went to bed. Lovemaking in the dim room, and all the time Marguerite thinking, I have no companion in joy. I can't live like this . . . the waste . . . the waste . . . I could die, honestly die of what I feel.

As the sun set over the sharp rock outlines of Ponza, and the aperitif hour settled on the pink town and ships in harbor, Signora Morosini took a poison dart from her handbag, and taking careful aim, made a bull's-eye on Signor Morosini's chest as he sat in bed reading *Thomism and Modern Theology*. She turned herself in to the hotel concierge and was in due time tried for murder. Her case was sensational in Italy. If it had been a crime of honor or passion there would have been sympathy and flowers tossed at her as she entered the courtroom. But Signora Morosini herself insisted to the court that she killed her husband because he had promised her a creative life and hadn't kept his word; because he still spoke poor English; because he spent summers at the sea without ever swimming or walking on the beach; because he drew the blinds on sun and light.

"I keep dreaming of skiing," Marguerite told Dr. Verdile, her psychiatrist in Rome.

"What does skiing mean to you?"

"Freedom—or maybe being alone, because Alberto doesn't ski. But mostly freedom: moving, flying, soaring."

"What kind of freedom?"

"Getting out of marriage."

"Why does your marriage keep you from freedom?"

"Because it's repressive; because I no longer believe in it; because no one should be made to stay on, hating the other, just to stick it out."

"And you hate your husband?"

"No, not even that . . . I'm just tired. He's so negative. I want an affirmative life, a positive one I can believe in before it's too late."

"And you think you can do this by ending your marriage?"

"Listen! I keep trying, giving it another chance. But there's the other thing, too—I need love."

"And your husband doesn't love you?"

In that moment there flashed across Marguerite's mind the image of Alberto watching her undress. "You're still beautiful," he was telling her, smiling with that mixture of lasciviousness and naiveté that made him so appealing. "You're like the women of Cranach, with your long legs and those high, small breasts. A perfect woman of Cranach." And he had caressed her and made love to her and all the while she had thought, I've never properly made love to him. . . .

"He loves me," she told Dr. Verdile. "That's why I could never leave him in all these years. I don't like to hurt him. It's me—*I* have to love someone."

"And where will you find this someone?"

"I'll go to America, Alaska, Australia," she laughed. "It's easier there for a woman to remarry and start over."

"You want to remarry?"

"Why not?"

"But you're saying marriage is repressive—"

"*This* marriage," she flung out impatiently. Facing Dr. Verdile she took the gold band inscribed M-A that she had worn continuously from the time Alberto had put it on her finger and she said, "I'm not going to wear this anymore. I'll only put it on again if I find freedom really does lie in this marriage. But if my way is out of marriage, don't obstruct me."

Dr. Verdile smiled easily as he tamped down his pipe. "I'm not a policeman," he said, "or a judge."

At home Marguerite threw the gold band into a box of old school charms, wrote out her declaration for Alberto, and put it in his studio. The house was empty. At his return he came to her with the paper in hand.

"You swore to maintain this marriage," he said. "You are breaking your word and you can do so, if you like, but it is part of my faith. I believe in the holy sacrament of marriage, of *our* marriage."

"Alberto, you can't force life and people into your beliefs."

"Very well, I accept your feelings—on the condition that you won't let pride keep you from coming back." His voice faltered. "This marriage is not ending for me. I will always be your husband. And this is your home. . . . Remember," he said as he turned away and his voice broke, "I love you."

It was true that he loved her. Not just on principle; he loved her enough to let her go. Though she rejected his solidity and his imperturbable view of the world, it was the only permanence of affection she had ever known. Sweet indeed to have a place of peace and permanence. Comforting to know exactly one's place in the world. But it was no longer time to stay protected in Alberto's shadow; it was time to move on.

Marguerite got a lawyer and started the separation action. She confided in her friend Angela Cambio—Angela, whose own husband had left her and who, by toughness and wit, had overcome all obstacles to become a noted journalist.

"You're mad, absolutely mad!" Angela exploded, her eyes cold with fury. "Why don't you just take a lover? How can you leave a good man like Alberto—how can you take away his children? You're a fool! You don't know what it is for a woman to be alone."

"I'd rather be alone than in a marriage I don't believe in, or that I make dishonest by having a lover."

"Incredible! A real American answer. You're going to sacrifice Alberto and your daughters and lose your status as Alberto's wife for something like integrity or whatever you want to call it. The reason you can do this," Angela said bitterly, her lips tight, "is because Alberto is so good. You know he'll be standing there like Jesus with his arms open to take you back when you've had enough."

Her home no longer interested Marguerite. From the outside things looked as they always had. She and Alberto even went out together occasionally; they were waiting until the separation was posted before she left and they gave word to their friends and her family.

One night they dined in Trastevere, invited by a wealthy doctor and his wife who liked to collect writers and artists around themselves.

"It's a vulgarity . . . an obscenity," Marguerite was saying to Lalla Fonti among the general conversation.

"What's that? Pasolini's new film?" Cesare Servi broke in from across the table. "Did you know he is now known as *pipi nazionale* —in part for his initials, in part for the signature piss-scenes in each of his films."

"No, no," said Lalla, "we're discussing Alberto's Catholicism. But maybe it's political," she said, turning to Marguerite; "maybe he doesn't really believe it at all."

"Oh yes, completely! The works. Whatever he is, he's not a hypocrite." ("That Alberto Morosini was not born modern," the poet Montale had written of him, "is known and accepted and irrelevant. More to the point, however, and more interesting is the fact that he's never lifted a finger to become so—has remained a poet adrift among men.")

"Then it's a question of belief," said Lalla, "and there's no explanation for that. But how do you two get on?"

"We don't anymore," Marguerite admitted.

"Children," the doctor at the head of the table was saying loudly, "are an indispensable experience in one's life, absolutely essential to completing one's being. Without this experience you cannot be said to have had a complete life."

It took Marguerite's breath away to hear this assertion that the childless are only half-beings, have only had half-lives. But, she wanted to cry, if I've given up a whole part of my life to make and care for children! How Italian, how male Italian to define life and completion in terms of children!

And for what a short time we have them, she thought. After the loss of her son she suffered Tina's departure—as if eighteen years of her own life had been whacked off when Tina departed on that Alitalia flight to New York. In fact, those years *had* gone: wrapped in an Indian scarf, jingling with gypsy earrings, clutching Katherine Mansfield's *Bliss* in one hand and an Ingres poster in the other. And wearing, all unknowingly, the colors of the Italian flag, from her red underpants to her white shirt and green suit. Tina had left for college.

Aloud Marguerite said, "It's not that the childless have missed an experience, it's that they've had a different one."

"But not the essential experience that leads to completion," the doctor said complacently. "The whole principle of marriage—of life itself—is based on the establishment of a family."

"Ah, it's bound to change and for the better," said Lalla, who was anti-family, anti-children, and anti–Italian cult of the male. Around her neck she still wore the familiar coral horn, the phallic horn of plenty that meant: Plenty of fucking, and so what? ("It's all written in her last book," Angela once told Marguerite; "Arnaldo knows, too. Lalla's made no secret of it; it's part of her sincerity and women's lib. She and Arnaldo consider themselves permanent and everyone else their pastimes—they understand each other completely.")

The doctor's wife had been talking to the artist Marco Segre, just back in Rome after working some years in New York. "But you can't say the Americans have made any real contributions in the arts," she was saying, composed, wide-eyed, transparent in black chiffon pajamas.

Segre appraised her. "You know," he said, "it's embarrassing to talk to someone like you. I mean you're so far out. I don't know what to say."

"Well," she answered beatifically, "I meant they've done nothing important, the Americans, nothing really great."

"Why, all the art of today, all the movement stems from there!" Marco exploded. "But not only in art—in life, too. All that violence and upheaval you read about—you must have read about it—that's America's giving birth to a new kind of person, one who's open to all the new stimuli, the new ways of living and feeling. Believe me, you're all dead over here! Even the hired help over in the States know more about what's going on than your so-called intellectuals here in Rome. Italian intellectuals! They make me laugh. Americans are a new kind of human being, not afraid to create disorder, violence even, in order to create new life."

At dinner on a late September evening on a terrace adjoining the Renaissance house where Raphael's mistress, La Fornarina, was said to have lived, dining superbly and drinking the good wine of the Old World, Segre's New World seemed irresistibly attractive to

Marguerite. The doctor, his wife, and Alberto could have their stasis. Upper and outer mobility was what she was after. Freedom.

There is no worse evil, said Sartre, than raising a specific into a generalization, an abstraction. Transforming, for instance, any faith from the art of the possible into a fixed concept. Jung had said it, too—no concept is a carrier of life.

"It's a terrible thing to be left without belief," her mother was saying from long ago. "Even when they're not perfect, they give meaning to life."

With Marguerite, like Simple Simon, to reply: "No, I think freedom is better than any faith. And 'meaning in life'—the more you pursue it, the more it escapes you. All we have is choice, each time over and over again."

But, her mind told her, if you make freedom your belief, you're back to the same thing.

Perhaps she was.

When Alberto came to her room and said, "We're due at court tomorrow morning," she had a moment of panic. How do you walk away after eighteen years? Shaking hands and saying *ciao*? Do you thank him for the good times? Do you run?

At nine in the morning, punctually, they entered the great Palace of Justice, in a stream of short, dark, southern lawyers who were duly saluted—*Buon giorno, avvocato.... Rispetti, avvocá.... Eccellenza, buon giorno*—by the guards and ushers on duty. A great cold mole, pompous and forbidding on the outside and squalid within; Justice as a concept. A figure of Italia, crown on head and sword in hand, watched those who, caught, oppressed, fraught with anxieties, the upsetters of the status-quo applecart—the outsiders and sidestreamers—entered the Palazzo di Giustizia to have justice meted out to them.

Panic passed into exhilaration. The months of shabby bickering had dissolved, and on that spring day of late March, hard by the bridge of the angels and Castel Sant'Angelo, where she had strolled years ago with Alberto who courted her reading Laforgue, she went to be certified free.

Dr. Verdile had never understood the need for, as he put it, "all those papers and documents." Marguerite, too, would have preferred a simple dissolution of marriage; she was perfectly aware of the sublime nonsense of her yearning for a freedom that had to be ratified by a court of justice and stated on a piece of notarized paper. That was Dr. V.'s point: If she were really free, inwardly, she wouldn't need authorization to do what she wanted. But first things first—she might still get there eventually.

Dr. Verdile seemed to think you could simply walk out after having made some kind of loose verbal accord with your husband, but then he was a Jungian. (Some weeks ago, one of Marguerite's Jewish-American friends in Rome had said sententiously, "Rome is full of Jungian shrinks—it's a good place for them to talk their mumbo jumbo. They're a sad bunch."

"Why?" Marguerite had asked, fascinated by the graceless remark and now knowing better, much better.

"They're nothing more than astrologers—for logic and a rational approach, it takes a Freudian."

Marguerite felt thankful to have learned before it was too late that there is more in the psyche than reason. There was swinging mumbo jumbo, too.)

In the meantime, the miserable decisions had to be attended to: child support, property division, car ownership.

Was it justice that she give up the home and its furnishings and take a furnished place in Florence decked out with all the sad discards of mean-souled landlords? Yes, she supposed it was just— in the sense that justice was requital.

Marguerite was a failure both as an American woman and as an Italian. She couldn't be one of those sharp, self-confident Americans who put their husbands through the wringer getting house, car, furnishings, special school allowances for children, high monthly support, and even the lawyer's fees paid. Back home, even when the woman wanted the end of the marriage it was always the husband, the good sport, who got out and went to a hotel someplace with a suitcase of clothes hastily thrown together. And she couldn't be Italian, sticking in no matter what.

Alberto was no sport; he was an old-fashioned, obtuse Catholic provincial who could only say, when she pointed out the finesse of other separating couples, "This is my home; I can't leave it. I must defend it. It will be here for you, and the girls, unchanged, when you want to return."

She personally wanted nothing except a few of her books. The rest she would leave; it was the price she was paying for her freedom and she accepted it. "Why don't you stick up for yourself?" her mother would have said if she had known what was going on. "Just think of how much you're giving up"—and she'd have meant the silver and furnishings, not Alberto.

A few nights before the formal separation, Alberto's old friend, the octogenarian critic Cesare Servi, called and asked her to dinner with him—just the two of them. He knew everyone and everything that went on in literary circles; she wasn't surprised when he asked why she was leaving Alberto. Was there another man?

"No, there's no one else. I'm not leaving for another man. I'm leaving for myself."

"That's very ingenuous, my dear. You can be sure no one in Italy will believe that. And if it were believed, it wouldn't be to your credit. Adultery can be understood, but nothing like saving one's soul; we're an old civilized people, but basically very elemental. That northern gloominess of wanting to achieve a soul, or whatever you want to call it, will never go here. It's perverse—worse than snobbery, cruelty, infidelity, extravagance—anything. An extreme presumption."

"I don't care what's going on at the moment or what anyone says or thinks; I care for what I have to do in this moment. And what I have to do is my business."

They talked about what she would do. "I thought of going to Florence," she said, "because there the girls won't be too far from Alberto. But first I'm going to the States. To see Tina and my parents."

"Alberto will suffer. Tell me what you do—what you want to do."

"I've worked in the library at St. Gregory's American school, but I'd rather do photography. Or translations—I've done that. You know what's going on in Italy; what new writers could I start translating when I get to Florence?"

"Keep in touch with me, I'll let you know."

Driving away from Cesare Servi, she saw her future clearly before her. The butt of cruel Italian jokes, she would be the scandal of a society that would judge her, not Alberto. She saw herself committed to the social limbo of separated women, while Alberto flourished like a younger, more attractive Cesare Servi. For Alberto was attractive to women. Widows, ambitious poetesses, the young daughters of his friends, hostesses all over town who always needed single men—they would all start calling him. I never wanted to be alone, she thought. Was this justice?

Yes, for she had broken the marriage. But no, she cried, he broke it too. Then why are you letting yourself be punished? Because I want to get out!

At the Palace of Justice, Alberto was in a state of tired depression. Marguerite, however, looked about intently, wishing to record this event in her life as accurately as her wedding day. *Già!* The day she had worn black and her mother had predicted disaster. Now, to sever the union, she wore a bright yellow sports coat and felt more like a girl than she had nearly twenty years before.

The walls of the *palazzo—palazzaccio*, the Romans called it, using the pejorative to signify not only their contempt of the ugly building, but of Justice, Law, everything official—the walls were dirty and pocked, as if they had been shelled. Marguerite and Alberto took an elevator filled with corpulent lawyers to the second floor and there went into a courtroom that was beginning to fill with people standing in groups. *"La Legge è Uguale per Tutti"* was inscribed above the judges' richly carved wood bench, and Marguerite regarded it silently. As if anything inflexible, any absolutism could be justice! she thought. And above the inscription, as if to render absurd the statement that the law is equal for all, hung the crucifix, present in every school, court, hospital, and post office of Italy and negating by its mere presence the idea of equality. This is a Catholic country, it said; this is a country run by interests that need to be lubricated by continual lip service to Catholic precepts; so it spoke to atheist, Jew, pagan, Protestant, and anyone else outside the structure.

The other women in the room aspiring to freedom were elegant, black-dressed, pouting or sullen women who stalked back and forth like the caged she-wolf on the Capitoline. Marguerite imagined they all had lovers somewhere waiting for them; they would all go on to elegant places for dinner with champagne after the separation was legally accorded. Or they would fly to London, Nairobi, Vienna for the weekend. Or perhaps just telephone to say "It's over and done with now, I'm free," and meet their man later that night in their own place.

Not she. She would go back to Alberto's home that night. She would prepare dinner as she always had, and sit at the table with him and Weezy as she always had. He had told her she could stay on as a guest there the few days remaining before her flight; she had her room to herself, he would sleep in the studio as he had done for all the past months. When she came back, she would make arrangements for going up to Florence.

Marguerite studied the inscription in a bronze wreath above the chief judge's seat: *"Lex."* She thought of Lex Barker. Lana Turner. Now there was someone who had gone through marriage as if she were trying on shoes. And not tight nun's shoes.

I should play the date of this day at lotto, she thought. All good numbers and a good year—1969. She thought of the New Year's Day cocktail party where the first 1969 jokes had already been exchanged: "Come on, guys, let's go!" "Where?" "To St. Peter's." "What for?" "To see how the pope will start his sixty-nine." Ignazio Silone had been there, too, gloomy as Eeyore and predicting that this year would be worse than the last; that there was nothing more to hope for from humanity; that things were in full decline everywhere, the horizons empty of hope, and that it was a useless perversity to continue to write. "Always serene, old Silone," Alberto said afterward. She laughed; at times like that Alberto was close to her.

Now she had a feeling of remorse as she stood in the dark courtroom. Despite everything, she and Alberto had lived a true, felt, shared human experience together. Marriage and motherhood were to have been her educators, he had thought. But he had not considered the deep frozen block of murk that had remained fixed in her; the matrix of countless hurts in her nature that needed, besides his warmth and affection, the heat of self-torment and conflict in order to dissolve.

Marguerite watched the rat-eyed lawyers and their flunkies running around the corridors. There was a small sad-faced young girl among them, the only person in the whole room who appeared to be feeling deeply what was about to take place. The other women carried shopping bags printed "Piper Market" or "Rive Gauche," smoked, talked among themselves or to their lawyers. Alberto seemed to be the only husband present, which was typical of his sense of duty and responsibility.

"You swore before God," he told her, staring at her with a kind of desperation, as if before the door opened to admit them to the separation rites he could stop it from happening. He was becoming flustered. His lawyer slipped the usher a folded bank note and came up to tell them they'd be first.

"But I'm first on the list," exclaimed another waiting lawyer, looking over the typed sheet of precedence in his hand. "Who is first before me?"

"The last shall be first," one of his colleagues laughed.

Suddenly Marguerite was standing before two men who asked her if she understood everything in the separation agreement, which lay on the table before them, and if she agreed. "*Si, si,*" she said and signed her name. Then she went out and it was Alberto's turn.

Five minutes in all and there they were, divided at last. Alberto's lawyer patted her on the cheek and said, "Good luck, *cara.*" Alberto took a cab. She walked across the bridge from the Palazzo di Giustizia and stopped at the first bar that had a telephone.

She called Dr. Verdile. "It's done," she said.

"*Va bene.* I'll see you Thursday at five."

Chapter Sixteen

Ontogeny recapitulates phylogeny: charismatic phrase of my education. Poetry and wisdom. The only thing I got out of college and it cost Dad three thousand dollars a word. Beautiful words and not even in *Bartlett's*. Suits me fine. Going back, taking the immigrant's route, seeking my fortune in the New World. Mad Marguerite, the end-product, recapitulating the experiences and history of my ancestors.

Going back to start again: like birds, lemmings, salmon—whatever fights wind and tides and countercurrents to follow instinct to the source. The urge of ineluctable necessity. My choice was always made.

I have cast auspices with V. and I dig the message: Do not force things, but be receptive to what comes. I should have done it years ago. I'm always late. "Late, late—my word I'm late," cried the white rabbit. . . . "Off with her head," said the Duchess. . . .

Hard to sleep the night before leaving; at dawn I wake to find myself curled in the fetal, defensive position. Hating life and the complexities of it, the hurting of people, the compulsive goddam need to be oneself—to chase the fucking ego all over the external world because it eludes us inside and we cannot find it there and be satisfied.

Darkness at dawn, and vague regrets. Sad, unsure, wavering. Hearing Alberto in the studio as he folds the grating hardware of his cot back to divan; the garbage truck in the courtyard, the fountain in the garden, and then, finally, the chime of the Quirinal clock sounding the hour: seven o'clock, rise and shine!

Everything's immediately better. Get breakfast, kiss Weezy and send her off to school, talk, move, act, dress. Affront a new day. Action.

Alberto at the airport: "At least if I knew you were going off with someone you loved," he says. His face is drawn and sad but composed. He is not emotional. "But you have no one. At least if I knew you could communicate with someone else, but in all your life who have you had except me? You've never opened completely, but the little you did was with me."

"But I've known what love is—I knew it before being with you."

"That idiot Verdile! He's done nothing for you if he's let you go on living in the past."

"It's not the past I'm concerned with, it's the future."

"The same mistake," says Alberto.

Fuchsia trees blooming near Keats's grave as he drives me past the Protestant Cemetery and Pyramid of Gaius Cestius. To the airport, en route to America. *Addio*, Rome. Good-bye, Alberto.

After the surliness, the sloppy food, and the general squalor of an El Al charter flight, the final relief of new promised land: flawless, smooth entry through customs; the swift-gliding rhapsodic traffic of the huge automotive monsters on the parkways; illuminated, transparent, gut-showing buildings springing from the flat land, guilelessly, like oldtime American candor. Signs everywhere promise everything: easy money to borrow, retirement on full income at an early age, a home in the suburbs, kids in college, vacations, trips, and permanence—the family that prays together stays together.

Off to Gloversville. It's Good Friday. Time for the passion to begin. I stare, famished, at the cuteness of American airline hostesses and compare their "My name is Jane" cozy hospitality and perky gingham cocktail aprons, as they pour drinks with impeccable bravura, to the down-in-the-mouth sullenness of their Old World sisters, wrapped in frowsy smocks and hating every minute of the flight.

Three in the morning for me, but the evening before for them and there I am—the comfortable big thick beds of the Tudor house. Its utter comfort: lush, deep-pile rugs; heat; jam-packed fridge and jam-packed freezer; drawers full of candy bars, chewing gum, cigarettes, and cigars; cake mixes by the dozens and liquor by the gallons in the cupboards; every cosmetic and toothpaste known in the bathroom cabinets; shrines of gold leaf–framed photographs of the grandchildren on the walls of the sunroom; bouquets of lush fake flowers on the piano, making a backdrop for the sisters-in-law who sit radiant, gazing steadily out from their studio photographs in white wedding dresses and veils. I must admit that I, too, would have made a beautiful bride.

Tina at odds with the grandparents because she's become a hippie. Sulking and vying for my attention as I greet the folks. "Wait till they hear what you're here for," she says darkly. "Cool it, Tina," I tell her. At Christmas when we talked about the separation she said she didn't care, it would be nice to live a bit in Rome with her father and a bit in Florence with me. Weezy, the same. So much for the traumas of the children of separated parents.

Tina is a bulldozer—no ego deficiency in her, she sucked whatever health still remained in me while I carried her and has flourished from my ground-up bones like some gorgeous wild bloom ever since. Eighteen and steady in her affections, her self-esteem, her nature. A beautiful girl. I love her. She is what I wanted to be.

First night back. I dream of my cousin Vic Vitale. It figures. He was mentioned earlier in the family rundown as outcast and ingrate in contrast to his brother, Tony, who gives Aunt Emma some satisfaction, at least, by being settled down and married and practicing law and going to church. So Vic equals me; both of us are outside approbation. "Why do you care?" Dr. V. would ask. Oh, Christ, if only I had him in my pocket like a transistor, to turn on when I need to hear him.

Easter Day. Resurrection. I break the news of Alberto and me. Mother's first reaction is gratification at the superb working mechanism of her ESP: "I *knew* you were different the minute you got off that plane! I kept telling your father. I knew something was in the wind. You even look different." How? I ask. "Better—more cheerful, younger. Even dressed smarter."

Good. She's said it now. No turning back. Old mother oracle, old sphinx and sorceress—of course you knew! You who hold all life and breath, you who can thwart and punish. And I knew that you knew. And I know that you will always know. But *non importa*; I'm not asking you now, I'm telling you. You're different, too, old folks at home. Now that you're off my back and out there where I can see you, you're not bad at all. Now I can love you as I always wanted to.

"If that's the way it was between you," Ma says, "why didn't you separate immediately, years ago?" So practical, so jumping with solutions. She's thinking, Years ago when you were younger and could remarry, before you had children. As if my children were mistakes, the results of procrastination and indecision. But I wanted my children! And Alberto, too.

"Well," she says, "you've always been the different one in the family. Now it's divorce."

"I'll fly over to Italy with you to put things right. . . . I'll take the girls and give them a home here," says Dad, trying, as in time past, to dominate the situation and command. But not this time. They see I'm different.

On rebirth day I go to church with them because I want to see old St. John's again, the old neighborhood. Sad. The beautiful elms gone, the old Victorian houses razed for parking lots or turned into boardinghouses, social welfare agencies, and doctors' offices. Where the old Fry mansion stood on velvet lawn there's now a motel with glassed-in coffee shop so you can watch the transients at breakfast. Gloom. It's progress, says Dad.

Easter brunch en famille with the cheery faces of Sammy and Betty, Steve and his wife, and all their brood. They start drinking the minute they get in the house and Betty eyes me furtively, measuring the length of my skirt against hers. Of course mine is shorter! Of course I'm more with it! Mom says I should see their beautiful homes. I already have—thousands of Saturday afternoons ago at the movies. Tina gripes at being there instead of with her friends. I feel sorry for all of us.

Gloversville is in its death throes. The folks lock the side door now when they go out; there is a burglar alarm at the garage entrance; drivers on buses won't give change for fear of being mugged; Aunt Emma's handbag was snatched in broad daylight downtown by a bunch of teen-agers. Everyone's afraid. "Love America or Leave It" says the sticker on Pa's car; he's still afraid of commies, but they're easier to spot now because they wear beards. Ma's afraid of blacks: "They're so pushy—why can't they be satisfied with their own schools and neighborhoods instead of spoiling it for others?" The folks can't remember when their own folks were Negroes.

They complain of Tina. "I can't take her downtown to lunch, she doesn't wear a bra or shave her legs," says Mom. And Dad, gravely, "She wanted to take a bus to Cape Cod with some boy on Thanksgiving instead of coming here to the family." Oh, my beautiful Tina . . . oh, my prophetic soul.

Tina and I leave the day after Easter. She has to go back to school, I head for the city. "What's down there?" Dad grumbles. Lining up work, I tell the folks, waving cheerfully. Mother's eyes are hard with suspicion . . . envy. I look at her with new understanding: Did she want to be me?

I skip the New York covey of ex-marrieds who sent me reading lists on their Christmas notes (*The World of the Newly Separated*, etc.) and condolences for the breakup: . . . men will use you . . . you will die of loneliness in your bed . . . separation is no substitute for marriage, even a bad one . . . be sure you get a settlement. I skip them and move in on an old college classmate: Emily Ordway, Midwest American, New York careerist, and private enterprise supreme.

"Well, now, I'll bet the Water-Pik hasn't come to Italy," says bright and brittle Miss Em, the tooth-flashing PR consultant for women's clubs and charities. The last thing I hear at night as I turn in on her sofa, determined not to answer her chipper, toothy, chattering well-meaningness. She stands there crunching an apple, skinny, ferret-faced, eye-goggling, grinning like she's been taught, blathering on and on.

"But I do like a male-dominated society!" she concedes magnanimously to poor Italy to make up for the Water-Pik.

Three days of information retrieval. "Now tell me everything you've been doing," says Emily Ordure, "in chronological order. What are your impressions of this country after having been away so long? . . . What do you think of the European mood at this moment? . . . Now just how does Alberto go about his work? . . ." I won't bare my soul to this correspondent for the alumnae news.

She's reading Updike's *Couples* ("I don't care much for the characters") and keeps a persistently open outlook on hippies and the copy of *Evergreen Review* Tina gave me. "Well, it's an exchange of ideas, anyway," says Miss Emily Ordeal of all the turbulence and turmoil, the revolutions and disasters, the violence and vehemence and human waste around us. Oh, Emily Ordway! The

world is full of you with your gadgets and efficiency and zeal for
self-improvement; with your fridge full of stuff stored in plastic
bags and one brownie stowed away in the freezer top and labeled
"one brownie"; with your sofa bed set thus, in the middle of the
floor, and not next to the wall as I'd prefer it because I might
mark the wall, and a lumpy flashlight under the pillow "in case you
have to go to the bathroom," which I won't. Careful, nut-storing
squirrels.

At morning coffee she pumps away, jotting all the names I mention on separate index cards, with brief notes on their work, special-
ties, outlooks. All followed by "friend of Marguerite." That's
public relations. I mention Giorgio Corsi: UN diplomat, NYU
professor, Italian intellectual, etc., etc. She's scratching away and I
add, "He's also gay."

Emily lives in a huge apartment complex just across the street
from where the neighborhood turns bad. She blinks lights with a
librarian in the facing wing to let each other know they're all right.
An Egyptian tapestry, bought because it was "Scandinavian in feeling," hangs in her entry; a Siamese fertility mobile of oscillating fish
hangs in the living room, chiding her barrenness; wine for meals
is measured by the half-glassful and the bottle carefully corked and
put away.

I skip out the third day when she's busy with clients, leaving her
$5 for the frozen foods I've used and my outlook for the future
written on an index card.

I go to Giorgio's in The Village. He's appalled to see me, but since
for years he's been telling Alberto and me to consider his place our
pad in New York, he takes me in and gives me his studio couch. Lots
of tips, too, on people to see for doing translations or other work
in Florence.

Meet an editor friend of Giorgio's and we talk about Italian
writers. Agree they all look like lightweights on the current literary
scene—they can't keep up the commotion on a global level because
they're so concerned with their provincial infighting. "The whole
Italian bunch is irrelevant in the world today and they don't know
it," says an editor. I think of Alberto, who knows it and doesn't care.
"They want to play the scene in their terms, the old thirties thing;
they haven't a clue to what's really new and popping." He tells me
to keep in touch if I discover any popping Italians.

Some of Alberto's old contacts take me to lunch, and they take the news of our breakup with the same interest as if I were giving up smoking. No—less. All want to hear of fresh Italian talent, as if we were talking of produce: tender Treviso lettuce, fragrant Sicilian lemons; luscious Verona peaches; and—why not?—Calabrian chestnuts. *Un fritto misto.* We talk. I suggest. They listen. Should have done this years ago. Something I learned from Alberto after all. Dozens of full-voweled Italian names roll off my lips. I'm connecting—they can hear me, see me. Me! A few months ago I was telling Verdile I didn't exist . . . I couldn't use the telephone because it increased to the point of terror my feeling of being detached from people, from the world.

Once in a while I remember Alberto. I walk through Bloomingdale's and see his jockey shorts, a gilded pocket toothpick, a foldaway mattress. I hear his voice: "My only fear is that when you realize your mistake, you'll be too proud to come back." At the airport I told him, "I didn't want it to be like this." He said, "It will be all right."

I wanted it to work. For years I worked at it, and maybe that was the trouble . . . laboring at something that should only have been accepted, without that uptight compulsion to better things that I, American, was born to. Better my life, my marriage, my husband. America the Betterful. "Every day, in every way, I'm getting better and better," says Mother You-Better-Better-Yourself.

New York is great, fantastic, everything's crackling. A yardstick of packaged matches with sun designs for Dr. V., only 59¢ in a Japanese emporium. Pastrami on rye at Lexington and Fifty-sixth Street—gorgeous! Serrated grapefruit spoons at Hammacher Schlemmer for Angela, Winnie-the-Pooh animals and Zen books for Weezy, sale dresses at Saks, apricot chew on Eighth Street, fabulous underwear, shoes that fit. Orgasm is everywhere. A whole new vision in the fifties from Seventh Avenue to Third. The vegetables in The Village greater than life, and the pastries enormous and death-defying. The public library—what can compare to it in Rome? Hot fudge sundaes. Cranberry juice. Spareribs. America the Bellyful.

Strangers call me sweetheart, dear, young lady. There are still anxious, blank, wearied faces but there are also newly cheerful ones. A bearded guy holding a red flower in one hand and his girl's arm in the other goes by singing a peace song while she struts in her flapping bell-bottoms, leaning close to him. Some blacks on a construction job at Columbus Circle stop to listen and one calls, "Make it a love song, brother!"

Giorgio introduces me to his friend Piero Paco, hero of the Italo-American breach into American literature. He looks like a massive gangster but turns out to be a plain, nice guy with a lot of folksy stories and no complexes. He doesn't feel guilty about blacks, doesn't care about elevating Italo-American prestige. He's no missionary for wops. No gripes about the Establishment. He just decided in the best American way to write a book that would make half a million bucks because he was tired of being ignored.

"You don't think struggling Italo-Americans should stick together and give each other a push up from the bottom of the pile where they've always been?" I ask him. But he's no struggling half-breed anymore. He's made his pile; he's all-American now.

"I'm not going to push that crap," he says engagingly.

We'll get no equivalent of the Jewish intellectual hero or the black martyr from him, I think. I like him. He's gross and good and sits like a big bespectacled Buddha in Giorgio's fussy little place asking for soda pop while we drink Scotch. He wears short socks, so a good bit of his thick white legs is always in view; he smokes stogies.

Giorgio says *andiamo* and we go to a Chinese restaurant where Paco's fortune cookie says he's lazy and mine that I'll achieve success.

Tina comes to town and crowds into Giorgio's with me. He looks like he'll cry, but I tell him we're leaving the next day. I take her to see *Hair*. Twenty-five bucks for our tickets, and she who contests American materialism and dresses in rags doesn't say a word. Sometimes even America works, is classic and good. A zippy audience in chain-mail boleros, see-through pants and skirts, loose hair, and tatters among the careful suits from suburbia. Tina and I get pelted with daisies.

I say, "Tina, do you care about what's happened to me and *papà*?"

She says, "I love you both. When you told me, I had to think of your problems as those of another person and not as my mother's. It was scary and it hurt and sometimes I felt it wasn't fair—but it was *good*. I got to know you as a person, to know what was going on in your mind. And then I came to love you more."

"*Ciao*, Giorgio, *mille grazie*. We'll see you in Florence." Tina and I get out of his hair and take the bus uptown. Three well-dressed black teen-agers are talking about their Fred Braun shoes, a leering creep across the aisle leans over and looks up my skirt. We pass a man jogging up Sixth Avenue. We get off at Columbus Circle —soft green and yellow forsythia in the park, a stupendous new glass building gone up, a bagel man. "America stinks," says Tina glumly. Some shrunken invalids in wheelchairs are taking the sun together at the park entrance. The banks are filled with dapper black employees who are marvels of efficiency and courtesy. Charge accounts still work: I rent a car and we drive off toward Gloversville. Beautiful George Washington Bridge. Beautiful country. Great roads. I head upstate. An apostate.

"Well, I suppose you went to see *Hair*," says Mother on the threshold, welcoming us back. I leave Tina to skirmish with her grandmother and go downtown to my childhood dentist, who asks, "How's Italy these days?"—amused that it's still there. He's installed in a super suite in crummy downtown and treats me the least bit coldly, as if it's not really nice to live abroad if you don't have to, like the military.

Tina gets a ride back to Bryn Mawr and I say good-bye till Florence. "Oh, Mumu," she says, kissing me good-bye, "just think of what you're giving up!"

The folks have had time to ruminate in my absence and are ready for the attack. "If you're set on this separation, then the best thing is for you to come back here to live, where we can help you. This is your country. You and the girls are Americans, after all." Back in Gloversville I might still give Mom a real wedding before it's too late.

"You have to think of the children," says Dad. "You've got others to think of beside yourself."

No, Great White Father, you're wrong. First me, this time.

Dad takes me down, in the bowels of his bank, to the vault to survey his domain of portfolios and see what will eventually be mine, the fruits of his labor. I feel real tenderness toward the fatigues of his life, his hanging on, his faith in America. America the Dutiful.

Even so, he lives in fear and dread of what's happening to his America: all those bums on welfare to support, the good-for-nothing hippies, the disrespectful college kids—"I'd rather have my boys in the service where they'd at least get some discipline and learn to be neat than in some atheist, hippie college," says Steve's wife—the traitors and cowards who won't die to defend the country from the communists in Vietnam, the pushy blacks who are getting as bad as the pushy Jews. Old America was going, leaving them all in the lurch.

Later I meet Mother for shopping. It is her world and she is expert in it. She is knowing, efficient, well dressed, and esteemed by the salesgirls. I enjoy it. The glittering insides of the stores are exciting; shopping is ecstasy. There is still a splendid American world of promises wafted on scented, melodic air; outside everything is seedy and squalid, but for an hour or two in Charles Brothers' I can believe once more in the old Saturday movies, in that grand old notion: America the Blissful.

That night at table: "I wonder why Louis and Irene haven't called to have you over for dinner. They know you're here. Your cousin Louis is an extremely successful psychiatrist. He's making a fortune and Irene's spending it—all on herself. When they moved here from Cato I put myself completely at her disposal to help her settle, practically taught her how to shop and dress. She comes from a very poor background. I've certainly entertained them enough here."

"You can't force gratitude from people, or even buy it," I say oracularly, and Mother's eyes narrow in on me suspiciously. In the old days I would have tried to defend myself, Louis, and Irene— thus lending point to her attack; now I don't care.

Then the New World is over.

But what world is there that's not beached first in ourselves?

Chapter Seventeen

Shades of Henry James: Now she was Isabel Archer. There she was concluding details for renting the shabbily furnished room in a sixteenth-century villa in the sweet hills ringing Florence that had been the setting for parts of *Portrait of a Lady*. She could see the flickering lights on a movie house: Marguerite Morosini in Portrait of a Loner.

"The place is charming," the real estate agent, a countess, had said, showing the rooms off the second-floor loggia to Marguerite. "Not everyone's cup of tea"—she smiled, tripping on a loose piece of the wood flooring—"but strong on charm, really, and very handy to the American school."

"This is called Florentine tacky," added Marguerite's friend, a secretary from the country day school across the way, as they took in the saggy, spiritless sofa and two amorphous mounds of chairs that were the only pieces of furniture in the living room.

Marguerite tried gaiety, too, along with them. The view was a Ghirlandaio landscape, and Weezy in her expensive school could feed her soul on views of Florence all day. And she? She would fix up the rooms, take walks in the pretty country, look for work, grow geraniums, and reread James.

Even so, Marguerite felt dispirited and ponderous as she sat there having the *contessa* and secretary present her appealingly to the owner, a wary old lady with a cigarette held tightly in bright red lips who had already had bad experiences with Americans, including several husbands. The villa had once been let as a high-class boarding school for American girls, and the girls had defaced it and left it bankrupt. "What a bore it all was," said the old lady, keeping the butt clamped tightly between her lips.

She wanted 90,000 lire per month, three months' rent in advance, and the lease made out for two years; she had, after all, to make some sort of kitchen in the rooms and move beds up from the cellar, she said (as visions of ancient damp-rot passed through Marguerite's head) and one didn't do that lightly with today's prices, but only when there was a certain guarantee. "It's a bore," said the old lady, wanting to be off to town to her bridge game.

Florence was depressing: a city of aging American and English women. For two weeks Marguerite had been there, living in a pension and taking meals with a Miss Cameron of Toronto, a retired teacher who was doing the art galleries and relayed back her sights at each sitting. It was a city of Miss Camerons; of resident widows who rented out rooms in their chilly villas; of touring widows. The city was filled with them at all the concerts and in all the tearooms. A glut of old women and college girls doing the Renaissance in their Junior Year Abroad.

Marguerite signed the lease, then returned to Rome to pack her things. No use spending money at a hotel, Alberto had told her, so she went to her old home to stay.

Angela was furious. "Are you crazy? A separation is automatically annulled when you sleep under the same roof—not even in the same bed."

"Who's going to report it—you?" said Marguerite. "You don't have to mention it all over town." The exhilaration of the trip to America had evaporated, leaving her beached in the late Rome spring. Florence weighed on her. The sense of being caught in a crevice between the Appennines was physically oppressive; the recollection of other, better times there, wearying.

"Why do you have to go to Florence?" Angela asked brusquely. Marguerite was irritated at this echo of her father's question, "Are you forced to go to Florence?"

Her irritation was the mark of her uncertainty. Why Florence? Why even Italy? Why anyplace? It would all be the same. She was part of the permanently dispossessed. She couldn't belong completely in the States anymore and had never belonged completely in Europe. Where *was* the goddam place her Senior Banquet had promised her in the world?

"But it's the only solution, Angela! I've told you. I know the town and can find work there. Weezy will be near enough for Alberto to visit and she has an American school there."

"Do you have to work?"

"Why, of course! How else can I manage? Alberto can't take care of a place in Florence plus the place here plus the schooling. Plus Tina's trips back and forth. But I've told you all this. *Basta.* I'm sick of talking about it."

"If you weren't so obstinate about Florence—and there's more work to be found in Rome, you *know* that—then you could have my place while I'm in England on my assignment. I don't want to rent it because I'll come down every so often, but you could stay there and keep an eye on it for me."

"No . . . no . . . the whole point is to get away. I even thought of America, Australia. Can't you understand?"

"No. You Americans are too businesslike for me. All plans and solutions and fresh starts."

Back in Florence, checking in again at the *pensione* of old ladies while she waited for work to be completed on her apartment at the villa, she met Richard Wareham, who had just arrived to take over the ministry of the Episcopal church there. The Reverend Richard Wareham, in a plaid sports jacket and deep orange turtleneck sweater, with the accent of Virginia, William & Mary, and Jack Daniel's bourbon.

He was sandy-haired, blue-eyed, slight, very socially adept with the ladies, and single.

"My daughters are Episcopal. You'll meet the youngest, Weezy, when she comes up after she finishes the last weeks of school in Rome," Marguerite told him in their conversation. It had been the fiery Tina, like a melodramatic Anna Magnani, who had gotten Weezy to go into the Church of England with her, in her own outburst of enthusiasm for the language of its ritual, which was a daily occurrence at St. Gregory's school in Rome.

In his rich voice, with his attentive southern regard, Richard had encouraged Marguerite. "I'm delighted! Lovely! Glad to have them. And you?"

As he talked Marguerite recognized one whose social ease came from generations of leisurely exchange in families whose language had always been theirs and the command of it exact. ("You can get topics for your discussions at home," Miss Stack, her sixth-grade teacher, had imagined years ago, not knowing that families like the

Scalzos were not like Warehams and didn't converse on Current
Events at the dinner table.) Marguerite had known these Virginia
families when she and Alberto had lived in Washington. She knew
their closeness of family, their relaxed association with the land
learned through centuries of ownership, their undeniable class in
manner and speech. They weren't endlessly occupied with finding
themselves and knowing themselves, for this had all been done for
them way back.

Self-assurance in others was magnetic to Marguerite. Richard
Wareham was someone who had never been alien anywhere: Wherever the Warehams had been, first in England and then for the past
three hundred and some years in Virginia, they had been the root-
stock, the gentry.

Her answer to his "And you?" was her self-introduction: ex-
Catholic, ex-wife, ex–American suburb.

They began to sit together at the pension for meals. They walked
about the city together, making purchases for the respective homes
they were setting up; she showed him Florence; he took her around
to meet friends of friends from back home. They sat around and
drank, and she, keeping up with his drinking, began to talk. She
told him everything.

"Honey, you're pure—pure as the driven snow," he told her.
"You're not out for tail or money or status. All you want is the pat
on the back, an affirmation of existence."

"That's it, Richard!" She leaned toward him, looking into his
clear blue eyes, eyes that had remained, somehow, candid in a face
lined and carved with wryness. "I have to know I exist, at least
that," she said intently, searching him to see if it were all a joke.
"But how did you know?"

"Honey, that's the ontological predicament. We're all in it. We
all need our daily pat on the back, along with our daily bread."

In talk they had become intimate: "This is soul-talk, honey, and
I need it as much as you," he told her. She knew he did. Beneath
the chuckles and courtliness, beneath the soutane and chasuble,
there was his own brand of fear as real as hers. With all his Wasp
assets what explained his being there, alone, a man in his forties, in
an outpost of his church and not in the American mainstream where
ambition and immediate advantage could have put him?

"I may come to your church, Richard," she told him. "I may
even make an offering to help pay for all the drinking we do."

"Why that would be great, honey, just fine. I'll sing and preach just for you."

"You're not a preachy man, Richard—Alberto probably was, more than you. And yet you're not just bluffing—you do believe, don't you? It isn't just a line of work for you like any other?"

"Nobody likes their work," he said, bemused. Then, in his rich, throaty, upper-class voice he said simply, "Yes, I do believe. It's my problem that no one else does. I'm doing my Father McKenzie bit, honey. You know that Beatles song 'writing the words of a sermon no one will hear, no one comes near'? That's me."

Laughing, his face spread in the rippling lines of a wide James Cagney smile, he sang in rich ecclesiastical voice: " 'All the lonely people/where do they all come from?/All the lonely people/where do they all belong?' That's me—that's you, honey."

She would have reached for him, but for all their talk he had maintained an absolute physical reticence that left her stranded on the shores of that new territory they might have explored together but never would. It was as if, talking, they had sighted those shores but could never decide to leave the comfortable, uninvolved places they occupied next to each other on the ship of their tentative cruisings, to put themselves on land where life began in earnest.

He was a charming host. His chaplain's residence was ready while she was still staying at the pension waiting to get into her place. He invited her for opening dinner. "Welcome to Turpitude Hall!" he exclaimed of his small ground-floor apartment set in a garden behind a high wall. "Here I am vying in ratty splendor with all the pensions in Florence thanks to the discards of my lady parishioners."

"My foot! You're elegant, Richard, look at you—nifty slipcovers and lampshades and even a picture wall. It's me who'll be living in genteel poverty, not you. You have all the old dames to dote on you and make you casseroles. That's why you're always fussing around them."

"I like the old. They know their place, finally, and have accepted it. Not like the young, always striving for something—something better or worse, but in any case different. All those young people and their existentialism can beat the be-Jesus out of any man."

Sometimes Marguerite would stop by his place while he was still in his old college sweat-shirt and pants watering the plants he was succoring through the heavy summer. "It's not what I'd call a mature garden yet," he told her, pointing out the empty places between the drooping plants, "but it will get there. I've thought of inviting my ladies for a pot party to help fill in the empty part."

"What kind of pot is that, Richard?"

"Flowerpots, my dear. Unless you can find the other kind, and then after the others go we'll take a little trip together."

Marguerite often thought of her mother saying, "The Episcopals are a social crowd. And the higher they are, the more they drink." It was certainly true. Richard drank like the Irish she remembered at the golf club; then he'd get expansive and tell jokes.

"Do you know this one, honey? About the traveling salesman on the New Jersey Turnpike who sees a huge billboard saying 'Mother Murphy's Whorehouse, five miles ahead to Exit 32, $5 a lay.' Oh boy, he thinks, what a bargain. And then after a while there's another sign: 'Mother Murphy's Whorehouse, one mile from Exit 32.' Then at Exit 32 there's a road marker saying 'This way to Mother Murphy's Whorehouse.' He follows the directions and arrives at a gracious old home where a little old lady in lavender is sitting on the porch knitting. 'Are you Mother Murphy?' he asks. And the old lady nods and holds out her hand. 'Five dollars, please.' He gives her the five and she points out the entrance, which is all set up with neon arrows pointing the way through corridors until he comes to another door. This he opens, and finds himself back outdoors in front of a big sign that says 'You've just been fucked by Mother Murphy.'"

Laughing at him laughing, Marguerite said, "Now why did you tell me that, Richard?"

"That's me, honey, always fucked by every Mother Murphy!" He laughed hard, but his expression was a grimacing wound.

"Sometimes I feel guilty," he would say—sitting in his garden propped against a packing box, an open book in his lap—"having it so easy here with all that's going on at home. It is, after all, a very easy life." And he'd wave his hand around to include his rooms, the quiet old countrywoman who served him, and the church beyond his gate, where he saw to the minimal spiritual needs of a congregation made up of transients and the few old residents he would, in time, bury.

"Have you ever been in love, Richard?" she asked one night.

"I was waiting for that," he said dryly. He was silent a moment, dragging on his cigarette. "Yes, yes . . . very much." He spoke haltingly, as if thinking out the words. "Too much so—it's all over and gone. 'Mr. Kurtz—he dead.' Mr. Wareham, too."

She began to wonder what arrangement was possible between them. And wouldn't the folks in Gloversville drop in their tracks if she did become a minister's wife. Richard lived on a small income and an even smaller wish to increase it. She could work. Could that be an arrangement? She had realized that there wouldn't be physical love between them. "After passion," he had told her, "there comes the better part of being together—that long abiding loyalty which leaves one free of one's senses." Theirs could be a comradely arrangement, an affectionate one, and not unpleasant for either of them.

Perhaps that's what freedom was all about. To look at things squarely, see they weren't perfect and never would be, and accept them gracefully for what they were—an arrangement. She and Richard's garden could come to maturity together.

"But goddam it, Richard, is this all!" she cried. "This is what bothers me. Here I am past forty and I've gotten nowhere. Everything I thought I wanted, I've had. But Jesus, is this all?"

"Yes, honey, this is it." He spoke quietly, and the very fixity of his answer reassured her. He knew. He had looked into the nature of things and it was a goddam horror and he had the nerve to accept it.

Their arrangement, she speculated, would require separate rooms —his at one end of the hall, hers at the other—and meetings in the garden for drinks. She didn't think that the inner secrecy he so cherished would stand the closeness of even breakfast together. They could only meet on a conversational level: "Yes, honey, this is all."

By the first of June, Marguerite had moved into her lodgings in the villa. She had lined up several possibilities of steady work with the American college programs for fall and in the meantime was doing a translation. It would work out. Going to Florence was working. That Richard was there seemed to be the main part of it.

She wondered how free he was of sensual urgency. She herself could imagine being in bed with Richard, had been ready for weeks to be there; but he, she could tell, would never be.

He came to her place one evening bringing housewarming bottles of Chianti.

"Now, take this McLuhan," he said as he looked through the books on her shelves—"this bit about us being so linear, so oriented to print and so on. I keep thinking about it when I give my sermons each Sunday. No one retains anything of what I've said because we're no longer receptive that way; unless it's written, we don't remember. We've lost our sense of hearing. But with Pina, all I have to do is translate aloud a recipe for her and she's got it the first time, retained for always. Not like you and me, honey, who have to see something in print to be sure."

"It's more than the sense of hearing that's been lost—it's all the senses. But the young are regaining them, Richard; they don't sit around just talking the way we do. They communicate in different ways: dancing, singing, looking at each other, reaching for each other, touching and feeling. They're recovering their senses."

"Oh well, my dear, they've gone too far in the other direction," he said quickly, just as she imagined he would. What else? He could only verbalize about immediacy, he couldn't act it.

Some vague clues were always there, though. "Violence, it's a real erotic factor! Something we sucked-out Americans have to get back to. All our troubles started with being considerate to women. Look at the Italians, they have no problems of authority or impotence. They treat women as they do and not only save themselves, they're respected and adored by their women."

"That's something, coming from a minister and southern gentleman like you."

"Gentleman, crap! That's our trouble, honey, being sucked out by our women."

They drank the wine and smoked through the night.

"How can you smoke so much, Richard?"

"Perfectly Freudian, my dear—it's my death wish."

"But why, why—"

"I've never thought I'd want to reach my fifth decade."

"For God's sake, what *are* you doing here, Richard? You had a cathedral back there and important work to be done with racial problems. What are you doing here preaching to old lady tourists?"

And though it was her own position she was throwing up to him ("What am *I* doing here? I had a husband and a home"), it was also his. The two of them, agonizing wittily over wine and small talk, pursued what Richard in his church jargon called the ontological predicament and what she, to herself, called attaining visibility.

Why, she wondered. Why don't you reach out to me, why don't we touch? Why, when we're both suffering, don't we at least have each other?

And then he said it: "Yes, Marguerite, I believe we could arrive at an arrangement. We are two sensitive people—we understand each other's limitations and we're civil enough not to clobber each other with them, but to accept things as they are."

But later, in bed, dizzy with too much drinking and sick to her stomach, thinking over his words, she knew it wasn't enough. And she thought of another of his stories, the story of the dying girl who wanted, before it was all over, the shaggiest dog in the world. And since the girl's father was the richest man in the world, he could and did send expeditions to every corner of the globe to bring back shaggy dogs. Finally the shaggiest of them all was found and brought to the girl. She looked at it for a moment, then said "It isn't shaggy enough," and turned over and died.

Marguerite felt sick and alone. Richard's drinking and vapid socializing were exhausting her. Before falling asleep, in the last effort of thought, it came to her that Richard's waspness was nothing new. In another form it was Alberto's thousand years of Venetian family tradition all over again. If nothing was ever going to be shaggy enough, why, for Christ's sake, had she given up Alberto only to make an arrangement with Richard? To be Mrs. Wareham instead of Signora Morosini when it was all the same thing, without, however, Alberto's warming physical need of her?

She hadn't been able to see Richard before for his charming accent and James Cagney smile, for the First Families of Virginia pin he pulled out to show her, for the stories of Aunt Maybelle, and the feeling of honeysuckled verandas at the ancestral home. Richard tooling around in a red Thunderbird, Richard sparkling with wit and courtliness, Richard living on private income like someone from a Trollope novel.

It just wasn't shaggy enough.

Weezy had already gone to Rome by train for the long All Saints' holiday weekend with Alberto when Marguerite decided to drive down.

The drive down was uneventful until she entered the city. Then, because she had left Florence in midmorning, she found herself entering Rome at exactly the worst time—the critical *ora di punta*, when the intensity of normal traffic (if anything mobile in that overtaxed conglomerate of jammed streets, fumes, cries, honking, insults, collisions, grazed pedestrians, crazed drivers, virulent policemen—if any of such could be called normal) was quadrupled by everyone's going home for the midday closing of everything.

Marguerite found herself on an abnormally sweltering October 31st under the noon sun in an enormous traffic jam, before, behind, to the right, to the left, as far as she could see.

A bus strike had augmented the usual throngs of Rome cars to a gigantic monstrosity, an incubus blown up to absurdity. Jean-Luc Godard's end of the world.

After fifty-five minutes of slow passage down Via Po, she found herself stuck in the narrow funnel that directed cars from Via Pinciana to Via Veneto; stuck there in the giant pile-up not really caring much anymore if she ever got out. It could be the solution to everything: buried alive in a Rome traffic jam. Her remains to be added to the other strata of history, to be excavated someday in a fever of excitement—and all it would be was she, Mad Marguerite, the white rabbit, late of Florence, having tried not to be too late for Rome.

Everyone was in the same mess, but maybe because her car was much larger than the others, and gave the impression of blocking more, a young, open-shirted guy from a little Fiat 500, infuriated, jumped up in the open sun-roof of his car and directed his wrath uniquely to her. "*Stronza!*" he called out in rage, shaking his fist at her. That she should have been so singled out in all that mass of stalled cars was the first surprise—then, following closely, the crudeness of the insult.

Stronza . . . worse than *merde*; the hard, bulletlike turd that comes from a begrudging bowel. A tough shit. The token of uptightness. And suddenly she understood.

That guy had picked her out, unerringly, for it was the costiveness of her life which gave her a badge of recognition. Of course. The traffic began a slow, tortuous crawl. And her mind, too, accepting the violence of the purgative insult hurled at her, began to move slowly.

She reached home. No one was there. There was a telephone message from an American friend she hadn't seen in a year or so, and she called back.

"Marguerite! What's up? Alberto was very vague, says you've been living in Florence."

"Peg—Alberto and I separated."

"Oh. Whose fault is it?"

Fault? What fault? she thought, irritated at the question. But what had she expected—instant approbation, immediate acceptance, and no questions asked? "Well, Peg, no one's fault, actually . . . it's just that it hadn't worked out. We decided to separate because it was no good staying on together."

"Poor Alberto. I just couldn't help feeling sorry for him. He sounded so low."

Marguerite was embarrassed. Besides being a nuisance this separation thing was getting embarrassing. Away from Richard's contained little world, she felt self-conscious about it. As if she had to keep apologizing and reassure everyone that Alberto would be all right.

"Alberto will be all right, Peg," she said. "Come up to Florence and see me when you can."

The heat broke in an enormous thunderclap, and it began to rain. She sat in the kitchen eating the leftovers of Alberto's last dinner and wondering where he was at the moment. Probably taking Weezy out to a great lunch, she thought morosely.

She was tired and went to her old room to rest on the bed until they got back. Listening to the rain, she thought of the heavy dragging depression of Florence that had blocked her feelings, had made her a *stronza*. And a Rome traffic jam had forced that miserable, punitive constipation of feelings to come unloosed. In relief, Marguerite admitted her feelings back into her life: I am *not* forced to stay in Florence. I am *not* forced to accept the legal bureaucracy of a homologated separation decree that says I am now free. Freedom is something else. I am *not* forced to leave Alberto. I can do as I feel.

It had come to her suddenly, and like all truth it was simple, self-evident, now that she could see. The freedom she needed was to accept Alberto freely—freely and not in the pinched, miserable sense of his being a lesser evil than Gloversville, or being alone. Oh, Christ Almighty, she thought. Who says I have to prove to the world that I can work and take care of myself? Or arrange a new classy marriage for myself? Florence would be me trying another time to prove to Mother and Dad that I am as hardworking, practical, and all-American as one of their sons; that once again Mad Marguerite is up to her old tricks. That's not what I want. I don't want to be the man of the family—alone, or with Richard. I'm not my father. I don't want to be him or what he wants me to be. I am me and *basta*. I accept everything. None of it was wrong, only necessary.

She called Angela. "I'm not going to stay in Florence."

"I always thought it was a terrible idea. Everything's here. You have a husband who still loves you—you don't know what it means to be really alone."

"I think I do. I've been alone all these years."

"Is it better to be alone out of marriage?"

"It was an alternative and it was necessary to know I had it. As long as there's an alternative, we have a margin of freedom."

"Have you told Alberto?"

"Not yet."

"I told you before: He'll take you back like Jesus with his arms wide open."

"What does that mean? That I should care about making a *brutta figura*? Well, I don't."

It was five o'clock; Weezy must have gone to a friend's house. Marguerite called Alberto's office and told his secretary to leave him a message asking him to meet her at Doney's around seven.

She was sitting at the Via Veneto *caffè* when he joined her and she told him she was giving up her plans to live in Florence.

"Then you're coming home?"

"Yes. Angela said I could have her place to work in while she's gone. I'd like to set up a darkroom and get into photography seriously."

"That could be a good solution."

She looked at him gratefully, smiling. "You're beginning to understand me."

"I've told everybody we're separated," he said.

"Do you care what they think?"

"No. Not a bit. And you?"

"Not a bit." She reached over the little table where they sat and took his face in both her hands to kiss him on the lips.

He was pleased. "It took a separation to do it. It's an expensive lesson for your education."

"And for yours. Do you think I'm reaching maturity?"

"Possibly."

"I think I've always had to break with things in order to accept them."

"And now what do you have to break?"

"Nothing. I feel good. Now I can see things as they are."

"They are no different from what they've always been."

"But now I can see."

That night he came to her bed and the separation was over.

"My one terror," he said later, "was that you wouldn't come back."

"It was no mistake, Alberto. It was the only way I had; the only way I could act. I'm sorry for you it was that way. But it was as it was and now it is as it is. It's all one. I can't explain—do you understand?"

"You made me suffer, but you suffered too and the important thing is that we have enough patience and tolerance with each other not to have resentments. None of the rest matters."

They dined out the next evening and ran into Cesare Servi. "But you're always together," he greeted them; "what kind of separation is it?"

"It's a paradox," said Marguerite.

"It's over," said Alberto.

And what was it Dr. Verdile had said once? "Before I knew Zen I thought the sea was the sea, the sky the sky, and a mountain a mountain; when I began to know I found that the sea was not the sea, the sky not the sky, a mountain not a mountain; now that I know I see that the sea is the sea, the sky the sky, and a mountain a mountain."

Chapter Eighteen

"We'll abolish emotions and feelings first," he'd say, his lips drawn tightly in a grim line, "and then the senses."

"And then what's left?" she'd laugh, caressing the soft, black, curled hair at the nape of his neck. "Without love and lovemaking what good is it?"

"Better for business," he'd say tersely, appraising her with his ironic, roguish smile.

But that was later, when they had been lovers for over a year. Even then, he was as sentimental as she, and as passionate in their relationship.

His skepticism made him deny it, or at least make the attempt to keep their affair in manageable channels. Here she trusted his sense, not hers. For she was impulsive and he cautious.

"Women are a great nuisance," he was always saying.

"But I'm not just a woman for you!"

Caressing her, smiling, he'd ask, "What are you for me?"

"Did you forget! Your companion, your friend, your colleague, your collaborator."

"That's right. I did forget."

Marguerite used to fantasize that the place of love's meeting might be a shared box at the opera, a line at American Express in Cairo, or a coach in that super train, the Settebello, which shared its name with Italy's favorite prophylactic. Instead it was at a supper party at Cesare Servi's that she met Massimo Bontelli.

"Be sure to come," Servi said, telephoning her. "There'll be new writers here both you and Alberto will be interested in meeting."

"I'm sure we would," she told him. "It's just that my cousins from the States are in Rome now."

"Bring them along," said Servi, and to Marguerite it seemed a good solution for entertaining Louis and Irene Longobardi, just arrived in Italy.

She and Alberto called for them at their hotel and found them in the patio-bar having whiskey sours. ("Irene likes her drink," Carla Scalzo would have noted. "She certainly was lucky to get Louis.") Louis Longobardi, successful analyst, puffed on his pipe contemplatively, looking solemn, professional, correct, and in total control. Too much control. As if he were reminding himself constantly to be poised and wise, the remote father figure, the compleat angler, Rin-Tin-Tin. ("How are you, Marguerite?" he had said on the phone. "Good, Lou, it's a good moment for me." "That's fine—Sam and Carla told me about things and I thought we'd be seeing you in Florence. But I'm glad it's all worked out.")

Louis Longobardi looked ten years older than he was, but Irene still affected the girlishness of her high school days. While he composedly exuded middle age—portly, graying, cuffed, and manicured—Irene had the tense bright look of all women who arrive in their forties not yet ready. She wore dangle earrings and a smart black dress and the too-bright lipstick of twenty years before, when for her, as for Marguerite, to be dressed like that meant "going out."

Marguerite had fixed into Alberto's lapel a little badge that had arrived in his mail that morning: *Fa l'amore, non l'editore.*

"What does that mean, Alberto?" said Irene.

"Make love, not books," he said, pleased as always at a woman's attention; charming as always.

Irene giggled happily. "Shall we start with a kiss?"

"There's the power of the printed word for you," said Marguerite. "Irene wouldn't have thought of it otherwise."

"That has nothing to do with it—it's because I want to," said Irene as she stuck a big red kiss to Alberto's willing lips. They laughed happily, drinking their drinks, because it was a fine night and they were in Rome.

"We're double adulterers, you know, Alberto and I. That's what's being said around town. Because we're officially separated but living together—and not just for our daughters' sakes."

"Basically, Marguerite," said Louis, "you're a healthy girl."

"Oh, Lou, that's beautiful!" Jesus, how the accolades were rolling in: the Rome gossip and now the pronunciation of health by a practicing psychiatrist.

It was one of those June nights Rome as stage-setting was designed for: suave, tender, unabashedly romantic, the pines giant statements in Cesare Servi's garden. If she were aware of anything besides the night, Marguerite might have acknowledged carrying with her that evening the omnipresent parasitic sense of expectancy that she had always hosted; the pearl of hope that had accumulated around the wound which was consciousness. The expectancy of something great, some moment of grace that could, if the wind lay right, blow her way. She asked only to recognize the moment. For grace lies totally in its acceptance.

At their arrival Alberto's lapel badge made a ripple of success that carried him off and away on the attentions of Aurelia Eccli. Louis, distinguished and poised, got taken in hand, along with Irene, by Cesare with his proficient English and his literary interest in the psychoanalytic process. Marguerite looked around: Whom did she know there? Leone Eccli. She took a long drink from a tray proffered by a waiter and started to make her way toward where Leone was talking to a serious, dark-haired man.

By the time she had crossed the room through the groups of guests, Leone had moved on and Marguerite found herself next to the serious, dark-haired man. "Are you a writer, too?" she asked.

"Among other things . . . Massimo Bontelli."

"I'm Marguerite Morosini."

"Alberto's wife?"

"Do you know Alberto?"

"By name of course." He was not as young as he seemed from a distance. His tanned face and full, dark hair and leanness made him seem so among the gathering of paunchy, balding, dark-suited men. Bontelli was different not only in his youthfulness but also in the kind of wary self-consciousness that again set him off from the confidence and aplomb around them.

He was nervous, his brow furrowed with some kind of anxiety, and he spoke in rapid, short bursts, his dark eyes wandering over the room restlessly as he spoke. "I met Morosini a few years ago when he was judge at the Viareggio awards. My first book was up for the prize."

"Did you get it?"

"No. They told me it was a winner. Then they switched at the last moment and gave it to some woman writer who hasn't written another word since."

"Oh, I remember that. Disgusting. I was there, too. But that was your first book?" she asked curiously.

"I'm forty-three, and I've just started writing."

And I, I'm just starting everything, she thought.

He was smoking, she looked around to see where Alberto was. Bontelli hadn't yet looked at her directly. She felt he was as alone as she in that room and as timid. It gave her courage.

"I'm looking for a new Italian writer," she told him. "I know publishers in the States who'd be interested in having me translate someone new from Italy."

"Morosini must have my books. I've sent them to him."

"Oh, he gets hundreds of books for review—and then I'm the one who gives them away before he's read them." She said this lightly, to see if Bontelli would relax and smile. He didn't. "What are your books like?"

"Very readable," he said with directness. "Simple, immediate, and fast." He spoke in spurts, as if talking impersonally into a telephone. "I'll send you copies tomorrow."

They were like two strangers sitting on the wood bench of a cold railroad station in the country, she thought. There was the same feeling of constraint. Not as though they were in an elegant room in Rome full of important men and beautiful women where bowls were filled with fragrant, old-fashioned cabbage roses as large as peonies. Soft, lush, and faintly decadent; overdone. But beautiful.

She wrote out for him the address of Angela's place, where she had set up a little darkroom for her photos, and glanced around the room again. Irene was sitting nearby looking bemused and watching them, lulled by lots of drinking. Marguerite moved away from Bontelli toward Irene. "Don't forget the books," she said to him.

"I won't forget," he said and smiled. The smile lit up his whole face. He's beautiful, she thought.

Platters of pasta were arriving on the buffet table, and guests were serving themselves and then moving out to little tables on the terrace among the potted lemon trees and oleander. Marguerite collected Louis and Irene and found them a table outside. Returning for Alberto, she saw Leone and Aurelia Eccli with Bontelli and went to greet them.

"*Cara!*" cried the handsome Aurelia expansively.

"*Ciao*, Margherita," said the dapper Leone, a successful and sophisticated writer of Alberto's age. "Do you know Massimo Bontelli?"

"We've just met. I'm going to read his books."

"He's a man of the future—you'll see."

"Future what?" laughed Aurelia.

Bontelli smiled in embarrassment, pleased at being praised and overcome with confusion at the same time. Marguerite felt like reaching to him and saying "*Coraggio!*"

So much for history. As strangers just meeting they hadn't thrown off the sparks of an Anna and Vronsky. Yet, in that moment, if she had been asked, Marguerite would have said yes, she was sure, she was in love with Massimo Bontelli.

Louis and Irene had a full day of touring coming up, so they left the party early. Marguerite suggested they stop by for cognac in the little room she worked in up on the roof-terrace of Angela's apartment. A fabulous place, such as Rome excels in, Angela's terrace overlooked the facade of Palazzo Spada with its exuberance of inscriptions, grotesques, and figures of Roman heroes. This night the palace and all of Piazza Capo di Ferro was floodlit and caught like sculpture by the lamps focused on it from an American movie crew.

They watched the shooting so that Irene could fill herself with impressions to relate back in Gloversville. Marguerite pointed out the cupolas of the Pilgrims' church and hospice, the dark mass of the Monte di Pietà, the imposing bulk of Palazzo Farnese. Against the moonlit sky the equestrian statue of Garibaldi and the trees of the Janiculum stood out clearly, and from everywhere came the soft sound of fountains in the night. Almost to herself, Irene Longobardi, who passed in Gloversville for a woman who had everything, murmured, "I wish I were you, Marguerite."

Below them were the sounds of the people who sat out on a mild night in the dark and narrow, odorous streets that led to Campo di Fiori.

Bontelli was right. His books read well, were full of spirit and humor and a freshness that had long been absent from recent Italian writing. Marguerite called to tell him.

"Let's meet," he said. "I'm free tomorrow—it's a holiday. We could meet at Caffè Greco."

When they met she said, "We're the only people around. What is it today?"

"Corpus Domini."

"What's that?"

"God's body."

"*Mamma mia!*"

"*Beh, pazienza.*" He smiled and shrugged.

They were almost alone in usually crowded Greco's; outside, the city was deserted, even there in Piazza di Spagna around the Spanish Steps. It gave their meeting a private, intimate aspect.

"What will you drink, *signora?*"

"Tea. It was chilly and a little damp in my room—I've just come from there."

"What room?"

"A place where I work. I've fixed up a storage space on the roof of a friend's apartment into a little studio."

"What's your work?"

"I started translating Alberto's work into English and I do some other writers, too, from time to time. That's my work, I suppose." She sounded almost apologetic, as if not convinced that anything she did could be called work. Then she brightened, and looking at him steadily, said, "But what I'd really do, if I could, would be to work as a photographer and travel around shooting everything I saw."

"Why don't you? That's a beautiful thing to do, you know."

"I have a family," she said. They fell silent. She tried to retrieve things. "Are you a real Roman, or like everyone else do you come from someplace else?"

"I come from a small place in the Marche, near the sea. I came to Rome after the war like everyone else—including the Americans."

"Do you know anything about us Americans?"

"Something—why?" He gave her his suspicious, furrowed look that meant he was being careful, going cautiously until he found out what was on her mind.

"Then you know we're not formal. Don't call me *signora*; my name is Marguerite. And I'll call you—what shall I call you?"

He thought for a moment. "Massimo. Yes, Massimo."

"Weren't you sure?"

"Some call me Max . . . my mother called me Mimmo. You can call me Massimo."

"I like your writing, Massimo. How is it you just started?"

"I've been busy surviving. I've never studied. I have no culture like Alberto Morosini or Leone Eccli. I've always worked. But I'd like to study, learn languages. . . ."

"Oh, no," she said strongly. "It would be a mistake. You'd lose yourself and become just like the rest of Italian writers. You've heard them speak on TV or at lectures—it's to die asphyxiated in the smog of their rhetoric and intellectualism! They know everything and keep burying the sense of it in language and ideas. They're like that everywhere—at conferences, at dinner parties, on the beach . . . everywhere. They're intoxicated with talk. You're not like that, you don't talk at all!"

He laughed and said, "Now you know me."

She surprised herself. Why was *she* talking—and so plainly?

"All the other Italian writers are professors, teachers, critics, or literary in some way or other. You're the first I've met who isn't. Don't ruin it."

"This meeting with you has been a lucky thing for me," he said.

"Let's hope it will be lucky. I'd like to translate some of your stories. You're a real writer."

They left, and going up the Spanish Steps she said, "I've always wondered how the generals and politicians and fat old bishops make it up all those flights of stairs at the Piazza Venezia monument to put wreaths and things there on holidays. I get winded just looking."

"Like this," he said. "Walk with your head and arms a little back. That keeps you from puffing." He had, in fact, an agile effortless stride. He was not much taller than she but his body was lean. Athletic.

"Look at all the things you know; you don't have to study anything. It's been a lucky meeting for me, too. Now I know how to walk up the Spanish Steps properly."

"With all this luck we shouldn't waste it. Shall we see each other again?"

"I'm taking my cousins to Pompeii. Shall I call you when I get back?"

"Not at home. This is the number of my office. I'm there in the late afternoon."

She drove Louis and Irene south for a week, amusing them with the old saying, "Anything below Rome is Africa." At Pompeii Louis thumped his chest as in the days of old when the bell rang at mass to announce the elevation of the host. "What a great civilization!" he said reverently, communicating with his Italic roots. Marguerite took them as far as Paestum and from there sent a postcard to Massimo telling him the day she'd be back in Rome. "*Arrivederci presto*," she wrote.

The day she got back he called, and they met that evening outside Otello's in Via della Croce. He was dressed in light slacks and a blue shirt open at the neck. He was tanned, and again looked beautiful.

"Is it you?" she said.

"How was Pompeii?"

"I think some of it shocked my cousins."

"Why?"

"Oh, you know—those murals. The guide showed us the sixty-nine one and asked if we had that in America, too. I don't know if he meant the painting or the sex act, but I told him it was against the law in any case."

"No wonder everything's gone wrong over there."

She laughed, and looked up as a couple passed their table. Marguerite nudged Massimo to call his attention to them. The short, stocky woman had grayish curls all over her head, wore high white glossy boots, and was quarreling with a tall man wearing a cowboy hat and chewing a long cigar.

"You see how badly some people get themselves up," Massimo said.

"They're Americans—just like me."

"Not at all! A man can feel proud to be seen with you. What have you to do with those relics?"

"You're right. Maybe they were Australians."

Under the leafy bower vines, seated next to the bright display of fruits and vegetables, they leaned toward each other and studied the menu.

"*Ciao*, Massimo. Marguerite! I thought you were living in Florence!" A huge female form loomed over their little table. It was Clotilde Guarino—self-styled national monument of Italian letters. One of a troupe of thick-skinned, aggressive, overpowering Italian women-cultivators of their own gardens who manure with contacts their meager crops of literature. Of all of them Clotilde was the worst because she was physically so vast, so present. Marguerite remembered the time a Christian Democratic deputy to Parliament had tried to intimate to Alberto that he'd do well to consecrate an issue of the review to Clotilde's poetry and Alberto told him to go screw himself—screwing Clotilde being too improbable, even for an insult. That was Clotilde: a site of pilgrimage for young provincials arrived in the capital, who, feeling her glory, fed their own hopes; pompous, dated as the last queen of Italy, omnipresent, and dangerous to rivals and the irreverent.

"No, Clotilde," said Marguerite. "I was in Florence only temporarily." There, take the news and stuff it, she invited her silently as the large woman hung over them inquisitively.

"I've been out of touch, of course," Clotilde answered swiftly. "An International Poetry Conference in Rumania—I was the only Italian representative—and looking over various translations of my books, plus preparing my new manuscript, the American adventures of Apuleius' Golden Ass. Sometimes I'd just like to give it all up and live simply like everyone else."

"You owe it to your readers to keep on, Clotilde," Massimo told her.

Marguerite busied herself with the bread to keep from laughing.

"Oh, I know it, Massimo, but I get so exhausted; my nerves are just worn down to nothing. Call me soon—we can go to the cabaret in Trastevere where some of my things have been put to music and are being sung. *Ciao*, Marguerite; tell Alberto I think he doesn't love me anymore. It's three months since I sent him a copy of my last poetry collection and I haven't seen a hint of a review yet."

"*L'Armadio*," said Marguerite dryly as Clotilde left. "That's what she's called and it suits her fine—she's as big as a wardrobe and just as crammed full. She drives Alberto crazy. Is she a good friend of yours?"

"Couldn't you tell?" he answered sarcastically. "I see her every so often. She's on the jury of some new prize and wants me to submit my new manuscript."

"Oh, don't get involved in that scramble for prizes," Marguerite burst out impetuously. "I mean . . . you're different . . . you can make it on your own merits." She knew how stupid, how foolishly ingenuous that remark must sound to an Italian writer, for whom intrigue was the soul of life. "What I really mean is your books are alive and pointed toward the future; the rest of them are *passé*

—that's why they have to deal out prizes to each other, to remind themselves they still exist."

"What you say is right, in principle," he said cautiously, still appraising her, "but in practice it's different. How can anyone get ahead in this country without keeping in touch, seeing certain people, competing for the prizes? It's the only way to get noticed, to get reviewed, to meet people who can help."

"Is that why you see Clotilde—to have her vote? I have no vote. You're wasting your time with me."

"No, I'm not."

Why should I care about Clotilde, Marguerite thought.

Clotilde had married the brilliant critic who had started her fame, old Rouge et Boire as he was known for his drinker's nose, but that had lasted only briefly and, everyone said, was a white marriage at that. Marguerite wondered how any woman could prefer literary glory to love when she had the choice.

To Massimo she said, "What does your wife think about these literary women?" It was the first time she had mentioned his wife.

"I'll ask her when she gets back."

"Where is she?"

"She's at the sea with the children. We have a little place near Ancona."

"How many children have you?" Marguerite asked.

"Two—one, the girl, is bigger than you."

"My oldest, Tina, is also bigger than I am!"

He looked startled. "You look so young! You must have been a girl when you married."

She looked at him quizzically, a half-smile on her lips. Actually they were both the same age, and he, too, looked younger than his years.

"It's my miniskirt," she said with a smile.

Later at Rosati's they sat for a while and looked at the beautiful night and the carnival of passersby. Every so often Massimo greeted someone and presented her: "Signora Morosini." He asked if she were cold, tired, thirsty, hungry. She felt his attentiveness. She felt something more.

When it happened that the bounds slipped from a conventional encounter into something else she wasn't sure. How it happened, when, where—nothing could she recall. There was always between them the question of his stories to translate. From his calling her at home every so often, they soon began to telephone each other at preestablished times when Alberto wasn't around; they met for dinner when Alberto was busy.

In some unfixed instant their interest in each other and feelings toward each other changed. Though Marguerite searched her mind, her diary, her pocket agenda, she could not place the hour or the day. Only the reason.

Chapter Nineteen

The women and children left for the sea first. The writers, intellectuals, artists, and cultural bloc in general started departing after the awarding of the Strega literary prize. By August the shopkeepers, clerks, and civil servants departed, too. Rome was once more in the hands of the outlanders. Tourists bathed their swollen feet in the fountains and huge Rome-by-Night buses passed incessantly, spewing their exhaust fumes and exhibiting the dull stares of old ladies framed in the windows to those who spent the long nights sitting in the piazzas.

Some oases remained. Piazza Navona, with its orangish facades and green ivy, was barred to traffic and turned back to strollers . . . the hippies . . . the kids on bikes . . . the torch-swallowing men.

Massimo was still in Rome, going to his family at the sea only on occasional weekends. Piazza Navona became their scene. Marguerite met him there to go on to the Trattoria Al Antiquariato. Never had summer been so prolonged. Way into September there were days of sun and blue skies for going to the sea at Ostia, near Rome; there were long, mild nights. They walked up and down the stilled summer center of Rome, hand in hand, or his arm around her shoulder. Lovers.

"Are we lovers?" she'd ask.

"No, we're more than lovers."

"Then we're less! That's what that means. More is less, like Gropius."

"No, we have more than lovemaking between us, even if that is the most important thing. We have our work, our friendship. . . ."

"Friends for life, *amici della pelle!*"

"That's it."

But later in the night, at her room, when she asked again "Are we lovers?" he answered, "*Si, molto.*"

At times, apart from him, she would play: Let us now reconstruct the past, and try to make history out of those bits of memory, conversation, images, meetings, and all the rest that made up their story. . . .

He had been circumspect at their first meeting at Angela's when he stopped by her room to bring her a folder of his unpublished short stories. He sat uneasily on the edge of the studio couch drinking the whiskey she offered him. His reserve increased hers and they spoke only of the plans for her translations of some of the stories.

One evening they went out to dinner together, again for the reason of conferring about the translation in progress. She put on a crepe mini and a Persian necklace and Tina said "Mom's going out with her boyfriend" as she went out the door. Alberto smiled. As if the thing were so impossible. As if the explanation of meeting Bontelli for the translations were so sufficient.

They had met at Rosati's. Both of them fitted their picture of each other: Both were well dressed, handsome, likable, clean, and healthy—just like a televised commercial. Except that they were real, and he was more: He was her bridge to a new reality even though he made her passage a slow, perplexing progress.

"I saw Alberto at the Strega, Marguerite, but I didn't see you." They were driving beyond the portal down Via Flaminia toward a restaurant on the river bank.

"I was there—splendid in a lamé dress I had made up in four hours while passing through Positano with my cousins. I was at a table in front; you probably saw Alberto when he was roaming around shaking everybody's hand. Or maybe you don't recognize me when we're not together."

"No . . . no. I know you now."

"And I know you—through your writing. Were any of your books up for the Strega?"

"No. I hope the next one will be, the one I'm working on now. It should be my turn by then."

"I hope you win because you deserve it, not because it's your turn."

"*Beh*," he said derisively, his mouth grim. "Here you don't count on winning anything because you've written well, but only if the right people are well disposed toward you or you've been able to do them a favor."

"Who else did you see there?"

"The usual. You and Alberto know them all."

"*Già*, always the same. . . ."

The place on the river was beautiful. They sat on a shaded terrace overlooking a Tiber that was not the dirty downstream river that flowed sluggishly through the city, but a green swirling stream overhung by willows. A man in a canoe was paddling beneath them; two boys on the opposite bank were poking sticks into the water.

"I like this place," she told him. "It's like being in the country. What I miss most of America are the trees."

"I saw Clotilde at the Strega, Marguerite."

"And?"

"She asked me if you were still separated from Alberto. I said I didn't know of any separation—that when I met you you were with him and I never heard any differently. Were you separated?"

He spoke deliberately. His eyes—light brown, large, shining, and curious as a boy's—those eyes that usually were so distant were now carefully fixed on her. He had two looks: the distant one when he was reflective, thoughtful; and the sharp one of trying to seize precisely on things and know them exactly. He is still from the provinces, she thought, smiling at him; he is still guarded, suspicious, wary of quick actions. He likes to know how things stand and where his place is among them. Imagine with me, not only a strange female, but that quintessence of menace, an American female . . . the symbol of all that is most demanding and devouring of men. Aggressive, authoritarian, overly intellectual and systemized. No wonder he was so ultra-controlled with her. Hadn't he for years, in his work as a journalist, been exposed to those odds and ends of information and newsbreaks that make up the pocket history of the American female? It was part of his culture. It gave him self-assurance and confidence to know things exactly—to fit her, for instance, into her slot. Fortunately, he also had resources of candor, humor, and irony. She recognized in him a fundamental integrity, the reserve of one who knows the value of things.

When he first came to Rome, he told her, just after the war, he had eaten at a mess set up near the station for those who had no work, no funds. And there each morning, early, when he arrived for his bread and *caffè-latte*, he would see an old woman put together the pieces of cardboard on which she slept each night, huddled against the remains of the antique wall that served as her shelter. With dignity, with exactness, she reassembled her cardboard dwelling, tucked it under her arm, and took her place in the food line. He had learned from her how one stayed attached to life.

"Massimo," Marguerite said, "I was separated from Alberto for a few months but not anymore. I've accepted things as they are. . . . I belong with Alberto." She returned his steady look.

In the next instant he was telling her of how he lived with, but, in effect, separated from, his wife; of the other woman he had loved for years and for whom he would have given up everything—wife, children, home, career—in order to go away with her. She had had a child she said was his, but in the end she hadn't had the courage to break from her own marriage. It was now almost ten years since he had seen her and almost as many since he had thought of her.

"No matter what," said Marguerite, "it's like a moment of grace in one's life to love."

"Until it's gone," he told her.

"If one is lucky, it can come again. Twice in life, maybe, or even three times. But you have to know and accept the moment when it comes and sometimes it's difficult to know. You have to be fortunate."

She felt as if in their slow progression they had passed a first barrier. "About my separation," she said uncertainly, looking away from him into the river, the words coming out like stammers, "I'm back with Alberto . . . I'm not looking for a way out. Is that what you wanted to know?"

"Yes."

She took a deep breath of relief and looked at him again, smiling. "We go well together," he said, smiling too.

How careful he is, she thought, to make things clear at the beginning—no illusions, promises, or traps.

Once, looking across the way from Angela's roof, she saw through a window a young man in the bottom half of his pajamas just getting out of bed and she had a fantasy of desire for him. And for no other reason than that she was feeling well and the man across the way was young and beautiful. Just sensuality and nothing else. Just because she was in old Rome on a rooftop and down in the narrow streets people called to each other and laughed and sang and hung their wash and watered their plants. In the young man's room she saw old-fashioned photographs of family groups on the wall, a large *armadio*, a crucifix above the bed, the crumpled sheets. Just for sensuality she would have liked to be in that bed— just once, without complications. A brief encounter and no further disrupting of her life. Her life was at a good point, a kind of longed-for normalcy, with things going well between her and Alberto. She didn't want to upset the balance. But just because she felt well she would have liked to have been in that young man's bed across the way. That was no paradox; that's how things were. Now she felt that for Massimo.

Massimo was to call her the next day at six. But at ten to six Marguerite could stand it no longer; her home was full of intruding presences—Tina ironing in the hall, Alberto in the studio dictating to his secretary, Russo the gardener fixing the vines on the terrace. One telephone was in the studio, the other in the hall where all could hear her. There was no place to be private and get his call in that house.

She dressed quickly, and went out: "I'm going to the library." She ran in the heat to the nearest bar.

"Marguerite! I was just about to call—where are you?"

"In some bar. Listen, Massimo, can you leave the office for a moment and meet me at Greco's. I can't talk at home with all those people around, or in this bar."

She stopped off at the American library to pick up a book, any book, and it was filled with people watching television sets in the darkened room. "What's happening?" she asked the librarian who stamped the date on her book.

"Why, it's the moon launching," said the other tersely, disapproving of her not being informed of such an American primacy.

Marguerite left the darkened room of spectators and thought, It's like a bivouac. People were sitting around eating bananas, smoking, and talking, and the librarians were circulating among them emptying ashtrays full of butts and lemon peels and regulating the TV sets.

Outside the sun was strong, and she was hot and strained by the time she got near Greco's. She felt a touch on her arm and turned:

Massimo. Beautiful. In his beige linen suit and dark brown shirt, no tie, he was smiling. "You said could I come down for a moment— it's impossible to get away, but I came anyway."

He led the way to the back and ordered two *granite di limone.* She studied him; he sat at his usual distance from her. He never, in any physical way, did anything to close the space between them. Yet she couldn't mistake the warmth and excitement in his voice when the sound of it came to her through the noise of some crowded bar from where she telephoned.

"What I don't understand," she said abruptly, "is how and why we're meeting."

He looked at her several moments before answering, "Listen, Marguerite," he said patiently, deliberately. "We've both had stories in the past from which we've suffered. Now I am studying to see where this could lead. To see what can come out of this as we begin to know each other better."

Jesus! Once he told her that in his wish to improve himself culturally he had spent a whole year studying French at the *lycée*— and had come out with a zero because he was always too involved with his work to do the lessons, and too tired to remember anything. And now if she were like his French? If nothing came of his studying her except another zero? But why should she be subject to study? Why must he be so ponderous, so heavy-handed with a moment in their lives of which the only thing he could be sure of was that it, too, would pass? Why this miserly circumspection?

"I want to go away with you," she said.

He looked at her and continued to spoon up the lemon. "Where do you want to go?"

"England? Greece? Mallorca?"

"Sardegna?" he ventured.

"Castagna!" she exclaimed as if just remembering something.

"Where's that?"

"In Calabria—it's the village my grandparents came from. I'd like to go and photograph it." She was momentarily exhilarated by the idea but then everything she didn't understand about him clouded her eyes as she looked at him. Perhaps he was an illusion, like the boy in pajamas across the way. Too far to reach.

"Marguerite. This is important. I don't want to make mistakes, to ruin everything . . . to lose you."

"Listen, Massimo, you don't have to be with me or feel obliged because of my sending your stories to New York."

"That doesn't even come into the question. That whole business can go to hell. I'm with you because I want to be. And you?"

"Yes, the same." But her voice was spent. She reached for another cigarette.

"I don't want to lose you; you're what any man would desire— beautiful, elegant, cultured. You're everything ideal."

She felt defeated. He was weaving the abstraction of the ideal woman, or as Dr. V. would put it, the projection of his anima. And all I wanted, she thought bitterly, was to be a sex object. The hell with this reverence; it's getting late. She should have stopped him then, for it was dangerous and wrong, but she was both fascinated and fatigued by this cobwebbery and let him talk.

They sat in the back of the *caffè*, not near each other, sipping lemon ice in a room now filled with other couples and tourists, and she let him go on talking because it hardly mattered, the damage was done. Beauty. Poetry. A man's ideal woman. Crap. And she remembered Dr. Verdile's saying sarcastically, "There's nothing dirtier than Platonic love."

"I meet you like this," Massimo was saying, "because of Alberto's name, because of your and my home situations." She didn't stop him. She was prefiguring the end: the wearing out of each other with unresolved encounters; his wanting to play for some long-term thoroughly studied goal that was too far, too impossible for her.

"Alberto is going to Venice on Sunday for some family matter and the girls will be away. Will you come for supper? We could eat on the terrace and go over the translation that I've just finished."

"Yes, I'll come."

It was hot, she couldn't think, she looked at her watch and said she had to go. Maybe he was right. He walked up the Spanish Steps with her, and at the top, as she extended her hand to say good-bye, he took it and kissed it. But he wanted too much and too little: the abstraction of her flesh and blood and tumult of nerves.

She looked down at the hippies lounging about the steps and the balustrades, camped on the landings: flaunting, costumed, stalking crotches. Immediate and free.

What was happening to her was too stupid to be happening in this day and yet it was happening. Where today was such a wooing as that between her and Massimo still being played out. Ireland? Afghanistan? Up there on the moon?

"Do as you feel," she heard the analyst's old refrain course through her. She left and walked home.

Sunday night men reached the moon and Massimo her bed.

They dined that evening on the terrace under a moon that hung as fulvous and fleshy above Rome as the slices of melon they ate with *prosciutto*.

"How well you look!" he said, greeting her; she wore geranium crepe pajamas in which she knew, in fact, that she looked well.

The house was empty—Alberto gone, Weezy and Tina off to Porto Ercole with friends.

Roses and jasmine were fragrant in the night; the sight of Palazzo Barberini below them was a testimony of what they were and could aspire to be; the sound of the fountain a soft splash.

"I look over there every day, you know," she told him, indicating Palazzo Barberini. "And I keep thinking of Milton, the English poet, when he stayed there. He was a Puritan and yet he stayed there, the guest of Cardinal Barberini."

"Why not?"

"It seemed strange to me in the beginning—as if he were betraying his ideals. But it was his humanism that saved him. At least in Italy. Here he could accommodate everything. That's the secret of Italy. What a night! Everyone should be out in the piazzas making love to celebrate the moon shot."

It was an old-fashioned scene of lovemaking, the kind not seen in the films anymore or written in any novel.

"If you keep moving backward you'll be out of the window and in that fountain down there," he said as she kept backing away from him toward the open full-length window in her bedroom that overlooked the Barberini gardens. He was loosening the chain around her waist and undoing the pajamas.

"Do you want me to tell you the truth?" she whispered as his hands found her. "I had planned to sleep with you this night."

"Was that your plan? You had already decided on it before I got here?"

"Yes."

"*Brava.*"

"And you?"

"I was oriented the same way."

"Truly?"

"Yes. Depending on how you acted." He took her head in his hands and kissed her gently, tentatively. He took her hand and led her toward the bed. She hesitated.

"But now . . . now I feel . . . I think. . . ."

"Don't think—it takes you away."

They made love with a moon orange and luminous as her desire visible through the window . . .

"You are beautiful as the sun," she said, feeling the strong warmth of his body, his exploring hands and tongue and eyes. A true collision of bodies, limb for limb; eyes stuck to eyes and mouth to mouth. No marriage of true minds, but a delectable physical feast.

"You are splendid, like a girl . . . firm and nervous, and you come strong like a girl."

"Why did we wait? Were you suspicious because I'm American?"

"Yes, maybe . . . and the fact that you're Alberto's wife—I don't want to risk losing you."

"Now do you know you won't?"

"Yes, now I know."

They didn't wait any longer. They had little time before he joined his family in the Marche. She began to suggest to Alberto that it was time for them to get a place away from Rome, at the sea —in the Marche region, for example, near Ancona.

Skills sharpened. She grew adept at calling and meeting Massimo. Sometimes he could arrange his time so that he found daytime hours to come to her place at Angela's. *Casa nostra*, he began to call that shed on the roof.

It was like being in a ship, or in some small log cabin in the wilderness. Even when, as they made love, the street sounds of passing boys and vehicles or the sharp tirade of the woman they called Principessa Spada pierced the walls, they were alone, contained, out of the world and time and pressure.

"Do you know what I think, Massimo?"

"What, *amore*. Tell me."

"That when we're both famous they'll put a plaque on this build-

ing to say that here we loved each other. But not a short plaque—
a long one covering the whole front wall and saying that in this
palace, a former *dépendance* of the princely Spada family, there
lived from the time of its renovation the following occupants: an
Italian deputy to Parliament; a young political-geographer working
hard to finish his dissertation so that he could marry his sweetheart,
who came to visit him on weekends; a young French dancer named
Philippe, whose naked torso appeared each evening in the large
window overlooking the piazza; an American guidance counselor
who had in his bookcase a volume called *The Honest Way to Sex*;
a lady called Portia Paradise; two call girls who arrived late at
night with gentlemen callers; and on the roof, above the top-floor
apartment of the famous journalist Angela Cambio, the American
photographer Marguerite Morosini, who was made love to by the
illustrious writer Massimo Bontelli. This was the moment of the
palazzo's chief glory. It was restored for rental by a diplomat's son
with a lot of time on his hands. It was cleaned by Maria. It was
cool in the summer and probably also in winter. But there were
fireplaces in each apartment, and the room on the roof had a wood-
burning stove; and as soon as the great Italian writer had been
translated into English and sold into American dollars by his love
they got a bundle of money with which to buy a Peruvian fur rug
to put on the floor in front of the stove where they made love from
the hours of two to five and nine to eleven—until the writer decided to retire from his work and spend all his time on his art. The
fire was incensed by the pinecones the writer and his love gathered
at Fregene. There were cushions and clothes all over the floor. The
sailcloth curtains were pulled down because the room was only an
arm's reach across the alley from the neighbors, who hung out of
their windows. The terrible voice of the fishwife known as Principessa Spada tore through the walls as she harangued her husband,
the prince. The writer and his love were usually wise and provident
enough to have bought a roast chicken, bread, and *castagnaccio*
from the *rosticceria* in Campo di Fiori, which they ate under their
blanket, like Bedouins, to restore themselves. But sometimes she
had to search the place for crackers and a can of sardines. Then
they showered downstairs in Angela's place, and he went to work
and she returned home. Thus was fame conferred on this palace
situated in Piazza Capo di Ferro."

"*Ti voglio tanto bene, amore.* You are a precious thing for me."

"Are we lovers?" she asked.

"Almost," he said, smiling.

"We understand each other, don't we?"

"Completely."

And as he showered, she thought, the best sign is that I can hardly remember the past; all the rest is hardly there . . . or, if there, finally weightless. Gloversville, London, Washington, Florence, the moving back and forth, the regrets—gone now.

"When will you bring your shaving stuff? I'd like to see it here," she called over the running water.

"The next time." Then he came into the room wrapped in a towel, drying himself and watching her put on her underclothes. "Let me see you, *amore*; let me see how elegant you are."

"What is it your son says?" she said, coming over to open the towel and put herself inside with him.

"He says, 'You have to be gentle with women—right, *papà*?' 'Certainly,' I say. And he, 'But we men command, right? We decide.' 'Yes,' I say."

"I like that. I like you." She stepped back and looked at him nude, his body brown and matted with wet hair.

"Friends for life," she said, hugging his damp body to her.

"For life," he echoed.

Chapter Twenty

Many externals imposed on their separate lives but Marguerite and Massimo pooled their network of friends and both managed to be at the same places together.

It was a wonder to her that they managed it in the complexity of their different lives. But they did. (*Squisitamente italiana*, old Bacchetti could have written of their relationship, for where else but in Italy could it have flourished so well?)

When fall came they left the piazzas and started meeting at Otello's.

"I had a tape all made and ready to switch on if by chance Alberto answered the phone tonight instead of you," said Massimo, greeting her.

"Why can't you talk to Alberto? He knows I've got this translation thing with you."

"No, I can't at the moment. Perhaps later. But it bothers me if he answers."

"What did the tape say?"

"How to vote in the coming elections—monarchist."

She laughed. "Is that what you'll do?"

"I won't vote anything. They're all the same—impostors. Most people I know woke one morning toward the end of the war and declared themselves socialists. The night before they had been fascist. Now they're warming up to communism. Look at Leone: He likes to act the man of the Left but he's the first to want to live in bourgeois comfort."

"When I tell this to Aurelia she says I'm a baby about politics—*un'innocente*. Alberto is certainly more honest than Leone and the rest of them. They think his Catholicism is only a sham to advance himself with the Christian-Democrats. And the Christian-Democrats abhor him because he's for the pill, for abortion, for abolition of religion in public schools, and even, in theory, for divorce. He writes as he wishes and no party wants him because he's too free. He is what he is from conviction, not from what's fashionable in politics."

"Alberto," said Massimo deliberately, "has his own reality, just as we have ours. No, he has more than we; he has his serenity, too." He looked at her with concern. "You're not eating. What do you want? Figs . . . melon . . . ice-cream . . . grapes?"

"Nothing, only to be with you."

In the car he pushed back her skirt, saying, "It gives me such a feeling of tenderness toward you—the way you come to meet me with such naturalness. As if you had no other problems, no worries, no other life. You have this directness that is very moving; it makes you incredibly young and fresh. But how can it be? You've suffered, too. Your life hasn't been easy."

"I have a whole inner life of my own." She smiled at her words.

"*Già!* That's what saves us!"

Up in her room they undressed in the light of a kerosene lamp. He was a tender lover, and a strong one—generous, expert, demanding. "What are you thinking of?" he asked afterward, as they lay entangled.

"You know—that you are as beautiful as the sun. More beautiful than . . ." She looked to the rafters, her hands tracing the space, groping for help.

"Than Cesare Servi? The pope?"

"That's it," she laughed, kissing him.

"You too."

"*Buffone!* . . . Are you a pirate?"

"Why?"

"You're so dark . . . like a Saracen, a Turk, an Etruscan."

"I was very light as a child. This is my real color," and he pointed to a minute strip of lighter flesh just above the groin, which was the only part of him not tanned by the sun.

"I like you dark, and your skin tasting so salty from the sea."

"I'll go to the sea every day until November to store it up, and during the winter I'll use a sunlamp if you like me like this."

"And I'll do exercises to keep my figure and have massages once a week."

"*Amore*, you don't need massages. Look at you—you're perfect as you are, firm and well made. Better undressed than dressed. What you have to arrange is some night course in something so that you can get out two or three times a week. We can go to the theater, or visit the galleries, or come here. Then in the spring we'll go back to the beach."

It sounded as if they were starting a lifetime together: November! the winter! the spring! Could she believe they would be together so long? That after each encounter there would be another chance to meet and love again?

"Massimo, Alberto's going to give a talk in Ancona, and he says that it would be a good time to look for a place in the Marche near the sea. Then you and I can be near each other in the summer, too."

"You have a great need for affection, haven't you?"

Marguerite shrugged her shoulders and looked away. He smiled, caressing her: "Yes, you strong American women can do without it!" His first American, he told her; and she answered, "My first Etruscan."

"I thought that night at Servi's that you were cold, businesslike, arrogant," he said. "Your face was so impassible, so resigned. Then you'd smile and it was like a flower opening."

"You're my sun. I keep asking myself what good I did in life to deserve these moments."

"*Esagerata!*"

"No, truly. Can't you tell what I feel for you? You are a beautiful thing for me. And now I know what I did—I waited, I never gave up hope."

"I feel a great tenderness for you, *amore*."

"Tell me."

"I feel well with you, we go well together. In every way. *Ti voglio tanto bene.* I am glad to have you—physically, above all physically."

At midnight they dressed and went out. "What will Alberto say about your coming in late?" he asked.

"I've already told him I'm going on a Rome-by-Night tour with some American friends."

They walked over to Piazza Monte di Pietà, where her Fiat station wagon was parked in front of the municipal pawnshop. "This car!" he said, amused, studying the hulk with its great rusty superstructure of a baggage rack, the chrome stripped from its side by innumerable encounters in Rome traffic, the broken tail-light and bent fender, and in the back, two antique candlesticks, stuck among beach mats, hats, and odd plastic bags from supermarkets.

"It's more like a dump truck; only a *signora* like you could drive it anymore."

"Let's go to Porta Portese, I want to sell the candlesticks and get some wood for my stove."

"*Amore mio, tesoro*, there's no one there now. I've told you and I'm sure—it would be impossible for something to be going on in Rome that I don't know about."

"Listen, Massimo, my American friend told me she got her best bargains going there on Saturday nights when everyone's just arriving and setting up their stands for the next morning. They sit around campfires, eating and singing. It's much better now than when the tourists go in the morning."

"Then let's go. Even if you won't get more than a thousand lire for both these candlesticks. How much did you pay for them?"

"Seven thousand each, or was it both? We'll sell them for twenty." He put his arm around her and laughed.

It was a still, mild night. He drove toward Palazzo Farnese, where the striped Gothic tower of St. Brigid of the Swedes was illuminated and the two giant fountain-basins were empty of the neighborhood urchins who swam there by day. The whole piazza was still. In front of Palazzo Farnese a young couple sat and clung to each other, kissing; further along the stone ledge two old men talked quietly. Campo di Fiori was deserted, all the commotion of the market now swept away with the garbage, leaving only the odor of the fish stalls permeated in the old cobblestone pavement, five centuries strong, despite the daily hosing. Giordano Bruno, hooded, stood brooding on his pedestal over the shadowy place where he had been roasted.

"Rome-by-Night," Marguerite called out as Massimo circled Palazzo Farnese, swung under the green-festooned archway of Via Giulia, and went over the bridge that joined the Tiber island to both banks and led into Trastevere. Rome swept clean of its traffic; emptied of exhaust, sweat, odor, closeness, frustration, nerves, rage. A fabulous city. Castel Sant'Angelo. The dome of St. Peter's. The leafy plane trees along the river. She thought, I'm sitting beside Massimo, my knees turned toward him as sunflowers turn to the light, and we're driving through Rome after midnight to go to the flea market and sell these crumbling candlesticks of the eighteenth century that someone stole from a church altar and sold to me.

But the long wide avenue at Porta Portese, so thronged and jammed on Sunday mornings with all the debris of the world, was empty and dark. "*Amore mio*, I knew there would be no one here at night."

"It was possible. . . ."

"Yes, it was possible; that's why I brought you. Do what I say—use the candlesticks for lamp bases. I'll get you wood for the winter."

Yes, the coming winter, when he foresaw them in front of the stove at her place. Again he spoke of a future she had never programmed. An encounter, yes—but this beautiful thing? To imagine spring seemed almost too much.

As their meetings went on and entwined the strands of their separate lives indissolubly together so that they talked of his work, her work, his children, her children, his wife, Alberto, and all their previous time before knowing each other, fashioning themselves joint dimensions—as, in short, they created themselves as a couple—she began to believe in them. She began to count on all the things he said they'd do together: go to his hometown in the Marche and drink the wine there with his friends, go photograph the castles of Apulia, go to the sea, to Rumania where his books were being translated, to America, to the shirt maker's and have matching shirts made.

"Our summer is over," Massimo said toward the middle of October. They were gathering dried stalks from among the beach pines at Fregene, and he was cutting her some that ended in feathery plumes.

He set out their program. "I don't want you at loose ends, missing me and turning sad again when there are no more beach days. While I work, you have to also. At least three or four hours each day on your photos, getting together material for a book and doing research so that you can have it set out in rough form by spring. We'll see each other the nights you can get out and whatever afternoons I can manage."

He believed in her project, encouraged her in it: for years she had talked vaguely about photography to Alberto but he had never been much interested, considering it a pastime.

"This time you'll do it," said Massimo sternly as they ate *grissini* and grapefruit from her beach bag. "You'll do it because I want you to. If you haven't finished by next spring, you won't come here with me again. Remember."

"Blackmail!"

"In between, in your free time, you can work on the translations for me."

"Jesus! There won't be time for lovemaking."

"There'll be all the holidays—the American ones as well as the Italian."

"We do spend all our holidays together," she told him as they went up the stairs to her room, "even if it is only by coincidence."

"What's today?"

"Armistice Day. And I've got pot to celebrate."

It was a Sunday afternoon. She brought, carefully wrapped in tissue, the bit of grass that a hippie friend of Tina's had offered her after being given dinner and a place to sleep one night.

They rolled two joints which they smoked, blowing the smoke into each other's mouths, dropping sparks, making faces at the dust that gathered on their tongues, and waiting to see what happened.

"*Tesoro*, this stuff is tea—*camomilla*," Massimo told her disparagingly. "Either you were given the wrong stuff or everything they say about marijuana is exaggerated like all publicity."

But they made love, and then again, laughing in the intervals while they stuck close to each other under the blanket.

"Massimo . . ."

"Ummm . . ."

"What are you thinking?"

"I feel very close to you, *amore*. In more ways, perhaps, than to anyone else I've known. I dreamed I was in the Marche being hunted by some kind of secret police and I fled from there to Rome, all the way over rooftops, to your place here. Our place. Because it was the only place I felt safe, and I knew you would take care of me. If you were to go or disappear my days would have no meaning, there'd be this monstrous emptiness; I'd feel lost, unsure, disoriented."

"I love you, Massimo. You see—I'm not afraid to say it. I love you. And you?"

"*Ti voglio tanto tanto bene.*"

"It's not the same."

"It's more."

"You've said that before. . . ." It was something she had always noted. The gravity of words between them was different—as if the intentions were different. Love/like, for instance. Or lovers/friends. She loved him, he liked being with her. He said it was more than love because there was their companionship, their work in common, their being friends, their dried thistles, their gathering wood together from the piles of pruned branches along the river like squirrels making provisions for the long winter before them.

She accepted it. She told him, "I am not for you what you are for me. But it's true in a relationship: One of the two always puts more into it than the other."

"Which of us is putting in more?"

"Why me, of course," she laughed.

"We're in this together," he said. "Just as with our work. Equally."

"We've only made three hundred dollars together so far on the stories of yours I've translated. About two hundred thousand lire, at the current rate of exchange. Not enough to live on."

"Enough for a month if we were careful."

"But we're not—we don't eat bread or pasta or rice or any of the other cheap things. And we drive two cars."

"We could sell one."

"But then we'd start to fight over who gets the only car."

"Well, at least the house is free. *Casa nostra,*" he said.

"What there is of it—two chairs, a table, a daybed, two forks, two plates, two glasses, a bottle of gin, carrots, stalks of thistle, a wood stove, and my darkroom stuff."

"You forgot all that wood I lugged up here."

She took his hands in hers and studied them. "I love your hands, Massimo. I noticed them immediately the night we met."

"They know every bit of you; they've explored every part of you. I'd know your body among any others even if I turned blind."

"And I know you." As, in years of marriage, she had never known her husband.

Thanksgiving Day night they made a fire, and roasted chestnuts and sausages in the stove. They threw some of the pinecones gathered at Fregene onto the flames, inhaling the fragrance of them as they sat on the rug before the fire; she slashed the chestnuts and wrapped them in foil to put in the embers, while he skillfully wound the sausages in a circular form on her knitting needle. Then they lay together under the blanket on the couch, watching the shadows on the wall and looking up at the branches of dried thistle and burrs that she had stuck among the rafters.

"Massimo, is it true for you that when you are working well, writing something that is going well, sex is not so important?"

"Yes, it's true. I could do without. . . . I don't even think about it."

"What are the big things in life, Massimo?"

"I don't know."

"Of course you do—your work. . . ."

"Yes, my work."

"I'm one of your works, too," she said. "You've given me hope for myself—for my work. It never happened before."

They lay in the light of the stove's soft, rosy glow. It made him as he reclined on his side, torso nude, his legs under the blue blanket, like an Etruscan sepulchral image, recalling those happy images of man and wife banqueting on the lids of their stone sarcophagi. Then she sat across him, leaning into the curve of his shoulder, her legs over his on top of the cover, white and long in the candlelight. And they banqueted too, picking up the sausages and eating them with their fingers till the fragrance of herbs and spices and the slipperiness of the grease was all over them. Then she got up and brought over a melon.

"A melon in this season, *tesoro*." He frowned, looking at it suspiciously.

"This is a Spanish melon and this is its season. Don't be afraid—it's delicious. I like to eat in bed. Like this. With you. And you?"

He smiled and caressed her hair, her cheeks. She leaned over to kiss him, to suck and bite the hollow of his shoulder blades, feel the thick mat of hair on his beautiful chest, slide her hands over the still-tanned musculature of his arms, hold his thickening penis against her breast.

He said, "I wish I had known you as a girl. I can imagine you there, in America, in the cold and snow, laughing, your cheeks red and your eyes glowing."

Marguerite said, remembering, "I miss the trees of my childhood—those beautiful tall leafy trees Italy doesn't have." The elms of Prospect Avenue shading the sidewalks and casting their generous shade in the still summer days as she sat at an orange crate in front of the house to sell lemonade; the spasm of fall—unbearable suspense as she tried to hold back forever that moment of color which, too soon, fell dead; the glossy horse-chestnuts collected by the pocketful, the leaves, the milkweed, the bicycle rides to the country to catch butterflies in an improvised net and smoke cornsilk in a field. The cold blue nights of winter, sad with streetlights already lit at five o'clock, and the peril of dusk, when frozen numb and holding back tears, she and Sammy trudged the long way home from sledding. The distance was immense, and the home when they reached it, a haven blissful beyond all imagining.

The ordinariness and peacefulness of that child's life lay, in memory, like a cooling shadow on the too-heightened moments of her present existence.

He made love to her and she to him, and she could feel her body drawing itself up from far off, coming closer and closer to that invisible point of her coming—like shock waves; she trembled all over. The little waves rippled over her and began to converge at her groin. She felt doors opening, whole abysses opening as her entire body flexed itself for ecstasy. And when it came over her it was an explosion of everything that had been held back, taut and trembling, to await that moment. She came strongly, spasms overcoming her and making her thrust him away in the excess of feeling. She pushed at him, clung to his hand in a fierce grip, heard him groan. To die like that—entwined, indissoluble, not alone.

From a distance came the screams of Principessa Spada; below them in the street, two loud jabbering women had passed by. Other voices came, filtered through the night from below, behind, around them. All those people walking, talking, discussing, raging, figuring, attacking, thinking, sublimating; and they, there, immobile now in each other's arms.

"I love fires," she said after a while. "I remember wondering why we never had them in our fireplaces at home. The fireplaces were all set up—logs on andirons and all the tools right there, but they were never lit."

"You didn't need them. Your house was heated by radiators, wasn't it?"

"Massimo! I don't mean for heat! I mean for love or friendship or just feeling good together. You know what I mean."

Like this, she thought; when before had she ever had this same balm of serenity? This beautiful understanding?

"I feel at such peace here," he said. "It's as if I leave all my afflictions outside these walls. My work . . . the book that's still to finish . . . all my problems . . . even my ulcer. Everything disappears. We go well together. If we had met sooner, we could have had our lives together."

"We can still have it—forevermore." But even as the syllables "forever" formed she knew the word shouldn't have been pronounced. What made her say it? What made her bring into their little room the notion of time? Of all the words in the love lexicon "forever" is the worst, and once it's said, it's like a sinister, reverberating echo that never stops. What pushes it into utterance is the beginning of doubt, the premonitions that happiness must have an end. Marguerite would have taken it back, but there it was, out of reach, among the shadows flickering on the walls. She put her hand in his. The best, as Massimo always told her, was not to think.

Forever. She wanted to preserve in perpetuum this instant of their lives. As if, the photo snapped, that moment could continue to be projected onto the screen of their future like some Andy Warhol movie that showed only one frame over and over. But it couldn't be. Each succeeding moment altered the one before. Nothing was constant.

"Massimo, do you really think your life would have been better if you and that woman you loved had gone off together?"

"If she had been you—yes."

Marguerite understood; that would have been the right combination of love and like. She alone wasn't.

"Let's not talk about the past," she said. "What can I do to make you laugh?"

"Tell me about your cousins in Pompeii."

For her, too, it was useless to think back to the mistakes of the past, to wish them undone, to wish she had made other decisions, been braver, more positive, affronted her life in a different manner. What was done was past; what was now was relevant.

What a pastiche, she thought, are the emotions. You can't depend on anything. She had thrust herself into his life, wanting him; but she hadn't planned on loving him.

No matter how it went, he was illuminating part of her way. Maybe she shouldn't ask more. And of whom could she ask it?

Chapter Twenty-one

"It sounds *poco* Zen," Dr. Verdile said, stomping the tobacco into his pipe with his usual irrefutable air. She might have given up analysis long ago if it hadn't also served as an alibi for where she spent evenings out. She told Alberto she was going to Dr. Verdile, and whether she did or not, she had those nights free to go to her place to meet Massimo. In the beginning she had stopped in first to see Dr. V. just to keep the thing going, and also because, despite her wanting to feel him extraneous, he was still the maestro, the guide, the wizard, the comforter, the interpreter. Even when he irritated her it was part of the necessary tension that generated the dynamics of their steady, evolving dialogue.

After the first year or so of her being with Massimo she began seeing Dr. Verdile regularly again.

She regarded him steadily, studying him, irritated as he pronounced her affair with Massimo not very Zen-like.

"It seems to lack spontaneity . . . serenity . . . joyousness," he continued.

"Naturally—the part you hear."

She was recounting the anxieties preliminary to each of her meetings with Massimo: the necessary machinations and the resulting intricacy her life had taken on. "After all, life is also contingent; it isn't just our good, inner resolves to be healthily egotistical that decide everything." Did he think she just walked out the door saying "*Ciao*, see you later, I've got a date with my lover now"? Is that what Verdile imagined? Couldn't he conceive the stresses implicit in her arranging her time within the network of Massimo's? Did he know what it was to have teen-age daughters?

"There are all these external pressures. . . ."

"You always tend to look outside either for the motivation or the excuse. What of inside?"

Già: her inner doubts. Her fear of not fulfilling Massimo's expectations of what she could do for him; the pressure of time and aging; her jealousies of the time she wasn't with him; her anxieties about his work and health; her momentary discomposure at Aurelia Eccli's brusque question, "Are you and Bontelli in love? I told Leone I bet you're already lovers"; and her growing dependence on Massimo. Somewhere she had lost her footing from that safe hold she had reached with Alberto. Somewhere the balance had tipped and made her no longer her own woman, but Massimo's.

There was more: the way Massimo referred to his wife. His domestic, he called her. Marguerite understood Massimo's estrangement from that woman, but it bothered her that on the one hand he despised his wife for not having evolved with him and on the other he put up with the situation for the sake of being served and seconded in everything. In comparison Alberto was a generous husband, and though Marguerite had jested with him about it for years, a faithful one.

Did she get along with Massimo only because they had no life in common? She didn't see to his shirts, his shoes, his special diets; she wasn't left home while he went to the theater, to art openings, to dinners and receptions as the escort of other women. "He's married according to municipal records," Aurelia said once, introducing Massimo at a party, "but you can consider him a bachelor." No one had ever met his wife.

Marguerite couldn't be jealous of such a wife, only of that previous great love for whom he would have given up everything; and then one day, in an inexplicable burst of apprehension that made her ask if there were others, she learned that, yes, there were other women he saw from time to time.

"Then I took this too seriously! Our being together is only another casual experience for you."

"How can you think that? This is serious!"

"If I had known . . . I would have never started with you."

"Listen, Marguerite, I had a whole pattern of life going before we met—other involvements. I can't suddenly undo the strands overnight. People are involved. It takes time."

"And what am I in this pattern?" she asked bitterly.

"You are the center! The one point in all the tangle. You have to be patient while I undo the rest. I can't hurt people."

"But what about me! Why did you start with me if you were already entangled?"

"That's why I went so slowly . . . I told you before, I didn't want to lose you."

She tried to tell herself she shouldn't suffer; it was she, after all, who had forced things, who had intruded into his already patterned life—but she did suffer.

"Massimo . . . I don't know . . . I'm confused. Maybe it's better if we don't see each other."

"Are you sure you aren't making one of your usual mistakes? You're the kind of woman who goes right to the end of something even with mistakes."

"Which is the mistake? Maybe being with you is the mistake."

"*Amore mio*, I know what we feel together. I have no regret about us. We've given each other something . . . have much more to give. We need each other."

"Massimo, I don't want to think about it. I don't want to struggle with this anymore."

"You're right. Accept it as it comes."

"It was my fault for taking it too seriously."

"But it is serious! This is no adventure, nothing casual. In a year, two years—five years from now, you'll think back to this time and laugh at your doubts. Everything else is meaningless. I'm not going to waste myself anymore. We have a long time ahead of us. You have to take it seriously."

He was right and yet he wasn't. It was all part of his waiting game, his keeping her involved with him while he refused total commitment. It made her demanding and unsure.

It made her, in her moments of deepest honesty, know that Verdile was right: Her situation was, by now, not very Zen. Because it had changed in a year from a free encounter into that last refuge of irreality, that last abstraction: the Love Affair. She was contriving her old error of casting her life into categories and trying to define herself. ("Are we lovers?" she asked, wanting to be systemized by a word, a slot. And for what? If she didn't feel what she was, what they were together, without Massimo's saying it, what good was it to be told?)

Loving Massimo, she had succumbed to the old affliction of fixing a point of arrival and, once arrived there, raising the old cry (hers and everyone's) "Is this all?" She remembered Richard's calm answer to that query: "Yes, honey, this is all."

So this was a love affair, she thought. For each joy you paid out huge sums in uncertainties, jealousies, the anguish of a predictable end, the loneliness of never being completely with your man, the rage of not being part of his life, the sadness of not having with him anything of the real stuff of life but only occasional moments of love.

Like Anna Karenina, all we have is our love, she thought.

"*Poco* Zen," said the analyst, drawing on his pipe. "You are like a teen-ager," he remarked ironically. "Why not?" she replied heatedly. Could she be more Zen than that? Without strain, just naturally, trusting her senses.

Like the time Massimo had asked about the melons.

"How do you choose a melon?" he had asked one late summer night as she rose from the daybed to go about the room gathering the pieces of her clothing she had flung off. He was lying there eating the slivers of melon she had prepared for him.

"What do you mean?"

"Do you pick it out yourself or take what they give you?"

"I pick it up and feel it and smell it. Don't you taste how good that melon is?"

"Superb. That's why I asked—you've gotten me used to having the best."

"The best of what?"

"Melons."

"*Sciocco!*"

It was through his questioning that Massimo knew her. Like the night on the river when he asked about her separation. She answered correctly both times—about her marriage and about the melon. She told the truth without calculating whether she should or not.

That was then. But how would she answer about her marriage now? It was as if she had congratulated herself too soon on achieving her liberation. Now that she loved Massimo, what had happened to the equilibrium she had reached with Alberto? Would she start a new upheaval? Yes, she thought; but only if she felt Massimo's love strong enough to strengthen her. If it wasn't an abstraction, but was real. And how would she know? Only with her senses? Unfortunately, no; there was more to it than that.

Somewhere she had been trapped: a little by his casual talk of the future (their future); a little by her need for security; a little by forgetting Dr. Verdile's prime injunction, "Nothing lasts"— everything changes in accordance with its own inner rhythm.

She had begun to play her own games, gambling on Massimo's vanity and ambition; if she gave him the satisfaction of being published in America, this of itself would tie him to her. He was driven by the need to succeed as a writer. He gave her clues for helping him: Alberto and Alberto's friends were influential figures in the literary world.

Yes, she had her problems. She couldn't let Dr. V. add to them with his *poco* Zen comment. Did he imagine that love could be only joy? The truer the connection between her and Massimo the more she would suffer, the more she would feel.

"Love isn't just a picnic," she told Dr. Verdile, and he looked at her through his pipe smoke and smiled.

Maybe he thinks it's not love, she thought, and began again to dislike the idea of being there to discuss things that were, after all . . . what? Personal? How absurd could she get. Everything she had ever told him had been personal, had been the very flesh flayed from her bones.

"I thought it was you who didn't want complications," he continued, smiling amicably and knocking the ash from his pipe. "Wasn't your idea a kind of lover with whom you could have a brief experience of purely sensual abandon and then he would obligingly disappear so as not to disturb your new freedom and your new balance?"

"It's my good fortune to have found more. Look at all the time we've been together."

"Why do you measure it in time? It's the intensity that counts."

"It is intense—it's everything."

"Then why don't you enjoy this relationship more? Why is it so full of anxieties for you?"

Oh, Christ! Would he never understand? Should she tell him only of the good times . . . of the conversations after lovemaking . . . of what Massimo was doing for her?

Like just last week, when he had come to the studio and had

gone over to her worktable and leafed through her pile of photos. "Your work is getting better and better," he said as she watched. "*Brava*! I knew something had to be born from us—a child, a book, something!"

"Madonna! Not a child—Audrey Hepburn just had one."

"And so?"

"And so I'm glad it wasn't me."

"You take the pill, don't you?"

"Of course."

"Still, something has to be born from us."

"*Your* book, Massimo. The one that will win the Strega."

"I'm pleased that you're working. This is important for you."

"I've always wondered why you've taken it so seriously."

"*Amore*," he said patiently, "what have you done in life up to now?"

"Two husbands, three children," she said, unloosing his tie. "And the library at St. Gregory's school."

"And?"

"I learned Italian." She unbuttoned his shirt.

"And?"

"I've done a part of Alberto, too."

"Now it's time to do yourself. You've tried to be an Italian wife, but now it's time for you to develop your own personality. The most important thing in all this business is our work."

"More important than life? Whatever I'm able to do now is only because my life is going well."

"No, *mia cara*, it's not like that. It's not that your life is going well but that you've come back to life from a long hibernation. Coming back, you're seeing things freshly and creating. It's this that makes you feel your life is going well."

First she thought, He's right; the work is important. But then, no; what good would any of it have been without him?

In her clear moments she knew that she was seeing the two of them disjointedly, only in the good scenes. Like editing her photographic shots and taking only the pleasing ones. As if the possibility of living with him in the future weren't also other images: waking in the morning with puffy eyes and bad breath and putting on an old bathrobe to make breakfast; his coming home at noon to the conventional Italian dinner, which would take up all her morning to prepare and mean sacrificing her freedom as she didn't with

Alberto, who was used to American ways; his going off in the evening, leaving her alone while he developed his contacts; their never being invited anywhere by the friends who would remain loyal to Alberto; her growing loneliness and resentment; her daughters' hate.

There was even the question of his shirts. He had his shirts made to order. Twelve to fifteen thousand lire each. He dressed carefully, he kept his body well. He looked like a boy. His one extravagance was those shirts—she loved especially his blue ones, or the warm brown and apricot ones. And if they were living together who would iron his shirts or squeeze the grapes he drank fresh in the morning?

No, they would never make it together. They could do so now only because, in their separate lives, they were free of each other.

Dr. Verdile was right. To have turned her encounter with Massimo into a Love Affair with all its attributes of irritability, explanations, questionings, and insecurity was *poco* Zen. Like that conversation after she had first learned of Massimo's other involvements with women.

"If I had a complicated life like yours," she had said, "and if from a feeling of sympathy, or loyalty, or simple attraction to a person I had once loved I found myself again—even if only for once—with someone from my past? Gillo, say, or the Englishman . . ."

He had pushed her away so that he could look at her directly in the eyes, his face serious. "Why do you joke like this?"

"I'm not joking, I'm asking. You've told me how it is with you."

"I told you with me it's different."

"Yes, I know, you're a man. An Italian."

"If you want to know, I'll tell you. I wouldn't make a scene. I wouldn't say anything. But you'd never see me again. I'd just go out of your life without a word."

"But that's cruel . . . that's terrible. Why? Even after all we'd had together? Why?"

"That's how it would be. Rationally I could understand you and forgive you and accept you, but on a visceral, physical level it would be over between us."

"You pretend a lot!"

"I pretend everything while we're together."

"Yes, and the irony is that you don't love me; it's Alberto who does."

"You did the best thing in going back to Alberto."

"But, Massimo, I love you . . . I want to be with you."

"I'm not free, *amore*. We're both buried in our separate situations, and this you knew from the start."

He told her then, as he had told her many times before, that all they could hope for was to bypass the worst part of their separate lives, holding each other by the hand in the brief time they could snatch from the rest. For as long as they could.

Dr. Verdile might be right. And likewise the words of old Maria, who cleaned her room on the roof: *Finchè c'è, vive il Re. Quando non c'è più, vive Gesù.* "As long as things last, three cheers for the king; when there's no more, pray to the Lord."

But a whole new tension had come into being. She had to prove herself to him. She had to get him what he wanted.

Chapter Twenty-two

What Massimo wanted was the Strega literary prize for his new book.

Marguerite knew him now. She knew his ambitions and his worries. It was true that he had problems to resolve: whether to give up one or all of his various jobs to concentrate on writing, which offer of new work to take, how to break into television. He was fragmented between all his concerns, tense and depressed with the sense of having worked hard all his life and still not having made it. It bothered him that youth was over and his family (the one of his boyhood) all gone.

Sometimes he came to her with a face that was drawn and grim, his eyes wandering nervously about the studio-room as if looking for landmarks to be sure where he was.

This night he was telling her that, in addition to everything else, just when he was in a fury to push his new book, he was being sent to Monte Carlo to cover the film festival.

"I'll go with you! I'll say I'm going to Florence."

He didn't even consider the possibility. "It's impossible. I'm going with other journalists. I'm not going to amuse myself, this is an assignment."

"Do you have to be with the others every minute? I can take care of myself while you're busy. We can have some time together—we've never been away together before."

"No . . . no . . . it's impossible."

She should have known it would be. He had his own terms

for their being together; he was cautious, he wouldn't do anything that would make Alberto wonder. It was as if she were learning how it would have been to be his wife, to live on the margin of his existence.

"Massimo, for a lover I'm really treated like a wife!"

"You're right. I'm not very attentive—I'm not like Alberto, am I?"

"It doesn't matter. You're tired, aren't you?" She made and handed him a Scotch-and-soda. "It's the letdown from having finished your book. That's natural."

"I'm worn out. I can't think . . . I can't plan. I lack the drive and energy to make the decisions I should be making now about my work, my future. I can't see anything clearly." He took a long drink from the glass. "How does Alberto manage!" he burst out bitterly.

"Alberto is generous toward life, Massimo. Receptive. Not diffident like you."

It had been her mistake to think that Alberto was negative; now she realized that he had a disposition toward life, a Franciscan grace, that was free from the ambitions and pressures of the closed, defensive Massimo.

How strange that the youthful Massimo who wrote so engagingly and spiritedly, with all the humorous malice of a Neapolitan urchin, should turn out to be ridden with dark moods, suspicions, and the inability to be other than alone. ("Not strange," the echoes of her Sicilian wizard, Dr. V., rebounded back to her; "we are all ambivalent, all our natures have two parts which alternate constantly, just as every question has its two sides." Yes, yes, the eternal paradox—the two sides of Massimo and Alberto, and her own to fit them both.)

Massimo had never opened himself completely with her; he held himself back from that total abandon and intimacy which is beyond sex. Of the men she had known, he had, however, come the closest to giving her herself. And he envied Alberto.

She understood. For all Alberto's seeming conservatism, his old-fashionedness, his inexpertise in the intrigues of Italian life (while Massimo and the others schemed and operated among the mazes, starting with the premise that life was devious and dark and you made your passage through it by vigilant suspicion), Alberto had gone his way confidently, lit inwardly by his acceptance of life. He had his own persuasion; he didn't have to bend or conform with what was expedient. This, in the end, made for the serenity that so puzzled Massimo.

Marguerite had her own taste of bitterness. She had wanted to be everything to Massimo—companion and colleague. But their lives were still separate. Sometimes they went four or five days a week without seeing each other, and she made lists of things she had to tell him so that they wouldn't break the fragile strands that bound them together. ("We never finish a conversation, Massimo; everything is left in fragments, like epitaphs." . . . "Because we meet to make love, we haven't time for the rest.")

Sometimes, discouraged, she asked herself if it wouldn't be better that he made no demands on her, left her the security of Alberto and her home without wrecking the little permanence she had in life. But instinctively the answer was no—it was better to have the best of both worlds, to divide herself between Alberto and him, to satisfy herself with what both, diversely, could give her.

The very best for her would have been Massimo completely. But it was clear to her now that Massimo would never ask her to leave Alberto for him because he needed Alberto as a friend.

It struck her as absurd that Massimo should care so much about a prize. But then she began to know him, to feel his torments, the weight of his work and ambition, the sense of insecurity that afflicted him in the company of eminent writers, his efforts to make up for lost time and the dispersion of his energy in countless other directions . . . the frustrations and regret that assailed him for having married the wrong woman and set his life in the wrong directions.

Actually, they both wanted the same thing: freedom. Hers was inner, his outer. Massimo's freedom had to be financial success, which would mean the end of his being tied down to odd jobs and the office schedules that eroded his time and filled his mind with concerns other than his writing.

She would help him get the prize he wanted for his new book. Everyone in Italy played the same game—even those who didn't need the money, as Massimo did. All he wanted to buy himself was time. A prize would keep him going long enough, perhaps, to produce another book; it would give him the luster to have the American publishers finally take notice of his other work. Then he'd have American dollars. A trip to New York.

"Alberto and I see people all the time," she told him. "I'll talk about your book; I'll mention that some of your stories have been translated in the States. That always makes an impression over here —look at what it did for Alberto."

"*Brava*," he said, pleased.

It was little enough to give him.

When Marguerite and Alberto met with the Ecclis, Clotilde, and Cesare Servi at Giggetto's for spring lamb, table talk centered on the most probable candidates for the coming Strega prize. The names of several writers, among them Massimo's, were mentioned.

"I've read the manuscript of Bontelli's new book," Marguerite told Servi, "and I'm going to send it on to an American publisher with the translation of a chapter or two. What do you think of him?"

"Very fresh and amusing—not much substance, of course, but that's not his style."

"He's something new in Italy, a real humorist. And he's unashamedly easy reading. I think Bontelli should get the prize for just being himself. Everyone else is so predictable and bland. The prizes themselves do that; they condition young writers to write in safe formulas."

"We didn't invent the literary prize, you know," said Leone Eccli a bit defensively; he was on the jury of almost every major prize in Italy—a calling as profitable in honorariums and paid vacations for him and Aurelia as his television job. "The French had them first, and even the English and Americans preceded us. But like everything else we do, we had to make it more splendid. Now we have more than three hundred prizes, and they've taken the place of the courts in the duchies and city-states. That's the only way they can be explained. Every little town and resort has its prize; jurors are like the nobility and writers take the place of courtiers vying for patronage. Instead of marriages of alliance and consolidation, there are love affairs according to which husband is on which jury and which wife has to be seduced. A very Italian phenomenon. Not at all like the British or American variety."

"You can't compare Italian prizes to American ones," said Clotilde with her wise-horse air and the fame of having used Servi and others to pick up a dozen or so prizes for herself. "American writers can live from their work, they don't need prizes, because there they publish a book in editions of ten or fifteen thousand copies. Then there is television, the movies, paperbacks. As with everything else, it's organized over there. Translations of my books are even in paperback. It's not like Italy, where an author would starve if he waited to sell ten thousand copies of his work."

"No one in Italy reads," said Leone disparagingly. "This is a country of illiterates. It has the literature it deserves."

Marguerite leaped into the conversation with an earnest look on her face. "Build public libraries and educate the people to read! You're publishing now for a tiny elite."

"Don't worry about literacy in Italy, *mia cara*," Leone said heartily. "It's already spreading too far. Today the maid cornered me in the elevator and said she had written a poem that she was going to send to the magazine *Annabella* and to the pope. But she wanted me to read it first."

"You Americans!" said Cesare, directing himself to Marguerite. "Always so practical. Who in Italy would give up the excitement and pleasure of intriguing and scheming and slandering to get a million lire in a prize just to earn it honestly? You think something as tame as public libraries and literacy is going to appeal to Italians? Prizefighting is a way of life in Italy—thrilling, passionate, corrupt, malicious, a testing of one's cleverness. After all, if it were only a question of the best book winning, what fun would there be in getting a Strega, for instance? What's important is not the book but all the background skill of arranging one's votes, getting to the voters, making important contacts, deploying oneself at the right receptions and cocktail parties. Italians have always esteemed cleverness in itself no matter toward what end it's used."

"I don't object to the prizes," said Aurelia Eccli. "How would writers live if they didn't have the prizes to help them along?" And in the cool night air she pulled over her shoulders the platinum-mink coat that represented Leone's last year of prizes.

"Who do you think will win the Strega this year?" Alberto asked Servi.

"There's no big name among the lists this year; there are four or five rather young new writers who are all about equal. Bontelli and a few others. It will be a question of personality in the end. Whoever can charm the most voters or whoever has the right contacts and influence. It should be interesting this year just for that, since there's no author from the established ranks who has to be paid off for sentimental reasons or because it is his turn."

"Too bad you don't have a book this year," Marguerite said to Alberto. "We could use the money to fix up the house in the Marche."

"Well, I've got the Pisa—some group up there has decided to give me half a million lire and a statuette of the Leaning Tower in gold for the poetry collection that came out a year or so ago."

"Give us this day our daily prize—eh, Alberto?" said Leone.

"Maybe we can pawn the tower," said Marguerite, thinking of the Monte di Pietà she saw from the roof at Angela's place.

"If it's worth anything. I seem to specialize in prizes that put me back instead of ahead. The last one I had to go all the way to Mestre to collect, paying my own train fare; and after dinner in a restaurant where they talked all night about my work, they gave me a figure of something in iron, an original sculpture by someone I'd never heard of, and that was it. You remember the Mestre prize, don't you?" Alberto turned to Marguerite for confirmation.

"Oh, yes, I remember," she said. How many things she remembered between them. Yes, they had a whole life together. A life that had intermeshed and made a rich, varied background of many-colored, many-textured strands. . . . This was Saturday. . . . Sunday Massimo spent with his family. . . . On Monday he had some special assignment that would occupy him completely; perhaps Tuesday, or failing that, Thursday for sure, they would see each other again. Once or twice a week they took up their life together, but the fabric on which they embroidered it was fragile. As Cesare Servi had said of Massimo's books, they were fresh and pleasing and immediately attractive but also slim and light, and in the end, of no substance. So, it seemed, was her being with him.

Look, she thought, at Alberto's generosity toward me; he gives me freedom and no questions asked. He'd never say anything even if he did suspect something between me and Massimo. He'd never accuse me; he would trust me even in that. And Massimo keeps worrying about Alberto—Alberto, who's freer and less conventional than either of us.

Alberto was saying, "There's the Fiuggi poetry prize next month at Castel Sant'Angelo."

"Oh, let's go! What a gorgeous place to have a party," said Aurelia.

"I never miss a party," said Clotilde. "We'll all go."

Massimo was there, too, on a splendid night made clear and fresh by drenching, cleansing afternoon showers. A great moon hovered benignly and solitarily in the rinsed sky and lit the angel-topped mausoleum on whose ramparts all the elite of the Italian cultural world were passing among stacks of Renaissance cannon-balls with drinks in their hands. Everyone was there. Massimo greeted Marguerite and Alfredo briefly and then went off to shake hands among the crowd. The old courtyards on top of the castle were filled with splendid girls, already tanned; and one wondrous beauty with Antonioni looked like Botticelli's *Primavera* with blue cornflowers twined in her long blonde hair. A superb champagne supper was served after the prize ceremony in the covered prome-nade of Pope Alexander VI. Looking out over the roofs of the city, Marguerite saw close by the white hulk of the Palace of Justice; the old *palazzaccio* was falling down. Here she was atop a two-thou-sand-year-old bastion, looking at the barely sixty-year-old court-house where she had been separated from Alberto, empty now, evacuated because it was falling apart. And farther away in the night she tried to discern her own roof across the river, the roof that sheltered her and Massimo.

"Did you see a lot of people at the Fiuggi thing?" Marguerite asked Massimo when they met next. "I talked about your book to everyone I met."

"*Brava.*"

"You're sure to get the Strega, no one else is so handsome."

"I don't even think of it anymore," he answered glumly. "It doesn't matter. Nothing matters."

"Why do you say that?" she asked, her throat beginning to tighten with tears. It was then that she could sense the end. Angela would be back soon.

"You know I'm not attached to living—I'm indifferent. I feel alone, without a faith. There is nothing important to me."

"Then that includes me," she said after a moment's silence. "Why do you say this? I love you. You aren't alone—how can you be alone when there are two of us?"

"*Ti voglio tanto bene,*" he said. "But let's not talk about this."

"It's something I've always known even if I wanted to hide it from myself. My coming into your life has resolved nothing for you, there's nothing I can do for you. That's what hurts."

"*Amore mio,* you are precious to me. Each time we meet I am amazed at your freshness . . . at what being with you does for me. But deep within, my character is what it is. I have always been like this."

"Always?"

"For the past ten years, anyway."

"Because you couldn't have that woman you loved?"

"That helped persuade me that nothing can change. But it wasn't just that. It's having the kind of family situation I have, the loss of youth, losing hope. I don't believe in anything. . . ."

"Then why do you bother to write? Why do you keep yourself looking good and run around so busily each day? Why are you ambitious for your work? Why do you bother to come to me— what would it all matter if you hadn't some hope, some attachment to life?"

"I don't know. I just hang on, that's all. Let's not talk about this anymore."

She let the tears come and they slid between them, cementing their embrace. Why should she try to understand? Was this her old mania of wanting to organize, to probe and sort? Massimo was simpler. He accepted what was, he wasn't set on understanding. Still, she tried.

"You will see . . . once you have the Strega prize, everything will be better. I love you, Massimo."

"You would like to be the dominant one, wouldn't you?"

"What do you mean?" she asked, raising her head a little to look at him in surprise.

"You would like to dominate men, have authority over them."

"Who—me?" she asked incredulously in the same instant that she recognized the truth he spoke. Of course she had been authoritarian with him: Hadn't she tried to buy him, to tie him to her by means of his books, the prize? Yet she had also been submissive. ("*Sei plagiata*," Massimo had told her once, semi-seriously. He had used "plagiarized" in the Italian sense of her becoming subjected to him, being totally absorbed in his influence, appropriated.)

"Sometimes I wonder," he went on, "if we could have ever married if we had known each other when we were both free. If things had gone right I would have been an Alberto—a completely faithful husband and family man. What do you think?"

"No, Massimo," she said, trying to change his mood. "I think we were made for other things. We'll run off to Mexico together when you get the Strega. You'll get a big advance for the film rights to your book, I'll pawn Angela's paintings and sell the car, and we'll go off for as long as the money lasts."

"That's what we'll do—*eh, tesoro*?" he agreed, smiling at last.

"*Detto!* Said and agreed."

"*Detto.* Then when we've spent everything, we'll come back, penitent, asking everyone's forgiveness."

"Clown!" And though she laughed with him, the tears were still in her throat.

Chapter Twenty-three

After Angela returned ("Neurasthenic and starving," she said; "just imagine a poor *romana* in England for three years!"), Marguerite found it difficult to meet Massimo.

"I could come to your place after your wife goes to the Marche with the children," she proposed.

But he objected. The *portiere* would see them, and the people in adjoining apartments.

What does it matter! she'd think wildly. She'd suggest his coming to her apartment when Weezy was in school and the maid out shopping; or he could come to her room at night while Alberto was working late in the studio; or they could go someplace for the weekends . . . or even use her car.

"You're mad," he'd say. "Sex isn't everything. We can still meet as friends."

This increased her despair. He didn't care! Maybe he was already meeting other women. And she? She was consumed by her need for him, not knowing how to find peace in the rest of her life without the part she shared with him.

"I haven't even time for the beach these days," he told her. "I've got the presentations of my book. The Strega is just weeks away."

The weeks and months she had counted on the rosary of her good fortune seemed to have all been said and told.

Massimo was involved in literary politics, seeing the people who could be of use to him for the Strega, taking them to dinner, talking to critics, and being seen everywhere. There was no room for her.

If Massimo got the Strega prize they'd be together again. Otherwise, she knew him; he'd sink back into his sense of futility and let himself not want anything or anyone. Hurting, anxious, she redoubled her efforts for his book, counting on Alberto's influence in the literary world to make things work.

Nothing else had worked out; Marguerite hadn't, as her parents would have put it, been able to capitalize on anything very significantly. Massimo's previous books had already been refused by several American publishers and were being read by still another; her room of her own was gone, and from it she had produced a few fine photos but not the assignments she had imagined; and from the exhilarating sense of freedom she had realized so briefly, she was now relapsed into emotional dependence upon a man who would always survive without her.

Her only accomplishment was a certain enlightenment; Alberto should have been the upright of her constructions. He was the safe clearing she had made in the jungle, a clearing tended and worked at and cultivated in all their years together; a place that was now secure, and ready to produce good fruits. Over this clearing Massimo, a note of dazzling grace, had come like a beautiful bird pausing a moment in flight. It was useless to pursue him far from the clearing. He would not be caught. Yet he was all she wanted.

There was a big send-off for Massimo's new book at his publisher's quarters in Piazza di Spagna. All Rome was there, and with them, Marguerite and Alberto.

"What was it I told you once?" Alberto said affectionately to Massimo, catching him for a moment while he was being filmed signing copies of his new book and smiling at the young actresses who were always in the background at such affairs. "I said, 'Here's someone who doesn't talk, but acts.' While all the rest of us talk about the books we'll write, you actually do them."

Massimo looked pleased at Alberto's attention and grinned at him. He looked marvelous, Marguerite thought, already tanned and dressed in a cream-colored linen suit with the psychedelic tie she had given him.

"He's the man to watch, Alberto," Leone Eccli said amiably, joining them; and Aurelia, smiling at Marguerite, added, "In more ways than one."

Marguerite stared back; Aurelia's words weren't meant to be malicious—only cognizant of something that Alberto had never taken the trouble to notice.

Looking about at the people who made up the firmament of sensibility in Italy in their day, Marguerite regretted the missing. Pavese was dead; Vittorini was dead; Ungaretti was dead; Calvino lived in Paris, discredited in Italy for having refused the five million lire of the previous year's Viareggio prize with a telegram to the jury in which he said that the time of such events was definitely over. He had cut through the collective vanity of literary Italy with all the candor of the child who didn't pretend to see the emperor's clothes, and his honesty was received in a rage.

All the climbers were there at Massimo's presentation; and all those who, having reached some perch, lived in fear and trembling of falling from it. The dowagers of literature were out in full force. Heavy-girthed lady novelists and poets bore down on Alberto and the other critics whenever a space opened near them.

In a flutter of salutes and handshakes, smiles and appraisals, Massimo's evening went on. Not only he but everyone present was in the business of being noted, of being remembered when their turn came up, of courting the powerful.

The men were alert and conservative; the women aggressively elegant. There was not an unconventional one among them. It was literariness without ferment or independence. "My beat is beatific," Jack Kerouac, on tour, had told them not long before, and no one had understood; they were long removed from a state in which poetry, disinterested poetry, was a condition of life. They were, that night, a gathering of shopkeepers merchandising themselves while the market was good.

The chattering went on as if they all hadn't met in the same place (or a similar one) with the same drinks and the same ideas just a week or so ago for another (but similar) author. Except, thought Marguerite, that Massimo is different if he'll only hold out. As lights centered on her, she turned to find him near her directing the cameramen to get her in the shot.

"You're a great sentimentalist after all," she said to him. "Is this shot supposed to be a souvenir for you?"

"*Antipatica!*" he said, laughing, in good spirits, before hurrying off to greet new arrivals.

"May I greet Signora Morosini," said a voice behind her. Marguerite turned into the half-embrace of Roberto Nardini, a public relations man whose first book, published the year before, had become a best-seller and just missed winning the Strega prize of that season.

"*Ciao*, Roberto," she said. "I see they're making a film of your book—you must be making a fortune. Are you writing another one?"

"Never again! Once is enough, like taking a cruise. To write seriously, to take one's self as a writer seriously is a vice, a sickness, like an itching that takes all your attention. Anti-life."

"That's what they all say. Look at Parise: He's always saying he'll never write another word and every week there's a report from him on some battlefront of the world, and every year a book."

"You can count on me to keep my word about not writing. There should be fines for writing books, just as there should be fines for those who add to the nightmare of our automobile traffic. Or at least a preliminary test to eliminate the really incapable if they haven't the good taste and elegance to do it themselves."

Everyone was there. Actors, astrologers, neurologists, and Vatican curia lawyers who specialized in expensive annulments for the rich and well connected. The towering Clotilde, accompanied by the dwarflike creature who was her secretary and attendant, stood pontifically in the middle of the room smiling her benediction. Another lady poet, known as La Béchamel for the white-sauce blandness of her verses, had managed to get hold of Alberto. The critic whose last name was the same as that of a laxative and whose slogan, they said, was "I work while you sleep" had come in. And Maria de Maria, the wild beauty of three decades past who still thought, with dark hair streaming over her curving shoulders, she could pass for a girl-writer of promise.

"Just what Italy doesn't need," Roberto muttered to Marguerite, "another Maria. Especially a black one like the Madonna di Loreto."

Trim as a Swiss au pair in her tailored black suit, with a coral penis dangling in the open neckline of her white blouse, Lalla arrived with the Great Man not far behind. And, ominous, like a slithery Carmine De Sapio, the publisher of a weekly scandal magazine circulated silently behind the thick glasses, like headlights, that gave him the nickname of Limousine.

"Always the same faces," Marguerite said. "Even the barmen are the same." They went to the table to get drinks from men who had poured for her all over Rome at public and private parties. Her own parties, too.

"Of course," Nardini agreed. "These receptions take the place of the old salons. Who could afford these days, or who has the time for, the open houses among the writers and artists that we used to have? That's how the Strega started. We used to meet each Sunday at the Bellonci place. Then the gatherings got too large and the Sundays at home were given up, but the prize has become a huge event. When I first came to Rome, just after the war, we used to meet in Mazzullo's studio in Via Margutta: Clotilde was there, Leone Eccli, Zavattini, Guttuso, Gianni Zanetti, Mario Soldati—everyone. We'd huddle around a wood stove and donate what we could to a hat set in the middle of the floor, and then someone would be sent out to get wine and fava beans and pizza. One of the younger ones, usually, like Massimo Bontelli. He was there, too. Always quiet, always listening."

"Yes, I can imagine," she nodded. She could see the beautiful twenty-year-old Massimo just in from the Marche and fascinated by the profusion of Rome and the illustrious names he met, and dreaming of making it as a writer.

Marguerite considered: You have to pretend the truth to children and keep your word to them because they don't know yet that life is flux; that nothing can be promised; that Absolutes are a mirage for desperate beings; that truth cannot be caught and redelivered, still living, at a future date. For each moment is a different truth, sliding into the next as in a kaleidoscope. Children can't understand that circumstances change . . . that different external factors act on decisions, relationships, ideas, like the natural forces on the earth . . . that persons act upon persons in a perpetual chain of being. Not because, no longer childlike, we want to be inconstant, changing, mobile; but because we are.

So we must be nimble to bend with the swirl or else we break. Maturity—what else is it but this flexing? We learn not to depend on anything, and with this nondependence comes the final freedom: the sense that all we see cannot be counted on to last.

At first, in childishness, Marguerite had wanted to freeze Massimo's words and intentions into beliefs. But their future, like everyone else's, was blank.

Alberto came up to Marguerite and Roberto, looking harassed. "*Ciao*, Roberto. I need a Scotch, too."

"Too much béchamel," Roberto said sympathetically.

"What a scourge on the world, these women writers!"

"This is nothing," said Marguerite. "Wait till Tina gets back in a few weeks and unleashes women's liberation on you."

"Speaking of women," said Aurelia, joining them, "have you heard the new definition of a virgin? A child of three—but *bruttissima*."

The next time Marguerite and Massimo met was the night of the Strega award. She had been unwell in the intervening week, and was pale that evening and strained-looking.

Over four hundred Sunday friends, plus their friends, had gathered in the courtyard of old Pope Julian III's splendid villa to cast their votes for the five finalists. Massimo was one of the five. The speculation was that he could be the winner but that Tomaso Campo's *Una Spirale de Bruma* ("A Spiral of Mist") was also a close contender. Nothing was sure.

Marguerite and Alberto were with Angela, Giorgio Corsi (back for the summer from New York), and the Ecclis. Angela, in a long white crocheted dress ordered sight-unseen from a peasant woman in Frascati and worn with nothing under it, was covering the affair for a woman's magazine. Already at ten o'clock, when they arrived at Villa Giulia, confusion reigned and crowds were thick. The friends had originally met in the delicious inner courtyard called Ninfeo after the sunken lily-pool set among mossy niches supported by graceful caryatids, which must have greatly consoled the old pope (a great *viveur*, said Angela) as he strolled there of an evening saying his office. But now, with the additional hordes of friends, reporters, public relations people, and aides from the contending publishing houses who were there to engineer the award, the nymphaeum no longer was sufficient, and tables were set in the large outer courtyard where the older cadre walked about frowning and grumbling, "Who are all these people?"

The evening proceeded with Roman nonlogic, according to Giorgio Corsi, for whose academic mind such bizarreness was mysterious, foreboding. The number on their invitation did not correspond to their table reservation, but by some hopelessly complicated system only indicated a place on another list which then assigned them to a differently numbered table. The confusion made for a lot of promenading about and exchanging of places, and to Marguerite it was no longer a charming ploy that put the stunning people into greater evidence, but a typical Italian debacle.

The women wore dashing *palazzo* pajamas or short Pucci prints in glorious bursts of hot midsummer colors. Tanned young women with perfect bodies wore slinky Jean Harlow–type slip-dresses and sequin sheaths cut straight and split up the back. The princesses wore no jewelry, the actresses no makeup except for their enormous ornamental eyes.

Luigi Barzini presided over the head table of referees on an elevation at the far end of the courtyard; it was from there that votes were tabulated and numbers chalked on a giant blackboard. The commotion, the handshaking, the table hopping, and the late arrivals protracted the voting past midnight. Now and then Barzini's voice would reverberate through the night soliciting voters. Hawk-eyed, he seemed to see everywhere. "Bassani!" he boomed through the microphone as that writer, like a communicant in a white summer suit, strode through the courtyard with his family trailing behind him. "Bassani, get up here, you haven't voted yet!"

Angela, roaming around to get news and gossip for her piece, came back to report that Campo's book was considered the safe one to win. "He's a visual projection of his book—safe, inoffensive, courteous. I asked him what he thought of the critics' charge about his provincialism, and he said, 'That's what they said about Verga, too.' In any case, it's a fait accompli—his publisher already had a hundred votes pledged in marked envelopes before the voting began."

"How is the Campo book?" Marguerite asked, forcing down her feelings of nausea and anxiety.

"Just like it sounds: spiraling mist."

"Actually, the title's not bad." And she thought of Dr. Verdile, who used to say we never close a circle, but, at best, evolve like an upward-tending spiral. To close a circle would mean full stop and then the mindless repetitive tracings of real despair. The spiral unloops slowly and each day makes its own course; nothing repeats, no track is exactly retraced. And so it goes.

Giorgio had gone off to the bar in the garden flanking the courtyard to get drinks. "No champagne for your upset stomach, and no gin and tonic for me," he told Marguerite in bemusement. "Now I know I'm back in Italy. The tonic people are on strike. All they

had was gin and lemonade, which might seem like a great innovation
over here but strikes me as being that old-fashioned thing called a
Tom Collins in the days I first went to the States to study. Seems
no point in remembering those days. . . ."

"None at all," Marguerite agreed. "It's like *Aïda*, isn't it?"

"What's like *Aïda*?"

"This triumphal procession of people all dressed gorgeously and
all parading around—in fact it's better than *Aïda*, which is always
a tacky production because they depend on everyone's liking the
music just the same." I'm bantering, she thought; talking aimlessly
to keep up my spirits.

Geno Pampaloni came by smiling slyly, critic and jury member
of all the prizes in Italy, more Cheshire cat than ever; and Goffredo
Parise, who had cured himself of a chronic fever by going to
China for two months and coming back with a new Chinese cast
to his features; and Flaminia Serranova, flouncing around in fuchsia
palazzo pajamas with a low cowl back and foot-long plastic earrings.
"There are only a few women who can carry off the names of the
consular roads—the Appia, the Flaminia, and all those—like our
Aurelia or Signora Serranova," said Giorgio, looking admiringly at
Flaminia.

"It's a fashion show," Leone quipped. "They could change this
from a literary event to a best-dressed one. After all, who reads
the books? But everyone does look at the women." Clotilde,
l'Armadio, came by in a beaded top and black skirt, making it
clear that the beaded top over the black skirt had been out for years.

Angela came back to have a drink and rest her feet from her
ramblings over the pebbly courtyard. "At Moravia's table they're
organizing a rebellion in case Campo wins," she reported. "And
Carlo Levi's just arrived from Piazza San Giovanni, where he led
the anti-American protest." A beautiful blonde in transparent black
organdy pajamas stopped by the table and Angela got out her
pen and pad: "Is that your own hair?"

"No, it's Chinese."

"Chinese blonde?"

"Why not? A cross between races."

Massimo stopped by. Marguerite had seen him earlier, circulating
among the tables. His smile was warm; he looked happy, exhilarated, and confident.

"How are things going, Massimo?" Alberto asked. "You've got
my vote anyway."

"Thanks, Alberto. A lot of friends have said they voted for me. But you never can tell."

"You'll win," said Aurelia, who just a moment before had conceded that Campo had it all tied up.

As Alberto got up to greet someone, Massimo sat down in his place next to Marguerite. "Are you all right? You look tired tonight," he said. "Do you remember the year we met when I missed seeing you at the Strega?"

"Yes, I thought you were saying that just to be polite."

"You know me better now. You know I say what I mean."

She looked at him and nodded. Yes, she thought, unfortunately.

Massimo glanced curiously at Angela, who was jotting notes, and at Giorgio, who was looking distractedly into the distance. Leaning toward Marguerite he said, "It's been three years."

"Yes, we lasted three years."

"You say that as if everything's over," he said defensively. "After tonight, once all this has ended, we'll be together like old times. I'll call you soon." He got up, kissed her hand, and then was gone, merged with the crowd in the Renaissance courtyard.

"How can he be so confident?" Marguerite murmured.

"I wonder," said Angela. "Campo's already got it."

But Marguerite hadn't been thinking of Massimo's book. She had been thinking of them. If he lost tonight, she lost, too. She felt sick, and a light sweat broke out on her forehead.

As she looked about at the setting of Pope Julian's splendor, the suave summer night an enchantment around them, the courtyard full of the new courtiers of culture and their women, she thought, How did I get here? And now where do I go? If she could have moved, she would have run from the scene. But she felt turned to stone, another of the stone caryatids in that setting.

And then Barzini's voice, doubly amplified, hit the night: "The winner of this year's Strega is Tomaso Campo with his *A Spiral of Mist.*" He had beaten Massimo by twenty votes, and in a great glare of light was being photographed for television. Some boos came from the tables. Marguerite felt dizzy. Then the sound of music came from the nymphaeum and everyone rose to dance, dissent softly dying.

As the five long-legged hippie players beat out a frenetic rhythm on their red electric guitars, oblivious of the machinations of the evening in the excitement of their own sensations, Marguerite looked down from the sinuous curving balustrade to the incredible scene below. The scruffy hippies had set up their instruments in the niches around the lily-pool. A girl in a tiny square of gleaming plastic skirt and long hip-boots was gyrating to the music and singing into the microphone in her hand. The elegant people were descending the twin staircases to do the shake, and nothing was out of place, nothing jarred. The old and beautiful biscuit-colored stone of the balustrades, the spears of silhouetted pines, the mossy rocks of the pool, the carved reclining figures of Father Tiber and Father Arno, the invisible shadows of Julian III and his cardinals—they all lent their benevolent presence.

And I used to wonder about Puritan John Milton being the guest of a cardinal in Rome, she thought. In this land where everything is accommodated. Where nothing is resolved because it's all an unfolding spiral.

"Well, this is finished, if God is willing, for another year," Alberto was saying. "What do you say, Giorgio and Angela? Leone and Aurelia?"

"I say let's direct ourselves toward Pallaro's for fettucine and end the evening on a serious note."

"What evening? It's already morning, Giorgio," said Angela.

"All the more reason! Let's go. . . ."

As she got up to leave, taking Alberto's arm to steady herself, somewhere from her memory Marguerite heard the pursy-mouthed refrain of her convent-school days. "Who pays the fiddler?" Sister Theresa was saying grimly to the class of girls in their blue-serge uniforms. "The girl pays the fiddler."

Nothing had changed.

Part Three

Tina, 1950–

Chapter Twenty-four

The telegram arrived at the 1920s Tudor house in the good part of Gloversville on a day when Sam Scalzo was getting ready to meet his golf foursome at the club and Carla Scalzo was thinking of going downtown to a sale. Her grandparents recounted the whole thing to Tina when they saw her at Christmas.

After the shock wore off, they agreed it was typical of Marguerite. Their daughter had always managed to upset them.

Sam had answered the ring at the door and taken the overseas cable. It was from Rome and read: "Marguerite killed in car crash STOP Weezy is with me in sorrow STOP Advise Tina compassionately. Alberto."

Carla, sitting at the breakfast table, looked up from the morning paper. "What is that?"

Abruptly, he read the message to her.

"Oh, my God!" she exclaimed, her eyes opened in alarm, her hands flying to her face. "Oh, my God . . . what is the world coming to?"

"What's that got to do with it?" Sam snapped in disgust. "We've got to know what happened before we call Tina. As usual Alberto doesn't say anything—when it happened, how, the funeral. . . ."

"He still calls her Marguerite," Carla got out in a strangled voice, the tears coursing down her cheeks. "She always said he never got anything right about her, not even her name."

"Always unhappy about something—that's what she was. But

what's the difference . . . what's the difference!" Sam looked about him, uncertain, nervous. He felt destroyed.

Difficult in life, now here she was in death, cut from the same cloth. Why? Sam looked out the window of the breakfast room where the sun was pouring in. The garden was filled with the color of peonies and roses, and Joe the gardener was trimming the hedges and clipping grass at the edges of the flowerbeds. It was a tranquil scene. Why couldn't she have lived a normal life?

"Alberto wants us to tell Tina about her mother's death," he said. "And what do we know? I'll have to call Rome before I can talk to Tina."

"She'll be buried in Rome, so far from home," Carla said. Her face seemed to wither from shock and Sam moved about, darting glances at her and swearing softly, shaking his head. "She had to marry an Italian and live in Italy!" he said.

"She was enjoying life these past few years in Rome. . . . She was happier, I could feel it . . . and now . . ." Carla's face dropped with weariness, the lines pulled downward against their grain, for it was a face given to much smiling and cheerfulness. Her face and shoulders sagged with the burden of being too late to make it up to the daughter she had not understood or approved of, or even, at times, liked. As if speaking to herself, Carla added, "What did she want? What was she looking for? . . . All that moving around. All those homes she set up and then tore down. And moving those girls around so they had no normal life at all . . . What was it all for? To punish us?"

"She had no sense, that's what it was!" Sam retorted angrily. "All that education and no practical sense—and it looks like Tina is headed the same way."

With Carla weeping in the background, Sam put through the call to Rome. Weezy, named Luisa for Alberto's mother but always called by Tina's baby name for her, said her mother had been alone in the car, making the trip over the mountains back from their summer place, which she had gone to open; the car evidently skidded out of control in the rain; there was no need for them to come over; her mother would be cremated and interred later when Tina returned to Rome; her father had gone to claim the body. Weezy seemed calm and tried to comfort her grandmother, who kept saying, "You girls will always have a home here with your grandfather and me—you know that, don't you?"

Then Sam put in the call to Tina in New York. He told the operator to make it person-to-person, because if Tina were out, he didn't want to speak to the young man she was sharing the apartment with.

There was another example, he thought angrily; as soon as that situation had been discovered, he had written to Marguerite and told her what he thought of it, of how she had brought up her children to have no decent respect for morality and appearances. That had resulted in an incomprehensible reply from Marguerite saying that Tina was well of age to make her decisions, that she was a graduate student and teaching assistant at Columbia making her own way, that she was the most moral and upright person she knew, and that she, Marguerite, wasn't going to interfere and tell her daughter what to do or make her feel guilty about the way she led her life as had been done to her.

That day, in New York, Tina answered the phone and heard of her mother's death.

Wordlessly, she heard out her grandfather until, stunned, she slammed down the receiver, cutting him off. She looked wildly around at the turmoil in the room and sank down on a disheveled mattress that was set on the floor. All around were piles of Duke's clothes, her books, their mugs of cold coffee, boxes of Kleenex and crackers, records, a hair dryer, a carton of cigarettes, and some rolled-up posters. It broke on her in waves of revulsion that in such a mess she had heard the news of her mother's death.

How often as a child had she heard the story of how she had been willed into existence by her mother despite the difficult pregnancy and the doctor's prediction of miscarriage. For three months her mother, her veritable lifeline, had lain motionless, fed intravenously and obstinately wanting the birth. Tina was born beautiful and christened Umbertina for a great-grandmother—to give her strength in life, her mother said.

"I remember my grandmother Umbertina," her mother used to say, "but I could never speak to her. She spoke another language. We could only look at each other and smile. Then she'd tweak my cheek. All my life I've missed speaking to her; she died when I was thirteen."

Tina was high-strung and apprehensive; shadows of the precariousness of things were embedded in her as if the hold she had on life were always up for grabs. There were threats to her in everything: distant earthquakes, floods, wars, and epidemics. And when she learned that President Coolidge's son had died from a blister on his heel that became infected, she thought of how tenuous her—anyone's—life really was. A matter of ill-fitting sneakers. She was intensely self-centered and pavid, she excelled in what she did, and thoughts of death were never far from her.

Womb-shock, she thought—some indelible fear of not being born must have imprinted her forever and created that strong bond between her and her mother. Tina had always wanted to make up to her mother for everything: for the grandmother she couldn't speak to, for the parents who didn't understand her, for the husband who was too old.

Now, as she heard of her mother's death, she sobbed out, "Oh, Mother, I'm sorry!" She was sorry for herself; she couldn't think of life without her.

Duke came back to the apartment and he had some grass. He rolled joints and she clung to him. She knew, she said, how her mother had died; she was driving over the mountains to Ancona to see her lover.

"You know," Tina related, huddled against him, as if telling a story, "I have this incredible memory of the time I first met Massimo—that was her lover. It was after junior year and I had been all summer with you in Tennessee instead of going back to Rome. Finally, *papà* insisted I come home. Before I left we tossed the I Ching—you remember, Duke?—and it said this incredible thing: 'Do not be sad, it is fitting to be like the sun at its zenith.' So I went back and there was my mother, whom I love a lot but have this terrible thing that I'd started to fight with her, too, and I didn't know why except maybe because she wanted to monopolize me and strap me with her own hopes for herself, and I wanted to be with you. She was exasperating at those times! Still, I knew she had to be handled carefully: *Papà* kept talking about her sickness because of all her resentments against him, her parents, the headmaster at St. Gregory's where she worked—everyone, it seemed, was trying to do her in, trying to keep her from being the great person she was supposed to be. But no one could figure out who she was supposed to be.

"Anyway. She sets out hell-bent over the mountains like she's fleeing the end of the world and has to get to Ancona before it overtakes her. She's got her bikini on under her clothes and she keeps saying, 'Let's get there before the sun's gone—let's get the last of the sun.' So there's the sign of the sun again! And I keep thinking of you and Tennessee as we drive all the way across Italy. 'Imagine,' my mother says, 'we can cross the whole breadth of Italy in four hours and it takes four days to cross America'—as if that proved something. That's what exasperated me about her. I was lonesome for you and feeling this culture shock; I had just been back in Italy one day and she's rushing me off to Ancona. I'm supposed to be there to help with the driving but she does it all, like a demon, and really scares me. I don't know what I'm along for except she says we'll have a nice weekend at our little place near the sea. I figure out later that she wants me there to keep my father from being suspicious.

"We got to Ancona and she drives right to the beach and jumps out of her clothes. We have a swim, then she walks up and down as if she's looking for someone. That night, at our place, we share the room with twin beds and I'm lying awake, unable to sleep, and she's awake, too, twitching around. I'm thinking of you in America and I didn't know then what she was thinking of, but now I do— she was thinking of her lover just a few miles away in his own place, in bed with his wife. My mother and I don't speak a word, but we each know the other is awake. Instead of counting sheep I'm thinking of you; I go back to the very beginning of how we met, Duke—every moment as far back as I can remember. What was my mother thinking to herself? I lay sideways and could feel your body pressed against mine. I kept thinking how much I loved you. It seemed impossible to have such feelings and not burst. I wanted some dope. I thought, As soon as I get back to Rome I'll have to find someone at Piazza Navona I know and get some. I wanted to bring some seeds and grow them on the terrace near *papà*'s laurel, but I forgot them. I wrote you every night—remember, Duke?"

She turned to look at him and he caressed her hair. "Go on, Tina, talk it all out."

"So in Ancona I met this friend of my mother's, a writer named Massimo Bontelli who lives there, and also in Rome. He took us to another beach, very isolated, and we had lunch there at some little shack with a thatched roof and great fish. He and my mother drank a lot of wine and laughed a lot. I went and lay down on the beach and closed my eyes and thought of you. And then it struck me! They're lovers, my mother and that guy. I began to act badly to him; I was rude. Later I cried. Then I thought of our toss and how it said DO NOT BE SAD! I hoped and prayed that we had not passed our zenith; that you'd be there shining like the sun when I got back. I didn't want to be sad, and think of the setting of the sun . . . *nox est perpetua una dormienda*—you know, that great line in Catullus. We had to meet again at the zenith.

"I decided to be kinder to my mother. Her suns would always be less high than mine. She was in her forties, though she looked much less. She looked great—all tanned and slim and wearing miniskirts and bikinis. I wanted to be like her, look like her, have her taste in books and music and travel. And that strange thing she had that we should chase the sun over the mountains and go find it at the opposite sea. It was a way I've never seen her. It was the first time I thought of her as happy. . . .

"Then I got sad back in Rome. I was thinking of my father. I wanted to stay near him a lot because I sensed my life was calling me away from Italy. I thought it was my father who was feeling his mortality, feeling death close because he's much older than my mother. My mother was so alive—death was so far from her.

"I loved them both. But I think I hurt her because I didn't understand until now about loving, about being a woman, about choices —about everything. Oh, Christ, Duke, I was so mean to her! She wanted to be a photographer, on her own, traveling around. She had a great eye for things. I used to tell her she was killing *papà* with her insane desires. We all thought the family should count more with her than her personal ambitions. God! That was so unfair! God, Duke, we all drove her to what happened!"

"It's all right, Tina girl," he said gently, "cry all you want. I'm here."

"Duke, I believe what Freud said—there are no accidents. All I have to do is think how my mother used to drive and I can tell she was carrying a death wish as long as I've known her."

"It just seems that way to you now, Tina."

"No, Duke, I can tell. She was always reckless and not paying any attention to traffic or anything. I'd get very nervous as a kid and say 'Mom, watch out' and she'd say 'Don't bother me, I'm thinking.' God! I'd be petrified! She'd go through stop-signs, make

U-turns, drive as fast as she wanted, and act as if she didn't have to obey any law. I remember when she got her license taken away for a while and that was terrible, 'cause my father hates to drive and she wouldn't put up with not being allowed to drive, so she'd take the car anyway. It was this defiance she had—which was also a way to taunt my father because she thought he was too cautious." Tina gave back the joint Duke had passed her. "But it was no accident. It was in the books from long ago."

"Tina. It was a mountain road on a rainy day. It could have happened to anyone."

"Yes, but it happened to her, and I bet, before the lights went out in her brain forever . . . I just bet, she had time to think, Well, I'm finally out of it!"

Tina gave way to sobbing. Then she became sick. As she lay back in bed, she thought with longing of her father.

In the years of separation from her family in Rome, first at Bryn Mawr and now at Columbia, distance had helped her love them all. In Rome it was a different story; it was hard, then, to put up with her father's old-fashionedness. And every time Tina got used to a place, she had to leave: She got to Italy, hated it, loved it, then had to leave for America, hated it, loved it, and so back to Italy.

She had a recurrent dream of some idyllic crossroads in an unnamed part of Italy where a white villa stood on a hill surrounded by green, near water. Was it the crossroads of her life—this way to America, or that way to Italy? She didn't know, except that the vision was more than a dream; it was the dim recall of something she had seen as a child while on a trip with her parents across the north of Italy. Where had they passed a crossroads? she would repeatedly ask her mother. And her mother would say, "I wonder if you mean Sirmione on Lake Garda, where we visited the ruins of what's called Catullus' villa."

Was that the moment she had become a classicist? Tina wondered. Or a split personality?

Rome became another dreamplace she carried off to the wilds of America; and there, burrowed into modernity and high-speed highways, and rebellions and vast space and too much of everything, she nursed the dream, fearing with each return that it would get shabbier.

After an outburst of nostalgia in a letter home from college her father had written back in admonishment: *"Non sempre è un utile esperienza rivedere i luoghi dove si sono vissute ore di fiaba che sono irrepetibile.*" Right. Correct. It's *not* always useful to see again the places where one has lived enchanted hours that are unrepeatable. But she clung to the illusion that what she did was in the name of survival, not usefulness.

Her father counseled Yoga. In college she had swiftly taken up pot smoking, protesting, nudeness, and hitching around to other colleges for weekends. She sought friends from Rome like Missy, or Tim Jowers who was at Yale—all of them alienated in the raw new world. The boys from St. Gregory's in Rome were buddies, not lovers, and they were all clinging together because they were outsider Americans and they felt strange and uneasy in their land that was not precisely their land because so much of their lives had been spent abroad. They hated America and were seduced by it: the great open stretches of the West, where they hitched during spring vacations; the casual friendliness of the people; the simplicity of life. But then there was ugliness, too: the gross cars, the overheated places and bad food, and the hideous Vietnam war.

She was overcome in America by the feeling of extension, of space, which coincided with her own internal feeling of uncontrol, of utter chaos, which, in her prayers, she hoped to be saved from at the last moment by some decree of direction. She put a poem by Thomas Kinsella that said this for her in her wallet:

> I choose at random, knowing less and less.
> The shambles of the seashore at my feet
> Yield a weathered spiral: I confess
> —Appalled at how the waves have polished it—
> I know that shores are eaten, rocks are split,
> Shells ghosted. Something hates unevenness.
> The skin turns porcelain, the nerves retreat,
> And then the will, and then the consciousness.

Something hates unevenness. That was it, she thought. That's me.

And she turned it into the classic temperament. I will be a scholar, she said. I will banish unevenness.

And then she met Duke. Jim Frank Dukane from Harvard. She was returning, sullen, from a Thanksgiving-weekend visit to

Gloversville. More than any others, her grandparents made her feel a foreigner in a foreign land, longing for the backward enlightenment of Italy.

In the off-campus house where she lived with five other students and the occasional others who showed up, she had just gotten into her room when she turned back toward the door and saw looking in at her quizzically the lanky fellow with the strawlike hair whom she had seen around and heard called Duke.

"Nice to have you back," he drawled in his soft, slow southern voice, looking at her intently.

She stared back, still sullen, and said, "Yah."

After that she saw him around more. They talked and she found him sensitive and intelligent; he saw things straight. He moved into her room, and managed to take the stairs away from the wall they were fastened to and turn them around so that the bed could be moved and faced toward the window. It was for her the metaphor of Duke in her life: He had turned her view from the steps to the window, where she could watch spring arrive on the bare-branched tree it framed. They listened to Bob Dylan records in that room; they tripped on mescaline and watched the bricks shifting in and out of the brick wall beyond the tree; they read poetry; and he started to write a book while she went to classes.

He was her first love partner; she thought they would spend their life together. She had no doubt of his talent and that he would be a writer like her father.

Then she saw some of what Duke's real world was like when she went with him to Tennessee; she could see all the reasons he should try to get away from it and be something else. But she could also see that he wouldn't.

Jim Frank Dukane would stay what he was—a poor white from Tennessee who had gotten a scholarship to Harvard, dropped out, been reinstated, and dropped out again. He was like some literary Huck Finn, a vagrant of the academic world, a person of sensitivity and brains who alone of all of them had the decency to get out of the system they hated without the courage to quit. Tina respected Duke for his honesty in that sense but despaired of him in another: What would he do with himself besides stay on the fringes and protest?

As she began to fall asleep, Tina thought, Now everything will be different.

The next morning Tina was sick again. She looked haggard and pale, and she asked Duke to throw the I Ching with her. This time it wasn't like when they threw #55, the sign of abundance called Feng, which Duke said really meant Fuck, so that the throw meant fuck a lot and love abundantly. Now it was the sign of oppression and exhaustion; the image was one of no water in the lake; the judgment, "A man must not lean on thorns and thistles." Tina, already filled with misgivings, accepted what she saw as the end of her being with Duke.

She remembered her mother, when she had met Duke at Tina's graduation from Bryn Mawr, asking worriedly what she saw in him and saying, "He has such a thin body—is he healthy? And what will he do with himself? Why has he thrown away the chance to go to Harvard?" Tina was arrogant then, and confident of Duke's genius.

Now she was not. She no longer thought of him like her father, a natural writer and self-disciplined enough to work on his own. The more she plunged purposefully into her graduate studies, the more his genius seemed wispy and thin as his hair.

Duke went with her to the airport, and though Tina was telling him they'd keep in touch while she was gone, she already felt estranged and as if the departure were for good. Maybe he felt it, too. He pulled a small object from his pocket and said, "This is for you."

"Shall I open it now?"

"You'd better," he said, and she wondered if he knew, or sensed, that it could be the last chance for her to open it with him present. She opened a box and took out a gold ring set with turquoise, her birthstone.

"Oh, Duke, you knew I wanted it. It's beautiful. And I don't have anything for you."

"Just come back from Rome; that's enough."

"Duke, you know what I told you yesterday. I want to be with my father now."

"That's right, Tina—but you've got to get back to finish your studies. I'll be here when you do."

"I want to be with my father for as long as he wants me. I keep wondering if he ever guessed about Bontelli; they were sort of friends in Rome. I have to be with him now."

"I need you, too, Tina."

"I can't bear it! You know what I've been saying for a while now, even before this happened—what future do we have together? None."

"Tina, girl, you're upset now. Don't try to make plans or think things out. Just remember I want you to come back. I'll be waiting —and if you don't come back in a decent time, why, I might even have to stir myself enough to get over there and get you back." He smiled his slow, mouth-stretching, lazy smile, the smile that had once given Tina such feelings of tenderness toward him. But what did she see now? A guy with a soupy smile and strawlike hair, the hair of which her mother had said, "So thin . . . it looks sort of dead." Maybe it was just from the moment those words were spoken that Tina had known she and Duke wouldn't make it.

"Duke, face it. We would never have made it. We're too different. You don't want anything, just lazing around in the summer catching fish and swimming in the river, or lying in bed and watching the world go by. How long can hanging around the *National Lampoon* and feeding your ideas to the others fill your time? You know me, I want a lot—most of all I don't want to end up like my mother. I don't want to live thinking of what I might have done or what might have been. It makes us inoperable, Duke."

"Why so, Tina? Whoever said that in a couple both had to be achievers? I'd just as soon let you do the achieving. That doesn't bother me. What bothers me is that there's this strong thing between us and you're going to let it slip for no good reason."

"I keep thinking of Mom," Tina said quietly, her eyes filling with tears. "She had a way of seeing into things and telling how they were going to come out."

"Oh, come on, Tina, don't be fatalistic. And besides, this is not the time for you to be deciding things. You've been through too much. Just come back from Rome."

"I'm not promising. . . ."

"Don't promise. You know what Weezy says: 'Have-to's aren't nice.' I don't want you to think you have to come back from Rome, I just want you to want to."

"I'll send you something from Rome."

"Make it from Pompeii."

She smiled, and thought of all the good times they'd had. Duke. The guy who had showed her an easy, relaxed way to live. Deceptive. Like some charming facade behind which there was nothing; like grasshoppers fiddling all summer and then being caught in long, long winters.

It had been good while it lasted and she had no regrets, but their time together had no seeds for the future. The guy with the thin hair would become a middle-aged and then an old guy with thin hair, and no more would have been accomplished in their life together than some good times in bed.

He put his arms around her as they heard the boarding announcement for her flight; they had a long embrace, then kissed. She moved away, took a look at him and waved, then turned toward the boarding ramp. She didn't look back again.

Chapter Twenty-five

How beautiful Rome is, Tina thought as she stood on the terrace in the late afternoon. The air was still thick and fulvous with sun, and swallows were swooping and wheeling through the Roman sunset as they had since the day the city first started on the Palatine.

"Duke sends his love, Tee."

Tina turned away from where she was watering fuchsias and begonias on the terrace ledge and glanced over her shoulder at Missy. Her friend was stretched out on a wicker lounge in the still-sunny part of the terrace beyond the overhead straw matting. To be like Missy, she thought; to be long and rangy, a dancer, with that wild blonde halo of hair and those guileless blue eyes that looked at the world as if it had been created that instant. Missy wore skin-tight faded jeans and a tight poor-boy sweater that didn't quite meet the jeans, showing a strip of her tanned firm flesh. She was as supple and indolent as Weezy's cat Romulus, curled nearby in the shade. Feline, thought Tina, felix. *Sis felix, Caeli, sis in amore potens.* That was it—happy Missy, potent in love. No hang-ups. Missy could love easily, and either sex. Not like me, who makes everything a crucifixion. I'm not a dancer, Tina thought.

Missy was her friend from the days at St. Gregory's in Rome. They had separated to go to different colleges but always came together again in Rome or New York.

They had even spent a semester together in Florence—Tina coming from Bryn Mawr all resolute and directed to do the Renaissance and tuck that away, accomplished, in her bag of tricks where Greek, Latin, and medieval and Provençal lyrics were stored; and

Missy arriving like a sprite from Bennington, forgetting why she was there except to dance in the amphitheater at Fiesole, love and leave Italians, or stand in front of Botticelli's *Primavera* at the Uffizi studying the arrogant and sensuous arch on the foot of that woman she resembled.

In the States, things were always wilder, more threatening. She and Missy had hitched to Massachusetts one fall, the leaves a torrent of color all around them, making them giddy, and they had made the mistake of getting out of a car right on the Mass. Pike, where a cop picked them up and acted as if they were runaways. Tina started a compulsive chatter about the leaves while he drove them to the next exit, put them out, and said to Tina, "You're too young for me, anyway." That was America—unsettling. Give her the bounds and forms of classicism anytime.

"Missy, you know what I love about you?" Tina said, moving toward her, watering plants as she went. "You have no existential predicament in your nature. You're pure."

"Oh, come on, Tee, cut out the crap." Missy leaned over lazily on her side, watching. Her body was perfect, long but forming rounded hillocks in the right places.

"I mean it, Missy. The same way Duke is pure. You're both outside things in a way I could never be. That's why Duke and I couldn't make it. I'm too involved in wanting things. I'm too split. What does coming back to Rome each vacation mean to you? Only the pleasure of being here because your father's at the Academy. You know who you are, Americans living in Rome as long as his work is here, and after that, back to the States to your house in Connecticut. I've never understood where I belong. It tears my whole life apart each time—I mean I go through this absolute trauma of trying to decide here or there: Italian like my father or American like poor Mom. Part of me loves this natural, human life over here and the other part sees that it won't get me anyplace and that I've got to go back and plug into the system over there. God, Missy, it drives me up the wall!"

"You're too serious, that's all."

"I know it! I know! Part of me doesn't want to be, but I guess the deepest part does."

Tina frowned as she faced into the lowering sun and aimed a spray at a large laurel plant near the doorway leading into the apartment.

The terrace was filled with terra-cotta planters holding thick greens, ivy, and flowering plants splayed against the rich warmth of umber walls. A huge riccasperma was in bloom, its thousands of white blossoms threading a jasminelike fragrance into the air from among the glossy, dark leaves. Under the straw matting with its warp of vines, a marble slab, carved with acanthus leaves and inset with crimson, had been set into a wrought-iron frame to make a table; wicker chairs were set around it, ready for dining. Opposite, where Missy was lounging, the sun was still touching the riot of geraniums, petunias, roses, and bougainvillea that swarmed over the walls and latticing.

The latticing created a shady and private area on the part of the terrace adjacent to the ministry building next door. Missy had pulled the chaise to the open part so that she could catch the last sun. She was in the line of vision of two soldiers who were at a ministry window on the same level as the Morosini apartment, and were leaning over the ledge smoking and looking into the gardens of Palazzo Barberini below.

They spotted Missy and smiled. Missy smiled back and waved. Seeing her, Tina said, "Missy, don't encourage them or I'll never be able to take a sunbath out here."

"Why not, Tina? They won't hurt you. They're just looking at the view."

"Well, I don't want to be part of their view."

"What could be better than just to be part of such a beautiful sight?"

"Oh, Missy, you're impossible! That's what I mean about you—total acceptance."

"Actually, this is a great place. That crowd of St. Gregory boarders who are always hanging out at the Fontana di Trevi looking for men should know about your terrace!"

"Poor soldiers," said Tina. "Always on duty and having to salute their stuffed-pants superiors. If I come back in the afternoon around two when the Ministero della Difesa is closing up for the day, there must be twenty thousand generals and admirals streaming down the street with all these poor soldiers going crazy saluting them all. More brass in Italy than in all the NATO countries—or all of Europe. Maybe the world. Then I think, What am I doing in this never-never land where life is like an operetta, where Sophia Loren pays no taxes, and the pope comes out in his white nightgown and capelet to tell people how to vote while they cheer and drop on their knees.

"Or I'll get on the bus to go someplace, and if I'm standing in a crowd I get dead-handed on the ass by some greaser until I get a seat, and then they're all trying to look up my skirt or down my shirt. I feel like Weezy when I get back sometimes—I want to throw bombs at the Ministero and join her *compagni* marching in the streets for the homeless and jobless.

"Then, after three or four days at the most, I get into the rhythm of the place. I go down to the kiosk on the corner to chat with the vendor while I look over the sensational titles of his gossip mags, then I go across the street to the bar for a *cappuccino* while I read *Gente* or watch the people go by. I walk up Via Sistina and look in the windows and know nobody knows how to dress or live better than Italian women. Yesterday I saw this woman in a hot pink shirt-and-skirt outfit coming down the street with her little girl; she looked down, noticed something not right with the girl's head-band, took it off, and dropped it in the street while the girl smiled at her. How natural these people are! In three days I could be a *romana di Roma*; I start dressing differently, eating differently, thinking differently—that's how easily I'm reabsorbed into this place."

"And why not, why not?" Missy murmured.

Tina knew why not. Her sense of the illimitable possibilities awaiting her could not stop at the softness and languor of Rome, beneath which, she knew, there were deadly poisons of unrest and discontent. Rome is too old, she thought; nothing matters anymore. In New York everything does.

In New York she felt competitiveness throbbing in the air and became frenetic because of so much going on, because of the sense of space to fill. In Rome she was squelched by the sense of time: Everything had already been thought of and done—it was time to rest and savor.

"You know, Missy, *papà*'s trying to get me to stay on in Rome with him instead of going back to Columbia in the fall. He says I can do better in the classics over here—get a fellowship at the Academy, or go to the University of Rome. And what can I say? In a practical way he's right. He's trying to hold me because Weezy is going off; she's already made her declaration. As a family we're finished."

"It happens to all families, Tee, sooner or later. I haven't felt like a real part of my family since I went away to college. I come back because it's a free place to hang out for a while and I love Rome."

"See that oleander, Missy," Tina said, pointing to a flowering white plant that stood in a huge terra-cotta pot in the center of the terrace. "Every time my mother brought guests out here she'd say her little joke: 'There's a Spanish proverb,' she'd say, 'that in the house where the oleander blooms, the girls of the house don't marry. I have two daughters and I can never tell whether to get rid of the oleander or the daughters.' "

At Columbia in her library cubicle, Tina would think of the blossoming oleander. Would she or Weezy ever marry? Weezy, according to her radical-feminist principles, had said she never would accept an obsolete bourgeois institution. But Tina couldn't tell. Symbolically there were implications about the oleander that perhaps her mother hadn't realized. Did it mean that in the kind of home Marguerite Morosini set up, her daughters were deliberately warned against marriage? Was it her way of saying, "My daughters, keep the plant which is pleasure and shun marriage which is prison"? For the oleander was always there, while her parents' marriage had become more tenuous than its falling blossoms.

"Look at this place!" Tina said to Missy, leaning over the ledge. "I'd have to be crazy to leave it." Her eyes took in the fountains and gardens and noble backside of Palazzo Barberini, whose serene proportions filled the view from this last of her mother's homes. The top-floor apartment, though in the center of Rome, was removed from the monstrous traffic, the noise, the throngs on the too-narrow sidewalks, and the overload of sweating, badly dressed tourists who added to the summer temperature. It was a time when, if her mother were here, they would be going to the Marche.

"You'll leave," Missy said. "I know you. Anyway, I called Duke from the airport to say hello before I left and he said he missed you. He sent his love."

"He should have sent grass," Tina said glumly. How distancing it was to stand there at that hour and think of Duke in New York, ambling down the paper-strewn, littered, and shabby Broadway up near Columbia to get a fix. How much older and more sinister New York always seemed compared to Rome.

"Missy, do you want a beer?"

"Sure, but then I've got to go. They want me back for dinner.

Some fat cat from the States is going to be there—it might make my career. Jesus!"

"You're too much," Tina said with a smile. "What *is* your career?"

"Beats me, but I guess it's something every nice girl should have. At least at home that's the way they talk. I'd just as soon go on pumping gas in Cambridge, living with Lou, and going to dance classes."

"That's what I mean about you—no existential problems."

"And no bread, either."

Tina went through the perfect rooms to the kitchen, soothed by the sight of familiar things all in their places, liking the tranquillity of old, known objects that turned up again and again in their homes even though so much was lost with each move.

With each move things had passed from their home to the homes of friends or to strangers who had come in response to an ad to buy. But always a nucleus remained: Morosini family things like the hand-rubbed walnut credenza and the round table with the flatiron scorch mark, the instruments and logs of the Venetian sea captains, the elegant Thonet armchair from the country law-office of some great-uncle, a grandmother's sewing table, a game table with green baize top and delicate tapered legs, and even *nonna* Catina's parchment bound boarding-school notebook with exercises in math, French, and morality.

Opening the door of the giant turquoise American refrigerator with its huge separate freezer compartment, Tina thought of her mother. Her strangeness was everywhere in that dark little Italian kitchen.

It was there in the Italian stove, whose oven was never meant to accommodate a Thanksgiving turkey or bake American birthday cakes but which was subjected periodically to Marguerite Morosini's wishful thinking. Over the stove hung the gleaming pans of Revere Ware that had followed them over the ocean and back, time and again. Most absurd was the attempt at American kitchen gaiety and efficiency in a land where it didn't matter, for a kitchen was the maid's place, and as long as it had a water faucet and some gas burners no one cared in what decor the elaborate meals were produced.

Her father had jokingly called the fridge the family idol. It was secondhand, bought from a departing American family through an ad in the *Daily American*, and it coincided with the firing of Giovanna in one of her mother's attempts at economizing. She had persuaded Alberto that they should replace Giovanna with a dishwasher and a big enough refrigerator so there didn't have to be daily food shopping and cooking. Tina had gotten the news at college: "Not that the new idol will do the dusting or prepare the vegetables or iron my shirts as Giovanna did," her father wrote, "but it's huge enough, at least, to contain for the moment all your mother's illusions."

The kitchen made a naive attempt at eat-in space for American-type breakfasts. Boxes of expensive imported cereals and some Campbell's soups stood on the shelf of the cupboard, below which was the washboard that Giovanna (rehired) used in the primitive sink. The Morosinis ended up with an incomplete American kitchen and a part-time maid. The worst of both worlds, Tina used to reflect.

"What are you doing this summer, Tee, going to the Marche?" Missy asked as they sat in the fading light drinking beer on the terrace.

"Don't know. Weezy's going to take off right after the service for Mom. I thought I should stick around with *papà*. None of us want to go to the Marche after what happened to Mom. I don't know. How about you?"

"I'm hitching to Yugoslavia and maybe Greece with this guy I met."

"What about Lou?"

"What about him? He's in the States, with a summer job."

"Well, I mean what about him in the sense that you've been with him so long and now you can just go off with someone else all summer?"

"Gee, Tina, that has nothing to do with my feelings for Lou. And I don't expect he's just going to be sitting there alone all summer waiting for me. We know we'll be together when I get back. It's always been that way with us."

"I wish I could be that way. . . ."

"Try, sweetie!" Missy laughed as she got up to go. "Let me know if I can help with anything."

Tina looked at her appraisingly. "Missy, there may be something." Could Missy help? No, it was absurd to think so. Like asking a butterfly to stand watch.

"What's up, Tee?"

"I'm not sure yet—I'll let you know."

Tina was thinking of how complicated things were between men and women and how things always got in the way, yet how, in the main, things had seemed mostly good with her mother and father despite the fact that they had both committed the great error of their times—total romanticism. As a child Tina had often heard her father's joke about America making her mother acceptable to him in marriage; as a southern Italian she would have been too foreign, he said.

"Money helped too," Marguerite would add sarcastically. "While the Morosinis were sinking with Venice, Umbertina was on the way up in America. Money is a great equalizer." The Venetian Morosinis might have had centuries of civilization and walnut furniture, but Tina's mother had had youth and optimism, and when Alberto Morosini, so much older than she and from such a different background, had said they would be artists together and asked her to marry him, she accepted. Then they struggled with the mismatch until one of them gave up.

But how do you know when it's right? Tina wondered.

She went back to the terrace and stood looking out over the ledge. Farthest away was the white speck of the Pauline fountain on the Janiculum, where she could imagine Garibaldi, mounted, looking down at the city; in the middle distance the dome of the Pantheon was like the shell of a giant turtle basking in the reddish light; nearby were the treetops and watchtower of the Quirinale; unseen, just beyond Palazzo Barberini, Bernini's triumphant Triton raised the conch shell of sensuality to his lips and sounded its notes louder than all the traffic that swirled about him.

She turned to go in, satisfied. As she did, her eye caught the overhead straw matting, which was sagging, and she thought, It won't last till fall. The terrace was perfect, yes, but no lighting for night had been thought of; as in all their homes, there was this visible edge of impermanence, of things falling apart. Was the matting made of straw instead of something more durable because her mother's taste kept her to the natural? Or was it because when setting up this terrace she would have sensed the futility of spending money for anything more permanent, since in a few years, at most three or four, they would be moving on? That's what they'd always

been, Tina mused—campers on the move, vagabonds with aristocratic baggage and topnotch pots and pans to drag behind them as
they traveled.

Each move, there it was: Some cherished books got lost, some
more of *nonna* Catina's china got chipped, some drawings got
marked by moisture and some family papers torn, and some more
ancient furniture, going from the chill of Italian apartments to overheated American interiors, burst its joints, cracked, and crumbled.
The daisy-backed Empire chairs from the Veneto *palazzo* of a
titled relative gave way regularly under guests at the dining room
table and were by now a patchwork of mends and underpinnings,
not meant anymore to sit on but kept for sentiment.

"I don't care where I live," her mother used to say. "All I need
is a roof over my head and a little place where I can work in peace
and put my books and things."

But she did care. She cared enormously for place, and each one
they came to and claimed, she worked at to make beautiful. And
then moved on. Tina remembered six: some in Italy, some in the
States, one in France. This one, her mother's last home, was the
seventh.

Alberto Morosini's literary trophies were among heaps of books
and magazines on the refectory table her mother had found in the
Marche—little statuettes and sculptured knickknacks that he had
won over the years. "A prize for each saint's day"—she could hear
her mother's ironic tone—"and your father is on his way to collecting them all."

Her mother, on the other hand, had collected stones with interesting patterns from beaches or classical ruins, boxes, vases, wooden
figures, dried plants, and branches; and these were spaced artistically
throughout the shelves of her book collection in English, which took
up one wall in the living room, while her father's Italian books ran
all the way down the long corridor onto which the bedrooms
opened. Two separate libraries, two separate worlds that had never
merged.

Tina went down the hall to her mother's room to begin going
over her things, as her father had asked her to. It was a large room
with an oversize bed, where for the past year or so her mother had
slept alone—like a mother abbess, her father said. *La madre badessa*,
he called her. She said it was because he snored. Every morning
she had awakened to the susurrant fountain in the gardens below

and had gotten out of bed to the same stupendous sight. On a long table at the wall opposite the bed were the souvenirs of many auspicious beginnings: the jewel-making books, the bits of interesting stones now used as paperweights that were to have been crafted into belts and necklaces; the jars of photographic stuff that were to have started her on her career. There were boxes of all sorts and shapes holding things. Everything was in order; there were no unsightly piles as if something had been in the works and was now interrupted forever. No, the main surface of the table was clear, still waiting for the work to begin.

Above the writing table, dangling from a piece of yarn, was the tin heart Tina remembered always having been in her mother's room wherever they had lived. "It's from my grandmother Umbertina," Tina had been told as a child. "She wore it when she was a goat girl in Calabria. Someday I'm going to find the place she came from." Now Tina took the crudely shaped piece and ran her fingers over the hammered design. She wondered how it was worn. Then she knew what she was going to do this summer—she would go to Calabria to find Umbertina. My namesake, she thought; a strong woman who had direction in her life.

Alongside the table was a velvet-covered chaise from some Morosini *signora* in the Veneto who had used it to recline on after the midday meal as ladies were supposed to do, to read or embroider or receive her husband's embraces; but in her mother's household, there was no family dinner at noon and the chaise was more a wistful relic than anything useful.

A dressing table held several more boxes, including a handsome eighteenth-century Venetian toilet-box decorated in découpage that held her mother's jewelry. Tina opened the box and looked at its contents as she had done since she was a little girl, coveting the beads and bracelets and especially the large ring set with a diamond and two emeralds on interweaving bands of white and yellow gold that was her mother's engagement ring. Ever since childhood Tina had loved and wanted that ring. "Mom, someday can I wear this?" she would ask. "Someday," her mother would answer.

Curious, Tina thought now, how attached her mother had been to drawers and boxes and to the idea of having everything contained, in place; she who tore it all apart so readily, ready to move on, sending them winging like birds of passage on the flights of her inquietude.

Against the far wall was the *armadio* that housed her mother's fashionable Rome wardrobe. Tina opened it. She pulled out a rich wine-colored suede skirt and put it on, remembering the first sight of her mother in that skirt with her wine-colored boots and how she had envied her. She once had envied everything about her mother—her clothes, her life, that perfect room. "Why do you have to have the best room in the house?" she had said when they first moved there, knowing how silly she was to say that, because all parents always had the largest and best room and what she was really saying in her petulant way was, "Why isn't that me sleeping in the large matrimonial bed with a husband and being the queen of this beautiful place?"

Instead, she and Weezy had always shared a room until Giovanna had been fired, and then Tina had insisted on having a room of her own and Weezy had gotten the tiny maid's room. Weezy! That silly waif . . . that waifish revolutionary! At least Tina would end up with something after she finished her studies.

As if her thoughts had summoned her sister, Tina heard the front door open and Weezy come down the hall.

"Weezy, I'm in Mother's room," she called. "I'm going through her clothes. *Papà* wants us to pick out what we want and pack up the rest to give away. What do you want? I'm going to take this suede skirt."

"You can have it all," Weezy said. She came in, slight, shabby, carrying her art gear, and sat down on the huge bed. She was dressed in a cotton skirt and an old shirt, and her bare legs were pale and unshaven. Her hair hung loose over her shoulders and bangs covered her forehead. She was fair-skinned—as white, she joked, as Carpaccio's Venetian whores.

"You could be more cooperative," Tina said.

"I should be more like you," Weezy answered sarcastically.

"I'm not about to take all this stuff back to the States," Tina went on. "Besides, how can you live in Rome and not want to look and dress better?"

"This is how I feel like looking and dressing," Weezy said pointedly. "Anything else wouldn't be me—it'd be you or Mom. You'd better take it all. I'm going to Spain and then maybe over into Morocco this summer. After that I think I'll move up to Bologna. *Papà* will probably go back to Venice."

"Oh, Weezy," said Tina, genuinely moved, "it's as if we've all

come unstuck now that Mother's not here. It's as if we won't even
be a family anymore."

"Families are the assholes of the world."

"Oh, you're so cool!" Tina said. "Remember how you used to
go around quoting French aphorisms when you were going to
Sainte Dominique? Well, as Molière said, there are fagots and
fagots—meaning there are families and families, and ours is different."

"That's right," said Weezy. "This family's all crazy in different
degrees."

"Wait till you're off wherever you're going, you'll miss this to
come back to. How can *papà* leave this beautiful place!"

"It's too big and it's too expensive," Weezy said dryly. "And
papà never liked Rome, anyhow. He'll be happy back in Venice
living with *zia* Lauretta and working on his dramatic poem."

Tina contemplated her sister. Weezy was pulling the strands of
her long hair, twisting her face around to view the ends, to see if
they were split. Her hair was lovely and thick, abundant, with
warm auburn lights. It was the best thing about her. A cute face,
Tina thought, but childish and vague-looking. An Italian girl would
have known how to make that face interesting, taking advantage
of plainness by becoming clever and using grace instead of beauty
to charm.

Weezy the weasel, Tina used to tease her as a child. And there
was something weaselly about her, something furtive and secretive
that made her father call her his mysterious daughter. Tina thought
she knew the type, she had seen it in the States: the dropouts, the
superior beings who were above everyone else in sensibility and
poetics of the soul, which was all, they said, education was about—
certainly not the rote learning and straining after grades and fel-
lowships that Tina was into.

In fact, Weezy played the flute and read the Russians. She was
also into real life. That was Weezy's big thing—that she gloried
in real work, sweat, the hard edges of existence, survival. She had
worked as apprentice to a bookbinder, as a dishwasher in London, as
a grape picker at harvest time in the Marche, and had been a cook
in a summer camp for mentally defective youngsters. To be bruised
and roughed up by life, to experience it all, that's what she wanted.
To go on long, enlightening wanderings, to keep from being stuck
in the academic world. Schools are now what factories were during

the Industrial Revolution, she said—dehumanizing. Even if life outside the Ivory Tower was mediocre, she wanted to feel it in its
reality.

Tina glanced at the portfolio that Weezy had dropped to the
floor. Speaking of mediocrity, she thought. Everyone had agreed
that Weezy's work was weak, unformed; at its most interesting it
had a grotesque edge that might, with a stronger talent, be developed. Tina thought of a letter Weezy had written her saying, "I
have the passion of an artist, but no art other than life." Life, that
was supposed to be Weezy's great thing. Even their mother had
fallen for it, rebuking Tina's bookishness by saying of Weezy,
"Well, at least she's out in the world."

Now Weezy was lighting a cigarette and lounging on the velvet
chaise. It angered Tina to see her where their mother should have
been. No, not anger, she acknowledged to herself, jealousy: because
their mother had admired the queerness in Weezy, her independence
and refusal to be cast in the mold that formed all the rest of them.
And yet as mother and daughter they hadn't gotten along. Maybe,
Tina thought now, because they were too much alike.

"Don't smoke in here, Weezy," she said.

"Oh, fuck off, Tina," Weezy said, looking up with a frown. But
she put out the cigarette.

How different they were. Tina remembered what she had told
Duke once when they were stoned: "I like words better than people." And it was true. Words—fat, articulate, latinized, weighty,
and scintillating—were her weapons and her skill. Weezy, instead,
lazy about words, was very intuitive. She could listen, not say
much, and them come out with immediate and true perceptions.
In some ways Weezy had a quicker intelligence than Tina's tough
grasp of facts and mechanical learning. The difference was that
Weezy stuck to nothing whereas Tina persevered and mastered.
Now, through their father, Weezy had been admitted to the Ac-
cademia delle Belle Arti. But her main interest was the women's
movement and leftist politics.

Weezy got up from the chaise and went over to the table, where
a series of notebooks of various colors and sizes were lined up.
She picked one out and flipped through the pages.

"Tina, did you know Mom had all these diaries?"

"When *papà* said to go through her things, I don't think he meant
those. I bet he doesn't know about them."

"Tina, this is when she's in college: *All these snooty, shining girls! They know who they are and where they're going. One of them is descended from Thomas Edison. I'm the only Italian name here. They're all saying they're going to be writers or doctors or go into the Foreign Service. Whoever told me I could do any of that?*"

"Poor Mom," said Tina, "her parents never let her think she could be anybody. They think I'm going to be a teacher but I'm taking awfully long about it; they don't understand anything about graduate school and my being a scholar."

"I don't much, either," said Weezy. "I don't know how you can stand so much institutionalizing. A few people get out after sixteen years of it still hanging on to themselves—maybe you can do it—but most come out with their minds plugged up. They've never even centered in on their own thoughts because they're so busy assimilating other people's. That's my objection to all social structures."

"What are you going to do, Weezy, wipe out all the schools— you and your gang?" Tina asked sarcastically.

"That's the kind of hairpin I am. Kinky."

"Obnoxious."

"I'll tell you something, Tina. When it got time for me to follow in your footsteps and go to college in the States, I got scared shit-less. I took a hard look at you and Mom and what could also be me, and all I saw was life centered around this awful contrived thing called getting ahead. That's when I said, No way. I had to keep out of it and save myself."

"Do what you want, Weezy, but don't pretend that your role is more socially committed than mine. Right now all you're really into is yourself. That wouldn't be big enough or interesting enough for me."

Tina's words made her uncomfortable precisely because she did feel out of touch. She had cast aside the protest and debates and idealism of her student days to fit into getting on and having a career. It was the recognition that she was not socially committed that made her ridicule Weezy.

Still, since their mother's death she had resolved to be closer to her sister.

She picked up an Italian school notebook covered in Raphael-esque wreaths and marked 1969 on the spine. "*I can't live like this anymore*," she read. "*Questo matrimonio non ci sarà.*" She looked up at Weezy and said, "That's the line from *I Promessi Sposi.*"

"Jesus, Tina, you're so literary! Here's Mom talking about ending her marriage and all you can do is make a reference to *I Promessi Sposi!* That's what I mean about you—literature comes before life."

"Don't be an ass, Weezy. Literature *is* life."

"Diaries are as bad as families," said Weezy. "They do more bad than good if we take them straight."

"Do you think *papà* knew how she felt? But these last years she was happy, I swear it! I really began to think of her as my friend, as a person more than just my mother. She was so much looser and funnier. I remember when she came for graduation. She was marvelous; she looked great and acted great."

"She had a lover by then," said Weezy.

Tina was surprised by Weezy's bluntness. It was something they had never discussed. "Did you know that, too?"

"Not in any absolute way. But it's something I knew and felt in my bones. If we want to, all we have to do it keep reading her diaries. We'll find Massimo, I know we will."

"You knew it was Massimo, too?"

"Sure, he used to come over in the afternoon and she'd send me all over Rome on some stupid errand. Or if *papà* was going to be out of town, she'd tell me I could stay overnight at a friend's. Still, I didn't catch on for a while."

"I only met him once," Tina said. "But I knew it. She must have met him when we bought the house in the Marche."

"Or maybe we bought the house there because she had already met him and decided that it was a way to be near him when he wasn't in Rome."

"God, Weezy, do you think so?"

"What's the difference?" Weezy was thumbing through another notebook.

"Do you think we should read any more?" Tina asked. "On the other hand, I'm glad she had a lover. I wonder if *papà* knew."

"If he did," said Weezy, "he didn't object. Maybe because things were finally going well at home. I think we were, for once, finally settled. . . . Here, listen to this."

"Weezy, that's enough. It's getting late and *papà* will be back soon. He shouldn't see these. We'll have to pack them away some-

place, until we can burn them. There might even be letters somewhere."

"Let's just read the very last entry," Weezy insisted.

The final entry was a week before Marguerite's fatal crash.

*"Is this the bill for happiness? Is this paying the goddam fiddler?
Now I'm pregnant and it's Massimo's child and who else but me is
going to pay? Now what? Ask him to leave his wife? And he's just
lost the Strega! A backroom abortion? A quick trip to England or
Switzerland? And where would the money come from? What
could I tell A.? What do women do in Italy . . . or anyplace? What
is this terrible thing that happens to us in our bodies where we grow
our own punishment, this living thing in our guts which is the
proof of shame, guilt, sin, anger, frustration, lust. There is no question about bearing this child . . . or is there? If Massimo wanted it,
we could go away; we might be able to do it. But no, at my age,
it's too late. Everything's too late—if I tell him, I'll lose him. I've
already lost him . . . now what? Angela—"*

Tina sat down at the chest at the foot of the bed, stunned. Tears
were in her eyes.

"Poor lady," said Weezy. "Can you imagine her driving over
the mountains all that way and what must have taken place between
them? You can just bet he must have rejected her—in some nice,
smooth, Italian-men's-style way, but rejection all the same. She
should have told me; I'd have helped her."

The light of sunset had faded in the room and Weezy moved to
turn on a lamp.

"What's going to become of us?" Tina asked with a quaver in
her voice that made Weezy look over at her.

"We'll just go our own ways, I suppose," Weezy said offhandedly. "You can just stay put in graduate school; that's safe
enough. That can be your family, your womb."

"My family? My womb?" Tina repeated. "Oh, God, Weezy,
why did you say that? Jesus, Weezy, I think *I'm* pregnant."

Chapter Twenty-six

Tina put down her copy of *Il Messaggero* and looked about her. Her view of Piazza Navona allayed the anxiety she felt about her coming appointment with Angela. Two women passed her table at the *caffè*; they were old, old, bent over, and they walked arm-in-arm chatting like two schoolgirls. Then a cigarette vendor with his contraband American brands came and approached her.

"*Buon giorno, signorina,*" he said pleasantly.

Tina let herself relish the civility and charm of the Mediterranean huckster, so unlike the American sell of whatever. Here you were greeted with a proper salutation before any business was thought of. In fact, "*Bella giornata,*" the smiling man continued. "A nice day and here's a good buy to go with it. Look—three packs for a thousand lire."

Tina bought the three packs just for the enjoyment of the exchange. She'd give them to Weezy. As the man smiled and pocketed the thousand-lire bill, he said he could tell she was *una ragazza profonda e sensibile.* Italians, she thought, always said things like that after a one-minute acquaintance. It used to make Tina shudder with impatience at their shallowness but now she didn't mind.

The cigarette man ambled over to other tables and the parade in the piazza went on: marketing housewives, tourists, vendors, nannies and babies, beggars, dealers, faggots, touts, feminists, schoolchildren, duchesses, lawyers, whores, petty clerks, and pimps, crossing and re-crossing the elliptical piazza, the old racecourse of emperors, on their errands.

The baroque facade of Sant'Agnese in Agonia undulated in the warm air; the phallic fountains thrust themselves upward in awesome jets. Tina ordered her breakfast: a *cappuccino* with a sprinkle of cocoa on the froth and a grilled *würstel* on a bun. She sat in the sun, loving its warmth on her bare arms and legs. She let her mind empty as her eyes swung round the ellipse just as they were meant to, circling the excrescences of rococo exuberance, moving and skimming like the swallows at dusk.

How could she think she could live anyplace else than in Rome, Tina mused, when all the world, the one she felt good in, was right here. Perfect. That was the trouble with Rome, she knew. Her part in it was too perfect, too easy. All she had to do was nothing— simply be her father's daughter and everything would be accessible and easy and she would only have to let things happen.

The thought of what was wrong with her fell like a shadow over the feeling of well-being that had suffused her; fear came back. Absurd, she thought, as she glared at the easy skirmishes of spiraling forms and wafting billows where the facade of Sant'Agnese undulated and the figures in the fountains swirled and played. A theater of the absurd. How could she see her life in terms of sitting in Piazza Navona and basking? Even reading a paper was too difficult in that spot.

She deliberately picked up *Il Messaggero* to read the news of the day, all terrible. At an adjoining table she recognized the banalities of American tourists. The waiter brought her order and Tina heard a man's voice: "Say, look at that, Grace, a hot dog!" Tina let her glance go over to the table where the Americans were sitting—a man in an open sports shirt, wearing sunglasses and a camera over his shoulder, and a woman with knee-length shorts and a hairdo static with spray.

"It's called a *würstel* here," she said, regretting it as she did, wondering why she felt compelled to help them.

"Say, aren't you American?" the man said. She nodded. "What are you doing reading that rag?" he kidded, pointing to her Italian newspaper.

She thought of replying rudely "None of your business" or "What's it to you?" But she never could with these people; much as she disliked the tourists, their very helplessness and candor made her unable to deal with them.

"I live in Rome," she said. "My father is Italian."

"Hear that, Grace? She's Italian, too. We're Italian," the man said, beaming proudly while Tina winced at the mistake she had made. "You speak Italian, huh? *Nyah poke?*"

"What?" Tina said. "Nabob? What's that?" But the minute she uttered the strange word she had figured it out. The man was trying to say *un poco*—meaning "You speak a little Italian?"—and she blushed for him and his pathetic words.

"You speak a different dialect, huh?" he said pleasantly, nonplussed.

"I speak Italian," she corrected primly, knowing it would not have any effect. Italian-American tourists all felt they spoke Italian no matter what wretched sounds they came out with. It offended her sense of things that they should connect her Italianness with theirs. "I've lived here for years and my father is from Venice," she went on compulsively, showing that she could have no possible kinship with *meridionali* like them (and feeling like Peter denying Christ as she wiped out, with her snobbery, all her mother's Calabrian ancestry). Her father occasionally spoke Veneto. She loved the sound of it—the lilting cadences of a dialect imbued with sea motion, but it was the language of doges and artists, not some southern pastiche from ignorant mountain recesses.

Oblivious, friendly, expansive, the man went on. "My father was from Fudge."

"Fudge?"

"Don't you know where that is? Down near Bari."

"Oh," Tina gasped, "Foggia!"

"Yah, Fudge."

They were ruining her morning, Tina thought sourly as she ate her *würstel* and sipped at the *cappuccino*. She thought of herself in the States angrily explaining that she was not Italian-American. My father is Italian and my mother is a third-generation American who never heard Italian until she got to Italy to study; I am part Italian and part American, *not* Italian-American. It was a splitting of hairs that convinced no one, not even Tina. But she felt obliged, each time, to put up her defense against being merged in the ethnic mess she saw and despised in the States. She thought of a bumper sticker that disgusted her: "Mafia Staff Car, Keepa You Hands Off." She looked around, wanting to get away, as the man said, "Guess you know this town pretty good, huh?"

"Jason!" Tina called out, beginning to wave frantically. "Jason

Jowers, over here!" She beckoned to a figure crossing the piazza not far from the *caffè* until he turned, squinted in the light, recognized her, and came over.

"*Ciao*, Tina," Jason said as he came over, and kissed her on the cheek. He was dressed in an Indian shirt and was carrying a shopping net full of peaches and rolls. "What's up?"

"Let's get out of here," she said quickly in Italian, counting out change that she left on the table, "before I get involved with these *deficienti. Andiamo.*"

"See yuh," waved the man from the adjoining table.

"God!" she muttered, and took Jason's arm, steering him through the tables out into the piazza.

"Do you want to come up and sit on the terrace?" Jason asked. The Jowers family had a penthouse apartment overlooking Piazza Navona. Tina, who had been a classmate at St. Gregory's of Tim Jowers, Jason's younger brother, had been to parties on the penthouse terrace. She pictured herself now at those high school parties, standing off by herself contemplating, a slight scorning smile turning the corner of her mouth as she gave in to anger and envy. Oh, to be one of the Jowers, she would think; it was not just their perfect place in Rome that got to her, since her home was beautiful, too—it was their perfect lives. The first year Tina and Tim were at college in the States, he had invited her for Thanksgiving weekend to the Cape, where the original Jowers homestead, much expanded from 1710, was still his grandparents' family home. It had given her a sense of stability she had never forgotten. For even though the Morosinis were a Venetian family for centuries past, there was no continuously inhabited dwelling place with which they were identified and where all their history was laid out to say to themselves, and others, who they were. The Morosinis were scattered away from Venice, their furniture divided and crumbling, their male line extinct after her father.

"No," said Tina, "let's just walk to the Corso. Am I glad you came along!"

"I am, too, Tina. I wanted to call about your mother. I just got back yesterday and Dad told me."

"Thanks, Jason." She was silent as they walked along, then said, "Is Tim back?"

"Tim's working out his CO duties in Boston. For a conscientious objector, he's got a great assignment—he's working for a museum.

Here, have a peach." He dug in the net and got out a couple of peaches that they ate as they walked along.

Typical of Jowers males, she thought, their ease in shopping for peaches as well as dodging the draft. "You both landed on your feet with the war business," she said. "Being active in the SDS didn't keep you from law school or Tim from graduating."

Something not as strong as resentment, but akin, welled up in her. Some people just knew how to live, she thought. They managed not to have commitments they couldn't throw off, or honesty, which was Duke's deadly virtue. She liked the whole Jowers family and envied them their easy sense of self. Yet she was the daughter of a poet, she reminded herself; a descendant of people who had been sea-captains in Venice long before the first Jowers, a Puritan, built his little shelter in the New World. And she was Umbertina's descendant, too. Somehow the knowledge made her feel both insecure and blessed above all others.

"Yes, we did it all," Jason was saying. "SDS, draft evasion, fighting Nixon and pollution and the corporations. We integrated, boycotted lettuce and grapes, and backed the New Left. And then we ended right back in the system. I've just passed my law boards, by the way."

"That's great, Jason. And I've just got my master's." Tina took a deep bite of peach and licked the juice that overran her lips. "Going on for my doctorate," she said awkwardly, lapping up the juice with her tongue curled at the side of her mouth. "I can remember my mother saying about Duke 'He doesn't have a core' because he kept dropping out of Harvard. And I'd get real angry and say, 'Who's got a core, these days? Even the big old elm trees I always remember at the grandparents' place in Gloversville are dead of inner rot.' God, I was *so* smart-assed! All the regrets I've got—God! Maybe we were just into pranks. Maybe my grandparents were right, after all, to think the protest was just kid-stuff. Where's all the protest now?"

"I know what you mean, Tina. In college we could march and sit in and hassle the administration. But once we're into big life choices like whether or not to go to law school or graduate school, then suddenly there's no room to maneuver and we're in the system. I had the same feelings when it was time for me to go to law school, and the only way I could handle it was to remind myself that I was working in Vista and that I wasn't going into corporate law; I was going to be doing civil rights and I was needed."

"Sure, *you're* needed. But what about me? I've got to justify myself in this day and age for being in the classics. It's sheer indulgence, everyone tells me. 'Who needs Latin and Dante?' Weezy says. My grandfather says, 'You should study something practical—be a secretary. You've got the personality for it,' he tells me, 'not like your mother.' I should be engaged in politics, or be an activist in the women's movement. How can I justify doing what I love?"

"Well, just because you are doing what you love, I suppose. That is the human ideal, isn't it? Someone must be willing to carry on the traditions of the past and that's your role."

"One of the things I remember my parents arguing about when I was younger was the Vietnam war," Tina said, squinting her eyes against the glare of the bright sun. "My father supported Johnson, which made my mother furious. He said she didn't understand anything of the reality of the world, and so forth. At first I sided with my father, thinking that because he was a man he must know better. Then I knew that my mother's feelings were correct and I hadn't trusted her just because they were a woman's feelings. I was a kind of Uncle Tom against my sex. That's how confused our roles are in this shitty society."

"We've all been up to here in tensions. My family's no different. My parents have practically not been speaking to each other for the past few years. My mother is Canadian, you know, and says Dad is an American imperialist; and he, of course, has to keep somewhat decently quiet because he's a government representative after all. The whole thing is pretty rotten, and it's a hell of a mess to be working for the government and having to hold your tongue. I can see both their points."

"Who can stand being American these days! I'm glad I'm half-Italian. There's a marvelous word I just learned for my lot: 'quaquaversal.' Isn't that great? You can hear the *qua* in it. The OED defines it as 'whithersoever,' but it's a turning here, then there, and back again here . . . forever on. It doesn't apply to you and your family because you're assigned duties when you go from one place to another. But me and my family—we have no rhyme or reason, my mother just kept *papà* moving back and forth. It's a paradox: My father's Venetian ancestors were roaming sea-captains, but all he ever wanted to do was to stay still someplace and take walks in the country. So what happens? He marries someone demonic like my mother who keeps us on the move like a band of gypsies. And the best-laid plans of her family in Gloversville went astray, too. She didn't marry an American doctor or lawyer in her hometown but an Italian poet, and started a life of shuttling back and forth between the States and Italy."

"Very sensible, I would say," said Jason cheerfully.

"But you don't see the existential problem, Jason!"

"I think too much is made of this whole family business. After all, once you're grown you can live where and with whom you choose and have the life you choose."

"Yes, sure, but maybe the point is you can't grow up to get out *for good* if the family isn't supportive in the beginning. A strong base is like a launching pad. But a weak one is just a swamp. I think that's why my mother never got wholly away—there was no push upward from behind her. She was meant to fizzle out."

"Oh, come on, Tina, she wasn't a fizzle; she was a charming and lovely lady. Maybe she really liked and needed the turmoil of her life. Would she have been happier if she hadn't tried a getaway?"

Tina walked silently for a bit, thinking of this. "Maybe you're right, Jason. She gave me so much nourishment, she must have had strengths I didn't see."

She was silent again, sucking on the peach pit, her brow furrowed with concentration. "But you know what, Jason, we didn't mean a thing."

"What do you mean?"

"I mean to the government, to the rotten system, to the Pentagon, to the generals, to old shit Nixon, to any of them."

"How about ourselves?"

"Well, that's different," Tina said emphatically. "I'll always be glad for what we did. If this war ever ends, we had our hand in its ending and we were the voice of reason, not the wild loonies they tried to make us seem. You and I and Missy and Tim and Duke can always be proud of that, Jason."

"How about Duke? Are you still with him?"

Tina thought of Duke's seed in her belly, and again felt like Peter denying. "No," she said. "We were never going to make it in the long run, in the big way. I want to do something with myself— I'm not going to just flop around a commune and make granola and boil organic cabbage all my life! I'm really into what I've been doing this year—medieval Latin and the *Comedy*."

"Maybe Duke knows better than we do what an education is.

He's still hanging on to what we were all about just a couple of years ago."

"Oh, come on, Jason, don't give me that!" Tina was irritated at the defense of Duke she herself had taken so many times. "I know about the Establishment, the System, and now Academia. It's a hard thing to square the intellectual purity I'm in with the external forms of Academia. But I am not going to let the externals of any system do me out of what I want and I know what I want—to be a scholar who teaches for a living, not a teacher who passively absorbs other peoples' culture. Of course it pisses me off that I have to sell myself to the Department as a good investment before they'll give me a fellowship! They hesitate with women 'cause they're scared we'll quit and get married, as if a woman's education didn't become as integral a part of her life as a man's . . . as if a woman couldn't marry and have her career, too! That's the unfair part—but that's real and I've got to live with it and live around it and not let it get me down or take my sights away from what's really important. But this much I know: I wouldn't go through this for any piece of parchment in the world. I go through this for Dante."

"Well, that's not so quaquaversal, after all," Jason said, laughing. "You've got your sights." She felt his admiration.

"It makes me very insecure, Jason, because all of us graduate students are in this amazing obstacle race—the paranoia is rampant."

"It's no different from the business world or any other world, probably."

"That's the sad part: Academia is another hierarchy like the military, and completely political. But what I love in it is greater than the rest and I guess there's nothing perfect. My father's always saying we have to love each other's defects as well as our qualities."

At the mention of her father, the torrent of Tina's words quietly subsided.

She was on her way to Angela's to make arrangements for an abortion; it seemed very unimportant that she should be thinking about graduate school.

"Let's have an *aperitivo* before you get on the bus," Jason said.

"You always know the right thing to say, Jason," she said, brightening. "That's because you come from a diplomatic background. And yet you look more and more like a pirate—in fact, you look great. How's that?"

"Not hard, really." He grinned. "I took off my glasses and got contact lenses and had my teeth filled with gold."

She laughed, and they went into a little bar on the Corso and had Punt e Mes. She speculated about Jason as they talked. What, in his solid English lineage, accounted for his full sensual lips and dark coloring—his head of thick black wavy hair and his deep brown eyes and swarthy skin? He was not at all like Tina. Had an early pilgrim father begot with an Indian or a slave and taken the child of such union into his own family? Or had some later Jowers female, when the family had become affluent in the nineteenth century, gone to Europe on the Grand Tour, become impregnated by some Spanish, Italian, or Rumanian nobleman, and returned in seclusion to the Cape, there to infiltrate into the family the genes that had produced Jason?

He was more Italianate, in a way, than Tina herself. She had the fine delicate features, light eyes, and height of the northern Italian, and the dark hair and sullen glower of southern women, who see the world as a hostile presence before which to be, at best, diffident. Her features were not perfect—eyes and mouth too small and forehead low—but she had a beautiful face with an intensity in her look as if she were always about to lunge, verbally or physically, into something. Her nerves were on the surface; not, like Jason's, well embedded within centuries of settled living and family peace.

The aperitif relaxed her.

"There's going to be a service for Mother at the Protestant Cemetery Thursday," she said. "I'd like you to come if you're here."

"I will, Tina. She was terribly kind to Tim and me that time we were wandering around Apulia looking for Norman castles and got to your part of the Marche. She put us up at your place in the country for almost a week. She was a lovely lady."

"She felt frustrated, I know that. I think if my father had been stronger with her, *made* her grow up and stopped protecting her, it would have been better for both of them. She wanted someone to tell her to stop, to make her work at her art, to make her be a real person and not just a wife."

Tina was silent, thinking about her mother's lover: Had he presented one more problem in her overloaded life? Instead of solving all the ambivalence had he so increased it and yet become so necessary that he made life and its choices finally too much? It would have been typical of her mother, she decided, to demand big and final decisions when all along she knew how impossible they were; had she demanded that Massimo leave his own family for her? Had she decided to leave *her* family for him? Was she mulling all this over in her mind when the car went off the road?

"I have to go now, Jason. *Ciao*."

"Let's get together, Tina. What about going to see Signor Agostini?"

"I'd like that, Jason."

"I'll give you a call. *Ciao!*"

He stood and waved as she went off. He does look like a pirate, she thought. She liked his looks.

They went to Signor Agostini's the hard way, taking the 62 bus from the Corso to the end of its line at the little San Pietro train station near the Vatican, where they got the train for all the small stops outside Rome. They had done it before, separately, as had most of the St. Gregory's students that Signor Agostini had in his Latin and Greek classes.

Guido Agostini was more than just a classics teacher. He had been for Tina a *maestro della vita*, the great teacher of her life. He was the reason she had found her life's work.

And now she was going to see him not as she had done in former years—as an excuse to have a day in the country hearing his witty and learned conversation and eating good things accompanied by his own wine—but as if she were casting auspices and he would read the divination. Somehow she expected from Signor Agostini a message which, like the sibyl's, could be variously interpreted; but she would divine the meaning intuitively and would follow it.

From the station at Porta Rossa, Jason and Tina walked the short distance over the countryside toward the hill where Signor Agostini had enlarged and renovated an old shepherd's cottage into a modern dwelling for himself and his wife. He was an idealist, he told his Latin classes, hopelessly practicing the virtues of the old Republic while engulfed in the vice of modern-day democracy. He was a tough old bird, a demanding and invigorating intelligence who had taught his select group of St. Gregory students—*gli scelti*, "the chosen," he called them—a toughness and discipline they didn't know they had until he demanded it from them.

"Why do you suppose we're tramping out here to see old

Guido?" Tina asked rhetorically, knowing that she wanted no answers, that the day itself and the country were answer enough.

"What we really should be doing is hitching to Greece and Turkey and seeing the places that Agostini has been preaching about to us since ninth grade," Jason answered.

"Maybe we can join forces; I was going to Calabria this summer and that's a start in the right direction—Magna Graecia, you know. But do you mean hitching with knapsacks and all that?" Tina asked.

"Sure. I've already done it to Yugoslavia. It's quite nice, actually. And Calabria's fine—right on the way to the boat at Brindisi."

"Will there be good food?" Tina asked. "I always remember my trips in terms of the meals I encounter. I have an almost exclusively gustatory memory."

"You're spoiled, Tina. What kind of an SDS person were you?"

"I'm two different people, Jason. The Italian part, when I get back to Rome, likes civilized comforts: eating well, having Giovanna go out and do the shopping and prepare the *caffè-latte* for me each morning while I sleep late. Here I like to get all dressed up and go shopping or have Mauro cut my hair. I dress in blankets and clogs when I'm in the States and sometimes don't comb my hair for days. I drive my grandmother in Gloversville crazy when I go see her because she says I'm a hippie. But in Rome I'm purely a sybarite."

"Well, you're not going to indulge your sybaritic side all that much with Agostini."

"Oh, yes, I am; I know we'll have his own chickens—the kind that peck around in the ground and not the hothouse type—and good wine, not the adulterated stuff from Frascati. And we'll sit on his portico and look out over the *campagna* and he'll be wise and witty. That's what I mean by sybaritic. It doesn't have to be luxury, it has to be the best in whatever circumstance."

"Well, I can see you'd be all right as an eating companion on a Greek hike because you'd be able to smell out the right eating places, but what would you do about sleeping on the ground or in some of the hostels?"

"I'll have to think about that," Tina quipped. And she did. Going off with Jason? She'd like it. But how could she plan anything until she heard more from Angela?

Guido Agostini's house was his work of art, patiently worked at little by little each summer on the land he owned that had been sheep pasture outside Rome. He had modified the original shepherd's hut, laid out a vegetable garden, and sown a small area with grain, and had acquired beehives, herbs, a few chickens and ducks, and a pool for carp. Two stones were corded together at the door latch to clink together as a knocker.

Inside, the stone house was one large room with windows and terrace overlooking the green hills and a ladder that went up to a sleeping loft; a studio and kitchen had been added to the side. The walls were filled with mementos of civilization: musical instruments, paintings and drawings, a carefully calculated sundial that measured time by where light struck plotted lines on the wall.

"Signor Agostini and his wife are a super-refined hippie commune," Tina said.

"They have more class than the hippies do," Jason answered.

"That's what I mean. They have the best of the natural world and the best of the intellect."

"It's a good way to live."

"Yes, I guess that's what we all aspire to."

"At least those of us who have had Agostini for Latin and Greek and have lived part of our lives in Rome. We're privileged. . . . Not everyone has that."

It was true. She thought with great pleasure of one special day in her Greek class when she and Agostini had both been on the same wavelengths of sensibility.

They were reading the beautiful passage of the *Iliad* in which Achilles, from whom Briseis, his companion, has just been taken away, sits by the shore and looks broodingly out over the boundless sea. Then, out of the blue, Signor Agostini asked, "What kind of a day do you think it was?" And only Tina, with utter assurance, had answered. "Misty," she had said without hesitation. "Why do you say that?" Agostini asked, obviously pleased. "Well, you see," she said, "Homer's phrase 'the boundless deep' gives the impression of limitless immensity—hence a day of obscured horizons when everything blends together and boundaries merge to create the impression of 'boundless.' "

As Tina recalled the day and scene, she felt again the thrilling quality of that exchange: Both she and Agostini had been together in the mind of Homer. It had not happened again.

Frieda Agostini was smiling when they came up to the house and Guido Agostini was stern-looking, more than ever the image of some great *condottiere,* Tina thought. He was a tall, big-shouldered, robust man who might have been a shepherd from the Abruzzi or a metal worker in a factory, not a teacher of the classics in an American prep school. His wife was small and gentle, a Swiss woman who made honey, bread, wine, and then rushed into Rome to deliver broadcasts of Italian news to Switzerland.

With his usual asperity, Agostini said, "Frieda's just made a *torta delle due farine.*" Then his face relaxed into a smile at the joke of the two-flour cake.

He always told his Latin classes at St. Gregory's that they hadn't mastered Latin until they had deciphered Horace's recipe for the ancient cornmeal cake and actually prepared it to his, Agostini's, satisfaction. Tina had often experimented with her versions. Besides white flour and cornmeal flour, it called for almonds and quantities of butter. The extravagance used to make her mother furious. But it was Agostini's idea of what cake should be: rustic, hearty, not overrefined—a test of character.

They had the *torta* with glasses of Agostini's homemade wine on the terrace he had carved from his hillside, overlooking the hills of the spare Lazio region.

"I am trying to get Tina back into the classics, Signor Agostini," Jason said. "I say she can't be a classicist if she's not been to Greece."

"Oh, well, before you even get to Greece, have you seen the wonders of Paestum? In fact, if you should go to Paestum you could go on further down to Staffa in Calabria, where we have a small house in the hills above the sea and can't get to just yet because of Frieda's broadcast schedule. Go there and stay at our place and contemplate the sea and hills after the temples of Paestum if you want a full classical experience. From there you can cross Calabria to Bari and set off for Greece."

"Is there good fish, or is it all polluted or sent up to Rome?" asked Tina.

"She has to make sure about the food before she'll go anyplace." Jason laughed.

"I'll give you the name of my fisherman and the man in the village who saves his best wine for me. What more could you want?"

"Nothing more," said Tina. "I'll go!"

Tina sipped her wine and looked out over the hills; I have what I came for, she thought. A direction, Guido's message.

It was evening when they got back to Rome.

"Let's walk," Tina said.

"We're not far from the Film Studio," Jason said, holding her hand. "They're doing oldtime films there. Want to see a silent film called *Cabiria* with subtitles by D'Annunzio?"

"We can try," she said.

They went to the little movie house in an alley off the street on which the Regina Coeli prison loomed. The place was half-full and they found seats toward the middle, slouching down on the hard wooden seats and looking up at the film that had already started. "Here," she whispered and handed him a capsule, "put this under your tongue and let it dissolve." Scenes of Carthage: children being burned in sacrifice to Moloch, Scipio Africanus and Roman legions to the attack, the suicide of the queen. Jason and Tina started to giggle. Soon they were laughing so hard the others started hissing and they got up to leave, stumbling over feet in the dark, clattering and banging and making gasping sounds as they choked down their laughter.

"What kind of trip is this?" Jason asked.

"Mescaline," she said. "Duke gave me some before I left. I feel itchy all over, let's walk."

Jason took her hand. They went off toward Santa Maria in Trastevere, stopping on the way at Via Garibaldi to see if a friend from St. Gregory's was home, but leaving after no one answered their knocks. At Santa Maria in Trastevere they sat on the steps of the fountain among the little groups of hippies and pushers and looked at the gold mosaic across the facade of the church that portrayed the parable of the handmaidens. Jason told the story of the wise virgins who trimmed their lamps and saved their oil. "Now, what should they do in regard to the six foolish virgins?" he asked.

"Share the oil?" She giggled.

"Ah, but that is not the Church's teaching," said Jason, assuming a stern look. "The Church frowns on foolishness and punishes transgression. Only heretics would forgive and share."

"That's me," she exclaimed. "I shared my stuff with you!"

They got up and went off toward the American movie house, Pasquino, where they saw a notice for a place to rent and called it. No one answered.

Then, as they crossed into Piazza Trilussa, she had a moment of super exhilaration and elation as she felt a joint bombardment of lights, sound, sights that left her standing there motionless. Jason came back and pulled her along.

"Let's call some more people," she said. "Let's call old Father Wadhams at St. Gregory's and tell him we're ready to be confirmed."

"Let's call Mr. Friedberg and go over to his place."

"Let's sit down and have a drink."

"My heart's thumping full-blast, Jason—what does that mean?"

"You're alive, I guess." They both started laughing and she leaned against him, gasping.

"Makes me itchy, I'd like to be rubbed up against something."

"Try me," he said.

She felt hilarious, good, springy. They sat in the light of Piazza San Giovanni di Malfa and looked up at a fresco in a cornice. In a window, a girl was moving back and forth, putting on clothes. It was possible to look into the room and see the rafters. Tina suddenly thought how good it would be to be in bed.

"You suppose she's in her bedroom?" said Tina.

"I suppose."

"How great."

"What's so great about being in a bedroom?" he asked, still straight, and she burst out laughing.

"Jason is a wise virgin," she started to chant.

"Did you know Kant died a virgin?" he asked. "And that's not all. Once, while teaching basic English to an Italian girl I said the word 'cunt.' 'Kant?' she repeated, 'like the philosopher?'"

"Oh, Jason," Tina gasped, leaning against him and laughing uncontrollably.

At the next piazza, with the lights whirling all around, she pointed to a store and cried, "Look!" The storefront read *Droghe e Pane.*

"*Droghe e Pane.* Drugs and Bread—isn't that great!"

"The motto of our day."

They crossed Ponte Sisto and were suddenly, unaccountably overwhelmed in a mass of suitcase-carrying tourists that left them weak with laughter. "Hooliganism!" she cried. When two soldiers passed them, she suddenly turned to Jason and said, "Do I look switched on? Will they pick me up and throw me in the clink?"

"You look great—all you need is a suitcase and you'd look like a tourist or a hooligan."

They laughed all the way up Via dei Pettinari. They rang the bell

of the two women French teachers from St. Gregory's, but there
was no answer.

They looked at the oak tree that gave its name to Piazza della
Quercia and then went to look at a building on Via del Governo
Vecchio that presented a kind of optical illusion of tapering levels.

"Let's go to bed now," she said.

"You're using me," he said, but seriously.

She looked at him in amazement.

"What good is it to go to bed under the influence of drugs?" he
asked her harshly.

"Is it any different from the influence of bread and wine?" And
she started to giggle. "Or *torta delle due farine*, or roast chicken?"

"You see, you're not serious. No *gravitas*."

"You're uptight, Jason. Always have been."

"You're using the drug as an excuse to use me—so you can go
back and tell Duke about a high in Rome."

"Phooey to the Duke—he's gone as far as I'm concerned. I
just feel good."

"Me too, so let's keep walking."

"God," she exclaimed, "isn't that obscene!" She pointed to a huge
red poster in Piazza Pasquino that read *Emulsio Regala*.

"Horrid!" he agreed, and took her hand as they went off to
Piazza Navona. They sat at the Fountain of the Four Great Rivers
and looked up at the undulating baroque that swam above their
heads.

"You seem to mistrust me, Jason Jowers."

"You're right."

"In that case, how can we be friends enough to go on this trip
together?"

"We'll have to work at it."

They got up and walked over to the Pantheon. "How magnificent—isn't that magnificent?" said Jason, appraising the pediment
and reading aloud "*M. Agrippa . . . fecit.*" He was solemn.

"A paradox, a paradox," she cried, clapping her hands.

"Where?"

"Look at that store on the corner," she said, pointing to Via del
Seminario. "It's a fancy men's shop and the name of the owner, up
there in big letters, is Cenci—Rags! A rags-and-tatters clothing
store!"

They stopped to ring a friend's bell on Via del Seminario but only
the grandmother was home.

"I'm starved," said Tina. It was about eleven o'clock and the drug had begun to wear off. They were tired from the long perambulation around the city. They stopped in a little *trattoria* and had beans and sausage. It wasn't a good trip after all, Tina thought, and started to cry.

Jason was startled. "What's wrong?"

"I'm pregnant, for God's sake!"

At home in bed, she wept tears of sadness at the meaninglessness of the night, at the friends who hadn't been home, at the squalor of the place where they had eaten badly, and at Jason's disapproval. It's all too hard, she thought.

Chapter Twenty-seven

"Your mother used to think I should be a lion," Alberto Morosini was saying composedly as he loosened the soil around a large potted laurel and then stood back and looked at his work. It was the laurel that Marguerite had given him on his sixtieth birthday because, she said, he was a poet and poets are crowned with laurel. "The leaves are also good to roast meat with in case the poetry fails," he had replied good-naturedly.

Tina thought of that as she glanced over at her father with a quizzical look. He liked his daughters to be there when he returned from his office in the evening, and to converse with him while he prepared himself a Scotch-and-water and went out on the terrace to relax in what he called his *paradiso* and to look about at his plantings. He would loosen his tie, take off his jacket, and remove his shoes while Tina or Weezy went to the study at the end of the hall and brought out his old leather sandals.

He had created the garden on the terrace. Patiently he had espaliered the riccasperma against the wall, set up the lattices and trained the vines along them, and looked all over Rome for the terra-cotta scallop shell that he had set into the wall as a catch-basin beneath the water tap. Each evening he watered and trimmed and poked. Sometimes he returned with plantings—daisies, *margherite*, were for his wife, he said, and of all his flowers she was his favorite, though the most difficult one. "*Come sei difficile, amore,*" he had written to her in one of his poems.

Tina made it a point of being home when her father got there since Weezy was acting so badly, straining with impatience to be away and going on about why did they have to be together at dinner . . . in fact, why bother with dinner? Tina wished she could be as tough when it came to deciding whether she'd stay there in Rome with him or go back to New York at the end of summer. She even wished she could talk about the abortion with him, but she knew it was impossible. He would try to persuade her to have the child and let him keep it, and that was something she could not live with.

This evening she was watering the plants while he puttered around. She always enjoyed his company; sometimes she met him for lunch at Café de Paris or they would go to a film together. It was, transparently, part of his campaign to keep her there and they both knew it and joked about it. "What you need is a vaccine against the States," he told her, "and I'm going to supply it."

"But I've got friends there and commitments in my work, *papà.*"

"All life is a question of recasting," he replied.

Her response to her father used to be invariably uncritical: She adored his charm and gentleness, she was proud of him. But now shadows began to worry at the edge of her acceptance as she saw him in a new light.

"When we were in the country," he went on, "your mother would get upset if I wouldn't set out with her at high noon to bicycle up and down the hills of Monterubbiano. Or she'd suddenly want to go down to the beach and swim at night. It was, of course," he added as if an afterthought, "part of her charm."

Funny, thought Tina, how her ear now caught the intonation of irony that had probably always been there. She could fit between his own words the desperate ones from her mother's diaries; together they made a dissonance that saddened her. For if their perfect marriage had been like that, what chance was there for ordinary ones?

"*Papà,*" said Tina, "she was also concerned for you. The doctor had told you after your heart attack that you should exercise, build up your resistance. She was concerned that you didn't get enough exercise. You still don't."

She looked at the slight figure of her father. She was taller now than he, and his thickening paunchy middle made him seem shorter yet. He was balding and what hair he had left was turning white. As a young man he had been beautiful; in the family albums he still was: polished, dark tan, his figure lean and flat with the slim muscular calves of a bicycler, his hair a mop of black ringlets. But, as her mother used to say, she hadn't known him then, she had taken him on faith for the boy he was.

"She was an activist, your mother. She didn't know the contemplative life. Sometimes I'm afraid you're the same way; you don't think things out rationally—you explode, act on impulse, and then are sorry. You must calm down."

Tina knew what he meant about thinking things out rationally; the height of rationality for him would be that she stay there in Rome with him, in their beautiful home with the classics right at hand, instead of going back to New York to pursue them in the stacks of the Columbia library. It seemed perverse, as he painted it, to want to go back to the grim gray world of upper Broadway and the dreary little hamburger shops, the cheerless dorms, the cold long winter, and the pinched living on a fellowship while being exploited as a graduate assistant to teach beginning language classes.

"Everything is here for you," he continued, stopping between words to give his characteristic snort. "You could translate my new novel and get a credit that would help you in your own career, besides earning some money." (Stay near me, he was really saying, and enjoy this high civilization; forgo the compulsion of trying to find your way in the jungle of self-realization that is New York and enjoy the fruits of being part of my success; start by translating. . . . Was that, she wondered, the beguilement he had used with her mother, too?)

She began to understand how her mother had been charmed and led from her own aspirations by the soft cadences of this Venetian poet. He charmed and pleased everyone; he had a great gift for gab and a gentle, humorous kind of fun-poking that was very Venetian in origin, like the oldtime *signori* who could with deep bows and the reverent greeting of "Your servant, sir!" poke fun at the person addressed. It was in the same vein of satiric irony, deceptive in its amiability and gentleness, that he spoke of his wife's silly pranks. He had never seen her as a woman, it occurred to Tina, but only as a deliciously perverse creature whose eccentricities and foibles he was fated to put up with.

Tina used to overhear at parties the clucking of Italian women when her father amusingly told them how he often had a "tost" standing up in a *caffè-bar* for lunch, or gulped down the various poisons of a *tavola calda* at noontime. They didn't have dinner at noon, he explained, because his wife worked in the library at St. Gregory's and his daughters had lunch at their American school. And she would sense the women wondering how he put up with a wife who had overturned the civilized Italian schedule of life in order to impose an American one on him.

Actually, as Tina knew, her father preferred the arrangement of a light lunch at noon, a habit he had picked up during his years in the States. And not coming back home at midday left him free to lunch with friends, call on his doctor at home and dine with him there, or go out with writers who might be in town. But he was not the man to say, "I prefer it this way." He didn't mind the kind of innuendo that presented him as a hapless victim.

He had always been a victim. A victim of the First World War, which left him fatherless at age nine; a victim of genteel poverty, of a guilt-laden and rigid Catholic education, and of his own romanticism. He would be a poet, he said, and his companion in life would be a gentle woman, the queen of his home.

Tina knew her father's story—through albums, the family artifacts, the charts and documents and letters that always followed them in their travels, and through his and her mother's accounts. From both sides of his family he inherited a love of order and routine but little or nothing of the commercial astuteness of the sea-merchants. He lived among the artifacts and paraphernalia of things past and let the present bear him where it would.

The shape of his future had been the American girl Marguerite Scalzo. Proposing, Alberto had said they would learn each other's language and be artists together, although it would be wise if they started a family soon.

There never was time, Tina remembered her mother saying, to live as artists, the two of them. The babies and moving absorbed Marguerite and slowly her vision of herself swerved. Alberto relied on words as Marguerite did on her feelings for truth. When he told her that she should be happy with things as they were— with her successful husband, her beautiful home, her fine daughters —and not pine after what was lost or the illusion of her fulfillment as an artist, she tried to examine why her feelings mistrusted him. It was not what he had said before! Not knowing what else to do, she kept them moving; and Alberto let himself become the victim of her unrest.

All this went through Tina's mind as she weighed her father's words about her mother.

"The immurement is already tomorrow," he was saying, almost to himself. He was pulling the dried blooms from the geraniums and dropping them on the terrace. A handwritten will had been found in Marguerite's desk which said that if she died in Rome she wanted to be cremated and put to rest in the Protestant Cemetery. Arranging her death aesthetically was like setting up one of her homes. "If she had been buried as Church tradition recommends, we could have planted some of these flowers she loved on the gravesite. But she wanted to be cremated."

Weezy had come out onto the terrace, and overhearing her father, she said, "It's her way of being recycled into the universe, *papà*."

"The soul awaits an afterlife, not a general recycling," he answered.

"Well, to each his own belief, *papà*," Weezy continued. "She didn't believe in the afterlife."

"The trouble is," he said, frowning and busying himself with sweeping up the withered blossoms which were scattered about on the terrace, "that it is *not* to each his own, with that facile kind of relativism that makes only for chaos and unhappiness in this world. There is a traditional order which the Church upholds and it guides us out of the anarchy of self, the concentration on one's own personal salvation. Your mother never understood the beauty and harmony of the great universal Church. She could not stand authority and she lost herself in the illusion of trying to realize herself."

"*Papà*," said Tina impatiently, "in this day and age not everyone can believe in the authority of the Church. The pressures of these days are different from just speculating about the afterlife and the soul's salvation. We have to save ourselves, the world . . . the environment. . . ."

"You will end up an activist," he said.

"Not Tina," said Weezy, sitting at the table and lighting up a cigarette. "She's too into the academic life and books."

"And you're the revolutionary, eh?" he said, addressing Weezy. "Ah, *bambina mia*," he said with an air of grievance, shaking his head. "Revolution, which you students want, won't solve anything—it takes a slow and fatiguing evolution whose results will be far beyond the generations immediately involved. It takes faith to work for the changes we'll never see. You cannot with impunity throw away the two thousand years of tradition and human experience that the Church represents."

"That's the old line, that's the old rationale. No one will go for that now."

"You are too much in a hurry," he said. "That was your mother's sickness—she was too much in a hurry. Even her death was a result of hurry: Why was she speeding on a wet day? What was it but another instance of her restlessness and lack of serenity? Death must be merited, not reached with defiance of all rules or chosen because one is tired."

Having swept carefully and made a tidy pile, he put the dead blossoms into a plastic bag and returned the broom to its corner.

They were arriving at one of her mother's favorite places in Rome: the Protestant Cemetery at Porta San Paolo near the pyramid of Gaius Cestius. Even in death she had managed superb surroundings for herself. Now she would be forever under Rome's clement skies in the same place that held Keats's body and Shelley's heart.

Tina looked about her before they went through the gate in the high wall. A half-block away Rome was filling the air with its normal clamor of siren sounds, trams, trucks, and late-morning traffic. Across the street from the walled cemetery, oblivious to the coming together to formalize loss, a stout Roman housewife was hanging wash on her balcony; she wore a bright, sleeveless dress and gossiped audibly to a neighbor on an adjoining balcony.

Of course everything goes on, Tina thought; Mother goes into the wall, an urn of ashes, and everybody else goes on washing, gossiping, honking horns, working, living. She thought of years earlier her mother reading to her and Weezy the story from *Winnie-the-Pooh* in which Eeyore has a birthday and says in his dour way, "Birthdays? Here today, gone tomorrow." So with mothers, thought Tina.

A few people had gathered outside the wall of the cemetery. Angela was there and some of Marguerite's American friends; the Agostinis, Missy and her parents, a few of her father's colleagues, and Jason. No Massimo Bontelli, she thought without surprise. It was a beautiful day, he would be at the sea. Her father was greeting people. He looked old and tired, his face drawn and lined. He had never been a tall man, or a strongly built one, but now he seemed shrunken and aged. His face was frowning and deep wrinkles were set in it. His thickset neck seemed more than ever drawn into his shoulders; his prominent nose was sharp.

"The last time I was here," Weezy said in an undertone to Tina, "it was the one hundred and fiftieth anniversary of Keats's death in Rome, and Mom told me to stay out of school so that we could go together to the ceremony at his graveside. I thought that was so cool of her. We were here and it was a beautiful day in February, I remember it, but I began to get restless when this English poet started speaking, so Mom started getting cross with me. I was doing it on purpose—I wanted to show how impatient I was with the formal ceremony and the British dignitaries and all that sort of official thing. I wanted to show how much closer I was to Keats than anybody else there by suffering through the stuffiness. And actually, all the time I rather liked it; I liked being there and hearing Keats's poetry read in English accents. But I didn't want Mom to know. I keep thinking of that now because so much of what we do is really dishonest—really putting on a front so that people won't know what we really feel."

"I know what you mean," Tina muttered. "I do the same thing at times, just so I can have the satisfaction of pretending to do my own thing; with Mom it was showing her I didn't need her, or that the things she did and said were outmoded. All we can do now is make it up to her by being good to each other."

Their father led the group into the cool grounds in the new part of the cemetery to the spot in the wall where Marguerite's urn would be immured. He gave a brief eulogy.

"She said she had no country, nor any religion," he intoned, "and yet she was one of the most religious spirits I've ever known, with a purity and candor that were both vulnerable and invincible. She was restless, as the person in search, the person of sensitivity must always be. . . ." As he spoke, his eyes squinting in the bright sun, his balding head hatless and exposed to a heat which, Tina knew, he would feel prejudicial to him, she thought of him not as her father but as the husband of her mother.

In her childhood he had been a perfect and tender and loving father. More recently he had begun to speak to Tina as a confidante, telling her that he could have been a happy man if it were not for her mother's sickness; she was his cross, he said, but still his woman, the creature that God had entrusted to him, and he would always love her. Tina thought of that love, the love that accepted a person no matter what, defects and sickness and all, and asked for nothing from the person—no growth or improvement or change—and knew that such a love had done her mother in. Massimo, who had stretched her capabilities and expectations, was the man she had loved. And yet, how would it have been if they had shared home and children and all the fraying things of marriage as well as the good times? Was it always true that marriage meant the end of love? Again Tina wondered if she would ever marry; or would she have only those series of encounters that the feminists called "little marriages"—all the advantages of sex and companionship without commitment or entanglements? She had thought she loved Duke for what he had given her in a new approach to life. Then she had absorbed the Duke experience and found it was not a partnership for life, but another learning situation.

As she stood there, she felt that at this ceremony not only were her mother's ashes being immured, but she was also silently walling off her own dependency on any man who would keep her from the fullness of her own life and expectations. Her mother had had to pass through death and demolition by flame to reach release. What rigor would she have to undergo? Whatever it was, she prayed, let me come out alive and whole. She looked at Weezy and was surprised to see her crying.

At the end, Tina went up to her father and embraced him. "That was beautiful, *papà*," she said. He went around and shook hands with those who were there. Tina singled out Angela, who was wearing a flowery dress and high white kid boots. They embraced and Angela murmured "*mia cara*" with feeling. From her bag she drew an envelope and said in an undertone, "This is what I received for the jewelry. Everything can be done tonight if you're ready."

"Tonight?" Tina repeated, startled. "Yes, why not? Shall I come to your place?"

"That would be the best . . . I'll accompany you to the appointment."

Tina took the envelope and glanced at it. "L 300,000" was penciled on it. That's all there was from the jewelry that had been left to her and Weezy.

Tina spoke to the Agostinis and some others and then found herself next to Jason.

"Are you all right?" he asked, looking apprehensive.

"Perfectly."

"I mean . . . you know, what you told me the other night."

"That will all be taken care of. Tonight, actually."

Jason looked worried, concerned, and took her hand. "Will you be all right? I mean, Jesus, Tina, I want to help if I can."

"Thanks, Jason. You *can* help—wait for me to go to Greece."

"You can count on it!" He embraced her, and she clung to him, feeling strength in him. "Can I call you tomorrow?" he whispered.

"I want you to."

Jason left with the others, and her father went into the office of the cemetery superintendent to see to various documents and other business matters. Tina walked with Weezy to the old part of the cemetery to the site of Keats's grave. Weezy picked some little field daisies from the patch there. "I want to take these back to her," she said. "I want to tell her I'm sorry for how I was the day when we were here together." She blew her nose and wiped her eyes.

"She knows, Weezy, she knows," Tina said. "I wish I had brought some of the shells from her bookcase. She loved the sea and the sun and was her happiest there." The shells were those picked from the beach on the day Tina had first met Massimo with her mother.

"It's all a symbol, anyway," Weezy said, "and it's all too late. All we're doing is acting out for ourselves, to make us feel better."

"Weezy, Angela said it's set for tonight."

"Good—get that over with and then I'm taking off."

How tough her soft little sister had become, Tina thought; or maybe just realistic, grown-up.

"Here's the money, Weezy. There's only 50,000 lire left over after I pay the doctor tonight. Take it now."

"This never had to happen—I mean selling Mom's jewelry and everything. You could have trusted me."

"You're right. I hope *papà* never finds out." She put her arm around Weezy. "I'll never forget your letting me sell your share, too."

"You're just lucky I'm not like you," her sister replied.

She must have been waiting all her life to say that, Tina thought.

Chapter Twenty-eight

There was a man at Angela's when Tina got there.

"Marco, Tina; Tina, Marco," Angela said briskly. "We were going out this evening anyway, so we'll drop you off and wait. The whole thing won't take long. Then we'll drive you back."

It humiliated Tina to be included this way on Angela's date—to be taken for her abortion like some child who, by misbehaving, was interfering with the grown-ups' plans. Weezy had wanted to come, but Tina told her to stay home with their father.

"Oh, God . . ." Tina began, feeling angry and confused and wanting to be anywhere but there.

"It's nothing, *cara*, nothing at all," Angela replied, and Tina could see that, to her, that's just what it was.

"*Mia cara*," Angela had said in her glib, brittle way at their previous meeting, "the test came out positive. You *are* pregnant and obviously you have to do something about it. An abortion is no more than going to the hairdresser's these days. Everyone I know in Rome has an abortionist. The question is, just like a hairdresser, you can't have just anyone, you have to have someone good. What an irony," she had gone on, fitting a cigarette into an ivory holder and lighting it, "that you have just left New York, where you can go easily to a modern clinic and have an abortion done safely and cheaply, and you get back to this place, where you are in danger of something like the Inquisition and have to risk your life to stop a pregnancy. *Che peccato!*"

It was more than irony; it was the perpetual mix-up of her life, Tina reflected.

"Just the other week," Angela was saying, "there was the scandalous case of the four-months-pregnant woman who had been beaten by her husband and fell into a coma. She was brain-dead but there was a great deal of commotion about keeping her body alive as an incubator so that the fetus would live. Well, finally she died, and the fetus, too. Then it came out that her husband had beaten her because she wanted to have an abortion. She was twenty years old and already had two small children. Naturally she was viewed as the monster, while the husband, who beat her to death, was looked upon as acting within his rights. At her funeral service the priest said, 'She was a mother who gave two lives into the world. She was also a wife. In the next life she will still be a wife and a mother.'"

Angela paused, jerked her head upward, and with a thin ironic smile let her words sink in. "That's Italy for you, *mia cara*. The men here are almost Arabs in their attitudes toward women."

Angela Cambio was a liberated woman, a journalist, a feminist, a pillar of the Left. She had been her mother's closest Italian friend. She lived in an *attico* in the center of Rome and had frequent parties, deliberately mixing a hodgepodge of political views and opposing types so that, as she said, her salon would ferment with exchange and not be just another boring gathering of safe people reinforcing each other's ideas.

"*Pazza*," her father said of Angela Cambio. "A crazy woman— one of those new restless types that come from some backward village in the middle of the mountains to Rome and imagine they can become someone they're not." But her mother had admired Angela; she was always speaking of her writing, her husband having left, her being sent as a correspondent to England for several years, her doing so many things and living successfully on her own in a man's world.

It was, in fact, her mother's admiration for Angela, whose name was written in that last diary entry, that had brought Tina to her to find out how to be tested for pregnancy. Weezy had been offended and angry. "If you need an abortion," she said, "I can arrange it for you through the feminist group. We have some trusted doctors who will do it for you safely, unhumiliatingly, and not expensively. But Angela Cambio!" Weezy sneered. "She's one of those dilettantes who's into everything superficially, but nothing seriously. She pretends to be a feminist, a leftist—anything that she thinks is fashionable or newsy at the moment. How could you get mixed up with her?"

"She was Mom's friend—Mom mentioned her name in her diary. It seemed like the right thing to do."

"You're always following Mom . . . trying to dress like her, live like her, be like her. Why don't you be yourself?"

"Well, it's done now."

Tina distrusted Weezy and her feminist friends with their garlic or yoghurt douches and their overemphatic ways. For snobbish and other reasons she had gone to Angela. Also because she did not like the feel of her little sister being in charge.

But already at that preliminary meeting the thought had entered Tina's mind that she might have been mistaken going to Angela. Small, fragile-looking, and with protuberant dark eyes, Angela had looked up at Tina and said in her deliberately offhand way, "You'll need about 250,000 lire. Do you have it?" Tina had stared at the sleek woman whose dark hair was long and streaked with blond lights; she wore the skin-tight jeans that the fashionable women of Rome had just discovered, and no bra under her open-necked silk blouse. Her face was tanned from days at the beach, her eyes carefully made up, her lips pale. She was an interesting-looking woman, and an intelligent one. But hard.

"No," Tina had said. "I don't have anything like that much money—and I can't ask *papà*. Where will I get it?"

"Did your mother leave you anything?"

Tina thought of her jewelry box and the engagement ring that her mother had said would someday be hers. "Yes," she said, "her jewelry—she left it to Weezy and me."

"Bring it to me," Angela said. "I can arrange it."

Tina was going to lie to Weezy about the cost of the abortion, ashamed to admit that she was paying 250,000 lire when the feminists had doctors willing to do it for so much less. But she needed Weezy's share of the jewelry in order to raise the money. Weezy, in disgust, had told her to do what she damn pleased. When Tina had taken the ring and some other things to Angela, she asked if Angela had known that her mother was pregnant. "No," said Angela, "Marguerite didn't tell me anything of the kind." Maybe her mother wouldn't have gone to Angela after all, was the thought Tina then had to live with.

Angela was a wretched driver, and all the way across town to the doctor's Tina wondered why the hell she hadn't just taken a taxi and gone by herself. In fact, when they got to the address, there was no place to park and so Angela asked Marco to accompany Tina up to the doctor while she found a place by circling around the block.

In the elevator Tina could feel Marco looking at her. He was a youngish man, certainly younger than Angela, and Tina wondered who he was. He didn't seem intelligent enough to be a colleague of Angela's, and the cursory way he was introduced meant that Angela herself didn't consider him important enough to give any more information about. Just someone to sleep with.

"Don't worry," he said to Tina, attempting to be friendly but increasing her distaste for him and for his open shirt-front with all his chains and gold horns dangling in the thatch of hairy chest. "It's very simple . . . and done very quickly. Nothing at all."

She glanced quickly at him, then away. She didn't answer.

A gleaming oviform brass plate at the door read "Prof. Brenta," and the *professore* himself answered the door and showed Tina into a large study. There he changed from his suit jacket into a white one while he motioned her to sit down. Then he sat facing her from behind a desk ornate with leather and silver frames.

"Have you brought the sum, *signorina*?"

She handed him the envelope with the 250,000 lire in it. He took the pack of bills, and as he counted them, held each of the ten-thousand-lire notes up to the light to see if it was good.

"*Benissimo*," he said cordially as if congratulating her on some accomplishment. He slipped the envelope into a drawer, which he then locked, and nodded at her brightly. He looked like any one of her father's friends. He could be her father.

"Very well," he continued, "now we proceed. Go into the bathroom across the hall, empty your bladder, and leave off your panties. Then go into the adjacent room."

Tina did as she was told, also running water into the bidet and using her handkerchief to wash herself. Like brushing one's teeth before going to the dentist, she thought, so as not to be offensive. Wondering what to do with them, she left her pink silk panties in the bathroom. Why had she worn them? Did she think she was meeting a lover? She had bought them in Florence the semester she was there—her first luxury. She had spent book money on a pair of panties and a matching slip handworked with appliqué embroidery. And she had never worn her silk things until this evening. They had been left in Rome in a drawer in her room because she was afraid they'd be stolen at college.

Tina went to the room where the doctor was waiting. He motioned her to get up onto the examining table. She slipped off her sandals, got onto the table, and following his directions, put her feet into the steel stirrups, uselessly trying to keep her knees together.

"Relax," he said, quickly forcing her knees apart and lifting her skirt up around her waist. She felt like one of the half-clothed dummies she used to see in storefronts on Broadway and she tried to make her features melt into dummy vapidness, to keep her feelings at dummy level.

"*Coraggio, signorina,*" the doctor was saying, giving her a pat on the leg. "You're a strong girl—nice legs. I'll bet you're a swimmer. Soon," he continued as he did his examination, "you'll be at the beach."

He was not a bad person; and he was quite unaware of the revulsion and anger he stirred in her as he patted and looked. By telling her to have courage he was, in his way, trying to keep her spirits up. Still, she hated him—as much as she hated the pope in his long unsullied skirts, or the fat-bellied old priests who told women they sinned, or the pigs in Parliament who daydreamed of women to fuck as they deliberated on laws that violated their bodies.

No matter how cordial, the doctor was a profiteer and a butcher, and she thought of herself, legs apart, as one of those carcasses hanging in all the meat markets of Rome—revoltingly explicit with their hairy bodies intact but split up the middle. Once, in a festive mood at Christmas, the butcher on Via di Ripetta had put in his front window a pig on skis with a pipe in his mouth and a wool cap on his head. And the poor dumb carcass had actually looked as if it were grinning.

Tina thought of Mussolini hanging like a pig by his feet and his mistress hanging alongside him, her crime having been that of loving him. But even in that bad time, someone had had pity enough to pin Clara's skirt together as she hung upside-down at that gas station in Milan.

To Tina's horror, Marco was entering the room.

She half-rose on the table and looked at the doctor wildly. "Tell him to leave," she said.

"I thought he was your fiancé," the doctor said.

"No!" Tina said, and turned her head away from both men toward the wall. "Fucking pigs," she said under her breath. That's what all men were and these two most of all. She wanted to say aloud what she thought, but was afraid to. The doctor was about to work on her insides, and if she offended him she was afraid of what might happen.

She had always been fearful. *Pavida*, she thought, feeling the word nail her to the table. From childhood on she had been apprehensive about the world and fearful of being hurt. The grim freakiness of nature and people had always hung over her. She was fearful of bums on Broadway. She would not go to Los Angeles because of the San Andreas fault; nor to Israel because war might break out.

Now as she lay, stiff with fear, she thought again of the mother who had willed her to life and whose death might have come because she was pregnant, just as Tina was. She was sharing with her mother for the first time the communion of womanhood. The doctor told Marco to leave. The door closed.

Tina's eyes sought something to fix on to. Her gaze, startled, rested on a crucifix hanging on the wall. God, she thought—here, too. Everywhere in Italy you could find a crucifix: in the post offices, in government offices above cheating employees, in banks, in schoolrooms, and in courts of justice. She thought of Weezy being made to stand in a corridor at the Italian school she briefly attended because she didn't want to participate in the religion class and was not allowed, during that time, to study but only to stand like a penitent and wait. And then she thought, Now I'm going to be cut into by a Catholic doctor who votes against legalized abortion and is sure his wife and daughters are above such things.

"Now, *signorina*, we can get to work," the doctor was saying. "Let me tell you first that you can have an anesthetic if you wish, but the aftereffects are liable to make you sick. On the other hand, without anesthetic you will feel some momentary discomfort, but after a good night's sleep you will be fit all the sooner."

Tina did not want to risk being sick and arousing her father's worry or suspicions. Poor man! she thought. He's had enough to make him miserable in these days without my adding to it. "Do it without," she said, almost smiling at the thought of how terrified she had been of getting her ears pierced when Duke had given her hoop earrings.

The doctor began. She tried to detach herself from the room, her eyes clinging to the crucifix as she tried to focus her thoughts on

Jews and women in Catholic countries. Then the pain went through her and made her call out. She could feel the instrument scraping inside her.

"Quiet!" the doctor said angrily. "It won't take long and I can't have you crying out here in my office at this time of night."

Jesus, she said to the crucifix, make me pass out.

But she did not pass out. She stayed there with the pain, gripping the sides of the table with her hands, repressing her cries into muffled groans.

It was over, and the doctor took her feet out of the stirrups, pulled her skirt down, and told her to rest a few minutes.

She closed her eyes. She thought of Duke back in the States—that poor, sweet, easygoing Duke who would have been the last guy in the world to want to bring her pain. And yet he had because he was a man, and she, no matter what she did to her brain and willpower, was still inhabiting a female body. Just one night that she forgot a pill, and this was what happened. She thought of her mother's jokes about "Who pays the fiddler? The girl pays the fiddler."

Yes, the goddam fiddler. He was always there waiting to be paid, just like the goddam doctor counting his money. He was there every time a man looked at her, every time she felt the surge of pleasure from an embrace, every time bed beckoned. Pleasure, even if it didn't always end in pregnancy, was always a trap. How often she had thought, I will be chaste and do my work. And how often she could not be, because it was in her nature to love and be loved. And then she thought of the graffito in the New York subway that she had seen scrawled on the poster of a Broadway play: "Love hurts," someone had written with a magic marker.

"*Cara*, are you all right?"

Tina heard Angela's voice near her and opened her eyes. Angela took Tina's hand in one of hers and with the other wiped her forehead with a handkerchief. Only then did Tina realize she was wet with sweat.

"I'm all right," Tina said. "We can go."

"You were really brave," Angela said. "The doctor said so."

"Screw the doctor," said Tina. She did not want to tell Angela about Marco. All men were alike—what would she have told Angela that Angela didn't already know?

With Angela and Marco on each side holding her arm, they left the doctor's office and stood outside in the corridor ringing for the elevator in its elaborate wrought-iron cage. Nothing came. Marco peered down the shaft. "Someone must have left a door open down there and it won't move," he said.

"Can you walk down?" Angela asked. "It's better if we get away from the doctor's office as soon as possible before we're noticed. He might get reported."

Halfway down the stairs, Tina remembered her pink silk panties in the bathroom and began to cry.

"*Su, cara!*" Angela murmured, putting her arm around Tina's waist and pressing her close for a moment. "It's over—you've been magnificent. Just a few minutes more till we get to the car."

Angela had finally double-parked in front of the building entrance and left her parking lights on with the flashing signal.

Marco got in the back, and just as they were about to pull away a car started up with a roar nearby and raced off down the street. A man ran up, opened the door on Tina's side, forced himself in beside and partly over her, and shouted, "Follow that car!"

"Oh, my God," said Angela, "this is all we need!"

"Sorry, *signora*," said the man. "It's a thief. I have to get the license number."

Tina felt bizarre, as if her life, like her insides, were out of whack, all control gone. She began to giggle in a hysterical way.

"It's not funny, *signorina*," the man sitting on her said as he tried to turn his head toward her. "They're thieves, and if we can get close at the next traffic light, I can get their number."

"I know it's not funny," Tina said, still laughing, "it's this crazy country."

Angela sped down a few blocks along the Viale Parioli into Via Flaminia but missed the changing of the light and slowed down.

"Go through the light, you can still overtake them!" Marco shouted from the back.

But it was too late, they lost the car. "I'm sorry," Angela told the man. "All I can do now is take you to the nearest telephone so that you can report it to the police."

The man was left at a bar, and Angela got Tina back home.

"What took so long?" Weezy asked. "I was getting worried—I thought *papà* would be asking about you. Just open the door to his study and say good-night. I told him you were at Missy's."

When Tina was in bed, Weezy brought her a cup of chamomile tea.

"Just like Peter Rabbit," Tina said, as she sipped the tea. "Do you remember, Weezy, when Mom used to read to us the story of Peter Rabbit who was bad and disobeyed and so was put to bed with chamomile tea, while Flopsy, Mopsy, and Cotton-tail got bread and milk and blackberries 'cause they were good?"

"Was it awful?" her sister asked softly.

"Yes," said Tina. "Awful. Humiliating. I should have trusted you and the feminists. I've done everything wrong . . . everything."

"Never mind. Will you be all right?" Weezy asked.

"Yes—thanks to Mom, I'm one of the lucky ones who had the money. The women who get it done on a kitchen table with knitting needles aren't so lucky."

"When we change things it won't be like this anymore, Tina."

"Change things, Weezy, change them."

"Good-bye, *papà*, take care of yourself while I'm gone. I'll send cards from along the way."

Tina picked up a duffel bag as the elevator doors opened. She had attached the tin heart from her mother's room to her shoulder bag. She turned and kissed her father.

"You're all leaving me," he said with a thin smile.

"Oh, *papà*," Tina said, "I'm not leaving for good—I'll be back. So will Weezy."

"Can you trust this Jason you're going with?"

"Perfectly."

Yes, she could trust Jason. He would take charge, he would be there, she would simply follow. The trip was like some safe isolating container for her; she always felt that way starting out for someplace—detached, disembodied mentally and physically from the surroundings she passed through. A surveyor, a noninvolved viewer of things. Distancing from Rome—from the fact of her mother, her father, her future—was what the trip meant. The trip was a reprieve from all the choices; it meant belonging nowhere and having no past, no future, just the day on the road to accomplish. The trip as container, as isolation ward, as safety compartment. The trip as tripping.

"Remember whose daughter you are," her father said as he kissed her good-bye and the elevator doors closed.

Chapter Twenty-nine

The trip was going well, Jason said.

They got a succession of rides as far as Salerno, and from there decided to take the inland country train to Paestum. It was a primitive train of prewar stock. They jounced on the hard wood benches of a former third-class car thronged with peasants and heaped with their bundles. It was dusk when they pulled into the unprepossessing station of that secondary line and read a sign that said Pesto.

"How do you like that for a name! They might just as well have called it Pasta al Pesto," Tina said indignantly. "Imagine changing it from dignified Paestum—"

"And before that it was Poseidonia, for the god of the sea, which was even better," said Jason.

"Anything's better than Pesto."

They walked from the station a kilometer or so along a wall-enclosed property on a road called Porta Sirena. They were walking seawards with the mountains to their backs and the sun setting before them. At the main road they turned a corner and saw what the wall had heretofore obstructed from sight: the plain of temples with Poseidon's huge one nearest to them and all of them glowing orange from the accumulated warmth and light of ancient times absorbed into the porous stone.

They both stopped, staring at the sight.

"It's so beautiful," Tina said. *"Era già l'ora che volge il disio/ai navicanti e 'ntenerisce il core."*

"What's that?" Jason asked, as he focused his camera to get a shot in the last light of day.

"From the *Comedy*, at the beginning of Canto 8, in Purgatory. It's this incredibly beautiful passage about the nostalgia sailors at sea feel at sunset toward those they love and are far from, and it's echoed by the souls in Purgatory who feel the same nostalgia for earth."

"You are certainly into Dante. Everything reminds you of something in him."

"But that's because he covers everything. He is the ultimate fascist—he imposes himself on all of us and will last forever."

"Is he as relevant to our time, say, as Shakespeare is?"

"They are the two most universal texts—we'll leave the classics out for the moment. Their approaches are opposite but they bring you to the same point. It's like this: Shakespeare has this great immediacy and makes his stage everything; Dante determines what his stage is and then brings everything onto it."

Tina felt elated with that insight. They were sitting on the front steps of the sea-god's temple; it was the perfect hour and she was with Jason, who could understand and appreciate what she was saying. He was lounging alongside her on the steps, fondling her arm and looking alternately at her and over the plain at the temples. This is a man I would be with, she thought; he is my equal and yet he is different. "I'd like to feel what you do about him," Jason said. "Maybe you'll read him with me."

"He takes at least three readings. You don't get to the point of awe until you get beyond the level of the 'story,' or reading the 'Inferno' at the level of punishment and mere dogma. You begin to see then that the *Comedy* operates at the level of human choice, which is always relevant—to whatever age. Then you won't make the mistake of reading Paolo and Francesca as the romantics did and feeling that they were unjustly punished; Francesca damned herself, just as Anna Karenina or Emma Bovary did, by going against the grain of herself. Put it this way, Jason: Hell is the materialization of a person's choices."

"You're going to be a great teacher, Tina."

He picked a buttercup from among the wild flowers and grasses growing near the steps and held it under her chin. "Let's see if you'll make money, too."

She laughed and looked down at him; their eyes held and he leaned up and kissed her.

"I wish I had known you better before," he said. "Back in the States. After all, you weren't really Tim's girl, so I wouldn't have been butting in."

"You never looked at me in the States—or at St. Gregory's either. You were beyond us then."

"Well, no matter, we're here now."

"Yes, and I'm getting hungry."

"Come on." He got up, reached down, and pulled her after him. They wandered among the temples until the last light had gone.

They found a place to stay for the night, a big room with twin beds in a third-category hotel down near the beach. We're both very cool, Tina thought; neither of them fussing about sleeping arrangements, but just taking things as they came. Jason, when they had started out, had simply said that they'd save money by sharing a room, but they didn't have to share a bed if she didn't want to. She didn't want to, she said.

Now he went out while she meditated. When he came back he handed her a yellow rose. "Here you are," he said, "one of Virgil's twice-blooming roses of Paestum."

She took it and sniffed deeply. "You're a nice guy, Jason."

"Ah! So you've finally noticed?"

"*Cretino!*" she laughed, nudging him. "I've known all along, or why would I be here? Still, you've really been great, Jason . . . you know, no moralizing or questions about that business of mine in Rome. And actually I thought you were such a righteous, uptight guy. I mean, you remember how you were when we took the mescaline in Rome? So disapproving?"

"I wouldn't look at it that way, Tina. Think of it like this: I like you a lot. And if anything catches between us, I want it to be naturally, because we both have the right feelings toward each other. Not because we're tripping and just getting it off with anyone who happens to be around."

"It's true, Jason, it wasn't the right time." She looked at him surmisingly, as she sniffed at the rose. "First I'll have to earn your approval," she teased.

"Right now I'm very approving."

"Well, I'm not!"

"*Oofah!* You're as grim as old Eeyore," he said in mock despair.

"One of my favorite characters, actually."

"Great! Winnie-the-Pooh will bring us together even if Dante doesn't."

"Silly old bear." She laughed, and tousled his thick, dark hair.

The next day they were scrambling like the proverbial mad dogs at noon over the heat-baked ruins of ancient Elea.

She was glad that he was there; that at the moments when she was moved by glimpses of the ancient world she had Jason with whom to share things. As when they saw the old black-and-white paving blocks characteristic of Magna Graecia leading to an archway called Porta Rosa at the acropolis of the Elea excavations, and no one else was there but they two. Over in the shade of an old gnarled olive tree, the custodian of the site sat and watched them. Finally he motioned to them with the flask that was at his side and indicated they should come and have a drink of water in the shade.

"It's too hot even for me," he told them. "Almost as hot as that day ten years ago when I unearthed the head of Parmenides. They gave me an award for that." The old man paused to let the import sink in, took a swig from his flask, and passed it.

"Tell us about it," Jason said.

"Once in a great while I get some sightseers here and then I can recite my speech about Parmenides. He was the greatest thinker of the Eleatic School of philosophy, I tell them. This place was the ancient Elea, a place of philosophers. And the head I found was the most important thing ever excavated here. When they took it off to the National Museum in Naples, I missed the old guy. He was like a friend when I found him and kept him in my little hut here, just him and me. Then the authorities finally got around to coming for him. A great thinker, Parmenides—I could tell by the wide brow. He was a concrete man, too, a man of facts. Being is here, he told his followers, in this rock, this olive tree, this wine and water we drink. What we see, that's reality."

"An existentialist philosophy back in those times," Jason said.

"That would grab you, wouldn't it, Jason?" said Tina as she fanned herself. "You're so much the essence of reason yourself. Even when you're tripping, you're reasoning."

He turned his head sideways and looked at her quizzically. "Still trying to collect points on that? Why don't you drop it?" For the first time she heard annoyance in his tone.

The old man looked at them both intently. "Are you Americans?" he asked.

"Yes," she said.

"*Fidanzati?*"

She smiled at his asking if they were fiancés; he wanted to know if they were lovers.

"Well, not really," Jason began.

"Friends," Tina said.

"More than friends," Jason went on.

"What, then?" the old man laughed.

"Sightseers," said Tina, laughing with him. "What a place!" she said as she lay back on the ground, her hands beneath her head, looking up at the sky through the branches of the olive tree. "It makes me understand why all Parmenides could see was reality— what's real is so good here. But take other places: If we didn't believe in what's not real and not out there in front of our eyes, we'd die of melancholy. Anyway, I don't believe in one hundred percent reality or reason because life doesn't work that way."

"In law school they say that reason is the life of the law, and the law is perfection of reason."

"Do you believe that, Jason?"

"Yes, I guess so. I believe that it is through law and reason that we can change for the better, and not through a constant storming of the Bastille and chopping off heads."

"Well, I don't know if I do. I see Weezy's feminists and what they're doing—they've gone out into the streets, marching and jamming up traffic and making people notice them and get angry. They wave banners and scream and make a real spectacle. And things *are* beginning to change. And where would they have gotten if they had all stayed home and waited, like ladies, for men to hear the voice of reason? And besides, *you* were marching and protesting yourself once. It just means that after the first shock of getting attention by assault, then you can put on your jacket and tie and look like a lawyer reasoning things out."

"Easy! Everything seems to set you off."

"Oh, I know." She sat up and faced him, her brow wrinkling with displeasure at herself.

"*La rughetta,*" said the old man, who had picked a clump of green and held it out to her.

"Ah, *rughetta,*" she exclaimed. They picked more of the pungent green leaves and then joined the old man, who put it with other greens into a salad and shared salad, bread, and cheese with them. As they ate together under the olive tree, the old man looked at them again and again, finally nodding his head vehemently and saying, "*Fidanzati, sì!*"

Jason took his harmonica out of his jeans pocket and played "Come Back to Sorrento."

They arrived the next day at Staffa, a site once sacred to Venus and so beautiful in its position that Tina felt the energy and motivation for going to Castagna drain from her. There was the sea, deep blue before her, and at her back was the yellow *ginestra*-blooming mountain. All was curves and dips and strong, bright colors. They went through the lower village down to what was known as the public beach, a small strand of sand between the rocky projections of the shore and a seedy-looking hotel. The sea was still and calm, and Tina waded in. A piece of eggplant floated nearby, a bean-pod, some tomato skins—refuse evidently of the hotel or of the small thatched-roof eating place built on stilts over the water.

Tina made a face of disgust. "I can't bear this!"

"Detritus," he grinned.

"*De trop*," she answered.

They walked back to Piazza Gesù, the center of the lower village, a square flanked by a pink church, a yellow Banco di Napoli, and a vine-covered bar. They stopped to have a beer and to find out, by talking to the waiter, exactly where Signor Agostini's place was.

As she looked about her, Tina felt the trap of her senses fold her in. Another beautiful place, she thought; another postponement of reality. She thought of her mother; that poor lady had always had to live in a perfect setting, there had to be beautiful views, things had to be just so. And yet when she stepped out of her setting, there was the real world all around her, ready to jar, like a too-swift change of scene in a movie. Did it make any sense to shelter oneself in aesthetics? Tina thought of the squalor of New York. Yet the streets there were charged with a vitality that was nowhere evident in the perfect, pastel square. It was going to be a question of compromise, she thought, of accommodating oneself to less than perfect solutions.

"I just want to stay here and not move anywhere," she said.

"We can stay," he said.

"No. I've got to get to Castagna. That's a magic name for me . . . you can't understand."

"Oh, but I can. I haven't told you yet, but there's a Castagna in my life, too. It just shows how we were meant for each other."

"Now don't tell me a quintessential Wasp like you has Calabrian ancestors. That's too much! Although I always did wonder about your dark looks. Do you suppose some of those Englishmen who were always walking through Calabria in the nineteenth century stopped off in Castagna and begot a love child who is your ancestor?"

"No, nothing improper, please. It's just that I always grew up hearing of the wreck of the Italian bark *Castagna* off Nauset Reef. My grandfather's place is not far away, and he was part of the rescue team when he was only fifteen. It was in 1914."

"That's incredible—an Italian boat named *Castagna*! What happened to her?" Tina was entranced; she believed in the synchronization of names and places and time in two different lives. Such signs were the magic that came out of the blue and brought two persons together, she was sure, more than any amount of tripping, sex, or good fellowship on the road. Now she and Jason had this powerful word between them.

"It was the most exciting story of my childhood because Grandpa took such a part in it. You remember where Nauset Light is, don't you, from that time you came to the Cape? Didn't Tim take you to see it?"

Tina nodded silently, absorbed in his talk.

"Well, all the Jowers men have always been part of the volunteer crew at the lifesaving station. Grandpa, since he was a boy, used to tag along when his father went to the scenes of wrecks. But the wreck of the *Castagna* was just about the worst in the station's history because it took place in a February storm and the stranded men were frozen in the rigging."

"My God! Did they live?"

"Grandpa used to say he never saw such battered bodies as were taken from that ship. The men had lashed themselves to the mast to keep from being swept overboard by the waves when they grounded. The waves were tremendous."

"I remember. Even at Thanksgiving, it was wild. That gray huge ocean—nothing like the Mediterranean. I love stories. All history should be told as people's stories, like your grandfather's. Now, start from the beginning."

"Well, Grandpa always called her 'the bark *Castagna*'—for that's what a small, three-masted sailing vessel is; it's not a ship. My grand-

father always used to say one should be precise in things. I liked
the term anyway; it made her seem more ancient and vulnerable.
Anyway, she was seventy-three days out of Montevideo with a
cargo of guano (that's bird shit), heading for Weymouth where
there's a big fertilizer plant, when she got into bad weather after
the Tropic of Cancer—and we all know what that is, thanks to
Henry Miller."

"Come on, Jason, I'm interested in this! That's not how your
grandfather would have told it. Tell it straight!"

"Yes, sir! She carried a crew of thirteen—and here my grandfather would pause and say in a suspenseful way, 'Now, I'm not a
superstitious man, but one might almost take that for an omen.' And,
in fact, later it was learned that one of the crew had to be left
behind in Montevideo after he broke his leg in a fall from the rigging. There was some muttering among the men about the number,
but the captain persuaded them and on they went. They got into
the trades and had fine sailing until they passed the Tropic of
Cancer, when they had nothing but wind and rain and snowstorms
and were driven here, there, and everywhere. They had been
plagued this way almost continuously until they got a brief spell
of good weather, when the captain made sightings for Massachusetts
Bay. They were almost in when a fierce storm broke over them and
they lost their direction to Boston Light.

"Early in the morning the wind broke on them from the north-
west in a regular blizzard, and they hauled to until they heard the
roar of waves breaking on the shore and knew they had headed
blindly in the wrong direction. It was too late to turn about and
they struck the outer bar, bounded over it, struck the inner bar and
the foremast snapped, and the sea swept over the vessel carrying
off the forecastle and flooding the boat.

"The decks became coated with ice and the captain ordered all
hands into the rigging. My grandfather said it was the mate who
told the story later because the captain had fallen, frozen over with
ice, from the mizzenmast and been instantly washed away by the
undertow. Then one of the crew fell from the rigging and was
rolled back and forth along the deck until he, too, was swept overboard. After the rescue, the cook, an old man, and the young cabin
boy were found frozen to death in the rigging—the young boy still
in underclothes. They were found near each other, their arms
clasped around the mast and frozen there.

"Grandpa said the fog was bad and the lifesavers' patrol didn't discover the wreck until around seven in the morning, when they had already been grounded a couple of hours. Well, they tried to launch a surfboat after one was hauled to the beach by horses from a couple of miles away. But the surfboat kept grounding because of the water surrounding the vessel being first deep then sucked away to a matter of inches by the undertow. It kept swamping. By then, one of the *Castagna's* sailors, with help so near at hand, took a chance on cutting himself loose from the rigging and dropping into the sea where he could be grasped by the rescue crew. But the undertow got him first, and he was carried out and drowned.

"Then the lifesavers tried shooting lines aboard. The first and second lines fell short, but the third one passed over the bark and a sailor managed to make it fast even though his limbs were practically immobile."

Jason paused and looked grave. "Now comes the part we always waited for. This is the part where Grandpa comes in. You see, he was the first person to board the *Castagna* from the lifesavers. They were all afraid that the frozen line thrown on board would not hold the weight of heavier men, and so he was sent on board to chop the frozen crew from the rigging. Grandpa said he'd never forget the terrified look in the eyes of a frozen crewman as he went toward him with his ax. The crewman was literally frozen stiff and couldn't move anything but his eyes, which rolled back and forth with this terrible fear as he watched Grandpa chop him loose. It was a tough job in bitter cold to get them all loose, and in the case of the helmsman, Grandpa couldn't get his fingers free from the ship's wheel so he chopped away the section in the man's grasp. Years later he heard that an antique dealer who collected all things nautical had a wheel alleged to be that of the wrecked *Castagna*. Grandpa said he alone of all people would be able to identify it as such, which he did, for a six-inch piece was missing, just as he had cut it away thirty years earlier!

"Of the survivors, one died before they got him to the Marconi station, and the others, in horrible condition, were bundled up, packed in snow, and put on a train to Boston for the hospital. A year later, the body of the captain was found, still frozen, near Nauset Harbor. My grandfather, every time he told me the story, would say of the rescued men that they were a fine-looking lot, despite what they'd been through. They looked like men who had sailed all their lives. They were bronzed and weatherbeaten and bearded, but wiry and strong or none of them would have survived; they looked like sea-rovers. That's what he called them, sea-rovers, and it's always stuck in my mind."

"What a story! But why was that ship called *Castagna*, of all things?"

"That's the one thing I never asked my grandfather. We'll have to go to your Castagna; maybe they'll know there."

"What will they know? It's up in the mountains, and the people there have never even heard of the sea."

"Well, then, it's just serendipity—just something, as I told you, to connect you and me."

"What a story, Jason," she repeated, and as she looked at him she thought, In terms of men, a Jowers man was the perfect aesthetic.

That night, for the first time, they slept together and made love in Agostini's little house up in the hills overlooking the sea. And he said, as they lay there, "Tina, come back with me at the end of this trip. Come back to the States with me and stay with me."

"Oh, Jason," she said, "that's too far away. Who wants to think about that right now?"

"All right, don't think about it now—keep it in your mind for later. But remember, I mean it."

Just like her father, she thought, who also made his demands on her.

Their days in Agostini's house took on a rhythm. They found the fisherman, they found the wine man, and they found the open-air market of the upper town. They bought heaps of fresh tomatoes and peeled them raw, sprinkled leaves of fresh basil over them, and then had them over fresh pasta that they bought from Zia Mariuccia. Or they went to Biagio's, which was a combination deli-grocery-eating place with a sign that said *A piedi o seduto, può mangiare in un minuto*, and bought mountain prosciutto to have with fresh figs.

They went to the beach; they walked through the old streets; they hitched up to the mountain sanctuary of San Biagio, where an immense figure of Christ stretched his arms to encompass all the land and sea before him. Tina found the local hardware store and bought the clenched-hand knocker they had seen on all the doors in town.

"What are you going to do with that?" Jason asked.

"Save it for some future door," she said.

"Who do you expect to knock at that door?"

"The highwayman!"

They were very close, by day and by night, in companionship and in love. When she was sulky or querulous, she was gloomy old Eeyore; when he was affable and charming, he was good old Bear.

"What shall we do today?" Tina might ask.

"Oh, nothing. It's a nothing sort of day—let's just go along, listening to all the things, and not bothering."

"Well, that's all right for you, Bear of little brain, but what I'd like right now is a book."

"And you call me the reality-junkie! What you are is a book-addict," Jason said. "Jacques Cousteau says that men who live most of their lives on the sea think more clearly, since they always have before them the clear cut of the horizon, one horizontal line of sea and sky. This is a good time for you to think, not read."

"Oh, Bear, I read like I breathe. In college I used to go around quoting Logan Pearsall Smith: 'They say life is the thing, but I prefer reading.' This place is beautiful but it's a backwater—I can't find a book around and I'm sick of Italian gossip magazines."

"The only place to live is a backwater. This reminds me in a lusher way of Cape Cod. That's really home to me . . . and that's a backwater, these days, despite the summer people and tourists. The great days of whaling and shipping are gone."

"Well, I'm not going to sit here and think about that!"

"Think about us."

"Oh, Jason!" she would exclaim. For she was growing restless and edgy. The more she felt herself loving him, the more it angered her to think that love was entrapment.

While it was still a trip, she was safe from those big decisions Jason wanted her to make. The Pooh language and allusions they used between themselves helped, too—it went back to her childhood, it had nothing to do with her future as a woman.

She tried to tell him.

"I don't want to be financially and emotionally dependent on marriage. My mother was more interesting than anyone I knew, yet in the eyes of the world she was no one except her husband's wife and her children's parent. She wasn't strong enough to be herself. Only old Umbertina seems to have done what she had to do in life. The other family women are like lost souls—only there to provide life-systems for the men and children."

"Come on, Tina, everyone knows that things are different these days. There's no danger, anyway, of anyone like you being submerged! Actually it's probably the other way around; any guy would have to be pretty strong on his own to take on a full-blown temperament like yours. All that Castagna toughness—God!"

She laughed. "Does it scare you, Bear? Does it scare the Wasps because you're the past but we're new and emerging? That's the great thing: You see, I have these two things in me that are beginning to be worked out, my work and my Italian-American identity."

Jason looked at her quizzically. "You never used to say you were Italian-American. You went to great lengths to make it understood that your mother was American and your father Italian—separate things. No mix. You didn't want any part of melting-pot Italian."

"I know. But you know what, Jason-Bear, I'm excited by being here at the beginning of Calabria. I was never so far south before. I'm excited by being near Umbertina's birthplace—and excited by her, by her story. Up till now I ignored all that part; my mother's family just wasn't up to my father's side and so I ignored them. But the fact is, you see, that my father's Venetian side is like being Wasp in the States: all well and good, but dying out, enervated, obsolete. The interesting part is the rise of all these new people who got where they are not by privilege or family or connections but just by sheer guts and working hard. I'm beginning to like the southern part of me."

"That's your trouble, Tina; you just don't let both things blend naturally—no, you've got to make dramatic decisions and take one side or the other. Now you've got this thing about Wasp wispiness, as if we're all dying out of sheer inertia."

She laughed and put her arms around his neck. "Oh, Pooh, I do love you!"

But, she wondered, was love enough?

Chapter Thirty

Jason came back from market one morning his arms full of bags, his mouth stretched wide in a broad grin. He had brought her a tee shirt with "Melt in Your Mouth" emblazoned in hot pink letters across the front.

"God!" she said, pleased.

They sat on the front steps against an arch of the veranda and began snipping beans from one of the market bags.

"You'd make someone a great wife," he teased.

"So would you."

"It's funny how you do all the essentials so well—you like to cook, make love, go with a guy on trips, talk, swim—and yet you have this hang-up about getting married."

"Jason!" she remonstrated in what he called her schoolmarm tone. "I promised myself not to marry until I had my degree. I'm not going to be just dragged along as baggage on my husband's career."

"Tina, you know I respect your educational commitment. Jesus! that's what I like about you. I don't want some dummy who has no mind of her own. I've told you I would never interfere in your plans for yourself. You can and should have your own career."

"How can I be free if you're 'bestowing' this gift on me?"

"I don't mean it that way—"

"No man does! But I don't want this kind of magnanimity from anyone. I just want to do what I have to. I can't commit myself to a man before I've even started my work. And my work isn't solely to be a wife."

"Well, then, I'll wait."

He reached for her arm, fondling it. "You've got this pouty look, you know, like you want to discourage anyone from getting close. And then you smile and it's like flares going off up in the mountains. God, you're so pretty!" He looked at her intently. "I don't see why you can't continue your studies with me, in Boston."

"And then what, Jason? After I finish all these years of graduate school and begin looking for a place, what happens if it turns out to be in Michigan or California, or even the University of Hawaii?"

He was silent for a while. "What happens about love?" he asked with a troubled look. "You know how I feel about you, Tina. You know I love you and we have all these things we share together. Yes, we could go on like this but it seems sterile, leading to nothing. No future."

"I don't want that future at this point, Jason."

He looked uncertain, hurt. She reached for his hand. "Oh, come on, Bear! It's not you I'm excluding—it's anything that gets in the way of my finishing and having my own life in hand. Maybe we got together too soon . . . maybe this should have happened later on. Listen, J.J.! I'll put on my new tee shirt and we'll go down to the Hotel Staffa."

They walked down to the low, white hotel on the point overlooking the sea and entered the reception rooms through the terrace. Huge overstuffed couches and armchairs in light cretonnes and lemon-yellow slipcovers filled the white-walled rooms and stood out against the deep tones of smooth ox-blood-tiled pavements. Bouquets of natural flowers garnished the tables and groups of old prints were hung over antique chests. It was simple and stylish.

"I love this place," Tina said to Jason as she looked around.

Stunning people in casual but expensive dress drifted through the rooms or sat in groups on the terrace.

"The Italians really know what luxury is," Tina said approvingly. "You'd never catch them doing something hokey like Miami Beach hotels or all those disgusting Hiltons and Sheratons."

"Yes," said Jason. "When you have money enough, then understated is the thing."

"This is the life . . . first class all the way."

"You haven't much of Weezy's asceticism, I notice," Jason said wryly.

"Oh, Weezy!" Tina said, frowning. "She'd like to be some modern version of a saint. Live in the country and make soup from thistles and jam from prickly pears—then run five kilometers into town to her class for preschoolers, reading the kids *The Little Flowers of St. Francis* in English to teach them a second language and spiritual socialism all at once."

"You sound a bit defensive."

"I'm more of a saint than Weezy any day, the way I've had to live in the States!"

Tina went over to the desk clerk, who smiled at her and nodded with barely perceptible movements of his balding head. Tina recognized Italian approval. The tee shirt was tight over her full breasts, and the rest of her curved and strained against her jeans. She looked good and knew it. The tan glow in her cheeks brought out the light of her hazel eyes, and heat made her long thick hair wisp around her face like curling grape tendrils. She was tall, not like the dark short women of the area, nor fair like the hotel guests from the North. She was both of the South and the North, something different.

"Do you have a bookstore or library in the hotel?" she was asking the clerk when a large blondish man in navy blazer, silk ascot, and white ducks came out from an inner office with papers in his hand and noticed her.

"Permit me," he said. "Signorina . . . ?" He hesitated.

"Morosini," she said.

"Related to the author?"

"His daughter," said Tina.

"It's a pleasure to have you here, *signorina*. I'm Count Rivolonovo, and I'm afraid there's not much in the way of books in this part of Italy, even at the hotel, but allow me to open my own library to you. I live in the tower at Punto Moresco, not far from here. Why don't you and your friend come to dinner tonight? Just an informal gathering, alfresco. And then you can choose a book for yourself—English, Italian, or whatever."

"We don't really have anything to wear to a dinner party," Tina said, stuttering somewhat, both pleased and self-conscious at the count's attention to her. "We're not even staying at the hotel, we're at Signor Agostini's place."

"You're perfect as you are, both of you. I'll have my driver pick you up at eight-thirty tonight."

The drive down to the point was through an old grove of olive trees, which then mixed with a strand of feathery pines and oaks as they approached the watchtower on a spur of rocky cliff above the sea.

The count greeted them in the grove, which had once belonged to a farmhouse that was now a gatehouse guarding the access to his preserve. In a cleared area, a greenhouse was spotlighted, displaying rich exotic blooms and serving as backdrop for a bar that had been built around a twisted olive tree. In the distance Tina and Jason could see the crenellated heights of the tower, which loomed in its impressive bulk against the somewhat opaque evening sky.

"Here is where we will have drinks," the count said as he greeted them.

It was an uncertain evening; there was what the Italians call *foschia* in the summer air: a kind of oppressiveness, not yet mist but heavy and dampish, a warning.

Jason and Tina were presented to the other guests—Tina as the daughter of the author Alberto Morosini and Jason as the son of an American diplomat in Rome. "If we aren't worth knowing in our right, at last we have the right connections," Jason muttered to her sarcastically.

Tina, as usual on such occasions, was a mixture of envy and scorn. Envy at the beautiful lives and poise of these people; scorn that they didn't know (how could they?) what she did.

The count was fussing. "I'm very nervous about whether we should dine out tonight, after all, or go into the tower. What do you say, will it rain? Oh, well, let's risk it for now."

A man in a handsome beige linen suit with a deep blue shirt and burnt-orange tie, who had been noticing Tina since her arrival, was now making his way toward them. He was tall and well-built with a full, smooth face and eyes that were rather protuberant and probing. His hair was thinning.

At the same time, two women, one in a burnoose and the other in a jump suit, had joined them. "Ah!" the count said, "let me introduce you to two ladies from the French Embassy in Rome." The women enclosed Jason, talking both at once, and just then the man in the linen suit reached their group.

"Here is a futurist, whatever that is," the count said offhandedly, "Professor Simongini, Signorina Morosini."

"I may be the futurist, count"—the man laughed as Tina's eyes were drawn to the nubs in his raw-silk tie—"but you must admit, even your sixteenth-century tower has a twentieth-century elevator to get you up and down."

The count laughed generously. "Speak to this charming young lady, Ferruccio, she might like your notions," he said as he went off.

"What are your notions?" Tina asked smilingly. It made her feel bold and confident when men were attracted to her, as this professor obviously was.

"Just what I've picked up at Harvard plus all the European cultural baggage I carry around in my head. Come, let's get a drink from that bucolic bar." With skillful use of his hand under her elbow, he nimbly steered Tina toward the greenhouse. As she looked back, she saw Jason laughing with the Frenchwomen.

"What are you doing in these parts?" he asked as he handed Tina a Campari with soda. He was looking at her with an amused expression, his eyes roving openly over her figure.

"I'm on my way to a village called Castagna to find my ancestral place. My great-grandparents came from there."

"Beautiful name—'a chestnut' in English, isn't it?—probably famous for beautiful women, too. Is your friend on an ancestor search also?" He nodded nonchalantly in the direction of Jason, who was still conversing with the Frenchwomen.

"He's not Italian. He's New England."

"Ah, I see. But what you need is an Italian to lead you through deepest Calabria. And especially in these days of *canicola*. The dog days!"

"And how did you get here?" Tina answered.

"Because our friend Count Rivolonovo, who is, perhaps, not as authentic as his watchtower, delights in sparkling guests. He goes over the register at the hotel to see who is here to embellish his soirées. I add dash to the evenings; others, like you, add beauty; still others come automatically because of wealth, power, connections. The count is from the North, you see, brought here on a stream of American dollars to revitalize this backward part of the South. He started a branch of his northern textile industry down here and gave jobs to everyone; he built the hotel, improved the beach, and used his connection with the prefect to have the harbor of the fishing port dredged to accommodate the yachts of his friends. There he is. . . . As you look at him, which of the northern tribes do you imagine endowed our elegant count with his dynamism? Was it the Longobards, the Vandals, the Visigoths, or the Huns? Or do you notice an uncanny resemblance to Christ the Redeemer, which the count commissioned for the sanctuary at the top of the mountain? Both Christ and the count encompass all the area around here."

Tina smiled, amused, and looked toward the count, whose broad shoulders and thickish neck and stature did resemble someone Teutonic, like Curt Jurgens.

"Well, *professore*, the count is right about your adding dash. Does he know what you say of him?"

"Ah, *mia cara*," he answered in mock horror, "don't call me *professore*! How could you . . . here, on such a night . . . on vacation! My name is Ferruccio. And yours?"

"Tina," she said. "And now that I know you"—she smiled at him —"tell me what a futurist is."

"A sociologist. That's what I am—what the count mockingly calls a futurist."

"Oh," said Tina, pouting in a show of disappointment. "I was hoping you were the kind of futurist who tells fortunes. A sibyl, or something like that."

"I can be that, too," he said easily. He was looking at her intently. She began to feel giddy under his look and the strange pressure of the evening air.

They were joined by the prefect of Cosenza and his wife, Donna Emilia, who both knew Ferruccio and were introduced to Tina. The prefect was saying that it was his duty as judge in the contest for the Best-Looking Legs of the Gulf of Castronoto which had brought him there. His wife, stunning and tanned and of the type called *formosa* by southern men, had the glowing, satisfied look of people who live well.

Count Rivolonovo came up to them with a woman whose graying hair was well cut in a thick, short bob; she wore a polo shirt and long skirt and held a cigarette in a holder. "And here is the Baroness Dall'Airone," said the count, "who lives in the part of Staffa that I call the chicken-coop village—a kind of modern development that's our only eyesore."

The baroness laughed loudly, and said in a well-cultivated husky voice as she pointed with her holder toward a man with a tanned, wrinkled face, "My Koko and I—there he is with those charming women—yes, Koko and I make our friend the count jealous because of the perfect freedom we have in our henhouse. I have a home *comme il faut* in Naples full of boring treasures, but here it's all plastic and freedom and I adore it. The count teases because he hasn't yet achieved the inner freedom to live in a henhouse."

"Clever woman, the *baronessa*," Ferruccio said under his breath to Tina. "And a real title."

There were a number of other guests: Dr. Arndt, a Jungian psychiatrist from Zurich who came each year to the hotel to purge himself, he said, of Swissness and to take in the pleasures of the South, a necessary balance in life; Gianluca Grondi, the Socialist leader, who was there to attest to the count's tolerant attitude not only toward the Left but toward local tradition, for the Grondis, after all, had been the original gentry in those parts; the well-known author Giorgio Fermo, all in white, his candid blue eyes shining from the brown of his face, and at his side a new companion, a tall woman who wore her hair in a chignon and her face with an expression of disdain; a woman administrator of Italia Nostra, an environmentalist group; and a short, dark couple from Sicily, just back from Alaska and the northwestern states, who would have been eager to speak of America with Tina, but Ferruccio deftly steered her away.

As Tina looked about for Jason she saw him now with some tall, blond young people. Ferruccio identified them as Sisi—the count's daughter, and his hostess while her mother was in Geneva finishing a course in cybernetics—and her two brothers. They were slim, pale blonds with cool looks of aloofness in their eyes, and they made a startling contrast to the dark Jason and to Filippo Merici, a collector of ethnic and regional music who was going to sing and play his antique lute-guitar later that evening.

Ferruccio, who seemed to notice everything, leaned very close to her and said in her ear so that his breath ruffled the wisps of hair around it, "Don't worry about your friend, he's in the best of company."

"But am I?" she retorted.

"Ah! you American women," Ferruccio laughed warmly.

So that's who I am, Tina thought as she sipped another drink and looked about at the groupings of handsome people in that splendid setting. Not one of these gorgeous Italians, but an acerbic American. She shrugged her shoulders, not unhappy.

She thought of rejoining Jason but suddenly she and Ferruccio were involved in a high-speed conversation going on in Italian, English, and French—all at once and with swift switches from one language to another, accurate and brilliant—about the upcoming beauty contest for the best legs of the region. All of those legs, declared the prefect of Cosenza, as well as the eleven bishops and other souls of the region, were under his special protection.

Somehow the silly chatter excited her, as did Ferruccio's closeness, which made him continually rub up against her, even as he kept saying "Pardon!"

Dinner for twenty was served under trees strung with lanterns at a long table set with plates bearing the count's motto: *Ex rivis novis maximum flumen.* Tina giggled at the motto and thought of a rhyme from long ago in a book her mother used to read to her and Weezy:

> Large streams from little fountains flow,
> Tall oaks from little acorns grow.

She told herself to remember to tell Ferruccio later. Or did she mean Jason? She gave herself over totally to the superb food.

Waiters with white gloves served plates of tiny stuffed eggplants and peppers, a timbale of macaroni and béchamel, and then a platter of roast boar from the count's own preserve at Belvedere Calabro, which was greeted by a round of applause.

In between courses and above the chatter of the other guests came occasionally the loud, authoritative voice of Count Rivolonovo.

"Of course they live better now that the factory is here: The girls can pick up dress-lengths for only 700 lire and make themselves two or three outfits a season where they once had only one. Everyone is employed, or could be, and the new income is spread through the whole community. There's a *casa di riposo* for the old people, and a hospital. Still, I wonder sometimes if progress is worth it all."

"Well, it's progress of some sort to have the women's legs out in the open," said Baron Dall'Airone.

"Indubitably!" laughed the count. "And the Artisans' Fair, and the staging of the two Pirandello plays in the piazza. But is it better for these people to have civilized pressures upon them when, before, they had their bread and a little oil to spread on it and the sun to sit in and were without competitiveness and anxiety?"

"What you're asking," joined in Ferruccio, "is whether affluence is good for everyone. Of course it brings TV, car jams in the little streets, hippie clothes, plastics, and the like. But it also means travel; the *sarta* told me this year she's going to France for her vacation. When could that have ever happened before? And it's not just a question of money—before when they had money they bought themselves gold earrings and bracelets—it's a question of a new mentality, of educating themselves to other expectations. They stock deodorants now in the *tabacchi*."

"But they don't have books," said Tina, though no one seemed to hear.

"It's cleaner in Staffa than in Rome and the people are not as rude —not yet, anyway," the count answered. "But it will come: Vulgarity and spoiling the environment always seem to come with progress and money. But the worst are the *americani*, the ones who go off to the Americas and break their backs laboring with picks and shovels and living like dogs in terrible climates. Then they come back with their money, acting like little kings, and making the others unhappy with things as they are. Even their countrymen and relatives here despise them—they say anyone could make money if they wanted to live badly like that. They think money is everything, and yet they are the same *cafoni* as when they left. They'll never change."

Tina recognized in the count's words about the *americani* her own anger and shame at them. They came over, uneducated and arrogant, to get even with Italy by showing how much money they had, to demand ice in their drinks, and to complain about the food. It was all those wretched *americani* who had always created the ambivalence of who she was. What had she in common with such types? And yet she felt compassion, if not toward them, at least toward their immigrant parents who had literally been in the same boat as Umbertina. If somehow America as Purgatory hadn't yet refined their dross and had become, instead, their false Paradise, on the other hand it had taught them who they were: American.

Now, surprisingly, she found herself saying, "Oh, yes, there can be change. New people are born from new situations, and it's education that recasts them. My father says all life is a question of recasting." The table was quiet and listening to her. It was as if the count's words had sparked some private illumination in her own uncertainty. It was a good sensation.

Then Giorgio Fermo broke the silence by quipping, "*Ex rivis novis maximum flumen.* Isn't it true that it takes new streams to build up the old? To keep things flowing? That's the function of the *americani*, too."

The others laughed at his boldness; only one of the literati would have dared, at the count's table, to identify the *americani* with the count's motto.

The tension was broken as the count laughed and pointed to the tower. "Yes," he said, "here I am, new wine in an old bottle."

Tina admired his sophistication. She admired the whole evening and thought well of herself for being there.

The count then led the way into the tower. The elevator took them to a terrace off the battlements overlooking the sea. A bar was built into the natural rock formation and a servant was there to pour liqueurs from it.

"Oh, Count Rivolonovo, you are a perfect conjurer," said the Frenchwoman in the burnoose. "You astound us with bars and music and lights in every rock and tree." And indeed, there was hi-fi equipment, so that the terrace could be used for dancing.

"Are you having a good time?" Tina asked Jason as Sisi finally left him to see about getting Filippo set up for his playing.

"Aren't you? You've been spending the whole evening with that Italian." There was a raspy tone of displeasure in his voice and she saw that he had a tense look. It instantly infuriated Tina to think that he could be jealous in a circumstance like this, and that he had such a sense of possessiveness about her.

At the table she had been placed between the prefect and Baron Dall'Airone, and Ferruccio had been directly across from her, with Jason on the same side but separated by a few other guests so that they had not been together the whole evening. But it hadn't been her doing—more like Sisi's. Before she could think of anything appropriately sarcastic, Sisi was inviting them to sit down for Filippo's songs.

People were grouping themselves on the low wall or in comfortable wicker chairs that looked out to sea or up to the mountain, where the dim outline of Christ was faintly visible in tenuous milkiness. Sisi led Jason to her group, and instead of following, Tina looked around for Ferruccio. He was right there, and with hand under elbow again, was guiding her to one side in the shadow of a huge umbrella pine that curved over the terrace.

Filippo played his astounding baroque instrument with its span like an eagle's wings and two sets of cords. He sang about Staffa, Sant'Antonio, and even the lucky Signora Beatrice, who had had no less than Dante as a lover.

Except for Jason's peevish behavior, Tina was content with the night. The opaqueness, the singing, and the softened views made it all dreamlike. A servant passed demitasses of strong coffee followed by cigarettes and chocolates. The rocks gave forth Mistrà, grappa, and brandy. They were at ease in a perfect setting not yet despoiled, and just over the mountains, farther down the boot but not that far, was the land of her people.

And yet how far! How far from the count's elegant domain and well-appointed table; how far from Venice, where her father's bourgeois family lines were so well rooted; how far from anything, except, strangely, the distant America that alone had wanted their labor and patience.

Tina reflected on her inland people born just hours away from that pleasant setting, but not on the sea where songs were sung to the moon and fishing boats went out at night with their lanterns to attract a catch. Her people had hoed miserable little fields of rocks or gathered *ginestra* from the mountainsides to make into cord. And then one day they had put their things in a shawl, together with their last bread for the journey, and had walked to the sea to get the boat to Naples and from there to America. A long trip, a long time ago.

Strange currents were at work in Tina. She was both elated and still tipsy from all the drinking. Ferruccio was holding her hand and pressing his body close to hers. The music rose and fell like the sea, like her heart.

"Well, what about this trip to Calabria. Don't you think you need an Italian?

"But what Italian?" she answered back, playing his game, smiling over her liqueur glass and looking at him full in the eyes.

"A futurist, of course. You should have a futurist in your present."

That was what stirred her about Ferruccio; he was so clearly a present excitement—something completely transient, uncertain, and adventurous. As different as possible from Jason, whom she loved and was afraid of because his very permanency and steadiness were making unanswerable demands upon her.

She looked around at the group and then at Ferruccio with a glance of complicity.

"Shall we go to Castagna? This very night?" he whispered close to her. "I'll be your Italian guide."

"What, in July? You have to be crazy!"

"Let's be crazy."

Life, her mother used to say, is no more than choices. The wine, the unsettled air of the evening, the setting of the old tower all helped Tina make her choice. *In amore, vince chi fugge*—that, thought Tina tipsily, is why I'm leaving Jason; because love was a trap; because it was too good being with him; because she was afraid it couldn't last or that it would last, and at twenty-three permanence was as bad as fleetingness. In love, as the proverb said, the one who flees wins.

Tina and Ferruccio slipped away in the shadows while everyone else was intent on the singing.

Chapter Thirty-one

"What do you say, shall we head for the sea or go straight to Castagna?" Ferruccio asked as they left the coastal town where they had spent the night in the creaky bed of a third-class hotel. They were heading inland toward the *autostrada*.

"Oh, I don't know . . . it's so hot and primitive here, I'd like to get to the sea . . . and yet I came to see Castagna," she said, fingering the tin heart tied to her shoulder bag. She slouched alongside him in the speeding red Maserati, emphasizing her irritation by pulling hard at her long hair and tying it back with a scarf, though strands continued to escape and cling to her face.

Castagna was going to be a hard nut to crack: That was the prevailing pun between them as they drove the forsaken mountain road of inland Calabria toward Morano.

"Ah, yes, Castagna, where your ancestors started from on their way to America. A 'chestnut,' in English, is some old stale joke, isn't it?" Ferruccio kept looking sideways at Tina's long tanned legs as she thrust them up under the dashboard. He was laughing, pleased with himself that he could use English so well.

"The joke's on me," Tina said with a shrug, her eyes fixed ahead of her on the barren landscape that stretched brown and endless in the scorching heat. All morning the disconsolate country through which they drove, the sight of the parched riverbeds so preposterously styled *torrente*, and the occasional grubby, fly-filled *caffè*s at which they stopped in dusty little villages had oppressed her.

"Oh, come on," he was bantering, "you're in Calabria, and that's what you want, isn't it—to see the place your people came from?"

I wish I knew what I wanted, Tina answered silently. She wasn't like Weezy, who, in her madness, had some crazy method; nor like Jason, who had no great purposes and was content not to; nor even like Ferruccio, who knew exactly what he was about. Tina had discovered that Ferruccio's seemingly spontaneous whim of the night before was not that at all—he intended to go south into Calabria all along to look up an antique dealer named Luluzzo in Morano.

"You were coming to Calabria anyway," she said accusingly. The mood of the party and the escapade was fading in the bright glare of the day and the harsh sight of the barren inland mountains.

"Let's say Morano is the antipasto and Castagna will be the main course," he said smoothly. "Luluzzo has the best buys in all of Italy because no one would think of coming down here to get them. Whenever I'm in the South I always stop to pick up things for my place."

So why shouldn't she be humiliated, Tina told herself glumly; hadn't she done the same, or worse, to Jason?

From the *autostrada*, Morano looked like a charming village perched on a mountaintop, faraway and inaccessible. But the moment they began the approach, it became another squalid town of the South. It offended Tina, as it did not in Rome, to see the still-visible effrontery of fascist rhetoric in such squalor. Along streets full of hen-shit and goat-turds, the walls proclaimed the slogans of forty years before: "Italy Above All and Over All" . . . "Obey, Believe, Fight, Win." They drove as far into the town as they could, and where the streets became cobblestoned warrens too narrow and steep for the car, they left it and proceeded on foot to look for Luluzzo.

The apathetic and listless people standing and staring after them in the streets were like relics from a place under siege, but Ferruccio, Tina noticed, was not making any sociological observations; he was too taken with the excitement of flushing out bargains to notice where he put his expensively shod feet. The whole thing made Tina furious as she picked her way through slop and various kinds of excrement up to Luluzzo's place. There, in the damp whitewashed rooms of the dealer's storehouse, Ferruccio began foraging through the heaps of furniture, doors, lintels, tiles, plates, framed paintings, statues, books, marble altarpieces, whole choir-stalls, vestments, and lavabos from sacked churches. He kept up a stream of talk with the emaciated and ragged-looking Luluzzo, who silently went about gathering up the things that Ferruccio pointed out. Finally Ferruccio had chosen: some antique tiles torn from the church pavement in a remote village, a piece of handsome wood carving, a pair of gilt baroque altar candelabra, a long rustic refectory table, and an ancient faience soup tureen with "Roma" written on one side and "Venezia" on the other.

Luluzzo was asking 50,000 lire for the lot, including delivery to Rome.

"Come on, Luluzzo, what kind of price is that for an old client?" Ferruccio countered. Tina knew that in Rome he couldn't have gotten any single item for that amount, even at the Porta Portese flea market. "For that amount you should throw in something else!"

"Everything's getting higher," the dealer complained. "Even up in the mountains women who can't read or write have begun to hear that their old things are worth money and they want more when I go to buy . . . and it's not easy to get priests to sell things from their churches anymore. They're waiting for the dealers from Florence. But here, I can add this painting of a priest—it's old, believe me."

"I don't care to have that painting in my home," Ferruccio said sternly. "I don't like priests."

Luluzzo looked genuinely shocked. "If you say that about priests, what is there left to believe in?"

Ferruccio laughed, paid Luluzzo, and they left.

"That was a pretty disgusting business," Tina told him in the car as they drove out.

"Don't be so disapproving," he said lightly, laughing. "This is where Count Rivolonovo gets his things. Luluzzo is known all over and if we who appreciate this stuff didn't pick it up, it would lie and molder in his storerooms. The ones to blame are the ignor-amus priests." He looked over at her and noticed the firm set of her lips. "*Bambina mia*," he chided, reaching over to rub her cheek with the back of his hand, "what is it? Aren't you enjoying your-self? You're not in the same spirits as last night. I think we should head for the Ionian Sea before taking on Castagna; that will cheer you up."

"I feel guilty about Jason," she said glumly. "We made a pact to go to Castagna together." Castagna had been their magic word. And now what was it? No more than what Ferruccio in his flippant manner called a hard nut to crack.

"I had a commitment to Jason," she continued stubbornly, feeling unsporting, becoming a nuisance. Now that she was on the road with Ferruccio, why bring up the rest? Because she had a headache and an upset stomach and the flies and heat and look of Calabria was getting to her.

"As for commitments, *mia cara*," Ferruccio was saying, "remember that nothing in life is irrevocable or conclusive."

"That's very handy," she retorted. "Italians make everything relative! But there's such a thing as one's word being good."

"Despite an Italian father I see you are more Anglo-Saxon than Latin in mentality."

"You really mean more puritanical, don't you? That's what all Italians mean when they laugh at Americans for being uptight about commitments."

"Well, are you so in love with the fellow after all? You must be, to be tormenting yourself like this."

"That's not the point. I don't necessarily have to be in love with a person in order to keep my word."

"Still, I think you are. Don't worry—it makes it all the more interesting in the end."

"Are you so cynical about everything?"

"Not about my food and wine; those, at least, must be absolutely dependable."

The dry, lunar quality of the land, burned out and dusty, matched the dryness of his words. It was too late to repent her flight; she tried to piece together again why she had done it. She had seen what living with Duke led to; she didn't want it to happen with Jason. She didn't want to be put in her mother's role before her own career was set, then ruin the lives of both Jason and herself.

Yes, there as always, at the bottom of it all was her mother; her beloved, foolish, dead-and-gone mother, whom she was emulating all along. Was this her own version of her mother's driving over the mountains to find love and finding, instead, death in an overturned car? Was it an attempt at self-punishment for not being able to stick to Jason as her mother had not stuck to her father? Tina wanted to think there was good reason for what she had done—

saving Jason from herself, or something like that—but how could she believe it was anything more than the banality of sex and too much to drink? She recalled vividly Ferruccio's making love to her as the bed creaked and groaned with his thrusts. And her inflamed response.

She closed her eyes, pressed her two fists hard against the sockets as if to wipe out sight and memory, and then flung out her arms with a deep sigh.

"I can't bear this," she said. "Let's go to the sea."

He grinned, reached over, and caressed the inside of her thigh. "Pleasure before duty, eh!

"It's rather a good thing I have you with me. The women of the southern coasts are not noted for their looks, and you, at least, are passable."

She gave him a quizzical look in reply—curious, because of the literal streak in her, about his statements. "Why is that? What's wrong with southern women?"

"The best types are in the mountains. The coastal people have been too mixed and hybridized over the ages by the sea marauders —Turks and Saracens—who invaded these coasts and impregnated the women. About the only thing these women have are large, dark cow-eyes. But that's not for me. I prefer squinty light-green eyes like yours."

"My great-grandmother came from the mountains. I want to go to where she came from—to see the people and know what they're like. I want to see if I recognize me in them."

"A kind of postponed identity crisis, perhaps," he said glibly. "I can tell you who your people are without your ever having to set foot in Castagna. They're mountain people—brooding, suspicious, reserved, reticent. Just like you, you see. They're the descendants of the old Bruttii tribes of antiquity, the ones about whom Horace made the pun 'Bruttii from their brutish manners.'"

"The Romans were prejudiced."

"No prejudice—the mountain people deserved that witticism. They were the only tribes of Magna Graecia who didn't mix with the colonizing Greeks. They kept to themselves in the mountains, uncontaminated by civilization, or later, malaria."

This pleased Tina. She was glad that Umbertina and Serafino, those unknown Calabrian progenitors of hers, were from the ancient Brutii. But where were the forests of Bruttium?

Out of the mountains, they took the direction that led to the sea, and signs began appearing in the plains announcing the *Bonifica di Sibari*, the Reclamation of Sybaris. It had a wry sound. "Two thousand years late," she said, and Ferruccio nodded. "Everything's too late down here: Garibaldi was too late, Fiat was too late, the twentieth century is too late."

They got to a place Ferruccio knew about called Bagamoyo, which was clean, he said, and well organized because it was run by a German who had stayed behind during the last war. It was a small resort on a gorgeous stretch of sand fronted by the Ionian Sea and backed by a strand of pines and willows, the first gathering of trees she had seen all day. They were told they were fortunate to find a room there, the place having been completely filled until just yesterday when a family left.

Ferruccio grinned and said, "The greatest blessing in life is not to be rich or wise, but to be fortunate." He was irrepressibly confident and high-spirited. Did he ever worry, get dejected, lose hope, Tina wondered, as she and Jason did?

Everything, as far as Tina could see, went well with him, and his incurable optimism seemed not so much a sign of shallowness as of an active receptiveness to being lucky. She began to relax; she was thankful to be there with him, for all the harshness of Calabria glanced off him and made no mark. She and Jason, alone in the desolate land, would have been overcome with conscience, pity, self-hate, and all the other signs of a compassion that gives nothing useful to those it's directed at.

At the sea it was different. She liked being there with Ferruccio. He knew how to deal with people, how to command the foods and wines of the region that never appeared on the menus, how to listen to the sounds of the sea and get the best part of the sun, how to get stories out of the shy local people, and how to become one with the time and place he was in.

It may have been the approximately fifteen years' difference in their ages, or his one hundred percent *italianità* compared to her being the confused product of an American mother and Italian father so that she was neither one thing nor the other; but no two sides battled in Ferruccio Simongini—he was all of a piece in his self-centered approach to life.

"A fine sociologist and socialist," she teased him. "Admit: You are only interested in yourself and your immediate pleasures."

"Of course, when I am here with you on vacation. What else? Would you expect me to do other than pay attention to our well-being after my having abducted you?"

"You are a futurist, tell me the future," she continued.

"What a bore, what a pest you are! Why would you possibly want the future when here we have this glorious present?"

"I want to know what to prepare for . . . what to expect."

"The team; expect to be part of a team, my little individualist. No more cult of the personality. To get on successfully in society, you will have to be part of a functional group. The personal identity crisis will be old-hat, perverse really—an expression of self-centeredness that will be very suspect." He drawled lazily, as they lay prone on the warm, white sand and listened to the sounds of the waves.

"Mmmm," she said, trailing her hand in the sand. "Sounds delicious. What else?"

"No more the two of us alone on this beautiful beach with no one in sight for miles. We will be lucky to have room enough to walk to the water among all the throngs . . . Calabria will be filled with skyscrapers as people begin immigrating here from more populated areas. Money will become more and more meaningless since there will be less to buy in terms of nonfunctional items. There will be lots of leisure, of course, as everything gets auto-mated. Lots of time for a lot of sporting sex."

"What's that?"

"What we're doing on this trip."

"Meaning?"

"No big meanings, no big romance. Recreational sex will be all."

"Why is that?"

"The mythology of love will have vanished—as completely as the forests of Bruttium."

In spite of herself she liked him. He had shed his arrogant, banter-ing self along with the expensive shoes and beige linen suit of his Hotel Staffa wardrobe and become a natural, easy person to be with. He was quiet, silent for long stretches, content to walk on the beach with her, swim, eat, nap, make love. There were no man-woman battles between them, no cultural clashes, not even passion. All the lasciviousness he had hinted at had only been part of the role he was playing when he was the clever Professor Simongini. When he was not playing, he was, in his way, as simple and natural as Duke.

He was resting, withdrawing from himself; when he put back on his expensive handmade leather shoes and Rome wardrobe, and got behind the wheel of his Maserati again, his eye flashing over the despoiled landscape to see if it held any other villages inhabited by Luluzzos for him to plunder, then he would be once more the Ferruccio who taunted her and set her on edge.

She was calm, content during the day, but once at night she woke with a start wondering where she was, remembering, and her eyes filling with tears as she thought of her losses.

Jason was surely as lost to her as her mother; she would never find him again, and even if they did meet again in the States, what could there be between them now? Would he understand that she had left him because she loved him and that it was because of her goddam restlessness, so different from his New England stability and his serene definition of himself, that she had to leave him, could not marry him? Would he know that? Or only the hurt of having been left? She would send him a postcard in the morning. She never did.

One night Ferruccio heard that Pasolini's *Canterbury Tales* was playing in a nearby town and they went to see the film. Tina was turned off by all the bare asses, the pissing, farting, sexual heaves and thrusts the film indulged in, and Ferruccio was amused at her reaction. "It's so noisy, so overdone, a big cluttered kermess of pranks and roistering as if all life were without any solemnity," she said.

"Yes," Ferruccio teased, "be sure to get in the solemnity."

She turned away from him. Jason would have understood her. His grandfather had been the serious boy who had gone aboard the *Castagna* and loosened the frozen mate from the rigging.

When they left Bagamoyo, Calabria was again a hard experience. She hated her ambivalence toward Calabria but feared the harsh country and stunted people who stared at her for having had the luck to be born elsewhere. She began to think of her coming to Calabria as in the nature of those age-old raids, a despoiling foray more than a sentimental journey back to her origins. She was going to descend upon a place, take of it what she wanted, and then leave it to its perennial state, as treacherous in her own way as the Saracens.

Brullo was the word for Calabria: burnt like a *crème brûlée*, nude, ravaged, scorched. Worse than a lunar landscape, for that is a natural phenomenon, and what Tina saw was a land despoiled by men and showing its scars. The occasional patches of scraggly green growth hardly took hold around sun-baked farmhouses on yellowed stretches of land; no garden or orchard or patch of grain ever was in sight of those dried-out hovels. When, in the distance, a few gnarled olive trees appeared on the bare hills, it made the shadeless country all the hotter by contrast.

They sped down the valley of the Busento, and in the dusty little villages where they stopped for gas Tina could always make out the *americani*—the immigrants who had made money in America and come back to spend out their old age in those anonymous places of their birth. She saw them in their short-sleeved plaid or patterned drip-dry shirts, and they looked forlorn, beached, miserable even if they had spent all their adult lives in America cursing the new land and waiting to have enough money to get back to the old. For it was always too late to go back, and they didn't fit in anywhere. Tina, who had always wondered why Umbertina had so completely relinquished her Italian ties, now saw the wisdom of that release. She had made a choice.

"Look at this country," she said testily, lashing out at Ferruccio because he, Italian, was accountable, "dry as a bone, bare, parched. Why doesn't someone preach trees to these people?" And she thought of the poplars of her father's Veneto, the cypresses and oaks of Tuscany, the sweet green hills of the Marche. "I'm sick of this official guidebook spiel about the austere beauty of Calabria, and the people living from wild asparagus and wild artichokes. There's nothing growing around here. Why don't they come right out and say, 'This is a plundered land'!"

"*Mia cara*, you haven't realized yet that Italians, especially official ones, do not have the addiction to truth that you Americans do!"

They passed sheep and goats being herded along the road, barefoot women in black with jugs or bundles of brush upon their heads, and donkeys tethered in village piazzas by the dozens. Even a few little Fiats with Turin license plates could be seen as they got nearer to Cosenza. "The immigrants to the North are back for vacation," Ferrucio said every time they passed one.

Then after Cosenza they began the ascent into the highlands, and to Tina's enormous relief trees began to appear, the first strands of oak and beech and pine.

"This is the Sila," Ferruccio explained—"called the Switzerland of Italy, as if Swissness will remove any southern stigma and bring visitors. It's said that this was where Jove spent his summers . . .

and now we're here, Jove in the guise of a Maserati bearing Europa away!" He laughed and looked over at her. "Or should I say 'America'?"

Tina began to dread the arrival at Castagna with Ferruccio and his sophisticated, detached ways. She began to feel protective about this unknown place, which in its own way would certainly be as miserable as all the other villages they had passed through, or why else would its people have started leaving a hundred years ago.

At Soveria Mannelli, a market town whose balconies were laden with geraniums and begonias growing twenty to thirty blossoms a plant, they stopped at the main piazza and Ferruccio bought some of the gorgeous figs and grapes that were heaped on cloths on the ground. Some of the older women were wearing long red pleated skirts covered with an apron and topped by a velvet bodice.

"Here you are," said Ferruccio, taking Tina's arm and guiding her to a building that fronted the piazza. "Read this plaque just to make an honest tourist out of you so that you won't be mistaken for a returning *paesan.*"

The building was called Albergo Garibaldi, and the plaque which Tina read said that in that dwelling, on August 30, 1860, Giuseppe Garibaldi, Cavalier and Hero, had spent the night before setting out to defeat the Bourbon tyranny, to liberate the South from its yoke, and to reunite it to a new Italy.

"That's great," she said, "I never knew Garibaldi came so close to Castagna." For they were now only twelve kilometers from the fork that would lead to the village.

At the crossroads, they turned from the main road to a small dirt one that followed the course of the Corace in the valley between hills thick with shadings of green. The air was fresh and leaves cut the heat of the sun. They crossed a bridge over the stream and passed several women beating sheets over rocks at the water's edge. It was as it might have been in Umbertina's day.

"What a scene!" Tina said. She called Ferruccio's attention to a man on a motor-bike going up the road ahead of them. "Just look at that—plastic baskets hanging from each side of him instead of the beautiful hand-woven reed ones that country people make. How ridiculous that looks . . . these people! No sense of authentic beauty."

"Don't you believe in progress for 'these people'? It may be pleasing for you to see the women wash in a stream or sit for hours to weave baskets from rushes, but would you do it? Plastic is not picturesque, but these people don't even know what 'picturesque' means. It's a tourist term."

"Yes, I know," retorted Tina quickly, hating to be caught up like that by Ferruccio. "Now tell me that this is a society in transition. I know how you sociologists talk. But I'm still glad to see something of how it used to be. And I still think it's too bad they are losing some of their natural ways of doing things. Sometimes, when I see the Italo-Americans, I think it's too bad they left at all."

"Yes, *that's* the really hard nut to crack, isn't it? You could never have come back to show off your superior taste if they hadn't gotten out in the first place. And they got out to better themselves and use plastic if they want to. But when you come back, you're sorry they're still not what they used to be. *That's* the conundrum of your trip. They advanced you to the middle-class—but you want them to stay peasants."

"Oh, come on, Ferruccio," she stuttered, embarrassed, because *yes*, that *was* the conundrum: How accept what she was and what they were? She was acknowledging something sterile and over-intellectualized in her life just by the fact of this strange journey back to her rude origins.

Then they turned a curve in the road and came onto an unexpected sight: Along the banks of the stream were the ruins of a monastery, Norman in origin and of the eleventh century, as Tina's guidebook told her. It was an ivy-covered shell from whose crevices and crumbling lintels tufts of flowering weeds were thrusting and reaching. Through empty ogival windows came the sound of running water. Behind the ruin, on a height above the valley and settled into the density of trees, was the place she sought: Castagna.

"*Che bello!*" Tina exclaimed. She was surprised at the beauty of the place and grateful for it. Their eyes saw this, too, she thought.

"The monastery of Corazzo," she read from the guidebook, "was built by invading Normans and shone through the eleventh and twelfth centuries as a faint beacon of enlightenment among those silent hills where the descendants of the hostile Brutii still kept to themselves."

"Who would have thought of finding a scene like this in Calabria," Ferruccio said, stopping the car and getting out his camera. "It's more like Scotland."

The road entered the upper fringe of the village, but most of

Castagna descended from the road, banked along the mountain, on a prospect above the valley. Ferruccio parked in front of a bar and they went into the small, dark place where a thin man with a stubble of beard on his face stood alone and looked at them with shy wonderment.

"Is there a place to eat here?" Ferruccio asked.

"No, nothing. Only in Soveria Mannelli," the man answered.

"Do you have postcards?" Tina asked.

He shook his head and again said the name of the larger town.

"What about these?" Tina asked, pointing to a jug on the counter. It was the classical terra-cotta amphora that could still be seen all over southern Italy, where women used it to draw water from fountains and men carried it into the fields to quench their thirst as they worked.

The man smiled shyly and repeated, "Soveria Mannelli." Above his head the clock on the wall had stopped. That day, Tina wondered, or two weeks ago, or fifty years past?

"Do you have a telephone book?" she asked him, hoping to find a listing for a Nenci or a Longobardi, Umbertina's maiden and married names.

The man was very patient. "No one in Castagna has a telephone, only the *tabacchaio*."

"Nothing here, only chestnuts, eh?" Ferruccio said pleasantly. And Tina remembered her grandfather's old joke about his wife's family origins—Castagna, where all the nuts come from. The thought of her mother made her close her eyes.

Ferruccio was ordering two cold coffees. They drank them at the bar, savoring the good strongness. "Excellent," he said to the shy man, and then pointed to some hard candies in a glass jar and asked for an *etto*. The man went to the back of the store behind a curtain and came back with a small bag, saying, "These are better."

"Let's go to the Sale e Tabacchi," Tina said, "and you can get some cigarettes."

"It's the one thing a traveler can be sure of finding all over Italy, no matter how poor and miserable the locality," Ferruccio said as they went down a steep cobbled street fronted by stone dwellings that were old and decrepit-looking. A few women looked out of doorways, a few children stopped their play and stared. Tina glanced quickly at them, looking to recognize herself or Weezy in their impassive faces. In one dark-eyed handsome, roguish-looking boy she thought she saw her Uncle Sammy.

Within the dark shop an old woman sat knitting. The place was absolutely bare except for a little shelf where the familiar blue and white bags of salt were lined up: *sale grosso* and *sale fine*. Nearby was a wall telephone and a sign saying that it could be used week-days 8–12 and 14–19 and holidays 9–12. There were no cigarettes at the moment, the woman said. Tina, wanting to have something from Castagna and conscious of the woman's glance, bought a package of salt.

"For wisdom?" asked Ferruccio sardonically, as they left.

"No, to catch birds."

He laughed and caught her to him and bit her gently on the cheek. "Always fighting, aren't you—*sempre in polemica*! I think I'll miss that fighting; in fact, I'll miss you. I hope you'll stay on in Rome, I'm quite attached to you, you know."

"I don't know what I'm going to do."

"Let's take it day by day. And for today there's Castagna."

They went down the steep passageway to where all the other alleys of the little village converged into an open space that was like a large balcony contained by a balustrade overlooking the valley. A huge chestnut tree whose light green burrs distilled the light into cool shadows stood in the center of the piazza, which was deserted except for a person in a long black gown and wide-brimmed hat sitting on a bench reading.

"Aha," Ferruccio whispered to her, "now we have come upon the village authority and gentry all in one. It's the priest—he can look up the records for you."

But more and more she seemed to herself an intruder in a place that was as much a ruin as the monastery below them. And what was the use of pursuing Umbertina? she asked herself. This coming to Castagna had been more to lose herself than to find Umbertina. What had she in common with the impoverished hovels of this place . . . with the isolation and backwardness? She was now a product of education. There was no return. Umbertina's message in fact was: Leave, take a direction, go forward, do not look back. And yet she was there because no message could overcome her feelings of having to be there.

In some primal way she felt connected to the place—even as if she had been there before, had experienced the landscape. Or was it remembrance from some fourteenth-century Italian painting in the Uffizi? She felt the rightness of standing there and yet she stood there as a stranger, the homeland now as foreign a place as others she kept traveling through.

Only connect! Only connect! She thought of Forster's *Howards End.* God! I'm so literary, she chastised herself; why can't I be as simple and easily pleased as these people. But there it is again: Who sees the virtue in simplicity except the overeducated?

Ferruccio had begun a conversation with the priest, telling him who they were.

The priest, an elderly man in a grease-spotted tunic and with several days' growth of beard on his flaccid face, nodded as his eyes went from one to the other. "It is not Rome or New York," he said finally, "but the air is pure here and there is peace."

"How many people enjoy this peace?" Ferruccio asked, while Tina looked at him sharply to see if he was teasing.

"Officially I was supposed to have twelve hundred souls in my care when I took up my duties. Now there are about half that number. Perhaps there are no more than five hundred. First the men go north, then the others. Yet it wasn't always so—my own grandfather was a charcoal burner from the next village down the road, Carlopoli. He settled in Castagna and made good. It isn't only in America that you can better yourself," he finished, addressing himself to Tina.

Tina felt her face flushing. A toothless old woman was grinning out at them from what seemed a cellar window; an urchin had come down to the piazza and was hopping about to get their attention. "*Acà, acà,*" the old woman's voice rasped at him. Other women and children were in doorways, behind windows, or standing in the narrow streets silently staring.

The priest's eyes were drawn to the tin heart fastened on Tina's shoulder bag. "That is of the old type that was done around here long ago. How do you happen to have it, *signorina?*"

"It was my great-grandmother's."

"Who was she?"

"Umbertina Longobardi."

The old man's eyes lit in recognition. "I have heard the name," he said.

Tina felt a tremor of excitement at his recognition. So, she *was* part of the place, connected by the tin heart which had come from there.

"She immigrated to America with her husband," Tina said. "And with others from this village."

"Yes," said the priest, "they never come back. They left because of *miseria* and they forget the others still here in *miseria*."

Tina flushed again, feeling the accusation. Now I've got guilt laid on me! Am I responsible? But how can I feel connected without the burden of responsibility? It all seemed too hard for her to resolve and her eyes darted around nervously, picking up the crone in the window, the staring children in the street. "I can't bear it," she muttered under her breath.

Ferruccio patted her arm protectively. "Easy, easy," he said in English. Then, turning to the priest, he said, "You know, this village has all the potential to be an excellent resort. You're in the Sila in a magnificent setting with good air, you have a stream, forests, ruins in the valley; all you need is someone enterprising to open an inn, a *trattoria*, an outdoor *caffè*. You must have someone in this village—someone like your grandfather was—who could start things going."

"These people don't see the place as you do," the priest answered. "No one would believe they could make money here. They believe all they have to do to improve their lot is to go north."

"What does the village need?" Ferruccio asked.

"We have nothing."

"Is there a school?"

"Only the elementary classes."

"May I send books?" said Tina.

"How could that help?"

"What do the people do?" Ferruccio continued.

"They leave; there is no work here."

And it was true that nowhere were there goatherds or shepherds to be seen, farmers in fields, artisans, cobblers, or bakers. Nothing but chestnuts to be picked and sold at market.

Tina tried to imagine Umbertina and Serafino as they left Castagna a hundred years before. Would the road have been there in their time? Or, laden with bundles and holding on to children, would they have taken the footpath at the piazza down into the valley, then crossed the bridge over the stream and walked away forever?

Children had gathered in the road, looking over the Maserati;

before getting in, Tina looked about desperately. If she couldn't buy anything here, or send books, or relieve *la miseria*, she could at least drink from the fountain and taste the water that Umbertina had called for on her deathbed.

Near the entrance to the village was a fountain with a spigot of running water. "Is it for drinking?" Tina asked a girl, who nodded and smiled.

Tina bent her head to the spigot to drink, but the water slurped all over her face and even cupping her hands and trying to drink from them was no more successful. She felt conspicuous. The girl, the boys around the car, the shy man in the doorway of his bar, and some others now standing in the road were all watching her.

Her eyes filled with tears that ran down her cheeks, merging with the water on her face. She had wanted to come to Castagna, stand on the same ground and breathe the same air as old Umbertina, who had made a success of her life and had been a strong woman. Some voice was always in her head saying, If only I could be Umbertina, I'd be all right; everything would go together; I'd know my place. Why couldn't she take a road, as Umbertina had, and follow it, not looking back? What was she doing there with Ferruccio anyway? Where was her place in the world?

It was time to leave.

She went back to the car, wiping her face. "I can't bear it," she said fiercely. "Give them something—give them the candies!"

The trip to Calabria had come to an end. And as she got into the car Tina knew that though she had physically located the where of Umbertina, the secret of why she was lost and Umbertina directed still eluded her.

Chapter Thirty-two

In Rome Tina found a letter from Weezy:

Dear Tee,

I'm betting you're not staying in Rome with *papà*, but moving on in your own direction.

So this is to say good-bye, because I won't see you before you leave for the States. I don't know when I'll be back, but when I do get to Rome it will only be to pass through, on my way to Bologna. That's where my friends and I will be organizing.

Spain was great; Morocco is, too. I'm not much of a letter writer—I want us to meet again, face to face.

In the meantime I hope you find something besides Dante in your life. I'm not saying we should all be Christs or Castros, but there should be something else, here and now, that you care about. We're all in this together.

Your way or mine, all knowledge is just a search for more wonder. Keep searching!

Love 'n kisses,
Weezy

Tina left for New York, telling her father she wouldn't wait out the summer. In Rome she had called no one; she didn't try to find out if Missy were around, she didn't go sit in Piazza Navona to see who would walk through. She wanted to be gone because she wanted something deliberately harsh and tough in her life and that's what the rest of the summer in New York would be: finding a place to live, eating alone, struggling with her laundry, coping, accommodating, making do. She had had enough of Italy. After indulgence came penance; she welcomed it.

On the plane she said good-bye to everything. With her own departure for New York, her father's decision to live in Venice, where he would move into his sister's place, and Weezy's plan to go to Bologna, the family was finally scattered and undone.

And wasn't it typical of each of them, she thought: her father in an emptying Venice whose last shoddy hold on life was the tourist trade, there to live on memories of his sea-captain ancestors' vigorous past; and Weezy heading for a leftist commune in Bologna because that city had a Communist mayor, and since the streets were clean and the buses ran on schedule she could think the future had arrived for all of them; and Tina herself? Back to the monastic cubicle in the library to wrest from her love for Dante and company the license to be a woman professional in a world of men.

They all had separate lives now. Where would they meet for Christmas, for birthdays, or just to be together as in the days when her mother had always planned outings, fêtes, trips, occasions?

And where was Jason? Perhaps in Greece, or back in Rome, or at his grandparents' place on Cape Cod. He might even be on that very plane with her. And Ferruccio?

After Castagna, she had told him she was not driving back to Rome with him, and he had left her at the railroad station in Nicastro. There she had started the long way back, speaking to no one, glum and absorbed until she arrived in Rome.

"*Figlia mia,*" her father had greeted her, surprised at the early return. "Back so soon!"

"It wasn't good, *papà,*" she told him. "I want to go back to New York, to my work."

He took her out to dinner that night.

He was looking old, vague as one of those dithery society women who try to be salesclerks in boutiques, vague but charming, and in their own way filled with sure taste. No facts, only taste. His brow wrinkled with concentration as he spoke to her.

"I believe in the power of thought to communicate over distance," he confided to her. "I will be communicating with you through magnetic thoughts, wherever you are in the world." And then, leaning toward her, he told her that while she was away he had dreamed of her one night; she was wearing the linen djerba he once brought her from Tunis and was looking angry about something. He had said "What's wrong, Tina *mia*?" but then the dream vaporized. When she told him that at the probable time of the dream she had been in a bad temper and that she had worn her Tunisian mantle in Calabria when nights were chilly, his face lit up with eager triumph. "Ah, so that's how it was!" he said, smiling, pleased that his dream was confirmed.

Christ, how beautiful he is, she thought. Can he really feel me so strongly? "Oh, *papà*," she said, as they walked home through the empty streets, "I'm not sure of anything. Do you think things will ever turn out right for me?"

"Have faith. Each of us has a moment of grace. Yours will come."

The trip to Castagna had not brought revelation. It was, in fact, the summary of all her trips: hapless.

All those childhood trips back and forth over the ocean, first in ships, then by plane; both she and Weezy had memory books their mother had started for them, each with a trip diploma glued in and places for seals enough to attest to ten trips over the ocean. But ten hadn't been enough, and she had stopped noting down the dates of her trips long ago. The point was, all that gadding about and no center. That's it, no center to hold on to.

It's all a question of moves and positioning, Tina reflected. In the family, only Umbertina's move had had at its center a firm purpose. She had positioned for survival; success followed on its own.

Umbertina's sons and daughters had engaged in other positionings—social ones that had as their steps better neighborhoods, bigger houses, the Rotary Club, country clubs, garden or bridge clubs, colleges.

By the time it came to Tina's mother, moves were not positioning but lack of it—an erratic, blind dashing around, away from every center and certainty. The fata morgana of her life was the conviction that someday, in the right place, she could start her work; yet each time she thought she approached it, it vanished.

Only Alberto Morosini's center had always held. No matter where his wife had led him, his center of family tradition and religion stayed still, embedded within him. Scenery didn't matter. Nothing outside was as important.

And now here Tina was, alone in the plane, not talking to anyone, not eating the plastic dinner, not looking at the movie or plugging music into her ears, but considering her own moves.

Although impermanence was the only outward style of life she had known, Tina could hear in her mind's ear her mother's call against the disorder she and Weezy created all over the house. "Don't increase the entropy around here!" that poor woman would shout at them, her love of boxes and containers and drawers to store and order things being her own futile effort against things falling apart. Entirely futile, because those selfsame containers were themselves always on the move.

Her mother used to tell Weezy and Tina the story of her first job as a department-store clerk during a vacation period when she was sixteen and put into Men's Underwear and Socks in Clark's basement. "Position in life is everything," her boss had told her. He was a thin, balding man with spectacles who wore a dark suit and somber air and had attained to the position of head of that section in Clark's Department Store. Her mother had laughed and told the story as another indication of the absurdity of life.

But Tina had remembered it and had put together a whole series of intonings on position, like the responses on a litany of beads. Her grandmother's statement, for instance, was "He (or she) has a wonderful position," and implicit was all the envy and regret that her own children hadn't gotten there; or that her husband had made money, yes, but not achieved position; or that she herself had been given the only one open to her—woman's place, in the home.

"Get in position, correct position!" Tina's ballet teacher would command when she was a child. And the words hung ominously over her after all these years. For one's position in respect to people, power, place was everything; the man in Clark's basement had been right.

And when Tina had spent that Thanksgiving at the Jowers' place on Cape Cod, Tim's and Jason's grandmother was always saying "A place for everything, and everything in its place" each time her grandchildren asked her where the car keys, umbrella, books, gloves, or whatever were. Place was like position for that woman, and she had made Tina feel unreal, shallow, because when asked where her home was Tina had stuttered "Rome, but before that we lived in D.C. and before that in Milan . . ." and then had simply petered out in embarrassment; she was reciting a record of shiftlessness to a stony-faced woman who, since her marriage, had lived in a house that had been occupied by the Jowers family continuously for two hundred years and had itself been raised on the spot where the previous dwelling, dating from 1676, had stood until it burned to the ground.

Tina remembered that Thanksgiving weekend as making her feel wildly uncertain and putting her in a deep depression—for *where* was her place? Tim and Jason could always go back to Cape Cod, but she might get a cable tomorrow saying that the family was moving again.

Obsessed with this, she had gone back to college and written a term paper on place and movement. She quoted Plutarch: "It is not the places that grace men, but men the places"; Shakespeare: "O place, o form/How often doest thou with thy case, thy habit,/ wrench awe from fools!"; Bacon: "As things move violently *to* their place and calmly *in* their place, so virtue . . ."; and Toynbee: "Civilization is a movement, not a condition, a voyage and not a harbor." The writing had given her peace. She had learned that Grandmother Jowers' saying was from Emerson.

In the plane, suspended once again between Old World and New, between one thing and another, it gave her the same peace to sort out her thoughts; to put them in some order in the container of her mind, at least for the moment.

It seemed that Umbertina's secret of success was her total uprooting, followed by total replanting. Positioning, thus, became dignified, while positioning which was merely the restlessness of the moment undirected by anything but whim was destined to be barren. Like, Tina realized, her womb, which had been scraped bare because the seed scattered there had been cast by chance, not planted to bear fruit.

Well, never mind. She would get it together. She would settle into her work. Her work was her permanence and her dignity. And then, after that, *Che sarà, sarà.*

The trip to Calabria, every so often, flashed through her mind like glinting pieces of mosaic that she tried to shape into a whole, a pattern of serious design. But it was surreal, like pieces in a kaleidoscope, which never regroup in the same configuration but with each shake of the memory go into some new interpretation of their parts.

So, Calabria. It was fragments only. Bits of color came to her mind: the hard, desolate yellow of the burnt-out plains; the bright blue of the sea where she and Ferruccio had swum and sunned; the bright white of the sand; the tender green of the chestnut burrs in the forests of the Sila and the deep green ivy-covered ruins of the abbey in the valley below Castagna; the splash of bright colors in the markets and flowering balconies.

Yes, she remembered the landscape, the food and wine, occasional snatches of Ferruccio's talk. But mostly she remembered the sense of Umbertina's having eluded her.

It was as if by storming into Castagna in Ferruccio's red Maserati she had tried to take the old woman and the place by force. She had tried to buy Castagna—its postcards and souvenirs, to appease it by promising to send things to the priest. But she had not found Umbertina with all that. She was only beginning to do so now that the distance grew between her and Italy.

Castagna had been a hard nut to crack, and the fault was not in the place but in her, the seeker. She had gone heedlessly with Ferruccio. But perhaps it would have been the same thing with Jason. For the revelation she had to find was not in the mountains of Calabria, but in her own mind. Knowing, the nut would be cracked, the kernel revealed.

God! she thought, I sound like Jason philosophizing. A deep pang of regret settled in her alongside her stomach's sense of emptiness. Dear old Bear and their childish games. The sadness of all aborted things came over her and she curled in her corner near the window, putting her head on a pillow against the pane and trying to sleep.

As her thoughts subsided, one last one drifted through the cloudy territory of her mind: Here I am, up in the air, midway between Italy and America. How funny. How prophetic.

It was almost Christmas. Tina stood in Rizzoli's bookstore responding to the warm wood paneling, the prints and fine books, the sound of Gesualdo madrigals, the entire atmosphere that looked and sounded Italy to her. She heard Italian spoken by elegant people: *"Facciamo un Korvette's,"* a stunning woman in mink said to her companion, and the words tossed off so nonchalantly kept ringing in Tina's ears with their echoes of great style and utter assurance.

She was in the bookstore to find a gift for her grandfather. At Bergdorf's she had seen a very plush scrapbook labeled "Give the

Gift of Immortality." It was meant to hold photos and had blanks
to be filled in with data: name, birthplace, marriage, children, etc.
Immortality, all packaged and giftwrapped as Americans like things;
for a moment she was tempted to get it for her grandfather. Then
it made her angry. Finally she wondered why she cared.

Tina thumbed through a splendid photographic volume on the
antiquities of Sicily and wondered if her grandfather would like it,
or if she would be trying again to browbeat him into an appreciation
of Italy that he had always resisted.

She was going to Gloversville for the holidays. She was going so
that she could get away from the little cubicle in the library where
she studied and the slightly larger one, on 114th Street, in the
nurses' quarters, where she slept.

Tina could hear her mother's voice tinged with its hysterical edge
of contempt as she spoke of Gloversville: "That terrible place . . .
it couldn't even keep its trees and beautiful old homes, the only
good things about it. They're all gone. The houses have been made
into offices and the lawns are parking areas. There's a motel on the
corner of Main and Elm streets where the Frys' Greek Revival
mansion used to be. You can look through the glass siding and see
people eating breakfast. That's progress . . . that's America!"

That was her mother. Always disappointed; nothing ever lived
up to her standards. The Nativity scenes of the season had jolted
Tina into a remembrance of her own fleeting pregnancy. She felt
no emotion over the abortion; it had been something to get through
on the same level as her Salk shots. The only things that touched
her in the buried realm of her feelings were her mother's death and
the loss of Jason, and those were private woes that she keened over
silently. The rest was arrangements.

She felt more miserable about her aloneness in the cold corridors
of the nurses' quarters, where she knew no one, than she had about
her abortion. She felt invisible in those gray corridors, an unnoted
presence among the nurses and their silly jokes of labeling food
packages "fecal matter" in the common fridge. They all shared the
kitchen facilities, and while the nurses sat over tea and discussed the
clap, Tina would fry her miserable egg and try not to hear. She
felt desperate loneliness, an uncertainty about everything, and the
chill of knowing she had been wrong to leave Jason.

There were times she spent the day without speaking anything
but perfunctory remarks—no conversations, no human exchanges

of thoughts and feelings. At times she went to bed hungry and thrashed around in her bed sleepless, feeling her emptiness, feeling the indifference of the city, which made all her best plans seem futile exercises. Or she'd look up from her books in the library with a start and wonder what life existed for her in the academic world she had chosen. There was no love like the *Liebestod* anymore.

Now, as she stood in Rizzoli's, musing, trying to decide on a book for her grandfather, she glanced over toward the end of the store where the Italian newspapers and magazines were stacked, and saw, with a surge of relief and gladness, the blond aureole of Missy's hair.

"No browsing allowed, *signorina*," Tina said, sidling up to Missy, who was standing there reading a copy of *Oggi*.

"Tina! How great to see you! I knew that if I wanted to run into you in New York all I had to do was hang out at Rizzoli's for a while."

"What are you doing in town, Missy?"

"Lou and I weren't getting on anymore. I decided to look for a place here and see if I can get into dancing. Where are you living, Tee?"

"I have a cell over in the nurses' quarters on 114th Street," she said. "It's clean and safe and there's a kitchen where I can cook an egg or instant soup."

"It sounds pretty grim," Missy said.

"It's the pits," Tina answered glumly.

"Listen, Tee, I'm staying in a friend's place in The Village—but that's only temporary. Why don't we get a place together?"

"Good idea, Missy. We'll do it as soon as I get back from Gloversville."

There was a gilt wreath on the door of her grandparents' Tudor house in Gloversville when Tina arrived. She thought irritably, Why gilt? Why couldn't it be natural greenery with some pinecones? Why were things always gussied up in Gloversville?

But as her grandfather opened the door and her grandmother came through the rooms toward her, her arms open, her mouth stretched in a warm, welcoming smile, Tina thought again of why she was there—for the human warmth they gave her, and if it came in gilt, well, *pazienza*. The wall facing the front door was a display of gilt-framed family photos, the brass screen and tools near the fireplace gave off a gold glow, the large mirror over the untuned piano was in an ornate Florentine frame, and on the piano was a huge vase of gladioli: the fakest of flowers, Tina could hear her mother saying.

And yet the house was warm and comfortable and no more pretentious, actually, than Missy's family home, or even the Jowers'. It was not her mother's romantic interiors of driftwood and shells and secondhand sofas from departing English noblemen, nor was it the crazy rococo of many other Italian-American families; but for what it was—a well-to-do American interior with hanging plants, boldly patterned wallpaper, and a cupboard of figurines—it was right and proper. It could have been photographed anytime in living color for the pages of *House Beautiful*. What Tina really objected to were the missing things: the missing shelves of good books to read; the missing sound from the piano; the missing conversations; the missing flames in the fireplace.

"There you are!" her grandmother called, bearing down on her as she wiped her hands on an apron. She was short-legged, round, and very active, as cheerfully American as her rooms. Her hair was done, she dressed well, and her eyeglasses were stylish but not garish.

Once in Gloversville, Tina let down her defenses and let herself be enveloped by the comfort and expansive sense of security her grandparents' home gave her. In all Tina's life, she had known them in the same house. Here you knew where you were, once and for all. Even as she succumbed to the smells of good cooking that came from her grandmother's super-equipped kitchen, she tried to keep some hold on her critical faculty.

"How was the trip up, Tina?" asked her grandfather. "Did I send enough money? Did you have any trouble?"

"Everything was fine, Gramp," she said, giving him a kiss.

"Your uncles and their families will be coming over for dinner," Carla said.

Tina nodded. At least this year she wouldn't have to answer Aunt Betty Burke's sour quip about where was her mother moving next.

"Do you have any boyfriends?" her grandmother asked, standing back to appraise Tina and looking up at her with the barefaced admiration that always made Tina feel so tender toward her. It was as if the old woman pinned everything on her—every dream, hope, and not-quite-lost illusion she still had about life.

"I can't bear it!" she retorted. "Is that all you want to hear about me, *nonna*?"

"I wish you'd find someone . . . a beautiful girl like you. You should be able to do very well."

"*Nonna*! Such ideas—how can you do well by marrying if you haven't got your own personal life together first? No one's rushing into marriage these days. It's much better to concentrate on one's work and have other interests."

"That's not natural," Carla went on, shaking her head. "I saw Ron Peters, who used to like your mother—he's doing so well! But she pretended she was never interested either. Now he drives a Rolls Royce, has a yacht, a house in Florida, one son in Harvard, and a daughter in Paris."

Tina looked at her grandmother as she recited this litany of blessings. It was useless to say to her that by wishing her mother had married the man with the Rolls Royce, she was wiping out Tina's own father and Tina and Weezy as well. Her grandmother would not understand.

There was no use, Tina thought, of imagining she was there to impose her values onto Gloversville; she was there to eat and sleep. All the rest could wash over her.

"Now let me ask you, Tina," her grandfather said, putting down his paper on the arm of the chair where he sat facing the turned-on television without looking at it. "What are your plans for the future?"

"Gramp," she said patiently, "I'm getting a Ph.D. in Italian. I want to be a scholar."

"But why Italian?" he said in real consternation, his face frowning in bewilderment. "What will that fit you for?"

"I can teach or write." Her ears were filled with the noise of talk from commercials, and her eyes kept darting involuntarily to watch the people on the screen exclaim, laugh, react to a deodorant. It made her jittery and tense.

"I don't understand this infatuation with Italy!" her grandfather was saying, rattling his newspaper and looking agitated. "Where will that get you? Italy has no future. What has Italy ever done for the world?"

"Civilization, Gramp." She thought with sad resignation of this useless old argument, and of how, paradoxically, non-Italians like the Jowers family were so Italophile. What was wrong with the immigrants' children that left them so distrustful of their *italianità*?

It was, she knew, the burden of the second generation, who had been forced too swiftly to tear the Old World from themselves and put on the New. They were the sons and daughters ashamed of their illiterate, dialect-speaking forebears—the goatherds and peasants and fishermen who had come over to work and survive and give these very children, the estranged ones, America. Tina was torn between compassion and indignation: She understood him, why couldn't he understand her?

"Yes, all right, Italy has had all those artists and Verdi and opera and all that. But let me ask you, what good has it done?"

"Well, I suppose you'd say what good does it do me to know Dante and to make the *Divine Comedy* the base of my future. All I can say is that it's my way, and I have to be doing what I want and know; otherwise nothing makes sense. It's like you, Gramp—you loved your business."

"And what about Weezy?"

"She's dropped out of everything and just lives as best she can—doing translations or giving English lessons when she needs the money and living very cheaply with a bunch of others like her."

"Is that any way for her to live?" he asked disgustedly. He was an austere man, a man of propriety.

Again Tina thought of Weezy and their mix of despair and anger at never being able to reach the grandparents: "It's so weird to have people like them treating me like an idiot!" Weezy would exclaim. Strange indeed, thought Tina, the way they could be so confident that only their lives were worthy of emulation.

"I'd like to see you both married," her grandmother said with a worried frown.

"*Nonna!*" Tina said in a tone of annoyance. "I want my life to have some meaning beyond just marrying; I don't want to be unhappy in the way Mom was. . . ."

"Your mother was never happy, married or not," Carla retorted. "Your mother, Tina, never knew what she wanted. But you're more like *my* mother, the Umbertina for whom you're named. She was a strong person and she stuck to her guns."

Tina understood. The thing was to focus and to stick to the sighting. Her mother had lost her way because she hadn't focused. No matter what the beginning losses, Tina wanted to end up satisfied with her life as Umbertina had been.

That night at the dinner table Tina saw the faces of her relatives:

relaxed, comfortable, unperplexed by existential problems, and for a few moments she envied their condition of security and well-being. They had never wrestled with an Italian identity—if you asked who they were, why, they were just American. They had never moved from Gloversville; except to go to college, her uncles had never been away from their hometown. They had been born there, and their children, too; they would spend all their days there. They had friends, continuity, and a sense of their living space. They were good people. Almost imperceptibly Tina shook her head as if consulting with herself: It was not enough. One had to get more out of life than the slot where one was born. Positioning meant moving.

"Well, Tina, still surviving in New York?" her Uncle Sammy boomed. "Been mugged yet?"

When she got back to the city, Tina had a call from Missy, who said she had found an incredible apartment to sublet through an incredible bit of luck. It was on West End Avenue, not far from Columbia.

Tina went to meet Missy there on a bright, cold day. "Sun and light!" she exclaimed as they stood in the living room of the apartment looking out.

"And a tiny view of the river if you stand on a chair in this corner," Missy said. "Isn't it great?"

"Just what my Italian soul needs," Tina agreed.

When they moved in, Tina bought some plants to tend.

Chapter Thirty-three

At times Tina thought of Jason. The time she came down with flu and was in bed a few days, the bunches of bright flowers on her patterned sheets filled her feverish head with threatening hallucinations. All she could think of was the poor dormouse of the Christopher Robin rhymes who lived in a bed of delphiniums (blue) and geraniums (red). And with the recall of the dormouse, Sir Brian Botany, naughty Mary Jane and rice pudding again, Pooh Bear and Piglet and all the other characters came trooping back into her mind. And with them came Jason.

The men Tina was meeting at Columbia had skipped *Winnie-the-Pooh*. Their education had taken them from comic books and science fiction straight into Henry Miller and New Left liberalism. They had caught the catchwords of student protest and wove their talk around them.

They were interesting the first few times she went out with them, but then she got bored. Her closest friend was a thin, fastidious gay named Allan Saltzman, who was in the graduate department of English and with whom she could have bookish, stolid, opinionated discussions and good food in his well-stocked apartment.

At the end of the school year she went directly to Venice to see her father. He now lived in his sister's small, old-fashioned flat. His studio was in the small bedroom at the end of the hall, and Tina shared with her aunt the large, high matrimonial bed that had belonged to the parents; made for the larger rooms of bygone homes, it now crammed the modest bedroom of the Morosini apartment.

Tina found her father and her aunt, their home and all of Venice

gently decrepit and woebegone and yet with a serenity and sense
of humor that was entirely missing in New York. *Zia* Lauretta, a
strong, handsome woman of about fifty with the pronounced Morosini nose and dark wavy hair that resisted graying, fluttered about
cooking soups and fish and commenting every so often to Tina on
Venice's state: "*Che peccato!*" she kept intoning. She kept strong
in the damp winters, she said, by drinking the water in which
seeped a curative mushroom sent all the way from Mexico. Tina
loved the sense of outdated and outmoded confusion *zia* Lauretta
exuded. She remembered what Jason had said about backwaters—
they were the best places to live. Here nothing more turbulent than
the city's gradual sinking touched them, and that they didn't have
to reckon with immediately. The Venetians fled to the mainland to
visit relatives or walk in the mountains when the summer tourist
hordes began in earnest, but in the fall and winter Venice was
theirs again, with its attenuated light and deep silences in the *calli*.
There was no rush, no hurry. They walked through streets empty
of motor vehicles and heard the plash of ages as the waters of the
canals lapped upon the stones; once in a while the sound of a motor
launch reminded them again of the adverse currents that the modern
age had brought them and of the sentence of death that hung over
them. But death is in all life, said the glory of the churches. And
there was good dining in small, out-of-the way *trattorie*, there were
caffès, the concerts at the Teatro Fenice, the meetings with friends
at gallery openings, the long evenings along the canals, talking.
Into this undemanding backwater Alberto Morosini had settled
without demur; it fitted his nature. Tina saw it and understood and
knew why neither she nor Weezy could live there. She would leave
soon to visit Weezy.

But while she was still in Venice a card came for her from Weezy
in Budapest. Tina read the message with a flush of anger:

> Greetings from Budapest, sister and comrade! *Al improviso*
> this trip came up through the Party and I really couldn't pass
> it up. Back in one week. The food is excellent and accompanied
> by music as passionate as the paprika. The toilet seats are of
> wood and much nicer on the ass than the capitalist plastic. This
> is a country to see—it seems to work so much better, healthier,
> and simpler than anywhere else I've been.
>
> Love and kisses,
> Weezy

Tina was furious; she thought of all the other cards she had received from her sister—from Trento, where she had gone skiing; from the island of Giglio, where she had gone to celebrate spring; even from Rome, where she had gone for the day to march in some protest. Tina was envious and sad. Weezy was on her own, she had a cause, she had convictions in the present. Is Weezy really right? she thought. Is this how life should be lived?

Meanwhile she roamed around Venice seeing all the churches and galleries, and came back when her father had finished work to sit at a *caffè* with him in the evening dusk.

"Tina *mia*," he said to her one evening, "have you been working too hard this past year? You seem pale and tired, not your old self."

"It's not that, *papà*."

"What is it then? Has it something to do with your companion from last summer? The Jowers boy you were going to go to Greece with? I never understood what happened on that trip. Do you want to tell me?"

"Oh, *papà*," she said in a burst, "how can I talk about him?" Her face was furrowed with the effort to keep back tears. Alberto looked at her with concern as he sat back in his chair, sipping a Scotch.

"But you do believe in your work? You do know where you are going?"

"Oh, yes, *papà*. I've always been sure about that. I love the feel of the Renaissance—all those contradictions. It's the tensions, you see; that's why we who are in the Renaissance love it so. All creativity is the result of tension, the conflict between the world as it is and one's imagination."

"*Già*," Alberto said, smiling at her. "I see you know your way."

It wasn't until her last day in Venice, before she left for Bologna to see Weezy, that he brought up the subject again. "Are you in love with that young man?" he asked as he accompanied Tina to see the church of San Paternian. An ex voto hung on the walls there, one of many primitive paintings, but this one recalled Sebastiano Morosini, a sea captain and Alberto's great-grandfather, who in a tremendous storm off the Dalmatian coast in 1820 had been miraculously saved by a vision of the Virgin Mary.

But she countered with her own question. "What did you think of Jason, *papà*?"

"He is a very intelligent young man, very agreeable. Fine family. But the question is, Do you love him?"

"Oh, *papà*, I don't know! I got along with Jason very well. We understood each other. But sometimes I get terrified—terrified that I don't know what love is and won't recognize it—and so while I'm waiting for some miracle, some vision like your great-grandfather saw on his ship (except that it could happen in those days and it won't happen now, or if it does, we haven't the eyes to see it), I'm afraid I won't know it. How did you and Mom know for sure it was love?"

"We put in the missing ingredient: faith. I don't think anyone knows for sure; the most one can do, after his heart is stirred and he thinks, This is the creature God has sent me and with whom I will share my life and create new life—the most one can do then is to forge together, day by day, links of loyalty and patience with each other and understanding. And slowly, gradually, you see that it is, indeed, a pattern of love. I loved your mother very much; she was, in some ways, like another daughter, like my eldest and most vulnerable daughter whom I had to protect. And I would worry that I couldn't do all that I wanted for her. She had a restless spirit, but she knew that I loved her."

"I know she did, *papà*. But I think love is different these days— no one is going to think of daily links as setting the pattern for love. They're going to think of them as making a chain to keep one from being free."

"That depends on what freedom is for each one. There is great freedom, you will see, in love that is also giving up part of yourself; in comradeship and in sharing. It is the freedom from the dominant I, the insatiable I that will never be satisfied no matter how much you try to appease it by not involving yourself with other lives. Children are the perfect expression of love, but are they freedom? Not in the sense the young people of today view freedom. No, *cara*, you must have courage to love—and you will know the right person to love."

"Oh, *papà*, do you think so? I'm sure I loved Jason. But he was talking of marriage and I told him I won't until I have finished my graduate work and see where I'm going. But all the time I'm think-ing that while what I say is reasonable, if I really loved him, what would it matter? I'm so confused. Sometimes I stop in the middle of teaching and wonder if I will know love when it comes or if I'll be so blind as to let it go right by me while I'm busy looking in all directions for it."

"Have faith in yourself, Tina. Keep in touch with your own

sense of truth and *pudore*. Keep your innocence. You will know it when it comes and you will know if you already have it. It is as in my art, a blend between the eternal and the contingent. That is what life is."

"Oh, *papà.*" She loved this gentle, aging man; he was her gentle guide as Virgil was Dante's. Keep your innocence, he told her; he presumed her innocent, though not, she knew, virginal. But innocence for him had always been of the spirit.

In the dark church interior where they found the ex voto, where she saw the naive expression of her ancestors' faith in the *imprevedibile*, the unforeseen, the thing beyond reason and fact that can glide into each life when it is summoned with enough faith and hope, she made her silent pledge: She would know love when it came and she would be strong enough to accept it though it meant ceding some part of her freedom.

"In the meantime, Tina, pursue your studies. Work, do useful things, and don't worry about false values. They're there like traps, but don't fall into them because others entice you that way with talk of money, success, fame, pleasure, or whatever. I know something of daily humiliation and self-discipline. Don't forget I had to work ten years in a bank to support my mother and sisters, and all the while I knew at bottom that I was not an ordinary man, that I was a poet caught for the moment in another responsibility. That responsibility disciplined me. Keep your life simple. Have faith in Providence as the miracle of your daily adventure; practice Yoga as I do to direct the energies of Providence toward acquiring what you need materially."

Her father had looked old when she had arrived, but to be in his presence was to discern that he was inwardly illuminated by a perpetually boyish ingenuousness. "Remember, *figlia mia,*" he said at their leave-taking, "that wherever I am is your home and Weezy's. Whenever you need me I will be with you, no matter what distance is between us. Things have worked out that we have gone a separate way for the moment—like the miller's sons in the fairy tale who, upon their father's death, were each given a small something and told to go out in the world and make it into a fortune. Just so I have come to Venice, you have gone to New York, and Weezy is elsewhere. But in spirit, which is all your mother and I had to bequeath you, we are together. And that is what counts. You are too emotional, *mia cara*; remember to discipline yourself. Remember to add life to life, to go on surviving in the ongoing compromise between one's beliefs and reality that is the daily game of living. Remember that life is generous when you are."

Tina knew her father's disappointments; she knew he had suffered from her mother's unhappiness and restlessness; "*la mama è bambina,*" "*la mama è difficile,*" he used to write to her in college, showing how protective he had to be, and all the time he was dead wrong—her mother wasn't a child, her mother was a woman. She saw disillusionment in his aging face, his creased brow; she saw his sense of failure in his human works and his realization that his writings remained but his children were gone. She saw his frailty and fear of death. And she honored him for his sensitive and gentle soul and knew that though he was not always right, even his mistakes had been generous impulses. Just as her mother's had been.

She felt compassion toward them both.

That fall, in New York and back to her teaching schedule while preparing at the same time for her orals in December, Tina began to feel out of sorts with Missy.

She took as the metaphor of her discontent the sight of paint hanging in huge obscene peels from the living room ceiling of their apartment and the sight of a broken rocker that still stood in a corner, unrepaired. Their sublease was almost up, they'd have to move soon.

Tina felt beset, restless, unhappy. She began to think of herself as the incarnation of her mother, always having to be on the move. She saw her life as a scaled-down version of her mother's: Whereas her mother had had great loves in great settings, she, Tina, had nothing but encounters in temporary quarters. She thought of Duke, Ferruccio. And Jason.

"What are you doing to yourself, Tee?" Missy asked her finally. "You're like this tormented soul—you're so jittery and tense."

"I'd like to turn on, Missy, do you have anything?"

"Not a crumb; I might have tonight when Benny comes but that's not what you need."

"I know, I know, but it would help."

"What's wrong?"

"I can't bear it. I hate living like this! I'm not like you and Weezy who can hang loose . . . I've got to have some structure, some terra firma, and instead I'm always in a swamp not knowing what to do. And where are we going next when we have to be out of here?"

Missy regarded Tina with an expression of near-irony. Lanky, unkempt, her hair in frizzled curls, Missy sat in a sagging armchair, her feet over the arm, and watched her friend stalk around the room. "You're in touch with your feelings, Tee, I know you are. You are the prototype Dionysian woman. You know what to do in the main—why do you have to have even the little things so set up?"

"I can't live this way, Missy, the way you do with no regular hours, men coming in and out all the time, things all over the place. . . ."

"Why don't you go back to Duke? He still keeps asking about you. He's a nice guy and he loves you."

"How could I do that when I don't love him? I'd never marry him and that's what he wants."

"You could just live in for a while without making it long-term. There are no rules to the game, Tee."

"Some things are the way they've always been, Missy. Outwardly there seem to be big changes, but not with internal concerns. What's complicated is that the whole thing is conducted in a more open and honest way, but the issues remain eternally the same— that is, do we want the security of long-term commitment in marriage or do we want to be ephemeral mayflies?"

After they left the sublet, Missy and Tina moved up to 106th Street. Tina let Allan Saltzman celebrate her passing her orals with a wildly expensive dinner at the top of the World Trade Center while she privately thought she would have chucked the whole pretentious thing for any number of little *trattorie* in Rome or Florence or Venice, or Féfé's outdoor grill on the Adriatic, where they had gone in the Marche for huge bowls of mussels in broth, fish grilled over the coals, and the sunlight wavering between the vines that canopied them in the shade of a summer's day. All the lost paradises of my life! she told herself as she looked out at the lights of Manhattan.

Still, she and Allan were good friends.

"What shall we do to celebrate May Day?" he asked one beautiful day in spring when they were walking to the library.

"Let's go to the Statue of Liberty," she said on the spur of the moment.

"That's so tacky it's almost cool," he said. "Why do you want to go there?"

"What could be more American? Besides, I think it would be fun to go on a boat ride."

On the boat over, they were with all the colors and types of people who are American. It made Tina remember old Umbertina, whom she hadn't thought of for some time. She had, in fact, turned her back on the old ancestor, forgetting the urgency she had felt in Calabria and withdrawing more and more into academic life. Now, as she stood among the Puerto Ricans and blacks and Indians and Orientals and tourists from all over, Tina recognized that her focus on her work was not all pure devotion but also the fear of facing the outside world—thus the reversal of Umbertina's aggressive assault on the world of her day, which she made produce for her.

On board, a couple in very sophisticated casual dress were talking. One said to the other, "With all this talk of equality of sexes, they shouldn't have Liberty be a woman anymore. It should be an angel and sexless."

"I agree," Allan said to her, winking.

They got to the top of Liberty and took each other's photos and then they visited the Museum of Immigration at the base.

Among the exhibits were figures of men, women, and children clothed in the original costumes of their native land at the time of their arrival in America. A special exhibit called the "Anna Giordani Collection" was made up of clothes, trinkets, and other belongings of the immigrants that one Anna Giordani, the collector, had assembled over her years of working with the poor on the Lower East Side. Tina stood entranced at the spectacle of a magnificent bright-hued gloriously woven bedspread that bore the motifs of Calabrian design she had seen repeated in modern-day spreads during her trip through her ancestral region. In fact, as she neared the glass of the case and read the card, it said "Origin: Calabria. Owner unknown. Acquired by Anna Giordani in 1886."

"Look at that, Allan, isn't it gorgeous? Calabria—that's where my grandmother's people were from. In fact I'm named for the immigrant named Umbertina. She should have brought such a spread with her—isn't it gorgeous! Then it would have been passed down to me, maybe." Tina stood before the glass drinking in the beauty and warmth of the old spread. Its colors irradiated her spirit; the woven designs of grapes and tendrils and fig leaves and flowers and spreading acanthus spoke to her of Italy and the past and keeping it all together for the future. It was as if her old ancestor, the Umbertina she had fruitlessly sought in Castagna, had suddenly become manifest in the New World and spoken to her.

Chapter Thirty-four

It was a fine day to be in Central Park, the kind that made Tina glad to be in New York. She was in a mile-long line waiting to get tickets for Shakespeare in the Park. Earlier she had told Allan she would spend the afternoon there doing some reading while she waited to get the tickets. He would come by later. She was prepared for the long wait; she had gone to Zabar's first and gotten crabmeat sandwiches, coleslaw, cheese, apples, and baklava. She had a blanket for sitting on the ground and her books.

She had everything but the expectation of seeing Jason Jowers there. He was ahead of her in the line, seemingly alone; it had been two summers since she had last seen him. He looked the same: tall, rangy, dressed in a lightweight suit the jacket of which he held over his arm; his short-sleeved shirt was open at the neck and the striped tie he had worn dangled out of his jacket pocket. He was glancing through a section of the *Times*. Should she leave? she wondered, suddenly confused. Should she put on her sunglasses and disguise herself so that he wouldn't recognize her? Should she be cool and do nothing, letting what would happen, happen?

Should she miss this chance to speak to him after not having seen him for so long? She wrestled with everything: her shame for the way she had run out on him in the past; her feelings about him, which she recognized as still with her and still strong; her own self-interest, which said Jason is the right one—do what's best for you.

The sight of Jason disturbed her; she found she couldn't get into her reading. She gave up trying to read and concentrated on the

life around and about her as her mind reeled with the possibilities
of a meeting with Jason, and she almost willed him to turn around
and see her. Immediately near her was a group of four playing
bridge on a straw mat; a young woman was feeding her baby in a
stroller; others were chatting, napping, just sitting. The day was
not completely clear, there was a faint haze that kept the sky
from blueness. It was hot. Tina continued to concentrate on the
life around her, trying to decide what to do about Jason. What if he
rebuffed her? She certainly deserved it, but how would it be, there,
in front of that whole crowd of people, if he turned on her and
told her what he thought of her? She was not into self-destruction,
and if Jason turned her away, that's what it would amount to.

A man was performing a headstand to the side of the line in front
of the park's castle and with skyscrapers as a backdrop; frisbee
throwing was going on, and a ball game in the field farther away.
Up and down the line an ordinary-looking man in a yellow polo
shirt and brown trousers was singing Elizabethan airs and then
passing his hat, saying, "Something for the singer?" Tina admired
his spunk and liked his ordinariness better than the costumed min-
strels who also passed by.

Petitioners came around asking the people in line to sign their
petition to be put on the ballot for the coming elections. Tina
signed for them all: the Communists, the libertarians, the gays. She
took in the noises of the ball players; she saw the lake a little way
off; she felt the gray soupiness and humidity of the day; she observed people picnicking and playing and overheard their snatches
of conversation.

"Well, that's the littlest one I've seen in a good while!" someone
was saying to the mother of the baby. "What is it—two months?"

"No, five."

"A boy?"

"A girl."

Vendors went up and down the line offering cold soup from the
Front Porch, homemade chocolate chip cookies, frozen yoghurt,
chilled sangría or Lambrusco. Farther ahead Tina could see the
ethnic-food brigade: One wagon dealt in stuffed pitas and shish-
kebab; another was into vegetarian falafel; there was an Italian
sausage-and-pepper man, and a Chinese wok full of good things.

The whole mélange of noise, smell, sight, attracted and delighted
her senses. She felt everything filtering into her consciousness,

pleasantly and effortlessly, at the same time as she wrestled with her private problem about Jason. Should she or should she not? What if he had already seen her before she noticed him and had deliberately decided not to speak?

A man in a black velvet jacket, loose beret, and boots was doing Shakespearian monologues. As he finished he rather dramatically declared that his name was Barnefielde, the same number of syllables and letters as in the Bard's name.

A woman singer came along, singing an old English carol, the refrain of which was:

> "For the Lord knows when we shall meet again
> To be Maying another year."

It struck Tina with a great sadness; it was true of all the lost opportunities of all their lives—who would ever know if there would be other meetings, other Mayings. Change and distance and time could put the screws into everyone's plan of Maying. The refrain came again and again after each stanza.

> "For the Lord knows when we shall meet again
> To be Maying another year."

And it decided her. She would not let this chance go by no matter what it cost her. She turned to the young woman with the baby: "Would you keep your eye on my blanket and things? I'll be right back." "Oh, sure," said the woman.

"Jason," she said as she drew abreast of him.

"Tina!" he exclaimed. He looked surprised, pleased, and hesitant. He didn't offer his hand, he didn't move toward her.

"I saw you—I'm behind you in the line, and I just had to come to speak to you. It's so good to see you again. And if it's not too late—well, of course, it's too late—but I still want to say that I'm sorry. You know, about our trip, when I left you. I really had to get it off my chest to apologize to you."

"Are you with someone now, Tina—I mean right now, here in the park?"

"No, I'm alone." She quickly resolved that she would stay alone, would not mention meeting Allan later if it meant a chance of being with Jason.

"So am I. This line is going to take hours. Why don't we wait together and catch up on some things."

"Great—why don't you come back where I am. I have a blanket on the ground. I was going to do some reading, but I can see that it's going to be pretty impossible."

He reclined on the blanket, one knee up and leaning on his elbow, and studied her. "You're looking good, Tina. What have you been up to?"

"I'm still into my studies—but what about you? Are you out of law school? Where are you living? Are you married or anything? Where's Timothy?"

"Tim's in Minnesota, got a job there with the local Arts Council. I finished law school, passed my bar exam, and will start with a law firm in Boston specializing in civil rights in a few weeks. Actually this is the last of my vacation since I took the bar; I'm only in New York for a short time, since I came down for interviews. I had a kind of tempting offer from a firm here, but I called Boston this morning and accepted the job there. It's for many reasons—so that I can do some work I believe in, not just become a legal mind; and so that I can be near the Cape and my boats. As for the rest, no, I'm not married, or anything . . . no time really."

"Jason, that's great about your work. It sounds as if you have it all together."

"Well, you too, Tina. There you are still pursuing your Dante. You always were determined to have your career, and on your own terms, remember?"

"Yes, I remember, and that doesn't mean I haven't made big mistakes along the way even though I've got the same end in mind. I wouldn't do everything over again that I've already done."

"Did you ever find your namesake, Tina? That great-grandmother who came from Castagna?"

"No, I didn't find her there. Only over here have I begun to be in touch properly. Lately I'm beginning to feel her strength—it's like she's helping me. Or maybe they're just my own projections."

He leaned toward her and looked closely at her, his lips compressed. Then he said, "You went to Castagna without me. That really hurt, you know."

"I know, Jason. It hurt me, too. Believe me, it's hurt me ever since. I did it because I was afraid of our getting so close that we'd be tied together before I even knew who I was or where I was going,

or wanted to go. I was too mixed up then—my mother had just
died, our whole family was coming apart, and I couldn't think
clearly. Can you understand?"

"Yes, I think so. But I would understand better if you had gone
on alone. But my God, Tina, with that guy you had just met
that night!"

"I know, Jason. It was a bad trip. It was my mistake. I have
wanted to tell you so ever since."

"I can't care anymore . . . so much time has passed. But at the
time, I swore I never wanted to see or hear about you again. I've
had some girl friends since then but I can tell you, Tina, there was
something special with you. I mean, we had certain things together that I can't have with anyone else. That business about
Castagna was truer than you think. Remember when I told you
it was a tie between us?"

"That's just what scared me, Jason! I didn't want to be tied into
anything at that time—I had my own problems to work out. It
never meant that I didn't care for you. Actually I cared too much
for you."

Her eyes pleaded with him, she reached for his hand, and he
grasped hers tightly.

The man in the yellow polo shirt and brown trousers came back
alongside their part of the line and sang again, and the words
lingered in the still, heavy air:

> "Western wind, when wilt thou blow,
>   The small rain down can rain . . .
>   Christ, if my love were in my arms
>   And I in my bed again!"

"Do you think you're ready for another try, Tina?"
"Oh, Bear, I do love you!"
They left the Shakespeare line, gathered up the blanket, books,
and bag of sandwiches, and went off into the park in another
direction.

They walked, they sat and ate, they got up and walked some
more. By evening they had put the past to rest. He stroked her
hair, she touched his face, they embraced and kissed.

"Come up with me to the Cape for Labor Day weekend, Tina," he said.

"Jason, it's just before I defend my dissertation. I don't know whether I should."

"Best thing in the world for you. I know. I did it just before my bar exam. Went up and sailed and just relaxed. It's the best thing in the world. You know, by now, that after all the years you've put into your work it's not just a matter of three or four days at the end that's going to make the difference."

"I guess you're right. You know, I reread the *Comedy* again thoroughly. You remember on our trip when we were talking about Dante and I said Hell is what a person does to himself when he goes against the grain of his own character? That's what it really is and that's what I went through, my own Hell, when I made my bad choices."

"And now you've finished your punishment?"

"Oh, Jason, don't ever think of Dante on the level of 'punishment'! The *Comedy* doesn't operate at the level of dogma, but at the highest human level—at the level of choice. That's why it is universal, why it will always be relevant."

A kind of excitement came into her voice as she spoke, an eagerness that touched Jason because he recognized in it the same commitment he gave to his work; the same kind of professionalism he felt.

"You were right, Tina," he said, "to wait to finish your studies. It wasn't fair of me to assume that you should give up what you wanted to do—and have to do—just because I was in law."

"Oh, Jason, if you understand that, you understand everything!"

" 'Let me not to the marriage of true minds/Admit impediments,' " he recited.

" 'Love is not love/Which alters when it alternation finds,' " she finished.

They kissed again, nipping and gliding over each other's lips, his hand ranging over her breasts, her arms around his neck to bring him closer to her. Then, drawing back, she braced her hands against his arms so that she could see his face.

"Jason," she said. "Will I ever love you as much as at this moment?"

"Yes," he answered, looking into her eyes and drawing her close again, "more and more, better and better. We're going to be married."

Chapter Thirty-five

Jason's grandparents' place at the Cape was a shuttered frame house at the end of a road. Tina loved what lay all around the dignified white house: the old red barn in the rear with its piles of sweet-smelling hay, the hilly meadowlands, the encroaching brush and forest growth, the tangle of wild sweet-peas and grapes, the marsh-lands, and then in the distance, the sea-cliffs and dunes.

The house was three-storied, white clapboard in front with gingerbread embellishments under the eaves and along the roofline; weathered wood shingling was on the sides and rear, in the thrifty way of Cape Codders. Two chimneys broke the gabled roofline. Two additions were on each side of the main structure, and there was a complete wing in the rear, where a large deck opened out onto a red-grass meadow stretching toward Nauset Bay. In front, roses clambered over a split-rail fence and a huge oak spread its branches toward the house. Near it was the bleached ghostly trunk of a second great tree, which had been felled. A huge thicket of wild roses, purple sweet-peas, and brambles swarmed wildly just below the neat apron of lawn.

The house had been built at the foot of a gentle hill in a meadow once used as pasture in the days when the Jowers family were farmers. Near the barn was a vegetable garden and a boat under canvas. The hill, which Tina and Jason walked up as soon as they arrived, looked to the ocean.

The sky was bright blue and the sun warm, but there was in the September air the unmistakable note of summer's end; the sound of the ocean waves reverberated differently now, indicating that the good season had gone, something else lay ahead. Tina heard the admonition of the waves, felt the change in the air, sensed the beginning of the wane.

"In a way our hardest times are just starting," she said as she looked at the beautiful sight of vivid green marshland against the bright blue water and the more distant creamy tones of the sand dunes and bars. "This is such a perfect place and time—but for us it's going to be anything but perfect from now on. In December I'll be setting up job interviews. I'll hope for an opening in the Boston area, or in the East anyway, but we may have to adjust to being apart until we get our careers together in the same place."

"We've been separated before," Jason remarked calmly, chewing on a long strand of grass and looking out to the water.

"It seems peculiar to tell everyone of our plans—to say that we're going to get married at Thanksgiving and then a month later I'll be going to the MLA convention in Chicago for job interviews that might be taking me God knows where."

"Tina," Jason said, taking her hands and looking at her ironically, "when have you ever cared how strange your plans seem to others?"

"You're right, Jason. Just as long as you and I know how things are and what we have to look forward to and what we have to live through before it works out."

She turned from the ocean view and looked down toward the house. "I love this place," she said. "No matter where we are, this will always feel like the home we'll come back to."

It was his grandparents' home, but also the place all the Jowers sons and daughters and grandchildren came back to. Jason's family was like her family in Gloversville; they were not artists or poets but good, solid people who could be counted on. "You cannot ask from people more than they are able or want to give," her father always said.

Preserved in an old drawing that hung in the dining room was a view of what the original cottage had looked like when Timothy Jowers set it up in the 1670s. Low, hugging the ground against the wind and storm of winter, it had provided shelter for the early Jowers families. Some beams and wide plank flooring from the

original one room were now encapsulated within the large surrounding structure that had grown up gradually in different periods. Somehow the resulting house achieved substance and dignity
without ever losing its original simplicity and honesty of line.

Like the house, the Jowers family had changed: They had
started by tilling the soil, and then, when the soil wore thin, had
gone to sea as captains for the import trade and the whaling industry. Those, too, had died and the Jowers men were now into
the professions—some in Boston, some in New Bedford, a few in
other parts of the country and world.

"You know what I like, Jason," Tina mused, "I like this sense
of the elemental and natural; yet it's all humanized. I mean, out here
there's the land, the barn, the ocean, and inside the house there are
the old charts and books and furniture—all the civilizing things.
That's what I like: balance."

Jason led Tina to the library, a room that had once been the
whole of the original dwelling and still showed the old post and
beam construction done by the immigrant Timothy Jowers. The
room was now the study of Jason's bachelor uncle, Professor Robert Jowers, who lived with his parents when he wasn't at Harvard.

"I remember this wonderful room," Tina said as she looked over
the snug, wood-paneled room that was filled with shelves of books,
a table full of sailing charts, albums of cabotage charts and harbor
soundings, globes, and sailing mementos. Over the fireplace was
the handsome carving from the sternboard of the whaling ship
Leonidas, which depicted that ancient bearded Spartan in helmet
and toga looking out stoically from amidst encircling wreaths and
furled banners.

Tina gazed bemused at the bust of the general who, from the
battlefields of Thermopylae, had been evoked as a namesake for
the Jowers' ships. Jason seemed to be reading her thoughts.

"The Jowers family have always had a classical bent," he told
her. "All through the family there has always been a Jason or a
Phidias, a Pallas Athena or Diana in between all those four-square
Faiths, Prudences, and Samuels. Pretty fanciful of those old Christians."

"Makes them like the Morosinis," she said. "My father would
love it here—we had a house full of the same kind of things from
his sailing ancestors: ships' models, a barometer, sextant, charts, the
works."

"Here, look at this," Jason said as he got an old ledger from the bookshelf. "It's the jou..nal that Phidias Jowers kept when he was at sea in 1852." He opened the ledger at random. "Listen to this. 'October 17: Nothing to do on ship but make ourselves canes to support our dignity when we are home.' "

"That's great, Jason. Do you still have the canes?"

"No, what we have is some scrimshaw that the captains collected among their crews when they were on a long whaling trip of a couple of years. I have a piece of it I want to give to you."

Jason went over to the handsome desk that had once stood in an accountant's office at the busy waterfront of New Bedford, the surface of it scarred by the writing and scratching of countless clerks toting up the fortunes made by the Cape captains on their whaling trips. He opened a drawer and got out an object, which he handed to her.

"I've already cleared this with my grandparents. I told them that instead of an engagement ring I wanted to give you something really special and part of our family. This is a piece of scrimshaw from the ship *Alexander* that was later lost in the Arctic with all hands. But before his last voyage, the Captain Jowers of that particular ship brought this back to his wife."

Tina looked at a delicately carved comb that Jason had handed her. Its high rim was carved into the undulating figure of a unicorn, whose graceful body ended in a mermaid's curled tail. In tiny figures on the front leg was carved "1828."

"Jason, it's exquisite."

"It's for you. You can wear it in your hair when you put it up."

"Now we have two powerful totems for our family-to-be," she said, wrapping her arms around him in a tight hug—"this and my Calabrian tin heart."

"Let me show you one more thing," he said, disentangling himself from her embrace. He took the photo of a sailing ship from the wall where it was hanging with other nautical prints.

"This is the *Castagna*," he said.

She took the picture from his hands and looked at the photo of a stricken ship, her masts bare and skeletal, foundering in high waves and listing badly. It was a gray and desolate sight. She looked and gave the photo back to him.

"Poor *Castagna*," she said, and she was thinking of the Calabrian one, too.

Later that evening, before sleeping, Tina wrote a letter:

Dear Weezy,
    I just had to write to you because of this incredible day. I have become engaged to Jason. I am so lucky—I have always loved him.
    We're going to get married here at the Cape at Thanksgiving. I happen to know that it was one hundred years ago that our great-grandmother Umbertina got married. That really makes me think some design she started is being completed.
    We've got different purposes, you and I, but I think we should be close. I am writing this news about Jason and me to you first of all. I'll write to *papà* and the grandparents, too, but I wanted to tell you first. I think it is important for us as women to cultivate our strengths, to grow, and to move on with purpose whatever our goals.
Remember me as your true sister,
Tina

It would not be worthwhile for her father and Weezy to come over for the wedding. It would be better if they all met there in the summer. It was like a forecast of her life with Jason: each to his own job and place, and then they would meet in the summer to be together at the Cape. And yet she was not dismayed, but hopeful; it would all work out because they wanted it to, and there would be no regrets of work left undone or chances not taken when they finally did achieve their place together to start their own family.
    The weather changed toward the end of their stay, bringing rain and wind. When it cleared enough one late afternoon, Tina and Jason bicycled over to the site that marked the place where the Marconi Wireless Station had stood. The sky was gray, a cool wind blew over the low scrub and beach grass, and the ocean waves were a steady roar on the long and empty beach.
    They stopped to read the plaques at a weathered lookout that commemorated the ships lost just off that beach. "Here's the one for the *Castagna*," Tina called to him, then read aloud: " '*Castagna*,

last square-rigger to leave her bones on Cape Cod, went aground near South Wellfleet on February 17, 1914.' "

They faced the ocean and yet they were not far from the bay. Only some three or four miles of land separated them on the east from the Atlantic and on the west from the bay. Those bodies of inexorable water, just a few miles apart, exerted a strange feeling of precariousness. And yet all of it was wondrous in that gentle fall—the marshes and meadows and ponds of Eastham just beginning to burnish with the quick touches of color, the drive through long strands of pine, the fragrance of grapes and plums, and the busy call of birds and waterfowl. And implicit in everything was the sound of the end: the roar of the water on the beach, which would, with time, wash everything away.

It was there, stated, in the signs put up at the Marconi Station, which pointed out where the first wireless towers had stood on the beach until endangered by encroaching water; now they had been completely removed, and scrub and beach grass were planted over the dunes to hold down erosion.

"Jason, it's scary," said Tina, as she looked, fascinated, out to sea. "Do you think someday the ocean will be here where we're standing?"

"Yes, surely. The only thing certain about this place is its constant changing and shifting. I can remember houses on the dunes that aren't there anymore. The sea cliffs crumble here and are washed away and are built up in spits on the bay side. Then inlets are plugged up by sandbars and marshes are formed. It's continuous change, and no matter what we do, the sea is in charge."

"It's terrible to think that someday this place where we're standing, or even your family home, won't be here."

"Oh, God, Tina, that won't come in our lifetime or in any lifetimes that we can conceive. It will come, but so far from now that it's as remote from us as the Ice Age was, and the glaciers that made the Cape in the first place."

"I know, I know. But it will come, and we know it—all we have to do is look out there at those waves and feel the wind. And then look about us and see how much was eaten away from the Marconi Station in not even a century."

"Come on, Tina, you don't have to get morbid about it," he laughed, and he held her against him in a tight hug.

"I'm not morbid, Jason, just fascinated. I like it for its honesty. It doesn't pretend to permanence as Egypt did with the pyramids, and Rome did and even still does with the Vatican, promising something eternal as if there were such a thing. The Cape tells the truth: It is not permanent, as nothing is permanent. It is changing, as everything is changing. That's not disturbing—actually there's great harmony and beauty in it. What I couldn't face would be some promise of everlastingness in a universe that shows us the dishonesty of such a notion."

But when they got back to the house, Jason paused in the front yard at the ghostly trunk and said, "Here is one change I really regret. This was a magnificent tree when I was a boy, and Tim and I climbed it, sat in it, swung from it, made it our own. Now it's gone."

As he spoke of the tree, Tina remembered other homes, trees, people of her own life. But the sadness and despair of a few years before was gone; she finally felt at peace, accepting it all.

"That's what makes me wonder about Weezy," she said thoughtfully, "she's so dogmatic. She seems to be stuck on the present, assuming that the world is finished but it all went wrong and so she's got to wreck it in order to start again. Basically she's anarchic, because she can't believe in the future. Yet it's all ongoing change—all she has to do is wait and see."

Tina's room had a handsome maple bed with a fishnet canopy and a cross-and-crown coverlet that was old and faded and beautiful. At the foot of the bed stood an old sea-chest used by a Jowers sea-captain on some trip to the ends of the earth. There were hooked and braided rugs on the floor and a child's Chippendale chair by the fireplace. The room was papered in a reproduction of an early style. Everything was right. It was the equivalent of the fine Italian hand among the old families of the Veneto. Both were seafaring families, both had accumulated wealth and possessions and pride; but her father's family had been on the decline since the First World War and their possessions decimated, the style become faintly seedy. The Jowers family, however, were still enjoying their New World vigor.

And yet, Tina thought as she went to bed in that room, isn't it strange to realize that both places are doomed to vanish. First Venice will disappear beneath the waters of the lagoon; and long after, but still inevitably, the Cape, too, will erode and go back to its beginnings at the ocean floor.

It was all the same, and all different. Drowsily, she recalled that Thanksgiving of six or seven years ago when she had first come to the Cape as Timothy's guest. She remembered the scene after dinner. They were sitting around the fireplace in the living room, where cabinets stood filled with Sandwich glass and the China Import plate of a century and a half ago, and the walls were hung with paintings of prosperous Jowers sea-captains and their patient wives.

A cousin called Emily had riveted Tina's attention by saying, "Every time it's Thanksgiving and I think back to those brave pilgrims, I give thanks for my heritage. I wouldn't have wanted to be born anything but of Anglo-Saxon stock."

Tina had been astonished, not only at the narrowness of the remark, but at its spuriousness.

"Well, I suppose I agree with Emily," Grandmother Jowers had said. "I suppose I would rather be of English descent than anything else."

"Mother, what nonsense!" hooted Professor Jowers. His field was not the Reformation, which had produced the Puritans, but the Renaissance, which had spawned humanists, and he had spent long periods in Europe on his studies. "We have here as Tim's guest a girl whose father is an Italian poet, in a country of great artists. And Tim and Jason themselves have lived in Italy. Are they supposed to think that all they have seen there is not as good as any common person whose surname happens to be Anglo-Saxon? What nonsense!"

The conversation had stopped there, more from courtesy than from conviction. Emily, Tina thought, had hit a note of self-congratulation that, whether the professor wanted to admit it or not, the Jowers family all shared. Tina would have liked to say that as far as she was concerned, glory was in being Italian. But it all sounded so pretentious and silly that she was embarrassed. They were worse than her grandparents.

Tina thought again of that evening. Was there more merit in being self-contained, reserved, unemotional, reticent in the Anglo-Saxon way of the Jowers', and of Jason? Or in her Latin excessiveness of emotion, her flights of fancy, her intensity of feeling?

It was a silly argument, she thought. Comparisons are odious. And futile. And so she slept in her New England canopy bed, dreaming of the swallows sweeping down over a terrace in the stupendous twilight of a May night in Rome.

"What are you doing?" Jason asked, as he came out the back way into the yard and found her planting something in a sunny area against the house where it indented into a small courtyard and was protected.

"It's something I always promised myself, Jason; I'm planting rosemary. There's a chance it can survive the winters here if it's well protected, and when it grows to a regular bush. I thought I'd better get it in before we come back at Thanksgiving."

"Why rosemary? For remembrance?"

"Well, yes," she laughed, "maybe that, too, but actually for old Umbertina. It's the family women's quaquaversal plant—wherever one of Umbertina's clan descends, there also will be rosemary planted, for where it grows, the women of the house are its strength."

"And what of the men?"

"They should grow fig trees, maybe," she laughed. "But seriously, don't give it a sexist interpretation! It doesn't take anything away from men if their women are as strong as they. Strong men deserve strong women."

"Agreed."

"We'll just pit our strengths together from now on."

"And the rosemary will help?"

"Yes, darling Bear, the rosemary will help. I'm planting rosemary here because our lives will soon be merging and here's where our roots will be."

"So you've finally learned how to cultivate your own garden."

She looked at him lovingly. "I guess that's what it is—my great-grandmother planted peppers and pole beans, I'm going to plant humanism. And don't be offended, Jason, by my keeping my own name when we're married. That's the name I want to write under."

"That's all right with me, Tina. You can have as long and Italian a name as you want, but what of our children?"

"Oh, Jason, you're so forward-looking—comes from your ancestors, I suppose, always looking out to sea at the long line of the horizon. Well, I guess we'll just hyphenate the kids."

"And I guess it's time to go now. Back to the grind once more."

"Yes, time to go," she said. "But we'll be back. The rosemary stays here to get rooted and the tin heart comes with me wherever I am. Just to remind me of the *imprevedibile* in life."

Tina smiled over her shoulder at him as she went into the house to get her things for the trip back to New York.

She had done her planting and a sense of well-being pervaded her. Her place was marked; all the positioning to come, between her and Jason, would have this as focus.

Afterword

An Immigrant Tapestry

All history should be told as people's stories.

Helen Barolini, *Umbertina*

I thought of my work as a thread in the fabric of the whole national literature. When it was written in the late 1970s, that fabric seemed receptive to new designs and figures, it held the promise of becoming a splendidly variegated tapestry of many strands and colors.

Helen Barolini, "*Umbertina* and the Universe"

Rummaging through a pile of books on the clearance table of a large bookstore in New Jersey, I see an old edition of *Umbertina*, half-hidden beneath cookbooks, collections of nursery rhymes, and self-help books. Ironically, only a couple of years ago I searched for *Umbertina* in this same bookstore without any luck.[1] In a second I can come up with a list of twenty people who have been looking for this novel, in bookstores across the United States, to no avail. Although I own a copy, I feel compelled to rescue and take home, for a dollar, this small book, its print so tiny as to discourage any potential readers not equipped with phenomenal eyesight.

A stubborn book, *Umbertina* has managed to make its way to readers in spite of its crippling publishing history. The hardcover edition, published by Seaview in 1979, was promoted as a "family saga" and achieved modestly respectable sales, but went out of print after only three years. Two more editions were subsequently published.[2] The first was a mass-market paperback published by Bantam, which misjudged the book to be a romance novel. The cover of that edition, which depicted "three women, hair streaming romantically . . . spoke of a work the book did not represent" (Barolini). As Barolini recalls, "the public for which the book was meant never saw it." Sales were poor, by mass-market standards, and in 1982 Bantam called Barolini to inform her that the book would be shredded. The American Italian Historical Association bought several hundred copies, which allowed for some distribution of the book among its members, but over 100,000 copies were shredded. Another paperback edition was published by Ayer in 1988, but it was so poorly produced—its type reduced to an almost illegible size—that the author agreed to forgo royalties in order to have the rights revert back to her.

Undoubtedly, *Umbertina* suffered, during this unfortunate history, from misguided positioning by its publishers. But even more essentially, it suffered at the hands of a literary establishment unable to conceive of a novel dealing with women's experience or Italian American experience as worthy of serious critical attention or a lasting place in American letters. It is interesting to note that while *Umbertina* was reviewed by numerous newspapers in smaller cities with large ethnic populations, it was virtually ignored by the kinds of prestigious publications capable of setting a novel on the path toward contemporary canonization. This fate—common to the works of Italian American women authors[3]—has deprived Umbertina, until now, of the recognition it deserves.

The history of Helen Barolini's first novel—the history of the material artifact itself—is sadly typical among works relegated to the category of "women's novels." While novels depicting men's quests for autonomy and identity dominate lists of "great books" and "contemporary classics," novels like *Umbertina*, which describe similar quests by women, seldom achieve anything close to such status. This is particularly true of novels that emerged from the reawakening of feminist consciousness in the 1960s and 1970s, of which *Umbertina* is certainly one.[4]

At the same time, *Umbertina*'s history epitomizes the predicament of the Italian American literary tradition—and particularly of the Italian American women's literary tradition—within which it must be placed. This tradition, while still in the process of being recognized—and recognizing as well as defining itself—is forcefully making its way onto the literary scene.[5] That books such as Tina De Rosa's *Paper Fish*, Dorothy Bryant's *Miss Giardino*, *Ella Price's Journal*, and *The Confessions of Madame Psyche*, Diana Cavallo's *A Bridge of Leaves*, and Josephine Gattuso

Hendin's *The Right Thing To Do* have recently been or will soon be reprinted testifies to the vitality of, and a new interest in, Italian American women's literature. As Alice Walker has demonstrated through her fruitful uncovering of Zora Neale Hurston's work, literary history cannot be transformed without the patient work of recovery; and without such recovery there would be no literature.[6] This long overdue reprint of *Umbertina*—part of a larger publishing project through which The Feminist Press is making available the literature of Italian American and Italian women—offers the opportunity to assess where Italian American women's literature stands through a retrospective look at *Umbertina*'s long journey.

Women writers from various ethnic groups—Toni Morrison, Alice Walker, Maxine Hong Kingston, Amy Tan, Cristina Garcia, Joanna Kadi, Leslie Marmon Silko—have shown how the telling of multigenerational stories helps the uprooted, the displaced, and the oppressed to maintain a sense of cultural belonging and legitimacy. The first novel by an Italian American woman to explore, in depth, intergenerational female relationships in an Italian immigrant family, *Umbertina* is set both in Italy and the United States, and provides a compelling exploration of life between different cultures and countries. Written during the 1970s—a time of ethnic revival, as well as feminist awakening—*Umbertina* is not concerned with ethnicity *per se*, but tells instead the stories of those who recognize themselves as "the poor of the earth" (41) and of their economically more fortunate descendants, revealing their conflicts, which are related to class as well as geographical mobility.[7]

While other Italian American works have also told these stories, *Umbertina* stands out for its understanding of the cultural and social implications of uprooting and for its concern with situating its characters' lives against clearly outlined historical events: the unification of Italy, the migration out of Southern Italy, the two world wars, the Great Depression, and the economic boom in post-war Italy. *Umbertina* privileges the stories of the quotidian struggles of immigrants, which have traditionally been left out of official historical narratives.[8] And most significantly, the novel foregrounds the seldom-heard perspectives and voices of women. An epic feminist narrative, Barolini's first novel offers almost a textbook case of immigrant history, as experienced by the women of a family that moves from the absolute poverty of peasantry to the oppression of being immigrant and working class to the material comfort of middle-class life, but remains haunted by the shadows of its past.

Umbertina has, over the years, been taught in several colleges and universities and written about extensively by a variety of scholars, including such Italian American scholars as Mary Jo Bona, Fred Gardaphé, Mary Frances Pipino, Anthony Tamburri, Carol Bonomo Albright, and Robert Viscusi. These critics have focused on issues such as the negotiation between Italian and American cultures and the figure of the grandmother as a recurring device that Italian American writers employ to mediate their relationship to ethnicity, as well as the quest for female selfhood that places *Umbertina* within the tradition of the feminist *bildungsroman*. Indeed, *Umbertina*'s status as an Italian American classic is undisputed. To make a case for *Umbertina* as an American classic, though, one must make a case for Italian American literature—and particularly Italian American women's literature—as American literature.

The attention recently received by Italian American women writers such as Rita Ciresi, Tina De Rosa, Louise DeSalvo, Sandra M. Gilbert, Maria Mazziotti Gillan, Diane Di Prima, Dorothy Bryant, Barbara Grizzuti Harrison, Donna Masini, Carole Maso, Cris Mazza, Marianna De Marco Torgovnick, and Agnes Rossi, to mention some of the most well-known contemporary authors, suggests that the intellectual climate is becoming more hospitable to both women writers and Italian American writers. Yet many readers and critics cling to anti-intellectual stereotypes against Italian Americans and are still reluctant to recognize some of these authors as Italian American.[9] Such stereotypes have been relentlessly exposed by Barolini in essays such as "Becoming a Literary Person Out of Context," "Buried Alive by Language," "Writing to a Brick Wall," and "After-Thoughts on Italian American Women Writers," some of which appear in *Chiaroscuro: Essays of Identity*, a book that confirms Barolini's place in the Italian American intellectual avant-garde.[10]

A vociferous supporter of the rightful inclusion of Italian American writers within the ever-growing and diverse American literary canon,[11] Barolini in 1985 published the award-winning *The Dream Book: An Anthology of Writings by Italian-American Women*. In her pathblazing introduction, she makes a brilliant and forceful argument on behalf of Italian American women's literature, and of all literature that is informed by the experiences of gendered culture:

> The Italian American woman writer . . . is stranded in a no-woman's-land where there is small choice; either follow the omnipresent models that do not speak to her own particular experience, or write of her expe-

rience and know that it will be treated as of no importance, too "different" for critical attention. Alice Walker asked the right question: why should anyone require more of a reason for the existence of *Sula* (or *Rosa*) than for *Jane Eyre*? (31)[12]

What Barolini would experience in the years to come, despite the praise that both *The Dream Book* and *Umbertina* received from readers such as Tillie Olsen, Cynthia Ozick, Ishmael Reed, and Alice Walker, indicated that the obstacles facing the emergence of Italian American women's literature would not be overcome easily. In 1997, just prior to the publication of *Chiaroscuro*, all of Barolini's books were out of print: the pioneer of Italian American women's literature was virtually absent from the contemporary literary arena, her books unavailable and thus doomed to remain unknown to younger readers as well as to a larger, non-Italian American reading audience. Although this is the sad plight of far too many books, it is especially pernicious in the case of an author such as Barolini who, in naming and bringing to the attention of readers Italian American women's literature, has been its courageous midwife. In the twentieth year after its original publication, this reprint of *Umbertina* acknowledges the place of its author and of Italian American women writers in American literature.

Helen Barolini was born in 1925 in Syracuse, New York, into a second-generation, middle-class Italian American family: her mother's parents had come from Calabria, while her father's were from Sicily. After attending Wells College and Syracuse University, where she majored in English, Barolini traveled to Italy in 1948. There she met and married the Venetian poet Antonio Barolini, with whom she had three daughters. The family lived in both Italy and the United States, and following her husband's death, Barolini moved back permanently to the United States in 1973. Her bicultural experience shapes her first novel as well as the body of work she has produced in the last three decades: a book of poems she co-authored with her husband entitled *Duet* (1966), *The Dream Book* (1985), the novel *Love in the Middle Ages* (1986), *Festa: Recipes and Recollections of Italian Holidays* (1988), a book on the fifteenth-century Italian scholar-publisher Aldus Manutius entitled *Aldus and His Dream Book* (1991), *Chiaroscuro* (1997), a radio drama on Margaret Fuller, myriad essays, stories and poetry published in periodicals and anthologies, and many translations from Italian to English.

Barolini began to work on the story inspired by her own maternal great-grandmother in 1969, although she did not work actively on what would become *Umbertina* until 1976, when she received a National Endowment for the Arts fellowship. Originally, Barolini conceived of the material in two separate parts—a novel that included the "Umbertina" and "Tina" sections, and a novel, entitled "The Last Abstraction," containing the core of Marguerite's story. Following her publisher's suggestion, she merged the two novels into one, organized around three sections—one devoted to each woman—and a prologue on Marguerite. *Umbertina* is a sophisticated mélange of social, familial, and personal histories: in preparation for the book, Barolini conducted extensive archival research on the "Great Migration" of the last century, during which Italians emigrated from their homeland, most of them to the Americas and Australia, as well as an oral history project with Italian American women. She integrated the results of this research into her fictional account of family history (interview with Bonetti). This archival research also paved the way for *The Dream Book*, which Barolini describes as her "literary manifesto" and wrote as a response to "the neglect of *Umbertina*"—that neglect representing for her "the neglect of all works by Italian American women writers" (interview with Ahearn 47). Through her choice of women's names as titles for the novel and each of its three sections, the author claims, immediately and unapologetically, the centrality of Italian American women's stories. Indeed, there is a certain calculated defiance in the choice of a name such as Umbertina, so unquestionably Italian—the kind of Italian that resists domestication by English pronunciation.

While from a structural point of view clear narrative and chronological demarcations exist between each character's story, *Umbertina* should be read as one woman's—Barolini's—complicated search for cultural origins and continuities, a search linked to the development of a feminist consciousness.[13] The structure of the novel makes it clear that the recovery of family and immigrant history is embedded within a feminist plot: The book opens not with Umbertina, but with Marguerite, the granddaughter who initiates the personal exploration that will lead her own daughter back to the origins, back to Umbertina. Marguerite's search is not what one would call successful—especially since it is tragically cut short. Yet she is the one who opens the Pandora's box that will make it possible for her daughter, Tina, to continue the journey.[14] Barolini's narrative of female development argues for the importance of ties between women and highlights the ways in which they can be sources of strength and resourcefulness for themselves and their daughters. But it also demonstrates the ways in which mothers can deplete their daughters' strength. Late in her life, Umbertina comes to understand how, in acting within the paradigms of the patriarchal culture that she both accepts and defies, she has not been able to pass on her own strength to her daughters. While a feminist consciousness does not reach maturity in Umbertina, in her daughters, or in her granddaughter Marguerite, it is more fully realized by her great-granddaughter Tina and especially by Tina's sister Weezy, who, though not a central figure, occupies an important place in the larger tapestry into which the novel itself is woven. And feminist consciousness is certainly evident in the book as a whole. The feminism of many of her characters may be ambiguous, and at times even reluctant, but Barolini's certainly is not.

Barolini carefully avoids the nostalgia and sentimentality that at times pervade immigrant literature. In *The Dream Book*, she writes, "There is a dark underside to the bright picture of the compact Italian American life so extolled by sociologists and onlookers" (16), and she is unafraid of exposing it—as unafraid as authors such as Louise DeSalvo, Rose Romano, and Mary Saracino, who have more recently offered unflinching depictions of Italian American family life, where nurturance and violence, tolerance and prejudice, go hand in hand. Referring to the racism suffered by the early Italian immigrants, but also to their subsequent assimilation into "whiteness," Barolini foregrounds the ties between race and class oppression. Thus Marguerite reacts to her parents' racism by thinking that her "folks can't remember when their own folks were Negroes" (204).[15] Barolini's fiction examines the interconnections between class and race that are central to the current debate on the construction of whiteness. "If the legal and social history of Jim Crow often turned on the question 'Who was Black?'" writes David Roediger, "the legal and social history of immigration often turned on the question 'Who was White?'" (182). *Umbertina* sheds light on the class transition and the process of cultural assimilation that made it possible for the so-called white ethnics, such as the Italians (or the Irish), to become white.[16]

Umbertina is a fictional account of the lives of working-class people and their middle-class descendants. Working-class literature is, in general, less interested in the self-contained story of the solitary individual struggling against, and overcoming, adversity than in the subtle ways in which the stories of individuals are interwoven with the stories of communities and their cultures. Working-class writers like Dorothy

Allison, Tina De Rosa, Esmeralda Santiago, and Janet Zandy have written of the high price, in terms of cultural loss, that upward mobility requires of working-class people.[17] "My parents, like most working-class parents, wanted a better life for their children," Zandy writes. "But they did not wish a better life that extracted as its cost familial and historic memory" (*Liberating Memory* 1). *Umbertina* tells of the pains of class migration: it is a story of simultaneous acquisition and loss, pride and shame, mobility and paralysis, victory and defeat—a story that, while specifically Italian American, cuts across the ethnic divide in its concern with gender and class.

Umbertina belongs to the tradition that has recently produced such works as Dorothy Allison's *Bastard Out of Carolina*, Louise DeSalvo's *Vertigo*, Joanna Kadi's *Thinking Class*, Kim Chernin's *In My Mother's House*, and Sandra Cisneros's *The House on Mango Street*. These memoirs and autobiographical novels are, like *Umbertina*, overtly gendered narratives informed by women's experience. They are also, like *Umbertina*, shaped by working-class identity, concerned with working-class history, and thus constantly merge personal and cultural memory.[18] *Umbertina* is about memory and the power of memory. Barolini traces the genesis of *Umbertina* to a trip to Calabria in 1969, during which she came across a traditional Calabrian bedspread, much like the one described in *Umbertina*, which in turn triggered a childhood memory of her grandmother. The bedspread that she found in Calabria, woven by women from the mountain villages on huge handlooms, was for Barolini "the most authentic" link to the times in which her grandmother had left Calabria.[19]

Umbertina begins with Marguerite at a point of crisis in her life, at a time in which she feels compelled to remember her maternal grandmother. And the novel as a whole pulls together the fragile threads of the stories of women immigrants and weaves them into a narrative tapestry, one that will "last forever," like Umbertina's "*coperta matrimoniale*" (44), her bedspread, which she takes with her to America in the bundle containing her family's few belongings. Barolini unfolds a chronologically linear story which nevertheless requires that the reader look at the three women's stories as the interconnecting pieces of one design.[20] The bedspread stands as a figure for this multigenerational story, for the structure in which it is embedded, and for the intersecting senses of longing and loss that both drive and thwart the lives of the characters. The artifact of Southern Italian American culture functions as a catalyst for the conflicts and ambiguities underscoring Umbertina's journey as well as that of her female descendants. In this journey, home becomes increasingly undefined and unreachable, expressing the perennial displacement experienced by those who leave their land.[21]

Umbertina's determination to leave a world of oppression, deprivation, and hopelessness leads her to accept willingly and without hesitation marriage to a much older husband, whom she does not love romantically but grows to respect and care for as the trusted companion of her life. Yet after his death, Serafino is the one commemorated for the family's economic success, while Umbertina is only mentioned as his "good companion" (128). She is not even a partner in the enterprise of Serafino Longobardi & Sons, which she has so single-handedly masterminded. The illiterate Umbertina starts out by selling freshly made *panini* and pizza for her husband's co-workers, keeping "the men's orders in her mind" thanks to her "great powers of concentration and a memory that took the place of reading and writing" (94). Encouraged by the profits her hard work reaps, she opens a *spaccio*—a space—in a storefront (95). After leasing a piece of farmland to grow her own provisions and purchasing a horse and wagon, Umbertina shrewdly transforms the *spaccio* into the Longobardi *groceria*, and later creates an importing business, a steamship agency, and a bank: she manages to build an economic security that protects her family even from the devastation of the Depression. Barolini's character thus follows a rags-to-riches journey, fulfilling—to all appearances, at least—the so-called American Dream.

For Umbertina, the goat girl of the Calabrian mountains, the bedspread embodies her struggle to extricate herself from poverty and her belief that she does not have to remain one of those with "resignation" painted on their faces, one of "those who have nothing to hope for" (43). It is significant that the bedspread has not been passed down to Umbertina by a mother or grandmother, who could never have afforded such an object. Instead, it has been especially made for and sold to Umbertina by Nelda, the housekeeper of Don Antonio, the village priest. A huge class gap exists between Umbertina's family and Don Antonio, who enjoys living conditions as foreign to people of Umbertina's class as the mythical New World to which she sails with her husband and their three children. It is important that Umbertina purchases the bedspread as a beautiful object she has desired, but also—and especially—as the sign of her belief in the possibility of better living conditions. For the same reason, she asks Nelda for rosemary from Don Antonio's garden—not paying homage to the traditional belief, voiced by Nelda, that women are strong in the houses in which the herb thrives, but rather aspiring to use rosemary as a condiment for the meat that she hopes she and her family will one day be able to eat. Yet Nelda's words about strong women strike a chord in Umbertina, who the people of Castagna say has had "character right from the womb" and is destined to be "the man of her family" (23). This tradition will be passed down to, and remembered by, her great-granddaughter as she plants rosemary in the garden of her future husband's family home.

The bedspread symbolizes tradition, female work, Umbertina's ambition, and the memory of her land sealed in the intricate design of leaves and flowers. The "traditional" design of the bedspread, with its "brightly colored yarn embroidered in bunches of grapes, fig leaves, twining ivy, flowers and the stylized hearts on the bright yellow-orange ground of thick homespun" (44), evokes the longed-for abundance and generosity of the homeland that Umbertina leaves with deliberation but cannot help missing and grieving over, despite her determination not to regret anything.[22] Umbertina's longing for the land she has left behind is not articulated through poetical reveries like, for example, Grandma Doria's imaginative stories in Tina De Rosa's *Paper Fish*.[23] In that book, Italy lacks any kind of geographical reality: it is instead a mythological reminiscence that is contrasted to the grim physical environment of the Italian ghetto in Chicago.[24] Wary of nostalgia and mythologizing, and paying scrupulous attention to the historical circumstances out of which the stories of her characters are born, Barolini never once loses sight of the social injustice that motivates her characters' emigration[25]: for Barolini, there is nothing romantic about poverty. Yet Umbertina's longing paradoxically resists the recognition that Italy has not been generous to her or the millions of its children forced to leave by devastating poverty, malnutrition, and disease.[26]

These hardships were the direct result of brutal exploitation by feudal landlords and the Italian government. In fact, Umbertina's story of inherited poverty is the story of Calabrian peasants and shepherds abused by the absentee landlords of the Calabrian *latifondi*. In the nineteenth century, "partnerships" between landlords and peasants and shepherds, always mediated by *fattori* and *caporali*, were an integral part of the feudal economy of the Italian South. Such "partnerships"— in which the baron provided grazing land and flocks to shepherds (which both Umbertina and Serafino are), and the shepherds provided labor—proved "immensely profitable for the baron": "the baron's income was assured even in bad years when the 'gain' in 'fruits of the flock' was meager and corresponded to starvation wages for the shepherds" (Petrusewicz 118–19).

> Of the baron's existence, Umbertina was quite sure even though she had never seen him; she grazed the goats upon his hills and gathered wood and nuts from his forests; he existed every time his *fattore* came riding through the village to collect payments and levies. . . . She knew that he and his wife existed, for they had to be fed prodigious amounts of food and wine her father and the others worked out of the land and turned over to the *fattore*. (28–29)

Peasants such as Carlo Nenci, Umbertina's father, were equally exploited by a baron who, "in return for doing nothing and knowing nothing, but for having the good fortune to be born who he was and thus owning all the land and trees and streams within sight . . . was given half of what was produced by Carlo Nenci and the other men of Castagna" (24).

The apparent promise held by the nationalists who had fought to expel foreign rulers and unify Italy came to nothing for impoverished Southern Italians like the peasants of Castagna. While Umbertina is considered Italian when she comes to the United States, she is one of many Southern Italian immigrants who had been baffled by the Italian citizenship thrust upon them in 1860, the year in which she was born. In any case, her new status as a citizen would have made little difference in her life, for the newly born Italian government failed to deliver "the poor of the earth" from their oppression and suffering.

> [It was a] thieving government . . . that took everything and gave back nothing—not a road, a school, or a sewer. . . . The *ladro governo* taxed the poor man's working mule but not the rich man's carriage horse. The *ladro governo* had sent Garibaldi into exile and made land distribution available only to those rich enough to buy great quantities. (29)

It is no wonder that Umbertina and many of her fellow immigrants feel no allegiance to the new Italian nation, with the exception of the socialist Domenico Saccà, a character who testifies to the fact that people left Italy for political as well as economic reasons.[27] While in her youth she despises Domenico's beliefs and idealism, as an old woman, Umbertina misses Domenico's "haranguing" and imagines what he would say: "You call this success, Tinuzza, but in Italy there's a different *benessere* and the word is more gracious, not so materialistic. Well-being of the total person—not just money, but spirit, too" (145).

Not even her doubts, however, prompt Umbertina to regret her pursuit of "well-being." If Umbertina shows little understanding of politics, she understands that the lives of people like her are of little value in the world, whether in the archaic Calabrian countryside or in the aggressively modern New World. With the intuition of one who has experienced exploitation, she does not fail to recognize the similarity between the oppression suffered in Calabria at the hands of the baron's *fattore* and that perpetrated by the American *padroni*, who hire the newcomers for little money, both "living and getting rich off the labor of others by taking from them part of what they worked for" (59).

In Italy, the bedspread had embodied Umbertina's hope for economic success and social ascent; in the United States, it also becomes a physical token of the ties to her culture of origin, to the village that she names before dying: "Castagna" (146). Feminist scholarship has emphasized the importance of women's domestic work in relation to women's creativity and aesthetics: "For women, the meaning of sewing and knitting is 'connecting'—connecting the parts of one's life, and connecting to other women—creating a sense of community and wholeness" (Hammond, quoted in Hedges 5).[28] The bedspread signals Umbertina's desire for connection to the traditions of her world, to the continuity of life among different generations and, more importantly, to a sense of cultural and familial belonging, a feeling of ease in a world in which one is a rightful citizen.

But Umbertina is forced to sell the bedspread that adorned the gloomy tenement room in New York's Little Italy, showering it with a wealth of light and beauty (pleasures from which the inhabitants of the slums are normally excluded). In doing so, she makes the unavoidable choice of the poor, who cannot afford luxuries such as these, as Anna Giordani, the social worker who offers to sell the bedspread on her behalf, sharply reminds her. Just as she was deprived of the opportunity to inherit such a bedspread from her mother, Umbertina will be deprived of the chance to pass it on as an heirloom to her own daughters and their daughters. While Umbertina's practical wisdom and economic astuteness enable her to prevail over the grim, fatal life of the tenement in New York, to move her entire family upstate, and to build her small economic empire, her pragmatism does not protect her or her female descendants from a chronic sense of displacement.

The bedspread resurfaces several times throughout the novel, primarily in Umbertina's reminiscences, but also in the continuous preoccupation with the search for patterns, forms through which the characters try to frame their confused actions. The material texture of Umbertina's bedspread, juxtaposed to Marguerite's self-destructive pursuit of "that last abstraction: the Love Affair" (258), marks the intergenerational and class differences among these women as they search for, define, question, relinquish, and rethink their place in the world. In the year 1900, the forty-year-old Umbertina feels as if "a design, like the rich intricacy of the long-lost matrimonial spread, was complete. Her life's pattern was outlined and it was satisfying and beautiful to her" (102). Yet the pattern would disintegrate. Towards the end of her life, alone in her own family, Umbertina feels as if she is holding something that no longer exists because she has no one to whom to describe the intricate patterns of her story: "She had won, but who could she tell the story to?" (145).

Umbertina's concern with providing the finest linen for her daughters' dowry captures her desire to endow her daughters with what they need to be strong, but also her own entrapment within, and collusion with, a world that she has always understood and accepted as a man's world (33, 134). The immigrant who cannot "sew a seam or do a stitch of embroidery" (132) recognizes fine *biancheria* and makes sure that her daughters' trousseau is full of the most exquisite linen, including items that her modernized daughters will not use in their American homes:

> dream stuff of another way of life that included damask dinner cloths with banquet-size monogrammed napkins, exquisite Madeira tea sets, blanket covers and tray sets for breakfast in bed, napkin envelopes with cutwork and linen hand-towels with long strands of flax fringe which, she told Sara and Carla, were to be used by the doctor when he washed his hands after a home visit: they also required, after laundering, the patient combing-out of fringe strands . . . several beautifully embroidered and hand-stitched capelets, called matinées, which were to be worn over garments for the morning brushing of the hair. (132)

With such a preposterous heritage, it is no surprise that Umbertina's daughters find themselves ill-equipped to cope with life. Purchased with the money earned through Umbertina's labor, none of these items can capture the significance and power of the lost bedspread, though their acquisition and bequest to her daughters indicates Umbertina's loss and her wish to protect them from the deprivation she has suffered. In his essay "Love in Italian-American Fiction," Robert Viscusi writes: "When parents and children do not speak the same language, they learn to communicate through bedposts and quilts, houses and trees, deeds and dollars" (170). This is certainly true of Umbertina and her descendants. Wanting to teach her daughters about tradition, continuity, and survival, Umbertina recounts to them the story of the long-lost bedspread and reminds them that they must pass on to their daughters the linen she has given them. Having provided, through her resourcefulness, economic security for her family, but incapable of truly questioning the structures of patriarchy, Umbertina leaves everything else to her sons. Without financial and emotional strength, her daughters grow to be passive and acquiescent women who quickly surrender—if they ever develop—any ambition besides that of pursuing middle-class consumerism and fulfilling the traditional feminine role in marriage. Like many daughters of immigrants, Umbertina's daughter Carla is committed to "marriage, motherhood, and American-style domesticity" (Gabaccia, *From the Other Side* 120).[29] Comfortably assimilated and unquestioning, Carla is too removed from the central questions of the novel, according to Barolini, to even warrant a section of her own (interview with Greenberg 95). And while Carla's daughter Marguerite will manage to break away from this insidious, depleting tradition, particularly through her own daughters, she cannot fully extricate herself from the entanglement of her own maternal heritage.

Weaving the significance of the bedspread into her immigrant narrative tapestry, Barolini foregrounds the importance of material culture and the very real consequences that the loss of artifacts such as the bedspread can have on the members of a cultural group. The study of material culture, *Umbertina* suggests, is imperative for women and working-class people, for their history is to be found in the history of objects such as the bedspread.[30] It is fitting that the lost bedspread appears to the dying Umbertina at the close of the section devoted to her:

> a sudden brightening came to her eyes as in a vision of light she saw the lost *coperta* of her matrimonial bed with all the intensity of its colors and bright twining of leaves and flowers and archaic designs in its patterns. "Ah!" she gasped at its beauty. (146)

The bedspread represents that "beauty" Umbertina had erroneously believed she could do without, but comes to crave at the end of her life's long journey. With seven living children, twenty-seven grandchildren, having survived the deaths of three of her children and her own husband, and having built a small economic empire, the almost eighty-year-old Umbertina has come a long way from the Sila mountains where, barefoot, she herded her goats. Yet on her deathbed, as the vision of the bedspread appears before her, she craves water from the spring of Castagna. There is no simplistic nostalgia about Umbertina's last craving, only the recognition of the deep scars that the trauma of poverty, geographical uprooting, and cultural and linguistic disconnection and isolation leave on immigrants.

If the first-generation immigrant craves, on her deathbed, water from the spring of her village—an impossible homecoming—then for the following generations things become even more complicated. While the dying Umbertina's request for water from Castagna is not understood by her children, the feeling it expresses is passed on as an unspoken desire, a profound loss for which they have no words. *Umbertina* makes a powerful argument for the importance of cultural memory, without which one is doomed to experience an all-consuming displacement, as Marguerite does. "Poetry is not a luxury" (37), Audre Lorde has taught us, and the bedspread is a source of poetry—the poetry of the mundane—and a figure for the hope that Umbertina cultivates like the plants she stubbornly grows in cans in the New York tenement. Umbertina's desire to keep the bedspread is rooted in the recognition that one's place in the world is related to familial origins. As Mary Saracino puts it, "Where you are born has far less to do with who you are than whom you are born to" ("Sunday Rounds"). This is the lesson that Umbertina's descendants need to heed in order to understand and counteract the chaos and powerlessness they so often experience.

While such crisis is already evident in the lives of Umbertina and her daughters, it reaches its moment of highest tension with Marguerite, who, unable to pull the threads together, dies prematurely, her pregnancy suggesting both the desire to create and the incapacity to do so. Marguerite's daughter, named after her great-grandmother, will begin to gather the scattered and broken threads of the stories of the women who came before her. But it is important to remember that the search for these threads begins with Marguerite, the "American transplant filled with fears and desires" (5), who likens herself to the Sicilian Persephone (16), the mythical maiden doomed to live between the luminous fields of Demeter and the shadowy kingdom of Hades. Persephone never becomes a woman, except as an embodiment of her mother. Yet she is the Queen of the Underworld—the place to which Marguerite and Tina symbolically need to journey to pose yet unasked questions to Umbertina—and an adept traveler who learns to move between two radically different worlds. That is the skill that Marguerite lacks, but is able to teach her daughter.[31] The importance of the novel's intergenerational focus becomes evident as the life stories of the four generations reveals the intricate and interwoven design of familial and cultural history.

As a feminist novel, *Umbertina* troubles the idea of romantic love, even as it closes with a traditional happy ending: Tina marries Jason Jowers, her fiancé of Anglo-Saxon ancestry with a family house on Cape Cod. Umbertina is utterly unsentimental—"She had no time in her life for romance and daydreams" (54)—but it is Marguerite who offers an explosive critique of romantic love as the thing that women turn to when incapacitated by familial, cultural, and societal circumstances to find communities and relationships in which they can thrive. While Marguerite's marriage to the Italian poet Alberto Morosini is on the verge of dissolution, she vainly seeks solace in analysis, with a male psychoanalyst, in fantasies that never fully develop into tangible creative work, although she does become a photographer. Finally, she becomes involved in a self-destructive love affair with a narcissistic writer. In the tradition of the feminist *kunstlerroman* (novel of the development of an artist), Barolini explores the circumstances that hamper female creativity. Her failed *kunstlerroman* indicts those forces that silence female creativity when it is directed outside domestic bounds.[32] Marguerite reaches a vague understanding of the sources of her depression, which the novel suggests lie in gender oppression, cultural displacement, the unfulfillment of artistic talent, and the strictures of both her petty bourgeois American family and the falsely progressive literary world of Rome. What underscores all of these factors is the tension rooted in the lack of a discourse to articulate the complicated consequences of class transition.[33] Class transition is less of an issue for Tina, who is born into the material comfort of bourgeois life and the social legitimacy of her father's Venetian family. But cultural and social roots are devastatingly complicated for Marguerite, and her journey comes to a tragic halt. The reference to Persephone proves ominous for Marguerite, but auspicious for Tina, who will travel South, to Calabria—once the site of Greek cults, including a cult of Persephone—to search for her great-grandmother. Tina will come to understand that she must travel the geography of memory to map out a story that incorporates the past, but she must do so without letting that past stifle her.

While Barolini unravels the significance of the bedspread in the lives of the Longobardi women, it is not until the end of the book that she fully exposes the vital interconnections between personal memory and working-class history. The lost *coperta* reappears on Ellis Island as an immigrant artifact preserved in the Museum of Immigration. Tina's brief encounter with her great-grandmother's bedspread points not to resolution, but to the possibilities open to the daughters of working-class immigrant women, whose silenced voices can be heard only through those of their descendants:

> Among the exhibits were figures of men, women, and children clothed in the original costumes of their native land at the time of their arrival in America. A special exhibit called the "Anna Giordani Collection" was made up of clothes, trinkets, and other belongings of the immigrants that one Anna Giordani, the collector, had assembled over her years of working with the poor on the Lower East Side. Tina stood entranced at the spectacle of a magnificent bright-hued gloriously woven bedspread that bore the motifs of Calabrian design she had seen repeated in modern-day spreads during her trip through her ancestral region. In fact, as she neared the glass of the case and read the card, it said: "Origin: Calabria. Owner unknown. Acquired by Anna Giordani in 1886." (407)

The silence that surrounds the "unknown" owner powerfully articulates the ways in which the history of the poor is written: the exhibit honors the name of the social worker, Anna Giordani, who never managed to "like" the immigrants, but "did her duty unflinchingly, as a kind of penance and discipline for her soul" (66)—and who clearly kept Umbertina's exquisite *coperta* for herself. In what can be described as a blatant case of cultural robbery, the immigrants themselves are relegated to the silent condition of namelessness. Tina cannot possibly recognize the bedspread as her great-grandmother's since the story has not been passed down to her. While she regrets that Umbertina did not bring a bedspread like the one displayed at the museum—"then it would have been passed down to me, maybe" (407)—an almost miraculous encounter with her dead ancestor occurs as the "woven designs of grapes and tendrils and fig leaves and flowers and spreading acanthus" speak to her "of Italy and the past and keeping it all together for the future" (408).

Tina's quest for selfhood, a quest that is intertwined with the understanding of one's cultural identity, remains, on the surface, only partially successful since she herself does not become a writer, a storyteller who can keep it "all together for the future." Tina instead becomes a Dante scholar, thus connecting to an Italian tradition that is dramatically distant from the story of the bedspread. However, Tina's journey traces the development of Italian American female identity. Tina, who at first rejects and is even ashamed of the appellation "Italian-American" (315), comes to embrace "Italian-American identity" (359) during her trip to Calabria. And while she feels that Umbertina has "eluded her" (393), once she is back in the United States the trip "flashes through her mind like glinting pieces of a mosaic that she tried to shape into a whole, a pattern of serious design" (392).

At the close of the novel, as Tina pieces together the "fragments" (392) of her memory of the trip like the colorful parts of a quilt, Barolini skillfully ties together two important strands of Italian culture: Persephone, who is referred to in the prologue, and Dante, who appears prominently in the final section.[34] Tina, who at times sees herself as an incarnation of her Persephone-like mother, must learn to trace her mother's steps in a symbolic descent into hell. This is a hell from which she comes back, like Persephone, but also like Dante, the pilgrim of the *Commedia* who returns from his journey to tell the story.[35] In Barolini's novel, Dante does not embody a literary tradition that was truly foreign to Italian American immigrants, but rather represents one gate through which an Italian American woman can begin to explore and incorporate Italian mythologies and histories into Italian American cultural life.

Traveling, which for Tina at first signifies "a reprieve from all the choices . . . belonging nowhere, having no past, no future" (347), becomes the means by which she finds her place, a sense of multiple cultural "belonging," a connection to her past and a key to her future. It is through Tina that we come to a better understanding of Marguerite's story, a story that her daughters can learn from the diaries she has left. Like many Italian American women writers, Marguerite is the first college-educated woman in her family.[36] In this century, access to literacy has made it possible for Italian American women to write their stories and the stories of their female ancestors, those who first crossed the borders and made the development of Italian American culture possible.

Umbertina explores crossings—geographical, cultural, social, chronological, ethnic—and the ways in which those who cross borders can learn to use their mutable identities as the rich soil for creative and transformative work. In telling the story of the Longobardi women and of the lost—and found—bedspread, Barolini has captured a larger history that could itself easily be lost. Ultimately, the one who ties everything together is the author herself, as she weaves a narrative fabric as radiant, evocative, and powerful as the design adorning Umbertina's *coperta*.

"I am not a bold person," Barolini has written. "But I have Calabrian ancestry, which means I am tenacious" (*Chiaroscuro* 37). For once, despite my profound aversion to stereotypes, I bow respectfully to the *testardaggine*, the stubbornness of the Calabrians, the resilience of *Umbertina*—its story, its characters, and its author. Umbertina, Marguerite, and Tina are for Italian American women what Zora Neale Hurston's Janie Woods, Alice Walker's Celie, and Toni Morrison's Sethe have become for African American women, and Sandra Cisneros's Esperanza Cordero for Chicana women: not cut-out figures or models to emulate, but complicated characters who capture the conflicts, failings, and achievements of their gender and their cultures. As Italian American literature takes its place in the American canon, Italian American women writers' stories will continue to speak to larger constituencies of readers, for these stories are rooted in the cultural history of America—a history that writers like Barolini do not merely recount, but challenge and transform.

Edvige Giunta
Jersey City, New Jersey
September 1998

NOTES

1. I have written about my symbolic and literal search for Italian American women's books in my essay "Blending 'Literary' Discourses: Helen Barolini's Italian/American Narratives."

2. A hardcover book club edition was also published by the Literary Guild. As sources for *Umbertina*'s publication history and for details of Helen Barolini's biography, I have used Barolini's interviews with Bonetti (American Audio Prose Library) and Greenberg (*MELUS*), in addition to my own personal correspondence and conversations with Barolini.

3. For a further discussion of Italian American women's exclusion from the literary canon see Giunta, "A Song from the Ghetto," the afterword to Tina De Rosa's *Paper Fish*. On Italian American women's literary history see Bona, *Claiming a Tradition*.

4. Among the books noted by many critics as missing from the Modern Library's 1998 list of the one hundred "greatest" twentieth-century novels in English (chosen by a committee of nine white men and one white woman) is *The Golden Notebook*, Doris Lessing's feminist classic of a woman's painful quest for livable life and a meaningful identity in

a resolutely patriarchal world. Other feminist "quest" novels by authors such as Marilyn French and Mary Gordon have achieved popular success, but similarly been written out of the "canon" everywhere but in women's studies courses. Also conspicuously absent from the Modern Library list is any novel by Nobel Prize winner-Toni Morrison, including the novel many consider her finest, *Beloved*, which traces the experiences and legacies of women over several generations of an African American family.

5. On the status and recent development of Italian American literary studies see Bona, "The State of Italian American Studies in the 1990s: Topics and Texts," Gardaphé, "The Evolution of Italian American Literary Studies," and Giunta, "Crossing Borders in Italian/American Women's Studies."

6. In *In Search of Our Mothers' Gardens*, Walker writes of her fortuitous encounter with Hurston's work, which in turn led to her pilgrimage to Hurston's unmarked grave in a Florida cemetery, to the reprint of the novel *Their Eyes Were Watching God* and the publication of the anthology *I Love Myself When I Am Laughing*, and to Hurston's enormous impact on African American literature as well as, more broadly, on American literature. See especially "Saving the Life That Is Your Own: The Importance of Models in the Artist's Life" (3–14), "Zora Neale Hurston: A Cautionary Tale and a Partisan Review" (83–92), and "Looking for Zora" (93–116). See also Mary Helen Washington's foreword and Henry Louis Gates Jr.'s afterword to *Their Eyes Were Watching God* (vii–xiv and 185–95) and Alice Walker's dedication and Mary Helen Washington's introduction to *I Love Myself When I Am Laughing* (1–5 and 7–25). The publication of slave narratives similarly testifies to the necessary relationship between literature as an intellectual phenomenon and literature as the material production of the books themselves. Barolini's own journey in search of Italian American women literary predecessors, described in her essay "Looking for Mari Tomasi" (*Chiaroscuro* 73–82), parallels Walker's journey in search of Hurston.

7. Janet Zandy, who is herself Italian American, has provided compelling critical discussions of working-class identity in the introductions to her two anthologies. See also the special issue of *Women's Studies Quarterly* on working-class studies edited by Zandy.

8. In *The Cheese and the Worms*, Carlo Ginsburg describes such histories as "microhistories." Catherine L. Albanese uses Ginsburg's theory in her work of recovery of immigrant history, *The Cobbler's Universe*.

9. See Cafarelli, "No Butter on Our Bread: Anti-Intellectual Stereotyping of Italian Americans."

10. On *Chiaroscuro* see reviews by Bona and Signorelli-Pappas.

11. See Barolini, "The Case of the Missing Italian American Writers" (*Chiaroscuro* 64–72).

12. *Rosa*, an autobiographical account of immigrant life by the illiterate Rosa Cassettari, transcribed and edited by Marie Hall Ets, is presently out of print. For a discussion of *Rosa*'s place in the Italian American canon see Gardaphé, *Italian Signs, American Streets* (31–36).

13. Another novel by an Italian American author that can, like *Umbertina*, be placed in the tradition of the feminist consciousness-raising novel of the 1970s is Dorothy Bryant's *Ella Price's Journal* (1972). See Barbara Horn, "The Education of Ella Price," the afterword to the 1997 reprint by The Feminist Press, and Pipino, "*Ella Price's Journal*: The Subv/mersion of Ethnic and Sexual Identity." In Bryant's novel the protagonist is not Italian American, though her best friend is (a tactic used by contemporary Italian American writers, for example, Agnes Rossi in *Split Skirt*). On strategies of ethnic self-identification see Gardaphé, "Narrative in the Philosophic Mode" and "Epilogue" (*Italian Signs, American Streets* 172–98), and Giunta, "Speaking Through Silences: Ethnicity in the Writings of Contemporary Italian American Women."

14. In an interview, Barolini stated that she saw Marguerite as *the* important character in the novel (interview with Greenberg 94).

15. The 1997 American Italian Historical Association conference was devoted to an exploration of the relationship between African American and Italian American communities. See the forthcoming published proceedings of the conference, *Shades of Black and White: Conflict and Collaboration Between Two Communities*, edited by Ashyk and Gardaphé.

16. By tracing the historical and linguistic processes through which the concept of "whiteness" has been constructed in opposition to "blackness," such a debate aims at destabilizing racial hierarchies and calling into question the idea of whiteness as "natural" and "civilized." Scholars have thus exposed the way in which the manufacturing of racial tensions camoflages class tensions and leads members of economically oppressed groups to lose sight of possible fruitful political allegiances with groups that share their economic and social concerns. For more on social constructions of whiteness, in addition to Roediger, see Dyer and Ignatiev.

17. See especially Dorothy Allison, *Skin: Talking About Sex, Class, and Literature*, and Tina De Rosa, "Career Choices Come from Listening to the Heart."

18. *Umbertina* is not a memoir, or even a faithfully autobiographical novel. But the seeds of the story Barolini tells in the "Umbertina" section are to be found in an autobiographical essay, "A Circular Journey," published in 1978, in which the author writes of her search for the story of her own grandmother Nicoletta (interview with Greenberg 100). Marguerite corresponds to Barolini's generation, and shares some, though not by any means all, of her life experiences. However, Barolini has lamented the fact that readers tend to draw excessively literal analogies between her life and her fiction. Marguerite represents the means by which the author broadly explores the questions faced by women of her generation and background, as opposed to a faithful autobiographical stand-in. Many critics who have written about Umbertina have discussed Barolini's use of autobiographical material. See, for example, Gardaphé's essay "Autobiography as Piecework." By drawing upon social, familial, and personal history in her fictional creation, Barolini has accessed some of the unique power that comes with the memoir form. As the current genre that recalls, with its popularity, the emergence of the novel— and the entrance of women into the literary arena—the memoir has proven a powerful tool, especially for women and minorities, to record traditionally unspeakable—and

unspoken—stories. On the radical potential of the memoir, see Giunta, "Teaching Memoir at Jersey City State College."

19. There is no known bedspread in Barolini's family history (through there is a tin heart), but she still has a few items from her grandmother's dowry, which inspired her later descriptions of Umbertina's daughters' trousseaus. Helen Barolini provided this information in a telephone conversation with me in July 1998.

20. The interconnectedness of the women's lives is immediately accentuated in the transition from the prologue to part one. With an abrupt chronological—and geographical —shift, clearly announced in the dates of Umbertina's birth and death (1860–1940) underneath the title of the first section, Barolini transports the reader from the fashionable bourgeois world of Rome and Florence of the early 1970s, which constitutes the setting of the prologue, to the rough peasant life in the small village of Castagna, on the Sila mountains, in Calabria (circa 1876) of the "Umbertina" section. At the same time, the change in tone and style—from the more unsettling and staccato rhythm of the contemporary Marguerite section to the slower narrative pace of the Umbertina section—signals the distance between their lives. In general, it is through innovative use of form as well as through content that Barolini captures the different consciousness and life experience of each of her female protagonists.

21. This sense of displacement is particularly strong in emigrants from a country like Italy, which is still relatively resistant to geographical mobility. There is additional irony in this, as well, since for thousands of years people from other countries have moved in and out of the Italian regions, while in the last two centuries the inhabitants of the South have been driven to emigrate abroad, so that the children of the area that was once called "Magna Graecia" (*Umbertina* 28) are now scattered across the globe.

22. In "Il Caso della Casa," Viscusi discusses the theme of departure in oedipal terms, focusing though on the guilt of the children who abandon the parent as opposed to the guilt of the parents (i.e. Italy) who have failed to provide for their children.

23. On *Paper Fish*, see Giunta, "A Song from the Ghetto," and Bona, "Broken Images." For a comparative discussion of *Umbertina* and *Paper Fish* see Bona, "A Process of Reconstruction: Recovering the Grandmother in Helen Barolini's *Umbertina* and Tina De Rosa's *Paper Fish*" in the forthcoming *Claiming a Tradition*. Gardaphé also discusses *Umbertina* alongside *Paper Fish* in "The Later Mythic Mode" (*Italian Signs, American Streets* 131–41).

24. While Barolini lived in Italy for many years, De Rosa has never traveled there, which explains, in part, their different representations of Italy.

25. That neither *Umbertina* nor any other comparable account of Italian American immigrants' lives—apart from Mario Puzo's much glamorized *The Godfather*—has been translated into Italian and published in Italy thus far is compelling evidence of a historical void that needs to be filled. If sociological and historical studies done in Italy provide important data, it is literary works such as *Umbertina* that give voice to the silent millions who have left that country in the last two centuries. For a sociological study of patterns of Italian emigration to the United States see Squier and Quadagno. On Italian

emigration and settlements see also Caroli; Friedman-Kasaba; Gabaccia *From Sicily to Elizabeth Street*; and Di Leonardo. On contemporary Italian American women see Anderlini-D'Onofrio.

26. While in the earlier part of the nineteenth century the immigrants came primarily from Northern Italy, towards the latter part of the century there was a shift as more and more Southern Italians left Italy. In addition to exploitation and agricultural depression, other factors must be taken into consideration—for example, "the role of the Italian state in encouraging temporary labor migration to the Americas . . . tied to the earnings emigrants remitted to their households and to Italian banks" (Friedman-Kasaba 77–78). (This exodus continued, at a decreasing rate, throughout the twentieth century, though it has more recently included primarily trained professionals, reflecting a change in the Italian economy as well as in American immigration laws, which now discourage the entrance into the United States of untrained laborers.)

27. Anna Giordani's family similarly leaves Italy for political reasons. In the introduction to his translation of Antonio Gramsci's *The Southern Question*, Pasquale Verdicchio writes: "Gramsci's analysis of North/South implicates the history of Italian unification, the first phase of which took place in 1860 with Garibaldi's 'liberation' of Sicily and the South from Bourbon rule. It soon became obvious to the Southern masses that the effort was to benefit them much less than they had been led to believe. The collaboration of Northern 'liberators' with Southern landowners further rooted the imbalances that had been established by the Bourbons" (4). For a discussion of North-South Relations in *Umbertina* see Tamburri, "Looking Back: The Image of Italy in *Umbertina*" in *A Semiotic of Ethnicity*.

28. For a discussion of women's art, especially sewing and quilting, see Roszika Parker, *The Subversive Stitch*, Hedges and Wendt, "Everyday Use" (1–73), and Walker, *In Search of Our Mother's Gardens*.

29. On domestic ideology in Italian American culture see Baker and Vitullo's discussion of Nancy Savoca's film *Household Saints*.

30. Mary Cappello's memoir *Night Bloom* highlights the importance of the recovery of material culture, as do the videos of Kym Ragusa and the sculpture of Nancy Azara (see Rando). On Italian American material culture see also Robert Anthony Orsi, *The Madonna of 115th Street*. This concept can be extended to reconfirm the importance of "recovering" Italian American books like *Umbertina*.

31. For a discussion of the myth of Persephone in the works of Italian American women see Giunta, "Persephone's Daughters" and Messina's "Soul-food and Transcendent Ways of Knowing in *Household Saints*."

32. On the female *kunstlerroman*, see Jones.

33. Marguerite's class transition is further complicated by her geographical move to Italy. See Tamburri, "Helen Barolini's 'Comparative' Woman: The Italian American Woman" and "Looking Back: The Image of Italy in *Umbertina*" in *A Semiotic of Ethnicity*.

34. At the beginning of the "Umbertina" section, Don Antonio addresses the villagers, quoting the famous line from canto 26 of *Inferno* in which Ulysses incites his companions to follow him in yet another daring journey: "*Fatti non foste a viver come bruti/ma seguir virtute e conoscenza*" (sic; 23–24). (In the English translation by Allen Mandelbaum: "You were not made to live your lives as brutes,/but to be followers of worth and knowledge," 231.)

35. In Ulysses' circle Dante also meets Guido da Montefeltro, who tells his story to Dante only because he thinks Dante is dead and thus will not be able to tell anyone on earth of Guido's damnation.

36. See Barolini, "Becoming a Literary Person Out of Context."

HELEN BAROLINI: A SELECT BIBLIOGRAPHY

Books

Aldus and His Dream Book: An Illustrated Essay. New York: Italica, 1992.

Chiaroscuro: Essays of Identity. West Lafayette, Ind.: Bordighera, 1997.

Ed. *The Dream Book: An Anthology of Writings by Italian-American Women.* New York: Shocken, 1985.

With Antonio Barolini. *Duet* (Poems in English and Italian). Venice: Neri Pozza Editore, 1966.

Festa: Recipes and Recollections of Italian Holidays. New York: Harcourt Brace Jovanovich, 1988.

Love in the Middle Ages. New York: William Morrow, 1986.

Umbertina. 1979. New York: The Feminist Press, 1999.

Radio Drama

Margaret Fuller, an American Heroine of the Italian Risorgimento. RAI. Rome. 1971.

Selected Essays and Stories

"Appetite Lost, Appetite Found." *Through the Kitchen Window.* Ed. Arlene Avakian. Boston: Beacon, 1997. 228–37.

"Becoming a Literary Person Out of Context." *Massachusetts Review* 27.2 (1986): 262–74.

"A Circular Journey." *Texas Quarterly* 21.2 (1978): 109–26.

"Going to Sicily." *Paris Review* (summer 1980): 178–87.

"Greener Grass." *From the Margin: Writings in Italian Americana.* Eds. Anthony Julian Tamburri, Paolo A. Giordano, and Fred L. Gardaphé. West Lafayette, Ind.: Purdue University Press, 1991. 39–45.

"How I Learned to Speak Italian." *The Best American Essays 1998*. Ed. Cynthia Ozick. Boston: Houghton Mifflin. 19–32.

"The Italian Side of Emily Dickinson." *Virginia Quarterly Review* 70.3 (summer 1994): 461–79.

"My Mother's Wedding Day." *Southwest Review* 77.1 (winter 1992): 34–47.

"Shores of Light." *Writers Forum* 19 (1993): 137–56.

"Shutting the Door on Someone." *Southwest Review* 75.4 (autumn 1990): 555–61.

Selected Interviews

With Carol Ahearn. *Fra Noi* (September 1986): 47.

With Kay Bonetti. Audiocassette. American Audio Prose Library. 1982.

With Dorothée von Heune Greenberg. *MELUS* 18.2 (summer 1992): 91–108.

WORKS CITED

Albanese, Catherine L., ed. *A Cobbler's Universe: Religion, Poetry and Performance in the Life of a South Italian Immigrant: Frank S. Spiziri.* New York: Continuum, 1997.

Albright, Carol Bonomo. "From Sacred to Secular: *Umbertina* and *A Piece of Earth.*" *MELUS* 20.2 (summer 1995): 93–103.

Allison, Dorothy. *Bastard Out of Carolina.* New York: Dutton, 1992.

———. *Skin: Talking About Sex, Class & Literature.* Ithaca: Firebrand, 1994.

Anderlini-D'Onofrio, Serena. "Neither 'White Widow' nor 'War Bride': The Discursive Construction of Italian Women in America." *Voices in Italian Americana* 8.1 (spring 1997): 11–31.

Baker, Aaron, and Juliann Vitullo. "Mysticism and the *Household Saints* of Everyday Life." *Voices in Italian Americana. Special Issue on Italian American Women* Ed. Edvige Giunta 7.2 (1996): 55–68.

Bona, Mary Jo. "Broken Images, Broken Lives: Carmolina's Journey in Tina De Rosa's *Paper Fish.*" *MELUS* 14.3–4 (fall/winter 1987): 87–106.

———. *Claiming a Tradition: Italian/American Women Writers.* Carbondale, IL: Southern Illinois University Press, 1999.

———. Review of Helen Barolini's *Chiaroscuro: Essays of Identity. Voices in Italian Americana* 9.1 (spring 1988): 202–06.

———. "The Status of Italian American Studies in the 1990s: Topics and Texts." Paper given at the MMLA Conference. Chicago. November 1997.

Bryant, Dorothy. *Confessions of Madame Psyche.* 1986. Afterword by J. J. Wilson. New York: The Feminist Press: 1998.

———. *Ella Price's Journal.* 1972. Afterword by Barbara Horn. New York: The Feminist Press, 1997.

———. *Miss Giardino.* 1978. Afterword by Janet Zandy. New York: The Feminist Press, 1997.

Cafarelli, Annette Wheeler. "No Butter on Our Bread: Anti-Intellectual Stereotyping of Italian Americans." *Voices in Italian Americana* 7.1 (spring 1996): 39–47.

Cappello, Mary. *Night Bloom.* Boston: Beacon, 1998.

Caroli, Betty Boyd, Robert F. Harney, and Lydio F. Tomasi, eds. *The Italian Immigrant Woman in North America.* Toronto: The Multicultural History Society of Ontario, 1978.

Cavallo, Diana. *A Bridge of Leaves.* Afterword by Mary Jo Bona. Toronto: Guernica, 1997.

Chernin, Kim. *In My Mother's House.* New York: Harper, 1983.

Cisneros, Sandra. *The House on Mango Street.* New York: Random House, 1984.

De Rosa, Tina. "Career Choices Come From Listening to the Heart." *Fra Noi* (October 1985): 9.

———. *Paper Fish.* 1980. Afterword by Edvige Giunta. New York: The Feminist Press, 1996.

DeSalvo, Louise. *Vertigo.* New York: Dutton, 1996.

di Leonardo, Micaela. *The Varieties of Ethnic Experience: Kinship, Class, and Gender among California Italian-Americans.* Ithaca: Cornell University Press, 1984.

Dyer, Richard. *White.* London: Routledge, 1997.

Ets, Marie Hall. *Rosa: The Life of an Italian Immigrant.* Minnesota: University of Minneapolis Press, 1970.

Friedman-Kasaba, Kathie. *Memories of Migration: Gender, Ethnicity, and Work in the Lives of Jewish and Italian Women in New York: 1870–1924.* Albany, New York: SUNY Press, 1996.

Gabaccia, Donna. *From the Other Side. Women, Gender, and Immigrant Life in the U.S., 1820–1990.* Bloomington: Indiana University Press, 1994.

———. *From Sicily to Elizabeth Street: Housing and Social Change Among Italian Immigrants, 1880–1930.* Albany, NY: SUNY Press, 1984.

Gardaphé, Fred L. "Autobiography as Piecework: The Writings of Helen Barolini." *Italian Americans Celebrate Life, the Arts and Popular Culture.* Eds. Paola A. Sensi Isolani and Anthony Julian Tamburri. Staten Island, N.Y.: The American Italian Historical Association, 1990. 19–27.

———. "The Evolution of Italian/American Literary Studies." *The Italian American Review. Italian-American Studies: The State of the Field and New Directions for Development.* Part I. 5.1 (spring 1996): 23–35.

————. *Italian Signs, American Streets: The Evolution of Italian American Narrative.* Durham, NC: Duke University Press, 1996.

Ginsburg, Carlo. *The Cheese and the Worms: The Cosmos of a Sixteenth-Century Miller.* Trans. John and Anne Tedeschi. New York: Penguin, 1985.

Giunta, Edvige. "Blending 'Literary' Discourses: Helen Barolini's Italian/American Narratives." *Beyond the Margin: Readings in Italian Americana.* Eds. Paolo A. Giordano and Anthony Julian Tamburri. Madison, N.J.: Fairleigh Dickinson University Press, 1998. 114–30.

————. "Crossing Critical Borders in Italian/American Women's Studies." *The Italian American Review. Italian-American Studies: The State of the Field and New Directions for Development.* Part II. 5.2 (autumn/winter 1996–97). 79–94.

————. "Persephone's Daughters." Paper presented at "Greece in Print—1997." Hellenic Literature Society. New York University. 20 September 1997.

————. "Speaking Through Silences: Ethnicity in the Writings of Italian/American Women." *Race and Ethnic Discrimination in American Literature.* Ed. Michael Meyer. Amsterdam and Atlanta: Rodopi Press, 1997. 49–69.

————. "Teaching Memoir at Jersey City State College." Lecture given at Berkeley College. New York. June 1997.

Gramsci, Antonio. *The Southern Question.* Trans. and introd. by Pasquale Verdicchio. West Lafayette, Ind.: Bordighera, 1995.

Hedges, Elaine and Ingrid Wendt. *In Her Own Image: Women Working in the Arts.* New York: The Feminist Press, 1980.

Hendin, Josephine Gattuso. *The Right Thing To Do.* 1988. Afterword by Mary Jo Bona. New York: The Feminist Press, 1999 (forthcoming).

Hurston, Zora Neale. *I Love Myself When I am Laughing . . . And Then Again When I Am Looking Mean and Impressive.* Ed. Alice Walker. Introduction by Mary Helen Washington. New York: The Feminist Press, 1989.

————. *Their Eyes Were Watching God.* 1937. Foreword by Mary Helen Washington. Afterword by Henry Louis Gates, Jr. New York: Harper & Row, 1990.

Ignatiev, Noel. *How the Irish Became White.* New York: Routledge, 1995.

Jones, Suzanne W., ed. *Writing the Woman Artist: Essays on Poetics, Politics, and Portraiture.* Philadelphia: University of Pennsylvania Press, 1991.

Kadi, Joanna, ed. *Food for Our Grandmothers: Writings by Arab-American and Arab-Canadian Feminists.* Boston: South End Press, 1994.

————. *Thinking Class: Sketches from a Cultural Worker.* Boston: South End Press, 1996.

Lorde, Audre. *Sister Outsider: Essays and Speeches.* Freedom, Calif.: The Crossing Press, 1984.

Messina, Elizabeth. "Soul-Food and Transcendent Ways of Knowing in *Household Saints*." *A Tavola: Food, Tradition, and Community Among Italian Americans*. Ed. Edvige Giunta and Sam J. Patti. West Lafayette, Ind.: Bordighera, 1998. 68–82.

Morrison, Toni. *Beloved*. New York: Knopf, 1987.

Orsi, Robert Anthony. *The Madonna of 115th Street: Faith and Community in Italian Harlem, 1880–1950*. New Haven: Yale University Press, 1985.

Parker, Roszika. *The Subversive Stitch: Embroidery and the Making of the Feminine*. 1984. New York: Routledge, 1989.

Petrusewicz, Marta. *Latifundium: Moral Economy and Material Life in a European Periphery*. 1989. Trans. Judith C. Green. Ann Arbor: University of Michigan Press, 1996.

Pipino, Mary Frances. "Creating a Context: The Fiction and Criticism of Helen Barolini." *I Have Found My Voice: The Italian American Woman Writer*. Currents in Comparative Romance Languages and Literatures. Vol. 71. Peter Lang, 1998.

———. "Ella Price's Journal: The Subv/mersion of Ethnic and Sexual Identity." *Voices in Italian Americana*. Special Issue on Italian American Women. Ed. Edvige Giunta. 7.2 (fall 1996): 35–54.

Puzo, Mario. *The Godfather*. 1969. New York: Fawcett Crest, 1970.

Ragusa, Kym, dir. *fuori/outside*. Video. Ibla Productions, 1997.

Rando, Flavia. "'My Mother Was a Strong Woman': Respect, Shame, and the Feminine Body in the Sculpture of Nancy Azara and Antonette Rosato." *Voices in Italian Americana*. Special Issue on Italian American Women. Ed. Edvige Giunta. 7.2 (1996): 225–29.

Roedinger, David R. *Towards the Abolition of Whiteness: Essays on Race, Politics, and Working Class History*. London: Verso, 1994.

Rossi, Agnes. *Split Skirt*. New York: Random House, 1994.

Saracino, Mary. *No Matter What*. Minneapolis: Spinsters Ink, 1993.

———. "Sunday Rounds." *Angie Loves Mary, Vinnie Loves Sal: Writings by Lesbians and Gays of Italian Descent*. Eds. Tommi Avicolli Mecca, Giovanna J. Capone, and Denise N. Leto. Toronto: Guernica, 1999 (forthcoming).

Signorelli-Pappas, Rita. "An Ambiguous Inheritance." Review of *Chiaroscuro: Essays of Identity*. *The Women's Review of Books* 15.2 (November 1997): 11–12.

Squier, D. Ann and Jill S. Quadagno. "The Italian American Family." *Ethnic Families in America: Patterns and Variations*. Eds. Charles H. Mindel, Robert W. Habenstein, and Roosevelt Wright, Jr. New York: Elsevier, 1976. 109–37.

Tamburri, Anthony Julian. *A Semiotic of Ethnicity: In (Re)Cognition of the Italian/American Writer*. Albany, NY: SUNY Press, 1998.

Viscusi, Robert. "Il Caso della Casa: Stories of Houses in Italian America." *The Family and Community Life of Italian Americans*. Ed. Richard N. Juliani. Staten Island, NY: The American Italian Historical Association, 1983. 1–9.

———. "Debate in the Dark: Love in Italian-American Fiction." *American Declarations of Love.* Ed. Ann Massa. New York: St. Martin's Press, 1990. 155-73.

Walker, Alice. *In Search of Our Mothers' Gardens: Womanist Prose.* 1967. New York: Harcourt Brace Jovanovich, 1983.

———. *The Color Purple.* New York: Harcourt Brace Jovanovich, 1992.

Zandy, Janet, ed. *Calling Home: Working-Class Women's Writings.* New Brunswick: Rutgers University Press, 1990.

———, ed. *Liberating Memory: Our Work and Our Working-Class Consciousness.* New Brunswick: Rutgers University Press, 1995.

———, ed. *Women's Studies Quarterly.* Special Issue on Working-Class Studies. 23.1-2 (spring/summer 1995).

CONTEMPORARY WOMEN'S FICTION
FROM AROUND THE WORLD

from The Feminist Press at The City University of New York

Allegra Maud Goldman, a novel by Edith Konecky. $9.95 paper.

An Estate of Memory, a novel by Ilona Karmel. $11.95 paper.

Apples from the Desert: Selected Stories, by Savyon Liebrecht. $19.95 jacketed hardcover.

Bamboo Shoots After the Rain: Contemporary Stories by Women Writers of Taiwan. $14.95 paper. $35.00 cloth.

Cast Me Out If You Will, stories and memoir by Lalithambika Antherjanam. $11.95 paper, $28.00 cloth.

Changes: A Love Story, a novel by Ama Ata Aidoo. $12.95 paper.

Confessions of Madame Psyche, a novel by Dorothy Bryant. $18.95 paper.

The House of Memory: Stories by Jewish Women Writers of Latin America. $15.95 paper. $37.00 cloth.

Mulberry and Peach: Two Women of China, a novel by Hualing Nieh. $12.95 paper.

Paper Fish, a novel by Tina De Rosa. $9.95 paper. $20.00 cloth.

Reena and Other Stories, by Paule Marshall. $11.95 paper.

The Silent Duchess, a novel by Dacia Maraini. $19.95 jacketed hardcover.

Songs My Mother Taught Me: Stories, Plays, and Memoir, by Wakako Yamauchi. $14.95 paper. $35.00 cloth.

The Tree and the Vine, a novel by Dola de Jong. $9.95 paper. $27.95 cloth.

Truth Tales: Contemporary Stories by Women Writers of India. $12.95 paper. $35.00 cloth.

Two Dreams: New and Selected Stories, by Shirley Geok-lin Lim. $10.95 paper.

What Did Miss Darrington See? An Anthology of Feminist Supernatural Fiction. $14.95 paper.

With Wings: An Anthology of Literature by and About Women with Disabilities. $14.95 paper.

Women Working: An Anthology of Stories and Poems. $13.95 paper.

To receive a free catalog of The Feminist Press's 150 titles, call or write The Feminist Press at The City University of New York, Wingate Hall/City College, New York, NY 10031; phone: (212) 650-8966; fax: (212) 650-8869. Feminist Press books are available at bookstores, or can be ordered directly. Send check or money order (in U.S. dollars drawn on a U.S. bank) payable to The Feminist Press. Please add $4.00 shipping and handling for the first book and $1.00 for each additional book. VISA, Mastercard, and American Express are accepted for telephone orders. Prices subject to change.